ing Arthur of Britain.

The Story of

KING ARTHVR
and his *Knights*

Written and Illustrated
by
HOWARD PYLE.

NEW YORK:
Dover Publications, Inc.

This Dover edition, first published in 1965, is an unabridged and unaltered republication of the work first published by Charles Scribner's Sons in 1903.

Standard Book Number: 486-21445-1

Library of Congress Catalog Card Number: 65-26022

Manufactured in the United States by Courier Corporation
21445126
www.doverpublications.com

Foreword.

✠   ✠

*A*FTER *several years of contemplation and of thought upon the matter herein contained, it has at last come about, by the Grace of God, that I have been able to write this work with such pleasure of spirit that, if it gives to you but a part of the joy that it hath afforded me, I shall be very well content with what I have done.*

For when, in pursuing this history, I have come to consider the high nobility of spirit that moved these excellent men to act as they did, I have felt that they have afforded such a perfect example of courage and humility that anyone might do exceedingly well to follow after their manner of behavior in such measure as he is able to do.

For I believe that King Arthur was the most honorable, gentle Knight who ever lived in all the world. And those who were his fellows of the Round Table—taking him as their looking-glass of chivalry—made, altogether, such a company of noble knights that it is hardly to be supposed that their like will ever be seen again in this world. Wherefore it is that I have had such extraordinary pleasure in beholding how those famous knights behaved whenever circumstances called upon them to perform their endeavor.

So in the year of grace one thousand nine hundred and two I began to write this history of King Arthur and his Knights of the Round Table and, if I am able so to do, I shall endeavor, with love of that task, to finish the same at some other time in another book and to the satisfaction of whosoever may care to read the story thereof.

Contents

The Book of King Arthur

PART I

THE WINNING OF KINGHOOD

Chapter First

Chapter Second

Chapter Third

PART II

THE WINNING OF A SWORD

Chapter First

Chapter Second

Chapter Third

PART III

THE WINNING OF A QUEEN

The Book of Three Worthies

———

PART I

THE STORY OF MERLIN

Chapter First

———

Chapter Second

———

Chapter Third

———

Chapter Fourth

PART II

THE STORY OF SIR PELLIAS

Chapter First

Chapter Second

Chapter Third

Chapter Fourth

Chapter Fifth

Chapter Sixth

PART III

THE STORY OF SIR GAWAINE

Chapter First

Chapter Second

Chapter Third

LIST OF ILLUSTRATIONS

The
BOOK
of
KING
ARTHUR

Uther-Pendragon.

Prologue.

I N ancient days there lived a very noble King, named Uther-Pendragon, and he became Overlord of all of Britain. This King was very greatly aided unto the achievement of the Pendragonship of the realm by the help of two men, who rendered him great assistance in all that he did. The one of these men was a certain very powerful enchanter and sometime prophet known to men as Merlin the Wise; and he gave very good counsel unto Uther-Pendragon. The other man was an excellent noble and renowned knight, hight Ulfius (who was thought by many to be the greatest leader in war of any man then alive); and he gave Uther-Pendragon aid and advice in battle. So, with the help of Merlin and Sir Ulfius, Uther-Pendragon was able to overcome all of his enemies and to become King of the entire realm.

After Uther-Pendragon had ruled his kingdom for a number of years he took to wife a certain beautiful and gentle lady, hight Igraine. This noble dame was the widow of Gerlois, the Duke of Tintegal; *Uther-Pendra-* by which prince she had two daughters—one of whom was *gon taketh to* named Margaise and the other Morgana le Fay. And Mor- *wife the Lady* gana le Fay was a famous sorceress. These daughters the *Igraine.* Queen brought with her to the Court of Uther-Pendragon after she had married that puissant King, and there Margaise was wedded to King Urien of Gore, and Morgana le Fay was wedded to King Lot of Orkney.

Now after awhile Uther-Pendragon and Queen Igraine had a son born unto them, and he was very beautiful and of great size and strength of bone. And whilst the child still lay wrapped in his swaddling clothes and lying in a cradle of gold and ultramarine, Merlin came to Uther-Pendragon with a spirit of prophecy strong upon him (for such was often the case with him), and, speaking in that spirit of prophecy, he said, "Lord, it is given unto me to foresee that thou shalt shortly fall sick of a fever and that thou shalt maybe die of a violent sweat that will follow thereon. Now, should such a dolorous thing befall us all, this young

Concerning the birth and perils of the young child. child (who is, certes, the hope of all this realm) will be in very great danger of his life; for many enemies will assuredly rise up with design to seize upon him for the sake of his inheritance, and either he will be slain or else he will be held in captivity from which he shall hardly hope to escape. Wherefore, I do beseech thee, Lord, that thou wilt permit Sir Ulfius and myself to presently convey the child away unto some place of safe refuge, where he may be hidden in secret until he groweth to manhood and is able to guard himself from such dangers as may threaten him."

When Merlin had made an end of speaking thus, Uther-Pendragon made reply with a very steadfast countenance in this wise: "Merlin, so far as my death is concerned—when my time cometh to die I believe God will give me grace to meet my end with entire cheerfulness; for, certes, my lot is in that wise no different from that of any other man who hath been born of woman. But touching the matter of this young child, if thy prophecy be true, then his danger is very great, and it would be well that he should be conveyed hence to some place of safe harborage as thou dost advise. Wherefore, I pray thee to perform thy will in this affair, bearing in thy heart the consideration that the child is the most precious inheritance which I shall leave unto this land."

All this, as was said, Uther-Pendragon spake with great calmness and equanimity of spirit. And Merlin did as he had advised, and he and Sir Ulfius conveyed the child away by night, and no one but they wist

King Uther dieth according to the prophecy of Merlin. whither the babe had been taken. And shortly afterward Uther-Pendragon was seized with the sickness as Merlin had foretold, and he died exactly as Merlin had feared that he would die; wherefore it was very well that the child had been taken to a place of safety.

And after Uther-Pendragon had departed from this life, it was likewise as Merlin had feared, for all the realm fell into great disorder. For each lesser king contended against his fellow for overlordship, and wicked knights and barons harried the highways as they listed and there levied toll with great cruelty upon helpless wayfarers. For some such travellers they took prisoners and held for ransom, whiles others they slew because they had no ransom to pay. So it was a very common sight to see a dead man lying by the roadside, if you should venture to make a journey upon some business or other. Thus it befell that, after awhile, all that dolorous land groaned with the trouble that lay upon it.

Thus there passed nearly eighteen years in such great affliction, and then one day the Archbishop of Canterbury summoned Merlin to him and bespake him in this wise: " Merlin, men say that thou art the wisest man in all the world. Canst thou not find some means to heal the *The Archbish-* distractions of this woeful realm? Bend thou thy wisdom to *op of Canter-* this matter and choose thou a king who shall be a fit overlord *bury advises* *with Merlin.* for us, so that we may enjoy happiness of life once more as we did in the days of Uther-Pendragon."

Then Merlin lifted up his countenance upon the Archbishop, and spake in this wise: "My lord, the spirit of prophecy that lieth upon me some-times moveth me now to say that I do perceive that this country is soon to have a king who shall be wiser and greater and more worthy of praise than was even Uther-Pendragon. And he shall bring order and peace where is now disorder and war. Moreover, I may tell you that this King shall be of Uther-Pendragon's own full blood-royal."

To this the Archbishop said: " What thou tellest me, Merlin, is a won-derfully strange thing. But in this spirit of prophecy canst thou not fore-tell when this King is to come? And canst thou tell how we shall know him when he appeareth amongst us? For many lesser kings there are who would fain be overlord of this land, and many such there are who deem themselves fit to rule over all the others. How then shall we know the real King from those who may proclaim themselves to be the rightful king?"

" My lord Archbishop," quoth Merlin, " if I have thy leave for to exert my magic I shall set an adventure which, if any man achieve it, all the world shall straightway know that he is the rightful King and overlord of this realm." And to this the Archbishop said, " Merlin, I bid thee do whatsoever may seem to thee to be right in this affair." And Merlin said, " I will do so."

So Merlin caused by magic that a huge marble stone, four square, should suddenly appear in an open place before the cathedral *Merlin pre-* door. And upon this block of marble he caused it to be that *pares a test of* there should stand an anvil and into the anvil he caused *Kinghood.* it that there should be thrust a great naked sword midway deep of the blade. And this sword was the most wonderful that any man had ever seen, for the blade was of blue steel and extraordinarily bright and glistering. And the hilt was of gold, chased and carved with marvellous cunning, and inlaid with a great number of precious stones, so that it shone with wonderful brightness in the sunlight. And about the sword were written these words in letters of gold :—

Whoso Pulleth Out this Sword from the Anvil
That same is Rightwise King-Born of England.

So a great many people came and gazed upon that sword and marvelled at it exceedingly, for its like had never before been beheld upon the earth.

Then, when Merlin had accomplished this miracle, he bade the Archbishop to call together all the chief people of that land upon Christmastide; and he bade the Archbishop to command that every man should make assay to draw out the sword, for that he who should succeed in drawing it forth out of the anvil should be rightwise King of Britain.

So the Archbishop did according as Merlin said; and this was the marvel of the marble stone and the anvil, of which same anyone may easily read for himself in that book written a very long while ago by Robert de Boron, which is called Le Roman de Merlin.

Now when the mandate of the Lord Archbishop went forth, summoning all the chief people of the land to the assay of that miracle (for, indeed, it was a miracle to draw forth a sword-blade out of an anvil of solid iron), all the realm became immediately cast into a great ferment, so that each man asked his fellow, "Who shall draw forth that sword, and who shall be our King?" Some thought it would be King Lot and others thought it would be King Urien of Gore (these being the sons-in-law unto Uther-Pendragon); some thought that it would be King Leodegrance of Camiliard, and others that it would be King Ryence of North Wales; some thought it would be this king and others that it would be that king; for all the world was divided into different parties who thought according to their liking.

Then, as Christmastide drew nigh, it presently appeared as though the entire world was wending its way to London Town, for the highways and the by-ways became filled with wayfarers—kings and lords and knights and ladies and esquires and pages and men-at-arms—all betaking their way whither the assay was to be made of that adventure of the sword and the anvil. Every inn and castle was filled so full of travellers that it was a marvel how so many folk could be contained within their compass, and everywhere were tents and pavilions pitched along the wayside for the accommodation of those who could not find shelter within doors.

But when the Archbishop beheld the multitudes that were assembling, he said to Merlin, "Indeed, Merlin, it would be a very singular thing if among all these great kings and noble, honorable lords we should not find some one worthy of being the King of this realm."

Unto which the Merlin smiled and said, "Marvel not, my lord, if among all those who appear to be so extraordinarily worthy there shall not be found one who is worthy; and marvel not if, among all those who are unknown, there shall arise one who shall approve himself to be entirely worthy."

And the Archbishop pondered Merlin's words, and so beginneth this story.

PART I

The Winning of Kinghood

HERE beginneth the story of the sword, the anvil, and the marble stone, and of how that sword was first achieved by an unknown youth, until then of no renown, whether in arms or of estate.

So hearken unto that which I have hereinafter written.

Sir Kay breaketh his sword, at $\overset{e}{y}$ Tournament.

Chapter First.

How Sir Kay did Combat in a Great Tournament at London Town and of How He Brake His Sword. Likewise, How Arthur Found a New Sword For Him.

IT happened that among those worthies who were summoned unto London Town by the mandate of the Archbishop as above recounted, there was a certain knight, very honorable and of high estate, by name Sir Ector of Bonmaison—surnamed the Trustworthy Knight, because of the fidelity with which he kept the counsel of those who confided in him, and because he always performed unto all men, whether of high or low degree, that which he promised to undertake, without defalcation as to the same. So this noble and excellent knight was held in great regard by all those who knew him; for not only was he thus honorable in conduct but he was, besides, of very high estate, being possessed of seven castles *Of Sir Ector,* in Wales and in the adjoining country north thereof, and like- *the trustwor-* wise of certain fruitful tracts of land with villages appertain- *thy Knight.* ing thereunto, and also of sundry forests of great extent, both in the north country and the west. This very noble knight had two sons; the elder of these was Sir Kay, a young knight of great valor and promise, and already well renowned in the Courts of Chivalry because of several very honorable deeds of worthy achievement in arms which he had performed; the other was a young lad of eighteen years of age, by name Arthur, who at that time was serving with good repute as Sir Kay's esquire-at-arms.

Now when Sir Ector of Bonmaison received by messenger the mandate of the Archbishop, he immediately summoned these two sons unto him and bade them to prepare straightway for to go with him to London Town, and they did so. And in the same manner he bade a great number of retainers and esquires and pages for to make them ready, and they likewise did so. Thus, with a very considerable array at arms and with great show of circumstance, Sir Ector of Bonmaison betook his way unto London Town in obedience to the commands of the Archbishop.

So, when he had come thither he took up his inn in a certain field where many other noble knights and puissant lords had already established themselves, and there he set up a very fair pavilion of green silk, and erected his banner emblazoned with the device of his house; to wit, a gryphon, black, upon a field of green.

And upon this field were a great multitude of other pavilions of many different colors, and over above each pavilion was the pennant and the banner of that puissant lord to whom the pavilion belonged. Wherefore, because of the multitude of these pennants and banners the sky was at places well-nigh hidden with the gaudy colors of the fluttering flags.

Among the great lords who had come thither in pursuance to the Archbishop's summons were many very famous kings and queens and noblemen of high degree. For there was King Lot of Orkney, who had taken to wife a step-daughter of Uther-Pendragon, and there was King Uriens of Gore, who had taken to wife another step-daughter of that great king, and there was King Ban, and King Bors, and King Ryance, and King Leodegrance and many others of like degree, for there were no less than twelve kings and seven dukes, so that, what with their court of lords and ladies and esquires and pages in attendance, the town of London had hardly ever seen the like before that day.

Now the Archbishop of Canterbury, having in mind the extraordinary state of the occasion that had brought so many kings and dukes and high lords unto that adventure of the sword and the anvil, had commanded that there should be a very stately and noble tournament proclaimed. Like wise he commanded that this contest at arms should be held in a certain *The Archbish-* field nigh to the great cathedral, three days before that assay *op declares a* should be made of the sword and the anvil (which same was *tournament.* to be undertaken, as aforesaid, upon Christmas day). To this tournament were bidden all knights who were of sufficient birth, condition, and quality for to fit them to take part therein. Accordingly, very many exalted knights made application for admission, and that in such numbers that three heralds were kept very busy looking into their pretensions unto the right of battle. For these heralds examined the escutcheons and the rolls of lineage of all applicants with great care and circumspection.

Now when Sir Kay received news of this tournament he went to where his father was, and when he stood before his face he spake in this wise: "Sire, being thy son and of such very high condition both as to birth and estate as I have inherited from thee, I find that I have an extraordinary desire to imperil my body in this tourney. Accordingly, if so be I may approve my quality as *Sir Kay asks permission to attend the tournament.* to knighthood before this college of heralds, it will maybe be to thy great honor and credit, and to the honor and credit of our house if I should undertake this adventure. Wherefore I do crave thy leave to do as I have a mind."

Unto these Sir Ector made reply: "My son, thou hast my leave for to enter this honorable contest, and I do hope that God will give thee a great deal of strength, and likewise such grace of spirit that thou mayst achieve honor to thyself and credit to us who are of thy blood."

So Sir Kay departed with very great joy and immediately went to that congress of heralds and submitted his pretensions unto them. And, after they had duly examined into his claims to knighthood, they entered his name as a knight-contestant according to his desire; and at this Sir Kay was filled with great content and joy of heart.

So, when his name had been enrolled upon the list of combatants, Sir Kay chose his young brother Arthur for to be his esquire-at-arms and to carry his spear and pennant before him into the field of battle, and Arthur was also made exceedingly glad because of the honor that had befallen him and his brother.

Now, the day having arrived when this tourney was to be held, a very huge concourse of people gathered together to witness that noble and courtly assault at arms. For at that time London was, as aforesaid, extraordinarily full of nobility and knighthood, wherefore it was reckoned that not less than twenty thousand lords and ladies (besides those twelve kings and their courts and seven dukes and their courts) were assembled in the lists circumadjacent to the field of battle for to witness the performance of those chosen knights. And those noble people sat so close together, and so filled the seats and benches assigned to them, that it appeared as though an entirely solid wall of human souls surrounded that meadow where the battle was to be fought. And, indeed, any knight might well be moved to do his uttermost upon such a great occasion with the eyes of so many beautiful dames and noble lords gazing upon his performances. Wherefore the hearts of all the knights attendant were greatly expanded with emulation to overturn their enemies into the dust.

In the centre of this wonderful court of lords and ladies there was erected the stall and the throne of the lord Archbishop himself. Above the throne was a canopy of purple cloth emblazoned with silver lilies, and the throne itself was hung all about with purple cloth of velvet, embroidered, alternately, with the figure of St. George in gold, and with silver crosses of St. George surrounded by golden halos. Here the lord Archbishop himself sat in great estate and pomp, being surrounded by a very exalted court of clerks of high degree and also of knights of honorable estate, so that all that centre of the field glistered with the splendor of gold and silver embroidery, and was made beautiful by various colors of rich apparel and bright with fine armor of excellent workmanship. And, indeed, such was the stateliness of all these circumstances that very few who were there had ever seen so noble a preparation for battle as that which they then beheld.

Now, when all that great assembly were in their places and everything had been prepared in due wise, an herald came and stood forth before the enstalled throne of the Archbishop and blew a very strong, loud blast upon a trumpet. At that signal the turnpikes of the lists were immediately opened and two parties of knights-contestant entered therein—the one party at the northern extremity of the meadow of battle and the other party at the southern extremity thereof. Then immediately all that lone field was a-glitter with the bright-shining splendor of the sunlight upon polished armor and accoutrements. So these two parties took up their station, each at such a place as had been assigned unto them—the one to the north and the other to the south.

Now the party with which Sir Kay had cast his lot was at the north of the field, and that company was fourscore and thirteen in number; and *Sir Kay takes* the other party stood at the south end of the field, and that *hand in the* company was fourscore and sixteen in number. But though *lists.* the party with whom Sir Kay had attached himself numbered less by three than the other party, yet was it the stronger by some degree because that there were a number of knights of great strength and renown in that company. Indeed it may be here mentioned that two of those knights afterward became companions in very good credit of the round table—to wit: Sir Mador de la Porte, and Sir Bedevere—which latter was the last who saw King Arthur alive upon this earth.

So, when all was prepared according to the ordination of the tournament, and when those knights-contestant had made themselves ready in all ways that were necessary, and when they had dressed their spears and their shields in such a manner as befitted knights about to enter serious battle, the herald set his trumpet to his lips a second time and blew upon it with might and main. Then, having sounded this blast, he waited for a while and then he blew upon the trumpet again.

And, upon that blast, each of those parties of knights quitted its station and rushed forth in great tumult against the other party, and that with such noise and fury that the whole earth groaned beneath the feet of the war-horses, and trembled and shook as with an earthquake.

So those two companies met, the one against the other, in the midst of the field, and the roar of breaking lances was so terrible that those who heard it were astonished and appalled at the sound. For several fair dames swooned away with terror of the noise, and others shrieked aloud; for not only was there that great uproar, but the air was altogether filled with the splinters of ash wood that flew about.

In that famous assault threescore and ten very noble and honorable knights were overthrown, many of them being trampled beneath the hoofs of the horses; wherefore, when the two companies withdrew in retreat each to his station the ground was beheld to be covered all over with broken fragments of lances and with cantels of armor, and many knights were seen to be wofully lying in the midst of all that wreck. And some of these champions strove to arise and could not, while others lay altogether quiet as though in death. To these ran divers esquires and pages in great numbers, and lifted up the fallen men and bare them away to places of safe harborage. And likewise attendants ran and gathered up the cantels of armor and the broken spears, and bare them away to the barriers, so that, by and by, the field was altogether cleared once more.

Then all those who gazed down upon that meadow gave loud acclaim with great joyousness of heart, for such a noble and glorious contest at arms in friendly assay had hardly ever been beheld in all that realm before.

Now turn we unto Sir Kay; for in this assault he had conducted himself with such credit that no knight who was there had done better than he, and maybe no one had done so well as he. For, though two *Sir Kay bears* opponents at once had directed their spears against him, yet *himself well in* he had successfully resisted their assault. And one of those *the encounter.* two he smote so violently in the midst of his defences that he had lifted that assailant entirely over the crupper of the horse which he rode, and had flung him down to the distance of half a spear's length behind his steed, so that the fallen knight had rolled thrice over in the dust ere he ceased to fall.

And when those of Sir Kay's party who were nigh to him beheld what he did, they gave him loud and vehement acclaim, and that in such measure that Sir Kay was wonderfully well satisfied and pleased at heart.

And, indeed, it is to be said that at that time there was hardly any knight in all the world who was so excellent in deeds of arms as Sir Kay. And though there afterward came knights of much greater renown and of more glorious achievement (as shall be hereinafter recorded in good season), yet at that time Sir Kay was reckoned by many to be one of the most wonderfully puissant knights (whether errant or in battle) in all of that realm.

So was that course of the combat run to the great pleasure and satisfaction of all who beheld it, and more especially of Sir Kay and his friends. And after it had been completed the two parties in array returned each to its assigned station once more.

And when they had come there, each knight delivered up his spear unto his esquire. For the assault which was next to be made was to be undertaken with swords, wherefore all lances and other weapons were to be put away; such being the order of that courteous and gentle bout at arms.

Accordingly, when the herald again blew upon his trumpet, each knight drew his weapon with such readiness for battle that there was a great *Of the contest* splendor of blades all flashing in the air at once. And when *with swords.* the herald blew a second time each party pushed forward to the contest with great nobleness of heart and eagerness of spirit, every knight being moved with intent to engage his oppugnant with all the might and main that lay in him.

Then immediately began so fierce a battle that if those knights had been very enemies of long standing instead of friendly contestants, the blows which they delivered the one upon the other could not have been more vehement as to strength or more astonishing to gaze upon.

And in this affair likewise Sir Kay approved himself to be so extraordinary a champion that his like was nowhere to be seen in all that field; for he violently smote down five knights, the one after the other, ere he was stayed in his advance.

Wherefore, beholding him to be doing work of such a sort, several of the knights of the other party endeavored to come at him with intent to meet him in his advance.

Amongst these was a certain knight, hight Sir Balamorgineas, who was so huge of frame that he rode head and shoulders above any other knight. And he was possessed of such extraordinary strength that it was believed that he could successfully withstand the assault of three ordinary knights at one time. Wherefore when this knight beheld the work that Sir Kay did, he cried out to him, "Ho! ho! Sir Knight of the black gryphon, turn thou hitherward and do a battle with me!"

Now when Sir Kay beheld Sir Balamorgineas to be minded to come against him in that wise—very threateningly and minded to do him battle—he turned him toward his enemy with great cheerful- *Sir Kay con-* ness of spirit. For at that time Sir Kay was very full of *tests with Sir* youthful fire and reckoned nothing of assaulting any enemy *Balamorgineas.* who might demand battle of him.

(So it was at that time. But it after befell, when he became Seneschal, and when other and mightier knights appeared at the court of the King, that he would sometimes avoid an encounter with such a knight as Sir Launcelot, or Sir Pellias, or Sir Marhaus, or Sir Gawaine, if he might do so with credit to his honor.)

So, being very full of the spirit of youth, he turned him with great lustiness of heart, altogether inflamed with the eagerness and fury of battle. And he cried out in a great voice, "Very well, I will do battle with thee, and I will cast thee down like thy fellows!" And therewith he smote with wonderful fierceness at Sir Balamorgineas, and that with all his might. And Sir Balamorgineas received the stroke upon his helmet and was altogether bewildered by the fury thereof, for he had never felt its like before that time. Wherefore his brains swam so light that it was necessary for him to hold to the horn of his saddle to save himself from falling.

But it was a great pity for Sir Kay that, with the fierceness of the blow, his sword-blade snapped short at the haft, flying so high in the air that it appeared to overtop the turrets of the cathedral in its flight. Yet so it happened, and thus it befell that Sir Kay was left *Sir Kay break-* without any weapon. Yet it was thought that, because of *eth his sword.* that stroke, he had Sir Balamorgineas entirely at his mercy, and that if he could have struck another blow with his sword he might easily have overcome him.

But as it was, Sir Balamorgineas presently so far recovered himself that he perceived his enemy to be altogether at his mercy; wherefore, being filled beyond measure with rage because of the blow he had received, he pushed against Sir Kay with intent to smite him down in a violent assault.

In this pass it would maybe have gone very ill with Sir Kay but that three of his companions in arms, perceiving the extreme peril in which he lay, thrust in betwixt him and Sir Balamorgineas with intent to take upon themselves the assault of that knight and so to save Sir Kay from over-throw. This they did with such success that Sir Kay was able to push out from the press and to escape to the barriers without suffering any further harm at the hands of his enemies.

Now when he reached the barrier, his esquire, young Arthur, came running to him with a goblet of spiced wine. And Sir Kay opened the um-bril of his helmet for to drink, for he was athirst beyond measure. And, lo! his face was all covered over with blood and sweat, and he was so a-drought with battle that his tongue clave to the roof of his mouth and he could not speak. But when he had drunk of the draught that Arthur gave him, his tongue was loosened and he cried out to the young man *Sir Kay bids* in a loud and violent voice: "Ho! ho! Brother, get me *Arthur get him* another sword for to do battle, for I am assuredly winning for *a sword.* our house much glory this day!" And Arthur said, "Where shall I get thee a sword?" And Kay said, "Make haste unto our father's pavilion and fetch me thence another sword, for this which I have is broken." And Arthur said, "I will do so with all speed," and thereupon he set hand to the barrier and leaped over it into the alleyway beyond. And he ran down the alleyway with all the speed that he was able with intent to fulfil that task which his brother had bidden him to undertake; and with like speed he ran to that pavilion that his father had set up in the meadows.

But when he came to the pavilion of Sir Ector he found no one there, for all the attendants had betaken themselves unto the tournament. And neither could he find any sword fit for his brother's handling, wherefore he was put to a great pass to know what to do in that matter.

In this extremity he bethought him of that sword that stood thrust into the anvil before the cathedral, and it appeared to him that such a sword as that would suit his brother's purposes very well. Wherefore he said to himself, "I will go thither and get that sword if I am able to do so, for it will assuredly do very well for my brother for to finish his battle withal." Whereupon he ran with all speed to the cathedral. And when he had come there he discovered that no one was there upon guard at the block of marble, as had heretofore been the case, for all who had been upon guard had betaken themselves unto the contest of arms that was to-*Arthur draw-* ward. And the anvil and the sword stood where he could *eth the sword* reach them. So, there being no one to stay young Arthur, *from the anvil.* he leaped up upon the block of marble and laid his hands unto the hilt of the sword. And he bent his body and drew upon the sword very strongly, and, lo! it came forth from the anvil with wonderful smoothness and ease, and he held the sword in his hand, and it was his.

And when he had got the sword in that way, he wrapped it in his cloak so that no one might see it (for it shone with an exceeding brightness and splendor) and he leaped down from the block of marble stone and hastened with it unto the field of battle.

Now when Arthur had entered into that meadow once more, he found Sir Kay awaiting his coming with great impatience of spirit. And when Sir Kay saw him he cried out, very vehemently, " Hast thou got a sword? " And Arthur said, " Yea, I have one here." Thereupon he opened his cloak and showed Sir Kay what sword it was he had brought.

Now when Sir Kay beheld the sword he immediately knew it, and he wist not what to think or what to say, wherefore he stood for a while, like one turned into a stone, looking upon that sword. Then in awhile he said, in a very strange voice " Where got ye that sword? " And Arthur looked upon his brother and he beheld that his countenance was greatly disturbed, and that his face was altogether as white as wax. And he said, " Brother, what ails thee that thou lookest so strangely. I will tell the entire truth. I could find no sword in our father's pavilion, wherefore I bethought me of that sword that stood in the anvil upon the marble cube before the cathedral. So I went thither and made assay for to draw it forth, and it came forth with wonderful ease. So, when I had drawn it out, I wrapped it in my cloak and brought it hither unto thee as thou beholdest."

Then Sir Kay turned his thoughts inward aud communed with himself in this wise, " Lo! my brother Arthur is as yet hardly more than a child. And he is, moreover, exceedingly innocent. Therefore he knoweth not what he hath done in this nor what the doing thereof signi- *Sir Kay keep-* fieth. Now, since he hath achieved this weapon, why should *eth the sword* I not myself lay claim to that achievement, and so obtain the *for his own.* glory which it signifieth." Whereupon he presently aroused himself, and he said to Arthur, " Give the sword and the cloak to me," and Arthur did as his brother commanded. And when he had done so Sir Kay said to him, " Tell no man of this but keep it privy in thine own heart. Meantime go thou to our father where he sits at the lists and bid come straightway unto the pavilion where we have taken up our inn."

And Arthur did as Sir Kay commanded him, greatly possessed with wonder that his brother should be so disturbed in spirit as he had appeared to be. For he wist not what he had done in drawing out that sword from the anvil, nor did he know of what great things should arise from that little thing, for so it is in this world that a man sometimes approves himself to be worthy of such a great trust as that, and yet, in lowliness of spirit, he is yet altogether unaware that he is worthy thereof.   And so it was with young Arthur at that time.

Chapter Second.

How Arthur Twice Performed the Miracle of the Sword Before Sir Ector and of How His Birthright Was Discovered Unto Him.

SO Arthur made haste to that part of the lists where Sir Ector sat with the people of his household. And he stood before his father and said, " Sire, my brother Kay hath sent me hitherward for to bid thee come straightway unto the pavilion where we have taken up our inn. And, truly, I think something very extraordinary hath befallen, for my brother Kay hath such a countenance as I never saw him wear."

Then Sir Ector marvelled very greatly what it was that should cause Sir Kay to quit that battle and to summon him at such a time, wherefore he arose from where he sat and went with Arthur. And they went to the pavilion, and when he had come there, behold! Sir Kay was standing in the midst of the pavilion. And Sir Ector saw that his face was as white as ashes of wood and that his eyes shone with a wonderful brightness. And Sir Ector said, " My son, what ails thee?" whereunto Sir Kay made reply, "Sire, here is a very wonderful matter." Therewith he took his father by the hand and brought him to the table that stood in the pavilion. And upon the table there lay a cloak and there was something within the cloak. Then Sir Kay opened the cloak and, lo! there lay the sword of the anvil, and the hilt thereof and the blade thereof glistered with exceeding splendor.

And Sir Ector immediately knew that sword and whence it came. Wherefore he was filled with such astonishment that he wist not what to do. And for a while his tongue refused *Sir Ector be-* to speak, and after a while he found speech and cried out *holdeth the* aloud in a great voice, " What is this that mine eyes behold!" *sword.*

To this Sir Kay made reply, " Sire. I have that sword which stood a while since embedded in the anvil that stands upon the cube of marble stone before the great cathedral. Wherefore I demand that thou tellest me what this may foretend?"

Then Sir Ector said, " How came you by that sword?"

And for a while Sir Kay was silent, but after a while he said, "Sire, I brake my sword in that battle which of late I fought, whereupon I found me this sword in its stead."

Then Sir Ector was altogether bemazed and knew not whether to believe what his ears heard. And after awhile he said, " If so be that thou didst draw forth this sword from the anvil, then it must also be that thou art rightwise King of Britain, for so the saying of the sword proclaimeth. But if thou didst indeed draw it forth from the anvil, then it will be that thou shalt as easily be able for to thrust it back again into that place from whence thou didst take it."

At this a great trouble of spirit fell upon Sir Kay, and he cried out in a very loud voice, " Who may do such a thing as that, and who could perform so great a miracle as to thrust a sword into solid iron." Whereunto Sir Ector made reply, " Such a miracle is no greater than the miracle that thou hast performed in drawing it out from its embedment. For who ever heard that a man could draw forth a sword from a place and yet would not thrust it back whence he drew it ? "

Then Sir Kay wist not what to say to his father, and he greatly feared that he should not be able to perform that miracle. But, nevertheless, he took what comfort to himself he was able, saying, " If my young brother Arthur was able to perform this miracle why should I not do a miracle of a like sort, for, assuredly, I am not less worthy than he. Wherefore if he drew the sword forth with such ease, it may be that I with equal ease shall be able to thrust it back into its place again." Accordingly he took such comfort to himself in these thoughts as he was able.

So he wrapped the sword in the cloak again, and when he had done so he and Sir Ector went forth from the pavilion and betook their way unto where was the marble stone and the anvil before the cathedral. And Arthur went with his father and his brother and they forebade him not. And when they had come to that place where the sword had been, Sir Kay mounted upon the cube of marble stone and beheld the face of the anvil And lo ! the face of the anvil was altogether smooth and without a scratch or scar of any sort. And Sir Kay said to himself, " What is this my father would have me do ! What man is there in life who could thrust a sword-blade into a solid anvil of iron ? " But, ne'theless, he could not

Sir Kay assays to put back the sword but faileth. withdraw from that impossible undertaking, but was constrained to assay that miracle, wherefore he set the point of the sword to the iron and bore upon it with all his strength.

But it was impossible for him to accomplish that thing, and though he endeavored with all his might with the sword against the face of the anvil, yet did he not pierce the iron even to the breadth of a hair.

So, after he had thus assayed for a great while, he at last ceased what he did and came down from where he stood. And he said to his father, " Sire, no man in life may perform that miracle."

Unto this Sir Ector made reply, " How is it possible then that thou couldst have drawn out that sword as thou sayst and yet cannot put it back again ? "

Then young Arthur lifted up his voice and said, " My father, have I thy leave to speak ? " And Sir Ector said, " Speak, my son." And Arthur said, " I would that I might assay to handle that sword ? " Whereunto Sir Ector replied, " By what authority wouldst thou handle that sword ? " And Arthur said, " Because it was I who drew that sword forth from the anvil for my brother. Wherefore, as thou sayest, to draw it forth is not more difficult than to thrust it back again. So I believe that I shall be able to set it back into the iron whence I drew it."

Then Sir Ector gazed upon young Arthur in such a strange manner that Arthur wist not why he looked at him in that wise. Wherefore he cried out, " Sire, why dost thou gaze so strangely upon me? Has thou anger against me ? " Whereunto Sir Ector made reply, " In the sight of God, my son, I have no anger against thee." Then he said, " If thou hast a desire to handle the sword, thou mayst assuredly make assay of that miracle."

So Arthur took the sword from his brother Kay and he leaped up upon the marble stone. And he set the point of the sword upon the anvil and bare very strongly upon it and lo! the sword penetrated *Arthur per-* very smoothly into the centre of the anvil until it stood *formeth the miracle of the* midway deep therein, and there it stood fast. And after he *sword and the* had performed that miracle he drew the sword forth again *anvil.* very swiftly and easily, and then thrust it back again once more as he had done before.

But when Sir Ector beheld what Arthur did, he cried out in a voice of exceeding loudness, " Lord! Lord! what is the miracle mine eyes behold ! " And when Arthur came down from the cube of marble stone, Sir Ector kneeled down before him and set his hands together, palm to palm.

But when Arthur beheld what his father did, he cried out aloud like one in a great measure of pain; and he said, " My father! my father! why dost thou kneel down to me ? "

To him Sir Ector made reply, " I am not thy father, and now it is made manifest that thou art assuredly of very exalted race and that the blood of kings flows in thy veins, else thou couldst not have handled that sword as thou hast done."

Then Arthur fell a-weeping beyond all measure and he cried out as with great agony of spirit, "Father! father! what is this thou sayst? I beseech thee to arise and not to kneel unto me."

So Sir Ector arose from his knees and stood before the face of Arthur, and he said, "Arthur, why dost thou weep?" And Arthur said, "Because I am afeard."

Now all this while Sir Kay had stood near by and he could neither move nor speak, but stood like one entranced, and he said to himself, "What is this? Is my brother a King?"

Then Sir Ector spake, saying, "Arthur, the time hath come for thee to know thyself, for the true circumstances of thy life have, heretofore, been altogether hidden from thee.

Sir Ector tell-eth Arthur the circumstances of his infancy. "Now I do confess everything to thee in this wise: that eighteen year ago there came to me a certain man very wise and high in favor with Uther-Pendragon and that man was the Enchanter Merlin. And Merlin showed me the signet ring of Uther-Pendragon and he commanded me by virtue of that ring that I should be at a certain assigned place at a particular time which he nominated; and the place which he assigned was the postern gate of Uther-Pendragon's castle; and the time which he named was midnight of that very day.

"And he bade me tell no man aught concerning those things which he communicated to me, and so I kept his counsel as he desired me to do.

"So I went to that postern gate at midnight as Merlin had commanded, and at that place there came unto me Merlin and another man, and the other man was Sir Ulfius, who was the chief knight of Uther-Pendragon's household. And I tell thee that these two worthies stood nigher unto Uther-Pendragon than any other men in all of the world.

"Now when those two came unto me, I perceived that Merlin bare in his arms a certain thing wrapped in a scarlet mantle of fine texture. And he opened the folds of the mantle and, lo! I beheld a child not long born and wrapped in swaddling clothes. And I saw the child in the light of a lanthorn which Sir Ulfius bare, and I perceived that he was very fair of face and large of bone—and thou wert that child.

"Then Merlin commanded me in this wise: that I was to take that child and that I should rear him as mine own; and he said that the child was to be called by the name of Arthur; and he said that no one in all the world was to know otherwise than that the child was mine own. And I told

Merlin that I would do as he would have me, whereupon I took the child and bare it away with me. And I proclaimed that the child was mine own, and all over the world believed my words, wherefore no one ever knew otherwise than that thou wert mine own son. And that lady who was my wife, when she died she took that secret with her unto Paradise, and since then until now no one in all the world knew aught of this matter but I and those two aforementioned worthies.

"Nor have I until now ever known aught of who was thy father; but now I do suspect who he was and that thou hast in thy veins very high and kingly blood. And I do have in mind that perhaps thy father was Uther-Pendragon himself. For who but the son of Uther-Pendragon could have drawn forth that sword from out of the anvil as thou hast done?"

Then, when Arthur heard that saying of his father's, he cried out in a very loud and vehement voice, "Woe! Woe! Woe!"—saying that word three times. And Sir Ector said, "Arthur, why art thou woful?" And Arthur said, "Because I have lost my father, for I would rather have my father than be a King!"

Now as these things passed, there came unto that place two men, very tall and of a wonderfully noble and haughty appearance. And when these two men had come nigh to where they were, Arthur and Sir Ector and Sir Kay preceived that one of them was the Enchanter Merlin and that the other was Sir Ulfius—for those two men were very *Merlin and Sir* famous and well known unto all the world. And when those *Ulfius appear* two had come to where were the three, Merlin spake, saying, *to the three.* "What cheer?" And Sir Ector made answer, "Here is cheer of a very wonderful sort; for, behold, Merlin! this is that child that thou didst bring unto me eighteen years ago, and, lo! thou seest he hath grown unto manhood."

Then Merlin said, "Sir Ector, I know very well who is this youth, for I have kept diligent watch over him for all this time. And I know that in him lieth the hope of Britain. Moreover, I tell thee that even to-day within the surface of an enchanted looking-glass I have beheld all that he hath done since the morning; and I know how he drew forth the sword from the anvil, and how he thrust it back again; and I know how he drew it forth and thrust it back a second time. And I know all that thou hast been saying unto him this while; wherefore I also do now avouch that thou hast told him the very truth. And, lo! the spirit of prophecy is upon me and I do foresee into the future that thou, Arthur, shall become the greatest and most famous King that ever lived in Britain; and I do foresee that many knights of extraordinary excellence shall gather about thee and that men shall tell of their marvellous deeds as long as this land shall continue, and I do foresee that through these knights thy reign shall be full of splendor and glory; and I do foresee that the most marvellous adventure of the Holy Grail shall be achieved by three of the knights of thy Court, and that to thy lasting renown, who shall be the King under whose reign the holy cup shall be achieved. All these things I foresee; and, lo! the time is now at hand when the glory of thy House shall again be made manifest unto the world, and all the people of this land shall rejoice in thee and thy kinghood. Wherefore, Sir Ector, for these three days to come, I do charge it upon thee that thou do guard this young man as the apple of thine eye, for in him doth lie the hope and salvation of all this realm."

Then Sir Ector lifted up his voice and cried unto Arthur, "A boon! a boon!" And Arthur said, "Alas! how is this? Dost thou, my father, ask a boon of me who may have all in the world that is mine to give? Ask *Sir Ector craveth a boon of Arthur.* what thou wilt and it is thine!" Then Sir Ector said, "I do beseech this of thee: that when thou art King thy brother Kay may be Seneschal of all this realm." And Arthur said, "It shall be as thou dost ask." And he said, "As for thee, it shall be still better with thee, for thou shalt be my father unto the end!" Whereupon so saying, he took Sir Ector's head into his hands and he kissed Sir Ector upon the forehead and upon the cheeks, and so sealed his plighted word.

But all this while Sir Kay had stood like unto one struck by thunder, and he wist not whether to be uplifted unto the skies or to be cast down into the depths, that his young brother should thus have been passed by him and exalted unto that extraordinary altitude of fortune. Wherefore he stood like to one bereft of life and motion.

And let it here be said that Arthur fulfilled all that he had thus promised to his father—for, in after times, he made Sir Kay his Sene-schal, and Sir Ector was to him a father until the day of his death, which same befell five years from that time.

Thus I have told you how the royalty of Arthur was first discovered. And now, if you will listen, ye shall hear how it was confirmed before all the world.

ow Arthur drew forth ẏ Sword.

Chapter Third.

*How Several Kings and High Dukes Assayed to Draw the Sword
Out of the Anvil and How They Failed. Likewise How Arthur
Made the Assay and Succeeded Therein.*

SO when the morning of Christmas day had come, many thousands
of folk of all qualities, both gentle and simple, gathered together
in front of the cathedral for to behold the assay of that sword.

Now there had been a canopy of embroidered cloth of divers colors
spread above the sword and the anvil, and a platform had been built
around about the cube of marble stone. And nigh unto that place there
had been a throne for the Archbishop established; for the Archbishop
was to overlook that assay and to see that every circumstance was fulfilled
with due equity and circumspection.

So, when the morning was half gone by, the Archbishop himself came
with great pomp of estate and took his seat upon the high throne that had
been placed for him, and all his court of clerks and knights gathered about
him, so that he presented a very proud and excellent appearance of
courtliness.

Now unto that assay there had gathered nineteen kings and sixteen
dukes, and each of these was of such noble and exalted estate that he entertained high hopes that he would that day be approved before the world
to be the right king and overlord of all Britain. Wherefore after the
Archbishop had established himself upon his throne, there came several of
these and made demand that he should straightway put that matter to the
test. So the Archbishop commanded his herald for to sound a trumpet,
and to bid all who had the right to make assay of the sword to come
unto that adventure, and the herald did according as the Archbishop or-
dered.

And when the herald had sounded his trumpet there immediately appeared the first of those kings to make trial of the sword, and he who came
was King Lot of Orkney and the Isles. With King Lot there came eleven

knights and five esquires, so that he appeared in very noble estate before
the eyes of all. And when King Lot had arrived at that place, he mounted
the platform. And first he saluted the Archbishop, and then he laid his
hands to the pommel of the sword in the sight of all. And he bent his
body and drew upon the sword with great strength, but he could not move
the blade in the anvil even so much as the breadth of a hair, for it stood as
King Lot of   fast as the iron in which it was planted. And after that first
Orkney maketh   assay he tried three times more, but still he was altogether
assay of the
sword and fail- unable to move the blade in the iron. Then, after that he had
eth.   thus four times made assay, he ceased his endeavor and came
down from that place. And he was filled with great anger and indignation that he had not succeeded in his endeavor.

And after King Lot there came his brother-in-law, King Urien of Gore,
and he also made assay in the same wise as King Lot had done. But
neither did he succeed any better than that other king. And after King
Urien there came King Fion of Scotland, and after King Fion there came
Sundry others   King Mark of Cornwall, and after King Mark there came
make assay and King Ryence of North Wales, and after King Ryence there
fail.   came King Leodegrance of Cameliard, and after him came all
those other kings and dukes before numerated, and not one of all these
was able to move the blade. And some of these high and mighty lords
were filled with anger and indignation that they had not succeeded, and
others were ashamed that they had failed in that undertaking before the
eyes of all those who looked upon them. But whether they were angry or
whether they were ashamed it in no wise helped their case.

Now when all the kings and dukes had thus failed in that adventure,
the people who were there were very much astonished, and they said to
one another, "How is this? If all those kings and dukes of very exalted
estate have failed to achieve that adventure, who then may hope to succeed? For here have been all those who were most worthy of that high
honor, and all have tried to draw that sword and all have failed. Who
then is there now to come after these who may hope to succeed?"

And, likewise, those kings and dukes spoke together in the same manner.
And by and by there came six of the most worthy—to wit, King Lot,
King Urien, King Pellinore, King Ban, King Ryence, and Duke Clarence of
Northumberland—and these stood before the throne of the Archbishop and
spake to him in this wise: "Sir, here have all the kings and dukes of this
realm striven before you for to draw forth that sword, and lo! not one of
all those who have undertaken that thing hath succeeded in his undertaking. What, then, may we understand but that the enchanter Merlin hath

set this adventure for to bring shame and discredit upon all of us who are here, and upon you, who are the head of the church in this realm? For who in all the world may hope to draw forth a sword-blade out from a bed of solid iron? Behold! it is be- *The kings and dukes are discontented.* yond the power of any man. Is it not then plain to be seen that Merlin hath made a mock of us all? Now, therefore, lest all this great congregation should have been called here in vain, we do beseech you of your wisdom that you presently choose the one from among the kings here gathered, who may be best fitted to be overlord of this realm. And when ye shall have chosen him, we will promise to obey him in all things whatsoever he may ordain. Verily, such a choice as that will be better worth while than to spend time in this foolish task of striving to draw forth a sword out of an anvil which no man in all the world may draw forth."

Then was the Archbishop much troubled in spirit, for he said to himself, " Can it be sooth that Merlin hath deceived me, and hath made a mock of me and of all these kings and lordly folk? Surely this cannot be. For Merlin is passing wise, and he would not make a mock of all the realm for the sake of so sorry a jest as this would be. Certes he hath some intent in this of which we know naught, being of less wisdom than he—wherefore I will be patient for a while longer." Accordingly, having communed thus within himself, he spake aloud in this wise to those seven high lords: " Messires," he said, " I have yet faith that Merlin hath not deceived us, wherefore I pray your patience for one little while longer. For if, in the time a man may count five hundred twice over, no one cometh forward to perform this task, then will I, at your behest, proceed to choose one from amongst you and will proclaim him King and Overlord of all." For the Archbishop had faith that Merlin was about to immediately declare a king before them all.

Now leave we these and turn we unto Arthur and his father and brother.

For Merlin had bidden those three to abide in their pavilion until such time as he thought would be fit for them to come out thence. And that time being now come, Merlin and Sir Ulfius went to the pavilion of Sir Ector, and Merlin said, " Arthur, arise and come forth, for now the hour is come for thee to assay before the whole world that miracle which thou didst of late execute in privacy." So Arthur did as Merlin bade him to do, and he came forth from the pavilion with his father and his brother, and, lo! he was like one who walked in a dream.

So they five went down from thence toward the cathedral and unto that

place of assay. And when they had come to the congregation there assembled, the people made way for them, greatly marvelling and saying to
one another, " Who are these with the Enchanter Merlin and
Sir Ulfius, and whence come they? For all the world knew
Merlin and Sir Ulfius, and they wist that here was something
very extraordinary about to happen. And Arthur was clad all in flame-
colored raiment embroidered with threads of silver, so that others of the
people said, " Certes, that youth is very fair for to look upon ; now who
may he be ? "

*Merlin bring-
eth Arthur to
the assay.*

But Merlin said no word to any man, but he brought Arthur through
the press unto that place where the Archbishop sat ; and the press made
way for him so that he was not stayed in his going. And when the Archbishop beheld Merlin come thus with those others, he arose and said,
" Merlin, who are these whom thou bringest unto us, and what is their
business here ? " And Merlin said, " Lord, here is one come to make the
assay of yonder sword." And the Archbishop said, " Which one is he ? "
and Merlin said, " This is he," and he laid his hand upon Arthur.

Then the Archbishop looked upon Arthur and he beheld that the youth
was very comely of face, wherefore his heart went out unto Arthur and he
loved him a very great deal. And the Archbishop said, "Merlin, by what
right doth this young man come hither ? " And Merlin made
reply, " Lord, he cometh hither by the best right that there is
in the world ; for he who standeth before thee clad in red is
the true son of Uther-Pendragon and of his lawful wife,
Queen Igraine."

*Merlin pro-
claimeth the
royalty of
Arthur.*

Then the Archbishop cried out aloud in great amazement and those who
stood nigh and who heard what Merlin said were so astonished that they
wist not what to think. And the Archbishop said, " Merlin, what is this
that thou tellest me ? For who, until now, in all the world hath ever heard
that Uther-Pendragon had a son ? "

Unto this Merlin made reply : " No one hath ever known of such a
thing until now, only a very few. For it was in this wise : When this
child was born the spirit of prophecy lay upon me and I foresaw that
Uther-Pendragon would die before a very great while. Wherefore I
feared that the enemies of the King would lay violent hands upon the
young child for the sake of his inheritance. So, at the King's behest, I
and another took the young child from his mother and gave him unto a
third, and that man received the kingly child and maintained him ever
since as his own son. And as to the truth of these things there are others
here who may attest the verity of them—for he who was with me when

the young child was taken from his mother was Sir Ulfius, and he to whom he was entrusted was Sir Ector of Bonmaison—and those two witnesses, who are without any reproach, will avouch to the verity of that which I have asserted, for here they stand before thee to certify unto what I have said."

And Sir Ulfius and Sir Ector said, "All that Merlin hath spoken is true, and thereunto we do pledge our most faithful and sacred word of honor."

Then the Archbishop said, "Who is there may doubt the word of such honorable witnesses?" And he looked upon Arthur and smiled upon him.

Then Arthur said, "Have I then thy leave, Lord, to handle yonder sword?" And the Archbishop said, "Thou hast my leave, and may the grace of God go with thee to do thy endeavor."

Thereupon Arthur went to the cube of marble stone and he laid his hands upon the haft of the sword that was thrust into the anvil. And he bent his body and drew very strongly and, lo! the sword came *Arthur draw-* forth with great ease and very smoothly. And when he had *eth forth the* got the sword into his hands, he swung it about his head so *sword.* that it flashed like lightning. And after he had swung it thus thrice about his head, he set the point thereof against the face of the anvil and bore upon it very strongly, and, behold! the sword slid very smoothly back again into that place where it had aforetime stood; and when it was there, midway deep, it stood fast where it was. And thus did Arthur successfully accomplish that marvellous miracle of the sword in the eyes of all the world.

Now when the people who were congregated at that place beheld this miracle performed before their faces, they lifted up their voices all together, and shouted so vehemently and with so huge a tumult of outcry that it was as though the whole earth rocked and trembled with the sound of their shouting.

And whiles they so shouted Arthur took hold of the sword again and drew it forth and swung it again, and again drave it back into the anvil. And when he had done that he drew it forth a third time and did the same thing as before. Thus it was that all those who were there beheld that miracle performed three times over.

And all the kings and dukes who were there were filled with great amazement, and they wist not what to think or to say when they beheld one who was little more than a boy perform that undertaking in which the best of them had failed. And some of them, seeing that miracle, were willing to acknowledge Arthur because of it, but others would not acknowledge him. These withdrew themselves and stood aloof; and as they stood thus apart, they said among themselves: "What is this and who can accredit such a thing that a beardless boy should be set before us all and should *Several of the* be made King and overlord of this great realm for to govern *kings and dukes* us. Nay! nay! we will have none of him for our King." *are angry.* And others said, "Is it not apparent that Merlin and Sir Ulfius are thus exalting this unknown boy so that they may elevate themselves along with him?" Thus these discontented kings spake among themselves, and of all of them the most bitter were King Lot and King Urien, who were brothers by marriage with Arthur.

Now when the Archbishop perceived the discontent of these kings and dukes, he said to them, "How now, Messires! Are ye not satisfied?" And they said, "We are not satisfied." And the Archbishop said, "What would ye have?" And they said, "We would have another sort of king for Britain than a beardless boy of whom no one knoweth and of whose birthright there are only three men to attest." And the Archbishop said, "What of that? Hath he not performed the miracle that ye yourselves assayed and failed to perform?"

But these high and mighty lords would not be satisfied, but with angry and averted faces they went away from that place, filled with wrath and indignation.

But others of these kings and dukes came and saluted Arthur and paid *Certain kings* him court, giving him joy of that which he had achieved; and *and dukes ac-* the chiefest of those who came thus unto him in friendliness *cept Arthur.* was King Leodegrance of Cameliard. And all the multitude acknowledged him and crowded around that place shouting so that it sounded like to the noise of thunder.

Now all this while Sir Ector and Sir Kay had stood upon one side. And they were greatly weighed down by sorrow; for it appeared to them that Arthur had, of a sudden, been uplifted so far from their estate that they might never hope to approach him more. For now he was of kingly consequence and they but common knights. And, after awhile, Arthur beheld them where they stood with downcast looks, whereupon he straightway went to them and took first one and then the other by the hand and kissed each upon the cheek. Thereupon they were again very glad at being thus uplifted unto him.

And when Arthur departed from that place, great crowds of people followed after him so that the streets were altogether filled with the press of people. And the multitude continually gave him loud acclaim as the chosen King of England, and those who were nearest to him sought to touch the hem of his garments; wherefore the heart of Arthur was exceedingly uplifted with great joy and gladness, so that his soul took wing and flew like a bird into the sky.

Thus Arthur achieved the adventure of the sword that day and entered into his birthright of royalty. Wherefore, may God grant His Grace unto you all that ye too may likewise succeed in your undertakings. For any man may be a king in that life in which he is placed if so be he may draw forth the sword of success from out of the iron of circumstance. Wherefore when your time of assay cometh, I do hope it may be with you as it was with Arthur that day, and that ye too may achieve success with entire satisfaction unto yourself and to your great glory and perfect happiness. Amen.

CONCLUSION

Now after these things had happened there was much talk among men and great confusion and tumult. For while some of the kings and nearly all the multitude said, " Lo! here is a king come to us, as it were, from out of Heaven for to bring peace unto our distracted land," yet other kings (and they were of greater number) said, " Who is this beardless boy who cometh with a claim to be High King of Britain? Who ever heard of him before? We will have none of him except upon further trial and upon greater avouchment." So, for the sake of peace, the Archbishop ordained that another assay of the sword should be made at Candlemas;

Arthur maketh sundry other assays of the sword and succeeds at all times. and here again all those who endeavored to draw forth the sword failed thereat, but Arthur drew it forth several times, very easily, in the sight of all. And after that a third trial was made at Easter and after that a fourth trial was made at Pentecost. And at all these trials Arthur repeatedly drew out the sword from the anvil, and no one but he could draw it forth.

And, after that fourth trial, sundry of the kings and many of the lesser barons and knights and all of the commons cried out that these were trials enough, and that Arthur had assuredly approved himself to be rightwise King; wherefore they demanded that he should be made King indeed so that he might rule over them. For it had come to pass that whithersoever Arthur went great crowds followed after him hailing

Arthur is crowned King of Britain. him as the true son of Uther-Pendragon, and rightwise overlord of Britain. Wherefore, the Archbishop (seeing how the people loved Arthur and how greatly they desired him for their King) ordained that he should be anointed and crowned unto royal estate; and so it was done at the great Cathedral. And some say that that Cathedral was St. Paul's and some say that it was not.

But when Arthur had thus been crowned, all those who were opposed unto his Kingship withdrew themselves in great anger, and immediately set about to prepare war against him. But the people were with Arthur

Arthur overcometh his enemies. and joined with him, and so also did several Kings and many of the lesser barons and knights. And, with the advice of Merlin, Arthur made friends and allies of sundry other kings and they and he fought two great wars with his enemies and won both of these wars. And in the second war was fought a very famous battle nigh to the Forest of Bedegraine (wherefore it was called the Battle of Bedegraine), and in that battle Arthur overthrew his enemies so entirely that it was not possible for them ever to hope to unite in war against him again.

And of King Lot, his brother-in-law, King Arthur brought two of his sons to Court for to dwell there and to serve as hostages of peace thereafter. And these two were Gawaine and Geharris and they became, after awhile, very famous and accomplished knights. And of King Urien, his other brother-in-law, Arthur brought unto Court his one son, Ewaine, for to hold as an hostage of peace; and he also became in time a very famous and accomplished knight. And because of these hostages *Arthur bringeth* there was peace thereafter betwixt those three kingly brothers *his nephews to* for all time. And a certain very famous king and knight *court.* hight King Pellinore (who was one of his enemies) Arthur drove out of his possessions and away from the habitations of men and into the forest. And King Ryence (who was another of his enemies) he drave into the mountains of North Wales. And other kings who were his enemies he subjugated to his will, so that all the land was at such peace that it had not enjoyed the like since the days of Uther-Pendragon.

And King Arthur made Sir Kay his Seneschal as he had promised to do; and he made Sir Ulfius his Chamberlain; and Merlin he made his Counsellor; and Sir Bodwain of Britain he made his Constable. And these men were all of such a sort as greatly enhanced the glory and renown of his reign and established him upon his throne with entire security.

Now when the reign of King Arthur became thus entirely established, and when the renown of his greatness began to be known in the world, many men of noble souls and of large spirit and of high knightly prowess—knights who desired above all things to achieve glory at arms in Courts of Chivalry—perceived that great credit and exaltation of estate were likely to be won under such a king. So it fell out that, from all parts, by little and little, there began to gather together such a Court of noble, honorable knights about King Arthur as men never beheld before that time, and shall haply never behold again.

For even to this day the history of these good knights is known to the greater part of mankind. Yea; the names of many kings and emperors have passed away and have been forgotten, but the names of Sir Galahad, and of Sir Launcelot of the Lake, and of Sir Tristram of Lyonesse, and of Sir Percival of Gales, and of Sir Gawaine, and of Sir Ewaine, and of Sir Bors de Ganis, and of many others of that noble household of worthy brotherhood, is still remembered by men. Wherefore, I think that it is very likely that so long as words shall be written, the performances of these worthies shall be remembered.

So in this history yet to be written, I have set it for my task to inform him who reads this book of many of these adventures, telling him, besides, such several circumstances as I do not believe are known unto everybody. And by and by, when I shall tell of the establishment of the Round Table, I shall set forth a tabulated list of a number of those worthies who at this time assembled at the Court of Arthur as men chosen to found that order of the Round Table, and who, for that reason, were entitled "The Ancient and Honorable Companions of the Round Table."

For though this entire history chiefly concerneth King Arthur, yet the glory of these great honorable knights was his glory, and his glory was their glory, wherefore one cannot tell of the glory of King Arthur without also telling of the glory of those noble gentlemen aforesaid.

PART II
The Winning of a Sword

HERE beginneth the story of certain adventures of Arthur after that he had become King, wherein it is told how, with great knightly courage and prowess, he fought a very fierce and bloodly battle with a certain Sable Knight. Likewise, it is told how he achieved, in consequence of that battle, a certain Sword so famous and glorious that its renown shall last as long as our speech shall be spoken. For the like of that sword was never seen in all the world before that time, and it hath never been beheld since then; and its name was Excalibur.

So, if it please you to read this story, I believe it will afford you excellent entertainment, and will, without doubt, greatly exalt your spirit because of the remarkable courage which those two famous and worthy knights displayed when they fought together that famous battle. Likewise you shall find great cheer in reading therein of the wonderful marvellousness of a certain land of Faerie into which King Arthur wandered, and where he found a Lake of Enchantment and held converse with a mild and beautiful lady of that land who directed him how to obtain that renowned sword aforementioned.

For it hath given me such pleasure to write these things that my heart would, at times, be diluted as with a pure joy, wherefore, I entertain great hopes that you also may find much pleasure in them as I have already done. So I pray you to listen unto what follows.

n the Valley of Delight

Chapter First.

How There Came a Certain Wounded Knight Unto the Court of King Arthur, How a Young Kinght of the King's Court Sought To Avenge Him and Failed and How the King Thereupon Took That Assay Upon Himself.

NOW it fell upon a certain pleasant time in the Springtide season that King Arthur and his Court were making a royal progression through that part of Britain which lieth close to the Forests of the Usk. At that time the weather was exceedingly warm, and so the King and Court made pause within the forest under the trees in the cool and pleasant shade that the place afforded, and there the King rested for a while upon a couch of rushes spread with scarlet cloth.

How King Arthur abided in the Forest of Usk.

And the knights then present at that Court were, Sir Gawaine, and Sir

Ewaine, and Sir Kay, and Sir Pellias, and Sir Bedevere, and Sir Caradoc, and Sir Geraint, and Sir Bodwin of Britain and Sir Constantine of Cornwall, and Sir Brandiles and Sir Mador de la Porte, and there was not to be found anywhere in the world a company of such noble and exalted knights as these.

Now as the King lay drowsing and as these worthies sat holding cheerful converse together at that place, there came, of a sudden, a considerable bustle and stir upon the outskirts of the Court, and presently there appeared a very sad and woful sight. For there came thitherward a knight, sore wounded, and upheld upon his horse by a golden-haired page, clad in an apparel of white and azure. And, likewise, the knight's apparel and the trappings of his horse were of white and azure, and upon his shield he bore the emblazonment of a single lily flower of silver upon a ground of pure azure.

But the knight was in a very woful plight. For his face was as pale as wax and hung down upon his breast. And his eyes were glazed and saw *How the wound-* naught that passed around him, and his fair apparel of white *ed knight cometh* and blue was all red with the blood of life that ran from a *into the forest.* great wound in his side. And, as they came upon their way, the young page lamented in such wise that it wrung the heart for to hear him.

Now, as these approached, King Arthur aroused cried out, " Alas ! what doleful spectacle is that which I behold ? Now hasten, ye my lords, and bring succor to yonder knight; and do thou, Sir Kay, go quickly and bring that fair young page hither that we may presently hear from his lips what mishap hath befallen his lord."

So certain of those knights hastened at the King's bidding and gave all succor to the wounded knight, and conveyed him to King Arthur's own pavilion, which had been pitched at a little distance. And when he had come there the King's chirurgeon presently attended upon him—albeit his wounds were of such a sort he might not hope to live for a very long while.

Meantime, Sir Kay brought that fair young page before the King, where he sat, and the King thought that he had hardly ever seen a more beautiful countenance. And the King said, " I prithee tell me, Sir Page, who is thy master, and how came he in such a sad and pitiable condition as that which we have just now beheld."

" That will I so, Lord," said the youth. " Know that my master is entitled Sir Myles of the White Fountain, and that he cometh from the *The page telleth* country north of where we are and at a considerable distance *the story of the* from this. In that country he is the Lord of seven castles and *wounded knight.* several noble estates, wherefore, as thou mayst see, he is of considerable consequence. A fortnight ago (being doubtless moved thereunto by the lustiness of the Springtime), he set forth with only me for his esquire, for he had a mind to seek adventure in such manner as beseemed a good knight who would be errant. And we had several adventures, and in all of them my lord was entirely successful; for he overcame six knights at various places and sent them all to his castle for to attest his valor unto his lady.

"At last, this morning, coming to a certain place situated at a considerable distance from this, we came upon a fair castle of the forest, which stood in a valley surrounded by open spaces of level lawn, bedight with many flowers of divers sorts. There we beheld three fair damsels who tossed a golden ball from one to another, and the damsels were clad all in flame-colored satin, and their hair was of the color of gold. And as we drew nigh to them they stinted their play, and she who was the chief of those damsel called out to my lord, demanding of him whither he went and what was his errand.

"To her my lord made answer that he was errant and in search of adventure, and upon this, the three damsels laughed, and she who had first spoken said, 'An thou art in search of adventure, Sir Knight, happily I may be able to help thee to one that shall satisfy thee to thy heart's content.'

"Unto this my master made reply 'I prithee, fair damsel, tell me what that adventure may be so that I may presently assay it.'

"Thereupon this lady bade my master to take a certain path, and to follow the same for the distance of a league or a little more, and that he would then come to a bridge of stone that crossed a violent stream, and she assured him that there he might find adventure enough for to satisfy any man.

"So my master and I wended thitherward as that damoiselle had directed, and, by and by, we came unto the bridge whereof she had spoken. And, lo! beyond the bridge was a lonesome castle with a tall straight tower, and before the castle was a wide and level lawn of well-trimmed grass. And immediately beyond the bridge was an apple-tree hung over with a multitude of shields. And midway upon the bridge was a single shield, entirely of black; and beside it hung a hammer of brass; and beneath the shield was written these words in letters of red:

Whoso Smiteth This Shield
Doeth So At His Peril.

"Now, my master, Sir Myles, when he read those words went straightway to that shield and, seizing the hammer that hung beside it, he smote upon it a blow so that it rang like thunder.

"Thereupon, as in answer, the portcullis of the castle was let fall, and there immediately came forth a knight, clad all from head to foot in sable armor. And his apparel and the trappings of his horse and all the appointments thereof were likewise entirely of sable.

"Now when that Sable Knight perceived my master he came riding swiftly across the meadow and so to the other end of the bridge. And when he had come there he drew rein and saluted my master and cried out, 'Sir Knight, I demand of thee why thou didst smite that shield. Now let *The page telleth* me tell thee, because of thy boldness, I shall take away from *of the Sable* thee thine own shield, and shall hang it upon yonder apple-*Knight.* tree, where thou beholdest all those other shields to be hanging.' Unto this my master made reply. 'That thou shalt not do unless thou mayst overcome me, as knight to knight.' And thereupon, immediately, he dressed his shield and put himself into array for an assault at arms.

"So my master and this Sable Knight, having made themselves ready for that encounter, presently drave together with might and main. And they met in the middle of the course, where my master's spear burst into splinters. But the spear of the Sable Knight held and it pierced through Sir Myles, his shield, and it penetrated his side, so that both he and his horse were overthrown violently into the dust; he being wounded so grievously that he could not arise again from the ground whereon he lay.

"Then the Sable Knight took my master's shield and hung it up in the branches of the apple-tree where the other shields were hanging, and, thereupon, without paying further heed to my master, or inquiring as to his hurt, he rode away into his castle again, whereof the portcullis was immediately closed behind him.

"So, after that he had gone, I got my master to his horse with great labor, and straightway took him thence, not knowing where I might find harborage for him, until I came to this place. And that, my lord King, is the true story of how my master came by that mortal hurt which he hath suffered."

"Ha! By the glory of Paradise!" cried King Arthur, "I do consider it great shame that in my Kingdom and so near to my Court strangers should be so discourteously treated as Sir Myles hath been served. For it is certainly a discourtesy for to leave a fallen knight upon the ground, without tarrying to inquire as to his hurt how grievous it may be. And still more discourteous is it for to take away the shield of a fallen knight who hath done good battle."

And so did all the knights of the King's Court exclaim against the discourtesy of that Sable Knight.

Then there came forth a certain esquire attendant upon the King's person, by name Griflet, who was much beloved by his Royal *Griflet craveth* Master, and he kneeled before the King and cried out in a *a boon.* loud voice: "I crave a boon of thee, my lord King! and do beseech thee that thou wilt grant it unto me!"

Then King Arthur uplifted his countenance upon the youth as he knelt before him and he said, "Ask, Griflet, and thy boon shall be granted unto thee."

Thereupon Griflet said, "It is this that I would ask—I crave that thou wilt make me straightway knight, and that thou wilt let me go forth and endeavor to punish this unkindly knight, by overthrowing him, and so redeeming those shields which he hath hung upon that apple-tree."

Then was King Arthur much troubled in his spirit, for Griflet was as yet only an esquire and altogether untried in arms. So he said, "Behold, thou art yet too young to have to do with so potent a knight as this sable champion must be, who has thus overthrown so many knights without himself suffering any mishap. I prithee, dear Griflet, consider and ask some other boon."

But young Griflet only cried the more, "A boon! A boon! and thou hast granted it unto me."

Thereupon King Arthur said, "Thou shalt have thy boon, though my heart much misgiveth me that thou wilt suffer great ill and misfortune from this adventure."

So that night Griflet kept watch upon his armor in a chapel of the forest, and, in the morning, having received the Sacrament, he was created a knight by the hand of King Arthur—and it was not pos- *King Arthur* sible for any knight to have greater honor than that. Then *makes Griflet* King Arthur fastened the golden spurs to Sir Griflet's heels *a knight.* with his own hand.

So Griflet was made a knight, and having mounted his charger, he rode straightway upon his adventure, much rejoicing and singing for pure pleasure.

And it was at this time that Sir Myles died of his hurt, for it is often so that death and misfortune befall some, whiles others laugh and sing for hope and joy, as though such grievous things as sorrow and death could never happen in the world wherein they live.

Now that afternoon King Arthur sat waiting with great anxiety for word

of that young knight, but there was no word until toward evening, when
there came hurrying to him certain of his attendants, proclaiming that Sir
Griflet was returning, but without his shield, and in such guise that it
seemed as though a great misfortune had befallen him. And straightway
thereafter came Sir Griflet himself, sustained upon his horse on the one
hand by Sir Constantine and upon the other by Sir Brandiles. And, lo!
Sir Griflet's head hung down upon his breast, and his fair new armor was
all broken and stained with blood and dust. And so woful was he of appearance that King Arthur's heart was contracted with sorrow to behold
that young knight in so pitiable a condition.

So, at King Arthur's bidding, they conducted Sir Griflet to the Royal
Pavilion, and there they laid him down upon a soft couch. Then the
King's chirurgeon searched his wounds and found that the head of a spear
and a part of the shaft thereof were still piercing Sir Griflet's side, so that
he was in most woful and grievous pain.

And when King Arthur beheld in what a parlous state Sir Griflet lay he
cried out, " Alas! my dear young knight, what hath happened thee to
bring thee unto such a woful condition as this which I behold?"

Then Sir Griflet, speaking in a very weak voice, told King Arthur how he
had fared. And he said that he had proceeded through the forest, until
he had discovered the three beautiful damsels whereof the page of Sir

*Sir Griflet tell-
eth how he
was hurt.*

Myles had spoken. And he said that these damsels had directed him as to the manner in which he should pursue his
adventure. And he said that he had found the bridge
whereon hung the shield and the brazen mall, and that he had there
beheld the apple-tree hung full of shields; and he said that he smote the
shield of the Sable Knight with the brazen mall, and that the Sable Knight
had thereupon come riding out against him. And he said that this
knight did not appear of a mind to fight with him ; instead, he cried out
to him with a great deal of nobleness that he was too young and too
untried in arms to have to do with a seasoned knight; wherefore he
advised Sir Griflet to withdraw him from that adventure ere it was too
late. But, notwithstanding this advice, Sir Griflet would not withdraw
but declared that he would certainly have to do with that other knight in
sable. Now at the very first onset Sir Griflet's spear had burst into
pieces, but the spear of the Sable Knight had held and had pierced
through Sir Griflet's shield and into his side, causing him this grievous
wound whereof he suffered. And Sir Griflet said that the Sable Knight
had then, most courteously, uplifted him upon his horse again (albeit he
had kept Sir Griflet's shield and had hung it upon the tree with those

others that hung there) and had then directed him upon his way, so that he had made shift to ride thither, though with great pain and dole.

Then was King Arthur very wode and greatly disturbed in his mind, for indeed he loved Sir Griflet exceedingly well. Wherefore he declared that he himself would now go forth for to punish that Sable Knight, and for to humble him with his own hand. And, though the knights of his Court strove to dissuade him from that ad- *King Arthur is very angry.* venture, yet he declared that he with his own hand would accomplish that proud knight's humiliation, and that he would undertake the adventure, with God His Grace, upon the very next day.

And so disturbed was he that he could scarce eat his food that evening for vexation, nor would he go to his couch to sleep, but, having inquired very narrowly of Sir Griflet where he might find that valley of flowers and those three damsels, he spent the night in walking up and down his pavilion, awaiting for the dawning of the day.

Now, as soon as the birds first began to chirp and the east to brighten with the coming of the daylight, King Arthur summoned his two esquires, and, having with their aid donned his armor and mounted a milk-white war-horse, he presently took his departure upon that adventure which he had determined upon.

And, indeed it is a very pleasant thing for to ride forth in the dawning of a Springtime day. For then the little birds do sing their sweetest song, all joining in one joyous medley, whereof one may scarce tell one note from another, so multitudinous is that pretty roundelay; then do the grow- ing things of the earth smell the sweetest in the freshness *King Arthur* of the early daytime—the fair flowers, the shrubs, and the *sets forth upon* blossoms upon the trees; then doth the dew bespangle all *his adventure.* the sward as with an incredible multitude of jewels of various colors; then is all the world sweet and clean and new, as though it had been fresh created for him who came to roam abroad so early in the morning.

So King Arthur's heart expanded with great joy, and he chanted a quaint song as he rode through the forest upon the quest of that knightly adventure.

So, about noon-tide, he came to that part of the forest lands whereof he had heard those several times before. For of a sudden, he discovered be- fore him a wide and gently sloping valley, a-down which ran *King Arthur* a stream as bright as silver. And, lo! the valley was strewn *cometh to the* all over with an infinite multitude of fair and fragrant flowers *Valley of De-* of divers sorts. And in the midst of the valley there stood a *light.* comely castle, with tall red roofs and many bright windows, so that it seemed to King Arthur that it was a very fine castle indeed. And upon a smooth green lawn he perceived those three damoiselles clad in flame-colored satin of whom the page of Sir Myles and Sir Griflet had spoken. And they played at ball with a golden ball, and the hair of each was of the hue of gold, and it seemed to King Arthur, as he drew nigh, that they were the most beautiful damoiselles that he had ever beheld in all of his life.

Now as King Arthur came unto them the three ceased tossing the ball, and she who was the fairest of all damoiselles demanded of him whither he went and upon what errand he was bound.

Then King Arthur made reply: "Ha! fair lady! whither should a belted knight ride upon such a day as this, and upon what business, other than the search of adventure such as beseemeth a knight of a proper strength of heart and frame who would be errant?"

Then the three damoiselles smiled upon the King, for he was exceedingly comely of face and they liked him very well. "Alas, Sir Knight!" said she who had before spoken, "I prithee be in no such haste to under-
The damoiselles greet King Arthur. take a dangerous adventure, but rather tarry with us for a day or two or three, for to feast and make merry with us. For surely good cheer doth greatly enlarge the heart, and we would fain enjoy the company of so gallant a knight as thou appearest to be. Yonder castle is ours and all this gay valley is ours, and those who have visited it are pleased, because of its joyousness, to call it the Valley of Delight. So tarry with us for a little and be not in such haste to go forward."

"Nay," said King Arthur," I may not tarry with ye, fair ladies, for I am bent upon an adventure of which ye may wot right well, when I tell ye that I seek that Sable Knight, who hath overcome so many other knights and hath taken away their shields. So I do pray ye of your grace for to tell me where I may find him."

"Grace of Heaven!" cried she who spake for the others, "this is certainly a sorry adventure which ye seek, Sir Knight! For already, in these two days, have two knights assayed with that knight, and both have fallen into great pain and disregard. Ne'theless, an thou wilt undertake this peril, yet shalt thou not go until thou hast eaten and refreshed thyself." So saying, she lifted a little ivory whistle that hung from her neck by a chain of gold, and blew upon it very shrilly.

In answer to this summons there came forth from the castle three fair young pages, clad all in flame-colored raiment, bearing among them a silver table covered with a white napkin. And after them came five other pages of the same appearance, bearing flagons of white wine and red, dried fruits and comfits and manchets of white fair bread.

Then King Arthur descended from his war-horse with great gladness, for he was both hungry and athirst, and, seating himself at the table with the damsels beside him, he ate with great enjoyment, discoursing pleasantly the while with those fair ladies, who listened to him with great cheerfulness of spirit. Yet he told them not who he was, though they greatly marvelled who might be the noble warrior who had come thus into that place. *King Arthur eats and drinks in the Valley of Delight.*

So, having satisfied his hunger and his thirst, King Arthur mounted his steed again, and the three damsels conducted him across the valley a little way—he riding upon his horse and they walking beside him. So, by and by, he perceived where was a dark pathway that led into the farther side of the forest land; and when he had come thither the lady who had addressed him before said to him, " Yonder is the way that thou must take an thou wouldst enter upon this adventure. So fare thee well, and may good hap go with thee, for, certes, thou art the Knight most pleasant of address who hath come hitherward for this long time."

Thereupon King Arthur, having saluted those ladies right courteously, rode away with very great joy of that pleasant adventure through which he had thus passed.

Now when King Arthur had gone some ways he came, by and by, to a certain place where charcoal burners plied their trade. For here were many mounds of earth, all a-smoke with the smouldering logs within, whilst all the air was filled with the smell of the dampened fires.

As the King approached this spot, he presently beheld that something was toward that was sadly amiss. For, in the open clearing, he beheld three sooty fellows with long knives in their hands, who pursued one old man, whose beard was as white as snow. And he beheld that the reverend old man, who was clad richly in black, and whose horse stood at a little distance, was running hither and thither, as though to escape from those wicked men, and he appeared to be very hard pressed and in great danger of his life.

"Pardee!" quoth the young King to himself, " here, certes, is one in sore need of succor." Whereupon he cried out in a great voice, "Hold, villains! What would you be at!" and therewith set spurs to his horse and dropped his spear into rest and drove down upon them with a noise like to thunder for loudness.

But when the three wicked fellows beheld the armed Knight thus thundering down upon them, they straightway dropped their knives and, with loud outcries of fear, ran away hither and thither until they had escaped into the thickets of the forest, where one upon a horse might not hope to pursue them.

Whereupon, having driven away those wicked fellows, King Arthur rode up to him whom he had succored, thinking to offer him condolence. And

King Arthur rescues Merlin from the three villains. behold! when he had come nigh to him, he perceived that the old man was the Enchanter Merlin. Yet whence he had so suddenly come, who had only a little while before been at the King's Court at Carleon, and what he did in that place, the King could in no wise understand. Wherefore he bespoke the Enchanter in this wise, "Ha! Merlin, it seemeth to me that I have saved thy life. For, surely, thou hadst not escaped from the hands of those wicked men had I not happened to come hitherward at this time."

"Dost thou think so, Lord?" said Merlin. "Now let me tell thee that I did maybe appear to be in danger, yet I might have saved myself very easily had I been of a mind to do so. But, as thou sawst me in this seeming peril, so may thou know that a real peril, far greater than this, lieth before thee, and there will be no errant knight to succor thee from it. Wherefore, I pray thee, Lord, for to take me with thee upon this adventure that thou art set upon, for I do tell thee that thou shalt certainly suffer great dole and pain therein."

"Merlin," said King Arthur, "even an I were to face my death, yet would I not turn back from this adventure. But touching the advice thou givest me, meseems it will be very well to take thee with me if such peril lieth before me as thou sayest."

And Merlin said, "Yea, it would be very well for thee to do so."

So Merlin mounted upon his palfrey, and King Arthur and he betook their way from that place in pursuit of that adventure which the King had undertaken to perform.

The Battle with the Sable Knight.

Chapter Second.

How King Arthur Fought With the Sable Knight and How He Was Sorely Wounded. Likewise How Merlin Brought Him Safe Away From the Field of Battle.

SO King Arthur and Merlin rode together through the forest for a considerable while, until they perceived that they must be approaching nigh to the place where dwelt the Sable Knight whom the King sought so diligently. For the forest, which had till then been altogether a wilderness, very deep and mossy, began to show an aspect more thin and open, as though a dwelling-place of mankind was close at hand.

And, after a little, they beheld before them a violent stream of water, that rushed through a dark and dismal glen. And, likewise, they perceived that across this stream of water there was a bridge of stone, and that upon the other side of the bridge there was a smooth and level lawn of green grass, whereon Knights-contestants might joust very well. And beyond this lawn they beheld a tall and forbidding castle, with smooth walls and a straight tower; and this castle was built upon the rocks so that it appeared to be altogether a part of the stone. So they wist that this must be the castle whereof the page and Sir Griflet had spoken.

For, midway upon the bridge, they beheld that there hung a sable shield and a brass mall exactly as the page and Sir Griflet had said; and that upon the farther side of the stream was an apple-tree, amid the leaves of which hung a very great many shields of various devices, exactly as those two had reported: and they beheld that *King Arthur* some of those shields were clean and fair, and that some *cometh to the* were foul and stained with blood, and that some were *castle of the* smooth and unbroken, and that some were cleft as though *Sable Knight.* by battle of knight with knight. And all those shields were the shields of different knights whom the Sable Knight, who dwelt within the castle, had overthrown in combat with his own hand.

" Splendor of Paradise! " quoth King Arthur, " that must, indeed, be a right valiant knight who, with his own single strength, hath overthrown and cast down so many other knights.   For, indeed, Merlin, there must be an hundred shields hanging in yonder tree!"

Unto this Merlin made reply, " And thou, Lord, mayst be very happy an thy shield, too, hangeth not there ere the sun goeth down this even-tide."

" That," said King Arthur, with a very steadfast countenance, " shall be as God willeth.   For, certes, I have a greater mind than ever for to try my power against yonder knight.   For, consider, what especial honor would fall to me should I overcome so valiant a warrior as this same Sable Champion appeareth to be, seeing that he hath been victorious over so many other good knights."

Thereupon, having so spoken his mind, King Arthur immediately pushed forward his horse and so, coming upon the bridge, he clearly read that challenge writ in letters of red beneath the shield:

$$\text{Whoso Smiteth This Shield}$$
$$\text{Doeth So At his Peril.}$$

Upon reading these words, the King seized the brazen mall, and smote
King Arthur   that shield so violent a blow that the sound thereof echoed
challenges the   back from the smooth walls of the castle, and from the rocks
Sable Knight.   whereon it stood, and from the skirts of the forest around
about, as though twelve other shields had been struck in those several places.

And in answer to that sound, the portcullis of the castle was immediately let fall, and there issued forth a knight, very huge of frame, and clad all in sable armor.   And, likewise, all of his apparel and all the trappings of his horse were entirely of sable, so that he presented a most grim and forbidding aspect.   And this Sable Knight came across that level meadow of smooth grass with a very stately and honorable gait; for neither did he ride in haste, nor did he ride slowly, but with great pride and haughtiness of mien, as became a champion who, haply, had never yet been overcome in battle.   So, reaching the bridge-head, he drew rein and saluted King Arthur with great dignity, and also right haughtily.   " Ha! Sir Knight!" quoth he, " why didst thou, having read those words yonder inscribed, smite upon my shield?   Now I do tell thee that, for thy discourtesy, I shall presently take thy shield away from thee, and shall hang it up upon yonder apple-tree where thou beholdest all those other shields to be hanging. Wherefore, either deliver thou thy shield unto me without more ado or else prepare for to defend it with thy person—in the which event thou shalt certainly suffer great pain and discomfort to thy body."

"Gramercy for the choice thou grantest me," said King Arthur. "But as for taking away my shield—I do believe that that shall be as Heaven willeth, and not as thou willest. Know, thou unkind knight, that I have come hither for no other purpose than to do battle with thee and so to endeavor for to redeem with my person all those shields that hang yonder upon that apple-tree. So make thou ready straightway that I may have to do with thee, maybe to thy great disadvantage."

"That will I so," replied the Sable Knight. And thereupon he turned his horse's head and, riding back a certain distance across the level lawn, he took stand in such place as appeared to him to be convenient. And so did King Arthur ride forth also upon that lawn, and take his station as seemed to him to be convenient.

Then each knight dressed his spear and his shield for the encounter, and, having thus made ready for the assault, each shouted to his war-horse and drave his spurs deep into its flank.

Then those two noble steeds rushed forth like lightning, coursing across the ground with such violent speed that the earth trembled and shook beneath them, an it were by cause of an earthquake. So those two knights met fairly in the midst of the centre of the field, crashing together like a thunderbolt. And so violently did they smite the one against *King Arthur* the other that the spears burst into splinters, even unto the *contests with the* guard and the truncheon thereof, and the horses of the riders *Sable Knight.* staggered back from the onset, so that only because of the extraordinary address of the knights-rider did they recover from falling before that shock of meeting.

But, with great spirit, these two knights uplifted each his horse with his own spirit, and so completed his course in safety.

And indeed King Arthur was very much amazed that he had not overthrown his opponent, for, at that time, as aforesaid, he was considered to be the very best knight and the one best approved in deeds of arms that lived in all of Britain. Wherefore he marvelled at the power and the address of that knight against whom he had driven, that he had not been overthrown by the greatness of the blow that had been delivered against his defences. So, when they met again in the midst of the field, King Arthur gave that knight greeting, and bespoke him with great courtesy, addressing him in this wise: "Sir Knight, I know not who thou art, but I do pledge my knightly word that thou art the most potent knight that ever I have met in all of my life. Now I do bid thee get down straightway from thy horse, and let us two fight this battle with sword and upon foot, for it were pity to let it end in this way."

"Not so," quoth the Sable Knight—"not so, nor until one of us twain be overthrown will I so contest this battle upon foot." And upon this he shouted, "Ho! Ho!" in a very loud voice, and straightway thereupon the gateway of the castle opened and there came running forth two tall esquires clad all in black, pied with crimson. And each of these esquires bare in his hand a great spear of ash-wood, new and well-seasoned, and never yet strained in battle.

So King Arthur chose one of these spears and the Sable Knight took the other, and thereupon each returned to that station wherefrom he had before essayed the encounter.

Then once again each knight rushed his steed to the assault, and once again did each smite so fairly in the midst of the defence of the other that the spears were splintered, so that only the guard and the truncheon thereof remained in the grasp of the knight who held it.

Then, as before, King Arthur would have fought the battle out with swords and upon foot, but again the Sable Knight would not have it so, *The knights* but called aloud upon those within the castle, whereupon there *break lances a* immediately came forth two other esquires with fresh, new *second time.* spears of ash-wood. So each knight again took him a spear, and having armed himself therewith, chose each his station upon that fair, level lawn of grass.

And now, for the third time, having thus prepared themselves thereof assault, those two excellent knights hurled themselves together in furious assault. And now, as twice before, did King Arthur strike the Sable Knight so fairly in the centre of his defence that the spear which he held was burst into splinters. But this time, the spear of the Sable Knight did not so break in that manner, but held; and so violent was the blow that he delivered upon King Arthur's shield that he pierced through the centre of it. Then the girths of the King's saddle burst apart by that great, powerful blow, and both he and his steed were cast violently backward. So King Arthur might have been overcast, had he not voided his saddle with extraordinary skill and knightly address, wherefore, though his horse was *King Arthur* overthrown, he himself still held his footing and did not fall *is overthrown.* into the dust. Ne'theless, so violent was the blow that he received that, for a little space, he was altogether bereft of his senses so that everything whirled around before his eyes.

But when his sight returned to him he was filled with an anger so vehement that it appeared to him as though all the blood in his heart rushed into his brains so that he saw naught but red, as of blood, before his eyes. And when this also had passed he perceived the Sable Knight that he sat his horse at no great distance. Then immediately King Arthur ran to him and catching the bridle-rein of his horse, he cried out aloud unto that Sable Knight with great violence: "Come down, thou black knight! and fight me upon foot and with thy sword."

"That will I not do," said the Sable Knight, "for, lo! I have overthrown thee. Wherefore deliver thou to me thy shield, that I may hang it upon yonder apple-tree, and go thy way as others have done before thee."

"That will I not!" cried King Arthur, with exceeding passion, "neither will I yield myself nor go hence until either thou or I have altogether conquered the other." Thereupon he thrust the horse of the Sable Knight backward by the bridle-rein so vehemently, that the other was constrained to void his saddle to save himself from being overthrown upon the ground.

And now each knight was as entirely furious as the other, wherefore, each drew his sword and dressed his shield, and thereupon rushed together like two wild bulls in battle. They foined, they smote, they traced, they parried, they struck again and again, and the sound of their blows, crashing and clashing the one upon the other, filled the entire surrounding space with an extraordinary uproar. Nor may any man altogether conceive of the entire fury of that encounter, for, because of the violence of the blows which the one delivered upon the other, whole *The knights* cantels of armor were hewn from their bodies and many deep *fight with* and grievous wounds were given and received, so that the *swords upon* armor of each was altogether stained with red because of the *foot.* blood that flowed down upon it.

At last King Arthur, waxing, as it were, entirely mad, struck so fierce a blow that no armor could have withstood that stroke had it fallen fairly upon it. But it befell with that stroke that his sword broke at the hilt and the blade thereof flew into three several pieces into the air. Yet was the stroke so wonderfully fierce that the Sable Knight groaned, and staggered, and ran about in a circle as though he had gone blind and knew not whither to direct his steps.

But presently he recovered himself again, and perceiving King Arthur standing near by, and not knowing that his enemy had now no sword for to defend himself withal, he cast aside his shield and took his own sword into both hands, and therewith smote so dolorous a stroke that he clave through King Arthur's shield and through his helmet and even to the bone of his brain-pan.

Then King Arthur thought that he had received his death-wound, for his brains swam like water, his thighs trembled exceedingly, and he sank down to his knees, whilst the blood and sweat, commingled together in the darkness of his helmet, flowed down into his eyes in a lather and blinded *King Arthur is* him. Thereupon, seeing him thus grievously hurt, the Sable *sorely wounded.* Knight called upon him with great vehemence for to yield himself and to surrender his shield, because he was now too sorely wounded for to fight any more.

But King Arthur would not yield himself, but catching the other by the sword-belt, he lifted himself to his feet. Then, being in a manner recovered from his amazement, he embraced the other with both arms, and placing his knee behind the thigh of the Sable Knight, he cast him backward down upon the ground so violently that the sound of the fall was astounding to hear. And with that fall the Sable Knight was, awhile, entirely bereft of consciousness. Then King Arthur straightway unlaced the helm of the Sable Knight and so beheld his face, and he knew him in spite of the blood that still ran down his own countenance in great quantities, and he knew that knight was King Pellinore, aforenamed in this history, who had twice warred against King Arthur. (It hath already been said how King Arthur had driven that other king from the habitations of men and into the forests, so that now he dwelt in this poor gloomy castle whence he waged war against all the knights who came unto that place.)

Now when King Arthur beheld whom it was against whom he had done battle, he cried out aloud, " Ha! Pellinore, is it then thou? Now yield thee to me, for thou art entirely at my mercy." And upon this he drew his misericordia and set the point thereof at King Pellinore's throat.

But by now King Pellinore had greatly recovered from his fall, and perceiving that the blood was flowing down in great measure from out his enemy's helmet, he wist that that other must have been very sorely wounded by the blow which he had just now received. Wherefore he catched King Arthur's wrist in his hand and directed the point of the dagger away from his own throat so that no great danger threatened therefrom.

And, indeed, what with his sore wound and with the loss of blood, King Arthur was now fallen exceedingly sick and faint, so that it appeared to him that he was nigh to death. Accordingly, it was with no very great ado that **King** Pellinore suddenly heaved himself up from the ground and so overthrew his enemy that King Arthur was now underneath his knees.

And by this King Pellinore was exceedingly mad with the fury of the sore battle he had fought. For he was so enraged that his eyes were all beshot with blood like those of a wild boar, and a froth, like the champings of a wild boar, stood in the beard about his lips. Where- *King Pellinore* fore he wrenched the dagger out of his enemy's hand, and *makes to kill* immediately began to unlace his helm, with intent to slay him *King Arthur.* where he lay. But at this moment Merlin came in great haste, crying out, "Stay! stay! Sir Pellinore; what would you be at? Stay your sacrilegious hand! For he who lieth beneath you is none other than Arthur, King of all this realm!"

At this King Pellinore was astonished beyond measure. And for a little he was silent, and then after awhile he cried out in a very loud voice, "Say you so, old man? Then verily your words have doomed this man unto death. For no one in all this world hath ever suffered such ill and such wrongs as I have suffered at his hands. For, lo! he hath taken from me power, and kingship, and honors, and estates, and hath left me only this gloomy, dismal castle of the forest as an abiding-place. Wherefore, seeing that he is thus in my power, he shall now presently die; if for no other reason than because if I now let him go free, he will certainly revenge himself when he shall have recovered from all the ill he hath suffered at my hands."

Then Merlin said, "Not so! He shall not die at thy hands, for I, my- self, shall save him." Whereupon he uplifted his staff and *Merlin lays a* smote King Pellinore across the shoulders. Then immediately *spell upon King* King Pellinore fell down and lay upon the ground on his face *Pellinore.* like one who had suddenly gone dead.

Upon this, King Arthur uplifted himself upon his elbow and beheld his enemy lying there as though dead, and he cried out, "Ha! Merlin! what is this that thou hast done? I am very sorry, for I do perceive that thou, by thy arts of magic, hath slain one of the best knights in all the world."

"Not so, my lord King!" said Merlin; "for, in sooth, I tell thee that thou art far nigher to thy death than he. For he is but in sleep and will soon awaken; but thou art in such a case that it would take only a very little for to cause thee to die."

And indeed King Arthur was exceeding sick, even to the heart, with the sore wound he had received, so that it was only with much ado that Merlin could help him up upon his horse. Having done the which and having hung the King's shield upon the horn of his saddle, Merlin straightway

conveyed the wounded man thence across the bridge, and, leading the
horse by the bridle, so took him away into the forest.

Now I must tell you that there was in that part of the forest a certain
hermit so holy that the wild birds of the woodland would come and rest
upon his hand whiles he read his breviary; and so sanctified was he in
gentleness that the wild does would come even to the door of his hermitage, and there stand whilst he milked them for his refreshment. And this
hermit dwelt in that part of the forest so remote from the habitations of
man that when he rang the bell for matins or for vespers, there was hardly
ever anyone to hear the sound thereof excepting the wild creatures that
dwelt thereabout. Yet, ne'theless, to this remote and lonely place royal
folk and others of high degree would sometimes come, as though on a pilgrimage, because of the hermit's exceeding saintliness.

So Merlin conveyed King Arthur unto this sanctuary, and, having
reached that place, he and the hermit lifted the wounded man down from

Merlin bring-
eth King Ar-
thur to the cell
of a lonely
hermit.

his saddle—the hermit giving many words of pity and sorrow—and together they conveyed him into the holy man's
cell. There they laid him upon a couch of moss and unlaced
his armor and searched his wounds and bathed them with
pure water and dressed his hurts, for that hermit was a very skilful leech.
So for all that day and part of the next, King Arthur lay upon the hermit's pallet like one about to die; for he beheld all things about him as
though through thin water, and the breath hung upon his lips and flut-
tered, and he could not even lift his head from the pallet because of the
weakness that lay upon him.

Now upon the afternoon of the second day there fell a great noise and
tumult in that part of the forest. For it happened that the Lady Guinevere of Cameliard, together with her Court, both of ladies and of knights,
had come upon a pilgrimage to that holy man, the fame of whose saintliness had reached even unto the place where she dwelt. For that lady had

The Lady
Guinevere con-
sults with the
priest.

a favorite page who was very sick of a fever, and she trusted
that the holy man might give her some charm or amulet by
the virtue of which he might haply be cured. Wherefore she
had come to that place with her entire Court so that all that
part of the forest was made gay with fine raiment and the silence thereof
was made merry with the sound of talk and laughter and the singing of
songs and the chattering of many voices and the neighing of horses. And
the Lady Guinevere rode in the midst of her damsels and her Court, and
her beauty outshone the beauty of her damsels as the splendor of the morning star outshines that of all the lesser stars that surround it. For then

and afterward she was held by all the Courts of Chivalry to be the most beautiful lady in the world.

Now when the Lady Guinevere had come to that place, she perceived the milk-white war-horse of King Arthur where it stood cropping the green grass of the open glade nigh to the hermitage. And likewise she perceived Merlin, where he stood beside the door of the cell. So of him she demanded whose was that noble war-horse that stood browsing upon the grass at that lonely place, and who was it that lay within that cell. And unto her Merlin made answer, " Lady, he who lieth within is a knight, very sorely wounded, so that he is sick nigh unto death! "

" Pity of Heaven! " cried the Lady Guinevere. " What a sad thing is this that thou tellest me! Now I do beseech thee to lead me presently unto that knight that I may behold him. For I have in my Court a very skilful leech, who is well used to the cure of hurts such as knights receive in battle."

So Merlin brought the lady into the cell, and there she beheld King Arthur where he lay stretched upon the pallet. And she wist not who he was. Yet it appeared to her that in all her life she had not beheld so noble appearing a knight as he who lay sorely wounded in that lonely place. And King Arthur cast his looks upward to where she stood beside his bed of pain, surrounded by her maidens, and in the great weakness that lay upon him he wist not whether she whom he beheld was a mortal lady or whether she was not rather some tall straight angel who had descended from one of the Lordly Courts of Paradise for to visit him in his pain and distresses. And the Lady Guinevere was filled with a great *The Lady* pity at beholding King Arthur's sorrowful estate. Wherefore *Guinevere bid-* *deth her leech* she called to her that skilful leech who was with her Court. *for to heal* And she bade him bring a certain alabaster box of exceed- *King Arthur.* ingly precious balsam. And she commanded him for to search that knight's wounds and to anoint them with the balsam, so that he might be healed of his hurts with all despatch.

So that wise and skilful leech did according to the Lady Guinevere's commands, and immediately King Arthur felt entire ease of all his aches and great content of spirit. And when the Lady and her Court had departed, he found himself much uplifted in heart, and three days there- after he was entirely healed and was as well and strong and lusty as ever he had been in all of his life.

And this was the first time that King Arthur ever beheld that beauti- ful lady, the Lady Guinevere of Cameliard, and from that time forth he never forgot her, but she was almost always present in his thoughts. Wherefore, when he was recovered he said thus to himself: " I will forget that I am a king and I will cherish the thought of this lady and will serve her faithfully as a good knight may serve his chosen dame."

And so he did, as ye shall hear later in this book.

xcalibur the Sword.

Chapter Third.

How King Arthur Found a Noble Sword In a Very Wonderful Manner. And How He Again Fought With It and Won That Battle.

NOW, as soon as King Arthur had, by means of that extraordinary balsam, been thus healed of those grievous wounds which he had received in his battle with King Pellinore, he found himself to be moved by a most vehement desire to meet his enemy again for to try issue of battle with him once more, and so recover the credit which he had lost in that combat. Now, upon the morning of the fourth day, being entirely cured, and having broken his fast, he walked for refreshment beside the skirts of the forest, listening the while to the cheerful sound of the wood-birds singing their matins, all with might and main. And Merlin walked beside him, and King Arthur spake his mind to Merlin concerning his intent to engage once more in knightly contest with King Pellinore. And he said, "Merlin, it doth vex me very sorely *King Arthur* for to have come off so ill in my late encounter with king *desireth to re-* Pellinore. Certes, he is the very best knight in all the world *new his battle.* whom I have ever yet encountered. Ne'theless, it might have fared differently with me had I not broken my sword, and so left myself altogether defenceless in that respect. Howsoever that may be, I am of a mind for to assay this adventure once more, and so will I do as immediately as may be."

Thereunto Merlin made reply, "Thou art, assuredly, a very brave man to have so much appetite for battle, seeing how nigh thou camest unto thy death not even four days ago. Yet how mayst thou hope to undertake this adventure without due preparation? For, lo! thou hast no sword, nor hast thou a spear, nor hast thou even thy misericordia for to do battle withal. How then mayst thou hope for to assay this adventure?"

And King Arthur said, "That I know not, nevertheless I will presently seek for some weapon as soon as may be. For, even an I have no better weapon than an oaken cudgel, yet would I assay this battle again with so poor a tool as that."

"Ha! Lord," said Merlin, "I do perceive that thou art altogether fixed in thy purpose for to renew this quarrel. Wherefore, I will not seek to stay thee therefrom, but will do all that in me lies for to aid thee in thy desires. Now to this end I must tell thee that in one part of this forest (which is, indeed, a very strange place) there is a certain woodland some-times called Arroy, and other times called the Forest of Adventure. For no knight ever entereth therein but some adventure befalleth him. And close to Arroy is a land of enchantment which has several times been seen. And that is a very wonderful land, for there is in it a wide and consid-erable lake, which is also of enchantment. And in the centre of that lake there hath for some time been seen the appearance as of a woman's arm—exceedingly beautiful and clad in white samite, and the hand of this arm holdeth a sword of such exceeding excellence and beauty that no *Merlin telleth* eye hath ever beheld its like. And the name of this sword *King Arthur* is Excalibur—it being so named by those who have beheld *of Excalibur.* it because of its marvellous brightness and beauty. For it hath come to pass that several knights have already seen that sword and have endeavored to obtain it for their own, but, heretofore, no one hath been able to touch it, and many have lost their lives in that adventure. For when any man draweth near unto it, either he sinks into the lake, or else the arm disappeareth entirely, or else it is with-drawn beneath the lake; wherefore no man hath ever been able to obtain the possession of that sword. Now I am able to conduct thee unto that Lake of Enchantment, and there thou mayst see Excalibur with thine own eyes. Then when thou hast seen him thou mayst, haply, have the desire to obtain him; which, an thou art able to do, thou wilt have a sword very fitted for to do battle with."

"Merlin," quoth the King, "this is a very strange thing which thou tellest me. Now I am desirous beyond measure for to attempt to obtain this sword for mine own, wherefore I do beseech thee to lead me with all despatch to this enchanted lake whereof thou tellest me." And Merlin said, " I will do so."

So that morning King Arthur and Merlin took leave of that holy hermit (the King having kneeled in the grass to receive his benediction), and so, departing from that place, they entered the deeper forest once more, betaking their way to that part which was known as Arroy.

And after awhile they came to Arroy, and it was about noon-tide. And when they had entered into those woodlands they came to a certain little open place, and in that place they beheld a white doe with a golden collar about its neck. And King Arthur said, "Look, Merlin, yonder is a wonderful sight." And Merlin said, "Let us follow that doe." And upon this the doe turned and they followed it. And by and by in following it they came to an opening in the trees where was a little lawn of sweet soft grass. Here they beheld a bower and before the bower was a table spread with a fair snow-white cloth, and set *Merlin and King Arthur* with refreshments of white bread, wine, and meats of several *follow a white doe.* sorts. And at the door of this bower there stood a page, clad all in green, and his hair was as black as ebony, and his eyes as black as jet and exceeding bright. And when this page beheld King Arthur and Merlin, he gave them greeting, and welcomed the King very pleasantly saying, "Ha! King Arthur, thou art welcome to this place. Now I prithee dismount and refresh thyself before going farther."

Then was King Arthur a-doubt as to whether there might not be some enchantment in this for to work him an ill, for he was astonished that that page in the deep forest should know him so well. But Merlin bade him have good cheer, and he said, "Indeed, Lord, thou mayst freely partake of that refreshment which, I may tell thee, was prepared especially for thee. Moreover in this thou mayst foretell a very happy issue unto this adventure."

So King Arthur sat down to the table with great comfort of heart (for he was an hungered) and that page and another like unto him ministered unto his needs, serving him all the food upon silver plates, and all the wine in golden goblets as he was *King Arthur is refreshed in* used to being served in his own court—only that those *a mysterious manner.* things were much more cunningly wrought and fashioned, and were more beautiful than the table furniture of the King's court.

Then, after he had eaten his fill and had washed his hands from a silver basin which the first page offered to him, and had wiped his hands upon a fine linen napkin which the other page brought unto him, and after Merlin had also refreshed himself, they went their way, greatly rejoicing at this pleasant adventure, which, it seemed to the King, could not but betoken a very good issue to his undertaking.

Now about the middle of the afternoon King Arthur and Merlin came, of a sudden, out from the forest and upon a fair and level plain, bedight all over with such a number of flowers that no man could conceive of their quantity nor of the beauty thereof.

And this was a very wonderful land, for, lo! all the air appeared as it were to be as of gold—so bright was it and so singularly radiant. And here and there upon that plain were sundry trees all in blossom; and the fragrance of the blossoms was so sweet that the King had never smelt any fragrance like to it. And in the branches of those trees were a multitude of birds of many colors, and the melody of their singing ravished the heart of the hearer. And midway in the plain was a lake of water as bright as silver, and all around the borders of the lake were incredible

King Arthur cometh to a strange land. numbers of lilies and of daffodils. Yet, although this place was so exceedingly fair, there was, nevertheless, nowhere about it a single sign of human life of any sort, but it appeared altogether as lonely as the hollow sky upon a day of summer. So, because of all the marvellous beauty of this place, and because of its strangeness and its entire solitude, King Arthur perceived that he must have come into a land of powerful enchantment where, happily, dwelt a fairy of very exalted quality; wherefore his spirit was enwrapped in a manner of fear, as he pushed his great milk-white war-horse through that long fair grass, all bedight with flowers, and he wist not what strange things were about to befall him.

So when he had come unto the margin of the lake he beheld there the miracle that Merlin had told him of aforetime. For, lo! in the midst of the expanse of water there was the appearance of a fair and beautiful arm, as of a woman, clad all in white samite. And the arm was encircled with several bracelets of wrought gold; and the hand held a sword of marvellous workmanship aloft in the air above the surface of the water; and neither the arm nor the sword moved so much as a hair's-breadth, but were motionless like to a carven image upon the surface of the lake. And, behold! the sun of that strange land shone down upon the hilt of the sword, and

King Arthur seeth Excalibur it was of pure gold beset with jewels of several sorts, so that the hilt of the sword and the bracelets that encircled the arm glistered in the midst of the lake like to some singular star of exceeding splendor. And King Arthur sat upon his war-horse and gazed from a distance at the arm and the sword, and he greatly marvelled thereat; yet he wist not how he might come at that sword, for the lake was wonderfully wide and deep, wherefore he knew not how he might come thereunto for to make it his own. And as he sat pondering this thing within himself, he was suddenly aware of a strange lady, who approached him through those tall flowers that bloomed along the margin of the lake. And when he perceived her coming toward him he quickly dismounted from his war-horse and he went forward for to meet her with the bridle-rein over his arm. And when he had come nigh to her, he perceived that she was extraordinarily beautiful, and that her face was like wax for clearness, and that her eyes were perfectly black, and that they were as bright and glistening as though they were two jewels set in ivory. And he perceived that her hair was like silk and as black as it was possible to be, and so long that it reached unto the ground as she walked. And the lady was clad all in green—only that a fine cord of crimson and gold was interwoven into the plaits of her hair. And around her neck there hung a very beautiful necklace of several strands of opal stones and emeralds, set in cunningly wrought gold; and around her wrists were bracelets of the like sort—of opal stones and emeralds set into gold. So when King Arthur beheld her wonderful appearance, that it was like to an ivory statue of exceeding beauty clad all in green, he immediately kneeled before her in the midst of all those flowers as he said, "Lady, I do certainly perceive that thou art no mortal damoiselle, but that thou art Fay. Also that this place, because of its extraordinary beauty, can be no other than some land of Faerie into which I have entered."

King Arthur meeteth the Lady of the Lake.

And the Lady replied, "King Arthur, thou sayest soothly, for I am indeed Faerie. Moreover, I may tell thee that my name is Nymue, and that I am the chiefest of those Ladies of the Lake of whom thou mayst have heard people speak. Also thou art to know that what thou beholdest yonder as a wide lake is, in truth, a plain like unto this, all bedight with flowers. And likewise thou art to know that in the midst of that plain there standeth a castle of white marble and of ultramarine illuminated with gold. But, lest mortal eyes should behold our dwelling-place, my sisters and I have caused it to be that this appearance as of a lake should extend all over that castle so that it is entirely hidden from sight. Nor may any mortal man cross that lake, saving in one way—otherwise he shall certainly perish therein."

"Lady," said King Arthur, "that which thou tellest me causes me to wonder a very great deal. And, indeed, I am afraid that in coming hitherward I have been doing amiss for to intrude upon the solitude of your dwelling-place."

"Nay, not so, King Arthur," said the Lady of the Lake, "for, in truth, thou art very welcome hereunto. Moreover, I may tell thee that I have a greater friendliness for thee and those noble knights of thy court than thou canst easily wot of. But I do beseech thee of thy courtesy for to tell me what it is that brings thee to our land?"

"Lady," quoth the King, "I will tell thee the entire truth. I fought of late a battle with a certain sable knight, in the which I was sorely and grievously wounded, and wherein I burst my spear and snapped my sword and lost even my misericordia, so that I had not a single thing lef tme by way of a weapon. In this extremity Merlin, here, told me of Excalibur, and of how he is continually upheld by an arm in the midst of this magical lake. So I came hither and, behold, I find it even as he hath said. Now, Lady, an it be possib^le, I would fain achieve that excellent sword, that, by means of it I might fight my battle to its entire end."

" Ha! my lord King," said the Lady of the Lake, " that sword is no easy thing for to achieve, and, moreover, I may tell thee that several knights have lost their lives by attempting that which thou hast a mind to do. For, in sooth, no man may win yonder sword unless he be without fear and without reproach."

" Alas, Lady!" quoth King Arthur, " that is indeed a sad saying for me. For, though I may not lack in knightly courage, yet, in truth, there be many things wherewith I do reproach myself withal. Ne'theless, I would fain attempt this thing, even an it be to my great endangerment. Wherefore, I prithee tell me how I may best undertake this adventure."

" King Arthur," said the Lady of the Lake, " I will do what I say to aid thee in thy wishes in this matter." Whereupon she lifted a single emerald that hung by a small chain of gold at her girdle and, lo! the emerald was

The Lady of the Lake summoneth a boat. cunningly carved into the form of a whistle. And she set the whistle to her lips and blew upon it very shrilly. Then straightway there appeared upon the water, a great way off, a certain thing that shone very brightly. And this drew near with great speed, and as it came nigh, behold! it was a boat all of carven brass. And the prow of the boat was carved into the form of a head of a beautiful woman, and upon either side were wings like the wings of a swan. And the boat moved upon the water like a swan—very swiftly—so that long lines, like to silver threads, stretched far away behind, across the face of the water, which otherwise was like unto glass for smoothness. And when the brazen boat had reached the bank it rested there and moved no more.

Then the Lady of the Lake bade King Arthur to enter the boat, and so he entered it. And immediately he had done so, the boat moved away from the bank as swiftly as it had come thither. And Merlin and the Lady of the Lake stood upon the margin of the water, and gazed after King Arthur and the brazen boat.

And King Arthur beheld that the boat floated swiftly across the lake to where was the arm uplifting the sword, and that the arm and the sword moved not but remained where they were.

Then King Arthur reached forth and took the sword in his hand, and immediately the arm disappeared beneath the water, and *King Arthur* King Arthur held the sword and the scabbard thereof and *obtaineth* the belt thereof in his hand and, lo! they were his own. *Excalibur.*

Then verily his heart swelled with joy an it would burst within his bosom, for Excalibur was an hundred times more beautiful than he had thought possible. Wherefore his heart was nigh breaking for pure joy at having obtained that magic sword.

Then the brazen boat bore him very quickly back to the land again and he stepped ashore where stood the Lady of the Lake and Merlin. And when he stood upon the shore, he gave the Lady great thanks beyond measure for all that she had done for to aid him in his great undertaking; and she gave him cheerful and pleasing words in reply.

Then King Arthur saluted the lady, as became him, and, having mounted his war-horse, and Merlin having mounted his palfrey, they rode away thence upon their business—the King's heart still greatly expanded with pure delight at having for his own that beautiful sword—the most beautiful and the most famous sword in all the world.

That night King Arthur and Merlin abided with the holy hermit at the forest sanctuary, and when the next morning had come (the King having bathed himself in the ice-cold forest fountain, and being exceedingly refreshed thereby) they took their departure, offering thanks to that saintly man for the harborage he had given them.

Anon, about noon-tide, they reached the valley of the Sable Knight, and there were all things appointed exactly as when King Arthur had been there before: to wit, that gloomy castle, the lawn of smooth grass, the apple-tree covered over with shields, and the bridge whereon hung that single shield of sable.

"Now, Merlin," quoth King Arthur, "I do this time most strictly forbid thee for to interfere in this quarrel. Nor shalt thou, under pain of my displeasure, exert any of thy arts of magic in my behalf. So hearken thou to what I say, and heed it with all possible diligence."

Thereupon, straightway, the King rode forth upon the bridge and, seizing the brazen mall, he smote upon the sable shield with all his might and main. Immediately the portcullis of the castle was let fall as *King Arthur* afore told, and, in the same manner as that other time, the *challenges King* Sable Knight rode forth therefrom, already bedight and *Pellinore to* equipped for the encounter. So he came to the bridge-head *battle again.* and there King Arthur spake to him in this wise: "Sir Pellinore, we do now know one another entirely well, and each doth judge that he hath cause of quarrel with the other: thou, that I, for mine own reasons as seemed to me to be fit, have taken away from thee thy kingly estate, and have driven thee into this forest solitude: I, that thou has set thyself up here for to do injury and affront to knights and lords and other people of this kingdom of mine. Wherefore, seeing that I am here as an errant Knight, I do challenge thee for to fight with me, man to man, until either thou or I have conquered the other."

Unto this speech King Pellinore bowed his head in obedience, and thereupon he wheeled his horse, and, riding to some little distance, took his place where he had afore stood. And King Arthur also rode to some little distance, and took his station where he had afore stood. At the same time there came forth from the castle one of those tall pages clad all in sable, pied with crimson, and gave to King Arthur a good, stout spear of ash-wood, well seasoned and untried in battle; and when the two Knights were duly prepared, they shouted and drave their horses together, the one smiting the other so fairly in the midst of his defences that the spears shivered in the hand of each, bursting all into small splinters as they had aforetime done.

Then each of these two knights immediately voided his horse with great skill and address, and drew each his sword. And thereupon they fell to at a combat, so furious and so violent, that two wild bulls upon the mountains could not have engaged in a more desperate encounter.

But now, having Excalibur for to aid him in his battle, King Arthur soon overcame his enemy. For he gave him several wounds and yet received none himself, nor did he shed a single drop of blood in all that fight, though his enemy's armor was in a little while all stained with crimson. *King Arthur overcometh King Pellinore.* And at last King Arthur delivered so vehement a stroke that King Pellinore was entirely benumbed thereby, wherefore his sword and his shield fell down from their defence, his thighs trembled beneath him and he sank unto his knees upon the ground, Then he called upon King Arthur to have mercy, saying, " Spare my life and I will yield myself unto thee."

And King Arthur said, " I will spare thee and I will do more than that. For now that thou hast yielded thyself unto me, lo! I will restore unto thee thy power and estate. For I bear no ill-will toward thee, Pellinore, ne'theless, I can brook no rebels against my power in this realm. For, as God judges me, I do declare that I hold singly in my sight the good of the people of my kingdom. Wherefore, he who is against me is also against them, and he who is against them is also against me. But now

that thou hast acknowledged me I will take thee into my favor.   Only as
a pledge of thy good faith toward me in the future, I shall *King Arthur*
require it of thee that thou shalt send me as hostage of thy *demands two of*
the sons of King
good-will, thy two eldest sons, to wit: Sir Aglaval and Sir *Pellinore for*
Lamorack.   Thy young son, Dornar, thou mayest keep with *hostages.*
thee for thy comfort."

So those two young knights above mentioned came to the Court of
King Arthur, and they became very famous knights, and by and by were
made fellows in great honor of the Round Table.

And King Arthur and King Pellinore went together into the castle of
King Pellinore, and there King Pellinore's wounds were dressed and he
·was made comfortable.   That night King Arthur abode in the castle
of King Pellinore, and when the next morning had come, he and Merlin
returned unto the Court of the King, where it awaited him in the forest
at that place where he had established it.

Now King Arthur took very great pleasure unto himself as he and Merlin rode together in return through that forest; for it was the leafiest time
of all the year, what time the woodlands decked themselves in their best
apparel of clear, bright green.   Each bosky dell and dingle was full of the
perfume of the thickets, and in every tangled depth the small bird sang
with all his might and main, and as though he would burst his little
throat with the melody of his singing.   And the ground beneath the
horses' feet was so soft with fragrant moss that the ear could not hear any
sound of hoof-beats upon the earth.   And the bright yellow sunlight came
down through the leaves so that all the ground was scattered *How King*
over with a great multitude of trembling circles as of pure *Arthur rode*
through the for-
yellow gold.   And, anon, that sunlight would fall down upon *est with great joy*
the armed knight as he rode, so that every little while his *and delight.*
armor appeared to catch fire with a great glory, shining like a sudden
bright star amid the dark shadows of the woodland.

So it was that King Arthur took great joy in that forest land, for he
was without ache or pain of any sort and his heart was very greatly elated
with the wonderfulness of the success of that adventure into which he had
entered.   For in that adventure he had not only won a very bitter enemy
into a friend who should be of great usefulness and satisfaction to him, but
likewise, he had obtained for himself a sword, the like of which the world
had never before beheld.   And whenever he would think of that singularly
splendid sword which now hung by his side, and whenever he remembered
that land of Faëry into which he had wandered, and of that which had be-

fallen him therein, his heart would become so greatly elated with pure joyousness that he hardly knew how to contain himself because of the great delight that filled his entire bosom.

And, indeed, I know of no greater good that I could wish for you in all of your life than to have you enjoy such happiness as cometh to one when he hath done his best endeavor and hath succeeded with great entirety in his undertaking. For then all the world appears to be filled as with a bright shining light, and the body seemeth to become so elated that the feet are uplifted from heaviness and touch the earth very lightly because of the lightness of the spirit within. Wherefore, it is, that if I could have it in my power to give you the very best that the world hath to give, I would wish that you might win your battle as King Arthur won his battle at that time, and that you might ride homeward in such triumph and joyousness as filled him that day, and that the sunlight might shine around you as it shone around him, and that the breezes might blow and that all the little birds might sing with might and main as they sang for him, and that your heart also might sing its song of rejoicing in the pleasantness of the world in which you live.

Now as they rode thus through the forest together, Merlin said to the King: "Lord, which wouldst thou rather have, Excalibur, or the sheath that holds him?" To which King Arthur replied, "Ten thousand times would I rather have Excalibur than his sheath." "In that thou art wrong, my Lord," said Merlin, "for let me tell thee, that though Excalibur is of so great a temper that he may cut in twain either a feather or a bar *Merlin tells* of iron, yet is his sheath of such a sort that he who wears it *King Arthur* can suffer no wound in battle, neither may he lose a single *of the virtues* *of Excalibur,* drop of blood. In witness whereof, thou mayst remember *his sheath.* that, in thy late battle with King Pellinore, thou didst suffer no wound, neither didst thou lose any blood."

Then King Arthur directed a countenance of great displeasure upon his companion and he said, "Now, Merlin, I do declare that thou hast taken from me the entire glory of that battle which I have lately fought. For what credit may there be to any knight who fights his enemy by means of enchantment such as thou tellest me of? And, indeed, I am minded to take this glorious sword back to that magic lake and to cast it therein where it belongeth; for I believe that a knight should fight by means of his own strength, and not by means of magic."

"My Lord," said Merlin, "assuredly thou art entirely right in what thou holdest. But thou must bear in mind that thou art not as an ordinary errant knight, but that thou art a King, and that thy life belongeth not unto thee, but unto thy people. Accordingly thou hast no right to imperil it, but shouldst do all that lieth in thy power for to preserve it. Wherefore thou shouldst keep that sword so that it may safeguard thy life."

Then King Arthur meditated that saying for a long while in silence; and when he spake it was in this wise: " Merlin, thou art right in what thou sayest, and, for the sake of my people, I will keep both Excalibur for to fight for them, and likewise his sheath for to preserve my life for their sake. Ne'theless, I will never use him again saving in serious battle." And King Arthur held to that saying, so that thereafter he did no battle in sport excepting with lance and a-horseback.

King Arthur kept Excalibur as the chiefest treasure of all his possessions. For he said to himself, " Such a sword as this is fit for a king above other kings and a lord above other lords. Now, as God hath seen fit for to intrust that sword into my keeping in so marvellous a manner as fell about, so must He mean that I am to be His servant for to do unusual things. Wherefore I will treasure this noble weapon not more for its excellent worth than because it shall be unto me as a sign of those great things that God, in His mercy, hath evidently ordained for me to perform for to do Him service."

So King Arthur had made for Excalibur a strong chest or coffer, bound around with many bands of wrought iron, studded all over with great nails of iron, and locked with three great padlocks. In this strong-box he kept Excalibur lying upon a cushion of crimson silk and wrapped in swathings of fine linen, and very few people ever beheld the sword in its glory excepting when it shone like a sudden flame in the uproar of battle.

For when the time came for King Arthur to defend his realm or his subjects from their enemies, then he would take out the sword, and fasten it upon the side of his body; and when he did so he was like unto a hero of God girt with a blade of shining lightning. Yea; at such times Excalibur shone with so terrible a brightness that the very sight thereof would shake the spirits of every wrong-doer with such great fear that he would, in a manner, suffer the pangs of death ere ever the edge of the blade had touched his flesh.

So King Arthur treasured Excalibur and the sword remained with him for all of his life, wherefore the name of Arthur and of Excalibur are one. So, I believe that that sword is the most famous of any that ever was seen or heard tell of in all the Courts of Chivalry.

As for the sheath of the blade, King Arthur lost that through the treachery of one who should, by rights, have been his dearest friend (as you shall hear of anon), and in the end the loss of that miraculous sheath brought it about that he suffered a very great deal of pain and sorrow.

All that also you shall read of, God willing, in due season.

So endeth the story of the winning of Excalibur, and may God give unto you in your life, that you may have His truth to aid you, like a shining sword, for to overcome your enemies; and may He give you Faith (for Faith containeth Truth as a scabbard containeth its sword), and may that Faith heal all your wounds of sorrow as the sheath of Excalibur healed all the wounds of him who wore that excellent weapon. For with Truth and Faith girded upon you, you shall be as well able to fight all your battles as did that noble hero of old, whom men called King Arthur.

PART III

The Winning of a Queen

So, having told you how King Arthur obtained that very excellent sword, Excalibur, for a weapon of defence, I shall now presently recount sundry other noble and knightly adventures whereby he won for himself a most beautiful and gentle lady for his Queen.

For, though all the world is very well acquainted with the renown of that perfectly gracious dame, the Lady Guinevere, yet I do not think that the whole story of those adventures by the which King Arthur won her good favor hath ever yet been told.

So as the matter hereinafter to be related contains not only the narrative of that affair, but also the account of a certain enchanted disguise which King Arthur assumed for his purposes, as well as sundry adventures of very knightly daring which he undertook, I have great hope that he who reads what I have written shall find it both an agreeable and an entertaining history.

he Lady Guinevere ℐ ℐ

Chapter First.

*How King Arthur Went to Tintagalon with Four of His Court, and
How He Disguised Himself for a Certain Purpose.*

NOW, upon a certain day King Arthur proclaimed a high feast,
which was held at Carleon upon Usk. Many noble guests were
bidden, and an exceedingly splendid Court gathered at the King's
castle. For at that feast there sat seven kings and five queens in royal
state, and there were high lords and beautiful ladies of degree, to the
number of three score and seven; and there were a multitude of those
famous knights of the King's Court who were reckoned the *How King*
most renowned in arms in all of Christendom. And of all *Arthur held a*
this great gathering of kings, lords, and knights, not one *feast at Car-*
leon upon Usk.
man looked askance at his neighbor, but all were united in
good fellowship. Wherefore, when the young King looked about him and
beheld such peace and amity among all these noble lords where, aforetime,
had been discord and ill-regard: "Certes," quoth he to himself, "it is
wonderful how this reign of mine hath knit men together in kindness and

good fellowship!" And because of such thoughts as these, his spirit took wings like unto a bird and sang within him.

Now while the King sat thus at feast, lo! there came an herald-messenger from the west-country. And the herald came and stood before the King, and said: "Greeting to thee, King Arthur!"

Then the King said: "Speak, and tell me, what is thy message?"

To which the herald made reply: "I come from King Leodegrance of Cameliard, who is in sore trouble. For thus it is: His enemy and thine enemy, King Ryence of North Wales (he who at one time in contempt of thee commanded thee to send him thy beard for to *An herald-mes-* trim his mantle), doth make sundry demands of my master, *senger comes* King Leodegrance, which demands King Leodegrance is al-*from the west-* together loath to fulfil. And King Ryence of North Wales threateneth to bring war into Cameliard because King Leodegrance doth not immediately fulfil those demands. Now King Leodegrance hath no such array of knights and armed men as he one time had gathered about him for to defend his kingdom against assault. For, since thou in thy majesty hath brought peace to this realm and hath reduced the power of all those kings under thee, those knights who once made the Court of King Leodegrance so famous have gone elsewhither for to seek better opportunities for their great valor and prowess at arms than his peaceful Court may afford. Wherefore my master, King Leodegrance, doth beseech aid of thee, who art his King and Overlord."

To these things that the herald-messenger said, King Arthur, and all that Court that feasted with him, listened in entire silence. And the King's countenance, which erstwhiles had been expanded with cheerfulness, became overcast and dark with anger. "Ha!" he cried, "this is, verily, no good news that thou hast brought hither to our feast. Now I will give what aid I am able to thy master, King Leodegrance, in this extremity, and that right speedily. But tell me, sir herald, what things are they that King Ryence demandeth of thy master?"

"That I will tell you, Lord," quoth the herald-messenger. "Firstly, King Ryence maketh demand upon my master of a great part of those lands of Cameliard that march upon the borders of North Wales. Secondly, he maketh demand that the Lady Guinevere, the King's daughter, be delivered in marriage unto Duke Mordaunt of North Umber, who is of kin unto King Ryence, and that Duke, though a mighty warrior, is so evil of appearance, and so violent of temper, that I believe that there is not his like for ugliness or for madness of humor in all of the world."

Now when King Arthur heard this that the messenger said he was immediately seized with an extraordinary passion of anger. For his eyes appeared, an it were, to shoot forth sparks of pure light, his *King Arthur* face flamed like fire, and he ground his teeth together like the *is very angry* stones of a quern. Then he immediately rose from the chair *which the* where he sat and went forth from that place, and all those who *herald bringeth.* beheld his anger shuddered thereat and turned their eyes away from his countenance.

Then King Arthur went into an inner room of the castle by himself, and there he walked up and down for a great while, and in that time no one of his household dared to come nigh to him. And the reason of the King's wrath was this: that ever since he had lain wounded and sick nigh unto death in the forest, he bare in mind how the Lady Guinevere had suddenly appeared before him like some tall, straight, shining angel who had descended unto him out of Paradise—all full of pity, and exceedingly beautiful. Wherefore, at thought of that wicked, mad Duke Mordaunt of North Umber making demand unto marriage with her, he was seized with a rage so violent that it shook his spirit like a mighty wind.

So, for a long while, he walked up and down in his wrath as aforesaid, and no one durst come nigh unto him, but all stood afar off, watching him from a distance.

Then, after a while, he gave command that Merlin, and Sir Ulfius, and Sir Kay should come to him at that place where he was. And when they had come thither he talked to them for a considerable time, bidding Merlin for to make ready to go upon a journey with him, and bidding Sir Ulfius and Sir Kay for to gather together a large army of chosen knights and armed men, and to bring that army straightway into those parts coadjacent to the royal castle of Tintagalon, which same standeth close to the borders of North Wales and of Cameliard.

So Sir Ulfius and Sir Kay went about to do as King Arthur commanded, and Merlin also went about to do as he commanded; and the next day King Arthur and Merlin, together with certain famous knights of the King's Court who were the most approved at arms of all those about him—to wit, Sir Gawaine, and Sir Ewaine (who were nephews unto the King), and Sir Pellias and Sir Geraint, the son of Erbin—set forth for Tintagalon across the forest-land of Usk.

So they travelled for all that day and a part of the next, and *How King Ar-* that without adventure or misadventure of any sort. So *thur came to* they came, at last, to that large and noble castle, hight Tin- *Tintagalon.* tagalon, which guards the country bordering upon Cameliard and North

Wales.   Here King Arthur was received with great rejoicing; for whithersoever the King went the people loved him very dearly.   Wherefore the
folk of Tintagalon were very glad when he came unto them.

Now the morning after King Arthur had come unto Tintagalon (the
summer night having been very warm), he and Merlin were glad to arise
betimes to go abroad for to enjoy the dewy freshness of the early daytime.   So, in the cool of the day, they walked together in the garden
(which was a very pleasant place), and beneath the shadow of a tall, straight
tower.   And all around about were many trees with a good shade, where
the little birds sang sweetly in the cheerfulness of the summer weather.

And here King Arthur opened his mind very freely to Merlin, and he
said: "Merlin, I do believe that the Lady Guinevere is the fairest lady
in all of the world; wherefore my heart seems ever to be entirely filled
with love for her, and that to such a degree that I think of her continually by day (whether I be eating, or drinking, or walking, or sitting still,
or going about my business), and likewise I dream of her many times at
night.   And this has been the case with me, Merlin, ever since a month
ago, when I lay sick in that hermit's cell in the forest, what time she came
and stood beside me like a shining angel out of Paradise.   So I am not
willing that any other man than I should have her for his wife.

" Now I know very well that thou art wonderfully cunning in those arts
of magic that may change a man in his appearance so that even those who
King Arthur   know him best may not recognize him.   Wherefore I very
openeth his   greatly desire it of thee that thou wilt so disguise me that I
heart to Merlin. may go, unknown of any man, into Cameliard, and that I may
dwell there in such a way that I may see the Lady Guinevere every day.
For I tell thee very truly that I greatly desire to behold her in such a wise
that she may not be in any way witting of my regard.   Likewise I would
fain see for myself how great may be the perils that encompass King
Leodegrance—the King being my right good friend."

"My Lord King," said Merlin, "it shall be as thou desirest, and this
morning I will cause thee to be so disguised that no one in all the world
shall be able to know thee who thou art."

So that morning, a little before the prime, Merlin came unto the King
where he was and gave him a little cap.   And the cap was of such a sort
that when the King set it upon his head he assumed, upon the instant, the
appearance of a rude and rustic fellow from the country-side.   Then the
King commanded that a jerkin of rough frieze should be brought to him,
and with this he covered his royal and knightly vestments, and with it he

hid that golden collar and its jewel, pendent, which he continually wore about his neck. Then, setting the cup upon his head, he assumed at once the guise of that peasant hind.

Whereupon, being thus entirely disguised, he quitted Tintagalon unknown of any man, and took his way a-foot unto the town of Cameliard. *King Arthur quits Tintagalon in disguise.*

Now toward the slanting of the day he drew nigh to that place, and lo! he beheld before him a large and considerable town of many comely houses with red walls and shining windows. And the houses of the town sat all upon a high, steep hill, the one overlooking the other, and the town itself was encompassed around about by a great wall, high and strong. And a great castle guarded the town, and the castle had very many towers and roofs. And all round about the tower were many fair gardens and lawns and meadows, and several orchards and groves of trees with thick and pleasing shade. Now at that time of the day the sky behind the tower was all, as it were, an entire flame of fire, so that the towers and the battlements of the castle and the roofs and the chimneys thereof stood altogether black against the brightness of the light. And, behold! great flocks of pigeons encircled the towers of the castle in a continual flight against that fiery sky. So, because King Arthur was a-weary with walking for all that day, it appeared to him that he had hardly ever beheld in all of his life so fair and pleasing a place as that excellent castle with its gardens and lawns and groves of trees.

Thus came King Arthur unto the castle of Cameliard, in the guise of a poor peasant from the country-side, and no man in all of the world knew him who he was. *King Arthur comes to Cameliard.*

So, having reached the castle, he made inquiries for the head gardener thereof; and when he had speech with the gardener he besought him that he might be taken into service into that part of the garden that appertained to the dwelling-place of the Lady Guinevere. Then the gardener looked upon him and saw that he was tall and strong and well framed, wherefore he liked him very well and took him into service even as he desired.

And thus it was that King Arthur of Britain became a gardener's boy at Cameliard.

Now the King was very glad to be in that garden; for in this pleasant summer season the Lady Guinevere came every day to walk with her damsels among the flowers, and King Arthur, all disguised as a peasant gardener boy, beheld her very many times when she came thither. *King Arthur dwelleth as gardener's boy at the castle.*

So King Arthur abode at that place for above a week, and he took no care that in all that time he enjoyed none of his kingly estate, but was only gardener's boy in the castle garden of Cameliard.

Now it happened upon a day when the weather was very warm, that one of the damsels who was in attendance upon the Lady Guinevere, arose all in the early morning whiles the air was still cool and refreshing. So, leaving the Lady Guinevere still sleeping, this damsel, whose name was Mellicene of the White Hand, went into the ante-room and, opening the casement thereof, looked forth into that garden of roses which adjoined the Lady Guinevere's bower.

Now there was at that place a carven marble figure of a youth, holding in his arms a marble ewer, and a fountain of water, as clear as crystal, flowed out from the ewer into a basin of marble. And the figure, and the fountain, and the marble basin into which the fountain flowed lay beneath the shadow of a linden-tree. And all around was a thick growth of roses, so that the place was entirely hidden, saving only from those windows of the castle that were above.

So it befell that as the damsel looked down thitherward out of the window, she beheld a very wonderful sight. For, lo! a strange knight *The damsel be-* kneeled beside the fountain and bathed his face and his bosom *holds a knight* in the crystal water thereof. And the damsel saw that the *at the fountain.* sunlight fell down through the leaves of the linden-tree and lay upon that strange knight. And she perceived that his hair and his beard were of the color of red gold—shining surpassingly in the brightness of the morning. And she beheld that his brow and his throat and his bosom were white like alabaster. And she beheld that around his neck and shoulders there hung a golden collar of marvellous beauty, so that when the sunlight shone upon it it flashed like pure lightning.

So, beholding this strange appearance—as it were a vision—the damsel Mellicine stood for a long while, all entranced with wonder and with pleasure, and wist not whether that which she saw was a dream or no dream, nor whether he who sat there was a spirit, or whether he was a man of flesh and blood.

Then, by and by, recovering somewhat from her astonishment, she withdrew herself softly from the casement, and, turning about, ran fleetly down the turret stairs, and so came out thence into that fair and blooming garden at the foot of the tower. So she ran through the garden with all speed and silence, and thus came down an alley-way and to the marble fountain and the linden-trees and the rose-trees around about where she had anon beheld that strange knight bathing himself in the crystal waters.

But King Arthur had heard the coming of that damsel, and had speedily set the cap upon his head again. So that when the damsel Mellicene
came thither, she found no one by the fountain but the gar- *The damsel find-*
dener's boy. Of him she demanded : " Who art thou, fellow ? *eth only the gar-*
And why sittest thou here by the fountain ? " *dener's boy.*

And unto her he replied: " I am the gardener's lad who came a short
time ago to take service at this place."

" Then tell me, fellow," quoth she, " and tell me truly. Who was that
young knight who was here beside the fountain but now, and whither
hath he gone ? " " Lady, whereunto," he said, " there has been no one at
this fountain this day, but only I."

" Nay, fellow," she cried, " thou art deceiving me, for I do assure thee
that with mine own eyes I beheld but now, where a strange young knight
sat bathing himself in the waters of this fountain." And the gardener's
boy said, " Lady, that which I have told you is the very truth, for indeed
there hath no one been here this morn but only I. Wherefore, an thou
deemest thou hast seen anyone else, thou art certainly mistaken."

At this the damsel set her look upon him, in great perplexity. Likewise, she marvelled very greatly, for she could not altogether disbelieve
him. Nor yet could she entirely believe him either, because her eyes
had beheld that which she had beheld, and she wotted that she had not
been mistaken. Therefore she knew not what to think, and, because of
her perplexity, she felt a very great displeasure at that gardener's boy.
" Truly, wherefore," she said, " if thou art deceiving me, I shall certainly
cause thee to suffer a great deal of pain, for I shall have thee whipped
with cords." Thereupon she turned and went away from that place,
much marvelling at that strange thing, and wondering what it all signified.

That morning she told unto the Lady Guinevere all that she had seen,
but the Lady Guinevere only laughed at her and mocked her, telling her
that she had been asleep and dreaming, when she beheld that vision. And,
indeed, the damsel herself had begun to think this must be the case.
Nevertheless, she thereafter looked out every morning from her casement
window, albeit she beheld nothing for a great while, for King Arthur came
not soon to that place again.

So, by and by, there befell another certain morning when she looked
out of the casement and, lo ! there sat that strange knight by the fountain
once more as he had aforetime sat. And he bathed his face and his bosom
in the water as he had aforetime done. And he appeared as comely and as
noble as he had appeared before ; and his hair and his young beard shone
like gold as they had shone before in the sun. And this time she beheld

that his collar of gold lay upon the brink of the fountain beside him, and it sparkled with great splendor in the sunlight the whiles he bathed his bosom. Then, after that damsel had regarded him for a considerable time, she ran with all speed to the chamber where the Lady Guinevere still lay, and she cried in a loud voice, "Lady! lady! arouse thee and come with me! For, lo! that same young knight whom I beheld before, is even now bathing himself at the fountain under the linden-tree."

Then the Lady Guinevere, greatly marvelling, aroused herself right quickly, and, dighting herself with all speed, went with the damsel unto that casement window which looked out into that part of the garden.

And there she herself beheld the young knight where he laved himself at the fountain. And she saw that his hair and his beard shone like gold in

The Lady Gui- the sunlight; and she saw that his undervestment was of pur-
nevere beholds ple linen threaded with gold; and she saw that beside him
the knight at lay that cunningly wrought collar of gold inset with many
the fountain. jewels of various colors, and the collar shone with great splendor where it lay upon the marble verge of the fountain.

Somewhiles she gazed, exceedingly astonished; then she commanded the damsel Mellicene for to come with her, and therewith she turned and decended the turret stairs, and went quickly out into the garden, as her damsel had done aforetime. Then, as that damsel had done, she straightway hastened with all speed down the alley-way toward the fountain.

But, behold! when she had come there, she found no young knight, but only the gardener boy, exactly as had happened with the damsel Mellicene aforetime. For King Arthur had heard her coming, and had immediately put that enchanted cap upon his head. Then the Lady Guinevere marvelled very greatly to find there only the gardener's boy, and she wist not what to think of so strange a thing. Wherefore she demanded of him, even as Mellicene had done, whither had gone the young knight whom she had beheld anon there at the fountain. And unto her the gardener lad made answer as aforetime: "Lady! there hath been no one at this place at any time this morning, but only I."

Now when King Arthur had donned his cap at the coming of the Lady, he had, in his great haste, forgotten his golden collar, and this Guinevere beheld where it lay shining very brightly, beside the margin of the fountain. "How now!" quoth she. "Wouldst thou dare to make a mock of me? Now tell me, thou fellow, do gardeners' boys in the land whence thou didst come wear golden collars about their necks like unto that collar that lieth yonder beside the fountain? Now, an I had thee well whipped, it would be thy rightful due. But take thou that bauble yonder and give it unto him to whom it doth rightfully belong, and tell him from me that it doth ill become a true belted knight for to hide himself away in the privy gardens of a lady." Then turned she with the damsel Mellicene, and left she that place and went back again into her bower.

Yet, indeed for all that day, as she sat over her 'broidery, she did never cease to marvel and to wonder how it was possible that that strange young knight should so suddenly have vanished away and left only the poor gardener's boy in his stead. Nor, for a long time, might she unriddle that strange thing.

Then, of a sudden, at that time when the heat of the day was sloping toward the cooler part of the afternoon, she aroused herself because of a thought that had come in an instant unto her. So she called the damsel Mellicene to come to her, and she bade her to go and tell the gardener's lad for to fetch her straightway a basket of fresh roses for to adorn her tower chamber.

So Mellicene went and did as she bade, and after considerable time the gardener's lad came bearing a great basket of roses. And, lo! he wore his cap upon his head. And all the damsels in waiting *The gardener's* upon the Lady Guinevere, when they saw how he wore his *boy weareth his* cap in her presence, cried out upon him, and Mellicene of *cap before the* the White Hand demanded of him: "What! How now, Sir *Lady Guinevere.* boor! Dost thou know so little of what is due unto a king's daughter that thou dost wear thy cap even in the presence of the Lady Guinevere? Now I bid thee straightway to take thy cap off thy head."

And to her King Arthur made answer: "Lady, I cannot take off my cap."

Quoth the Lady Guinevere: "And why canst thou not take off thy cap, thou surly fellow?"

"Lady," said he, "I cannot take off my cap, because I have an ugly place upon my head."

"Then wear thy cap," quoth the Lady Guinevere. "Only fetch thou the roses unto me."

And so at her bidding, he brought the roses to her. But when he had come nigh unto the lady, she, of a sudden, snatched at the cap and plucked it off from his head. Then, lo! he was upon the *The Lady Gui-* instant transformed; for instead of the gardener's boy there *nevere discovers* stood before the Lady Guinevere and her damsel the appear- *the knight of* ance of a noble young knight with hair and beard like *the fountain.* threads of gold. Then he let fall his basket of roses so that the flowers were scattered all over the floor, and he stood and looked at all who were

there. And some of those damsels in attendance upon the Lady Guinevere shrieked, and others stood still from pure amazement and wist not
how to believe what their eyes beheld. But not one of those ladies knew
that he whom she beheld was King Arthur. Nevertheless the Lady
Guinevere remembered that this was the knight whom she had found so
sorely wounded, lying in the hermit's cell in the forest.

Then she laughed and flung him back his cap again. "Take thy cap,"
quoth she, "and go thy ways, thou gardener's boy who hath an ugly place
upon his head." Thus she said because she was minded to mock him.

But King Arthur did not reply to her, but straightway, with great
sobriety of aspect, set his cap upon his head again. So resuming his
humble guise once more, he turned and quitted that place, leaving those
roses scattered all over the floor even as they had fallen.

And after that time, whenever the Lady Guinevere would come upon the
gardener's lad in the garden, she would say unto her damsel in such a voice
that he might hear her speech: "Lo! yonder is the gardener's lad who
hath an ugly place upon his head so that he must always wear his cap for
to hide it."

Thus she spake openly, mocking at him; but privily she bade her
damsels to say naught concerning these things, but to keep unto themselves all those things which had befallen.

Two Knights do battle before Cameliard

Chapter Second.

*How King Ryence Came to Cameliard and How King Arthur
Fought With the Duke of North Umber.*

NOW, upon a certain day at this time there came a messenger to
the Court of King Leodegrance, with news that King Ryence of
North Wales and Duke Mordaunt of North Umber were com-
ing thither and that they brought with them a very noble and considerable
Court of knights and lords. At this news King Leode-
grance was much troubled in spirit, for he wist not what such
a visit might betoken; and yet he greatly feared that it boded
ill for him. So on that day when King Ryence and the Duke
of North Umber appeared before the castle, King Leodegrance went forth
to greet them and they three met together in the meadows that lie beneath the castle walls of Cameliard.

*King Ryence
and Duke Mor-
daunt come to
Cameliard.*

There King Leodegrance bade those others welcome in such manner as
was fitting, desiring them that they should come into the castle with him
so that he might entertain them according to their degree.

But to this courtesy upon the part of King Leodegrance, King Ryence
deigned no pleasing reply. "Nay," quoth he, "we go not with thee into
thy castle, King Leodegrance, until we learn whether thou art our friend
or our enemy. For just now we are, certes, no such good friends with
thee that we care to sit down at thy table and eat of thy salt. Nor may
we be aught but enemies of thine until thou hast first satisfied our
demands; to wit, that thou givest to me those lands which I demand of
thee and that thou givest unto my cousin, Duke Mordaunt of
North Umber, the Lady Guinevere to be his wife. In these
matters thou hast it in thy power to make us either thy friends
or thine enemies. Wherefore we shall abide here, outside of
thy castle, for five days, in the which time thou mayst frame thine answer,
and so we may know whether we shall be friends or enemies."

*The King and
the Duke send
challenge to
King Leode-
grance.*

"And in the meantime," quoth Duke Mordaunt of North Umber, "I do

hold myself ready for to contest my right unto the hand of the Lady
Guinevere with any knight of thy Court who hath a mind to deny my
just title thereto; and if thou hast no knight in all thy Court who can
successfully assay a bout of arms with me, thou thyself canst hardly hope
to succeed in defending thyself against that great army of knights
whom King Ryence hath gathered together to bring against thee in case
thou denyest us that which we ask."

Then was King Leodegrance exceedingly cast down in his spirits, for he
feared those proud lords and he wist not what to say in answer to them.
Wherefore he turned and walked back into his castle again, beset with
great anxiety and sorrow of spirit. And King Ryence, and Duke Mordaunt and their Court of lords and knights pitched their pavilions in those
meadows over against the castle, so that the plain was entirely covered
with those pavilions. And there they took up their inn with great rejoicing
and with the sound of feasting and singing and merry-making, for it was
an exceeding noble Court King Ryence had gathered about him.

And when the next morning had come Duke Mordaunt of North Umber
went forth clad all in armor of proof. And he rode up and down the
field before the castle and gave great challenge to those within; daring
any knight to come forth for to meet him in knightly encounter. "Ho!"
he cried, "how now, ye Knights of Cameliard! Is there no one to come
forth to meet me? How then may ye hope to contend with the Knights
of North Wales, an ye fear to meet with one single Knight from North
Duke Mordaunt Umber?" So he scoffed at them in his pride, and none dared
rides before the to come forth from Cameliard against him. For the Duke of
castle. North Umber was one of the most famous knights of his day,
and one of exceeding strength and success at arms, and there was now, in
these times of peace, no one of King Leodegrance's Court who was at all
able to face a warrior of his approved skill and valor. Wherefore, no one
took up that challenge which the Duke of North Umber gave to the
Court of Cameliard. Meantime many people gathered upon the walls of
Cameliard and gazed down therefrom upon that proud and haughty duke,
all bedight in his splendid armor, and all were grieved and ashamed that
there was no one in that peaceful town to go out against him. And all
the lords and knights of King Ryence's Court came and stood in front
of the King's pavilion and laughed and clapped their hands together, and
cheered Duke Mordaunt, as he so rode up and down before them. And
the greater they were expanded with mirth, the more abashed were the
people of Cameliard. "Ho! Ho!" cried that proud Duke. "How now!
Will no one come forth to meet me? How then may ye of Cameliard hope

to face the King of North Wales and all his knightly array of which I am but one man?" And the people of Cameliard, gathered upon the walls, listened to him with shame and sorrow.

Now all this while King Arthur digged in the garden; but, nevertheless, he was well aware of everything that passed and of how that the Duke of North Umber rode up and down so proudly before the castle walls. So, of a sudden, it came to him that he could not abide this any longer. Wherefore he laid aside his spade and went out secretly by a postern way, and so up into the town.

Now there was in Cameliard an exceedingly rich merchant, by name Ralph of Cardiff, and the renown of his possessions and his high estate had reached even unto King Arthur's ears at Carleon. Accordingly it was unto his house that King Arthur directed his steps.

And while he was in a narrow way, not far from the merchant's house, he took off his magic cap of disguise and assumed somewhat of his noble appearance once more, for he was now of a mind to show his knightliness unto those who looked upon him. Accordingly, when he stood before the rich merchant in his closet, and when the merchant looked up *King Arthur* into his face, he wist not what to think to behold so noble a *seeks armor to do* lord clad all in frieze. For though King Arthur was a stran- *battle.* ger to the good man, so that he knew not his countenance, yet that merchant wist that he was no ordinary knight, but that he must assuredly be one of high degree and in authority, even though he was clad in frieze.

Then King Arthur opened the breast of his jerkin and showed the merchant the gold collar that hung around his neck. And also he showed beneath the rough coat of frieze how that there was an undergarment of fine purple silk embroidered with gold. And then he showed to the good man his own signet ring, and when the merchant saw it, he knew it to be the ring of the King of Britain. Wherefore, beholding these tokens of high and lordly authority, the merchant arose and stood before the King and doffed his cap.

"Sir Merchant," quoth the King, "know that I am a stranger knight in disguise in this place. Ne'theless, I may tell thee that I am a very good friend to King Leodegrance and wish him exceeding well. Thou art surely aware of how the Duke of North Umber rides continually up and down before the King's castle, and challenges anyone within to come forth for to fight against him in behalf of the Lady Guinevere. Now I am of a mind to assay that combat mine own self, and I hope a very great deal that I shall succeed in upholding the honor of Cameliard and of bringing shame upon its enemies.

"Sir Merchant, I know very well that thou hast several suits of noble armor in thy treasury, for the fame of them hath reached unto mine ears though I dwell a considerable distance from this place. Wherefore I desire that thou shalt provide me in the best manner that thou art able to do, so that I may straightway assay a bout of arms with that Duke of North Umber. Moreover, I do pledge thee my knightly word that thou shalt be fully recompensed for the best suit of armor that thou canst let me have, and that in a very little while."

"My Lord," said Master Ralph, "I perceive that thou art no ordinary errant knight, but rather someone of extraordinary estate; wherefore it is a very great pleasure to fulfil all thy behests. But even an thou wert other than thou art, I would be altogether willing to equip thee with armor, seeing that thou hast a mind to ride forth against yonder duke."

Upon this he rang a little silver bell that stood nigh to him, and in answer to its sound several attendants immediately appeared. Into their hands he intrusted the person of the King, bidding them to do him extraordinary honor. Accordingly, certain of those attendants prepared for the King a bath of tepid water perfumed with ambergris, very grateful to the person. And after he was bathed in this bath and was wiped with soft linen towels, other attendants conducted him to a hall all hung with tapestries and 'broideries, and at this place a noble feast had been spread ready for his refreshment. Here that lordly merchant himself ministered to the King's wants, serving him with various meats—very dainty, and of several sorts—and likewise with fine white bread. And he poured him wine of various countries—some as red as ruby, others as yellow as gold; and indeed the King had hardly ever enjoyed a better feast than that which the merchant, Ralph of Cardiff, had thus spread for him.

And after he had entirely refreshed himself with eating, there came six pages richly clad in sarsanet of azure, and these, taking the King to an apartment of great state, they there clad him in a suit of Spanish armor, *King Arthur is* very cunningly wrought and all inlaid with gold. And the *armed by Ralph* like of that armor was hardly to be found in all of the land. *of Cardiff.* The juppon and the several trappings of the armor were all of satin and as white as milk. And the shield was white, and altogether without emblazonment or device of any sort. Then these attendants conducted the King into the courtyard, and there stood a noble war-horse, as white as milk, and all the trappings of the horse were of milk-white cloth without emblazonment or adornment of any sort; and the bridle and the bridle rein were all studded over with bosses of silver.

Then after the attendants had aided King Arthur to mount this steed,

the lordly merchant came forward and gave him many words of good
cheer, and so the king bade him adieu and rode away, all shining in white
and glittering in fine armor, wherefore he resembled the full moon in
harvest season.

And as he drave down the stony streets of the town, the people turned
and gazed after him, for he made a very noble appearance as he passed
along the narrow way between the houses of the town.

So King Arthur directed his way to the postern gate of the castle, and,
having reached that place, he dismounted and tied his horse. Then he
straightway entered the garden, and there, finding an attendant, he made
demand that he should have present speech with the Lady Guinevere. So
the attendant, all amazed at his lordly presence, went and delivered the
message, and by and by the Lady Guinevere came, much wondering, and
passed along a gallery with several of her damsels, until she had come
over above where King Arthur was. And when King Arthur looked up
and saw her above him, he loved her exceeding well. And he said to
her: "Lady, I have great will to do thee such honor as I am able. For I
go forth now to do combat with that Duke of North Umber who rides up
and down before this castle. Moreover, I hope and verily believe that I
shall encompass his downfall; accordingly, I do beseech of thee some
token, such as a lady may give unto a knight for to wear when that knight
rides forth to do her honor."

Then the Lady Guinevere said: "Certes, Sir Knight, I would that I
knew who thou art. Yet, though I know not, nevertheless I
am altogether willing for to take thee for my champion as *The Lady Gui-*
nevere accepts
thou offerest. So, touching that token thou speakest of, if *King Arthur*
thou wilt tell me what thing it is that thou desirest, I will *for her cham-*
pion.
gladly give it to thee."

"An that be so, Lady," said King Arthur, "I would fain have that necklace that thou wearest about thy throat. For, meseems that if I had that
tied about my arm, I would find my valor greatly increased thereby."

"Pardee, Sir Knight," said the Lady, "what thou desirest of me thou
shalt assuredly have." Thereupon speaking, she took from her long,
smooth neck the necklace of pearls which she wore, and dropped the same
down to King Arthur where he stood.

And King Arthur took the necklace and tied it about his arm, and he
gave great thanks for it. Then he saluted the Lady Guinevere with very
knightly grace, and she saluted him, and then, straightway, he went forth
from that place, greatly expanded with joy that the Lady Guinevere had
shown him such favor.

Now the report had gone about Cameliard that a knight was to go
forth to fight the Duke of North Umber. Wherefore great crowds gathered upon the walls, and King Leodegrance and the Lady Guinevere and
all the Court of the King came to that part of the castle walls overlooking
the meadow where the Duke of North Umber defended. Wherefore, so
great a concourse was presently assembled, that any knight might be encouraged to do his utmost before such a multitude as that which looked
down upon the field.

Then of a sudden the portcullis of the castle was lifted, and the bridge
let fall, and the White Champion rode forth to that encounter which he
had undertaken. And, as he drave across that narrow bridge, the hoofs of
his war-horse smote the boards with a noise like to thunder, and when he
came out into the sunlight, lo! his armor flamed of a sudden like unto
lightning, and when the people saw him they shouted aloud.

Then when the Duke of North Umber beheld a knight all clad in white,
he rode straightway to him and spoke to him with words of knightly
greeting. "Messire," he said, "I perceive that thou bearest no crest upon
thy helm, nor hast thou a device of any sort upon thy shield, wherefore I
know not who thou art. Ne'theless, I do believe that thou art a knight
of good quality and of approved courage, or else thou wouldst not have
thus come to this place."

"Certes, Sir Knight," said King Arthur, "I am of a quality equal to
thine own. And as for my courage, I do believe that it hath been approved in as many encounters as even thine own hath been."

"Sir Knight," quoth the Duke of Umber, "thou speakest with a very
large spirit. Ne'theless, thou mayst make such prayers as thou art able,
for I shall now presently so cast thee down from thy seat, so that thou
shalt never rise again; for so have I served better men than ever thou
mayst hope to be."

To this King Arthur made answer with great calmness of demeanor:
"That shall be according to the will of Heaven, Sir Knight, and not according to thy will."

So each knight saluted the other and rode to his assigned station, and
there each dressed his spear and his shield, and made him ready for the
King Arthur   encounter. Then a silence fell upon all so great that a man
overthrows Duke might hear his own heart beat in the stillness. So, for a
Mordaunt.   small space, each knight sat like a statue made of iron. Then,
of a sudden, each shouted to his war-horse, and drave spurs into his flank,
and launched forth from his station. And so they met in the midst of the
course with a noise like unto a violent thunder-clap. And lo! the spear of

the Duke of North Umber burst into splinters unto the very truncheon thereof; but the spear of King Arthur broke not, but held, so that the Duke was cast out of his saddle like a windmill—whirling in the air and smiting the earth so that the ground shuddered beneath him. And indeed he rolled full three times over and over ere he ceased to fall.

Then all the people upon the wall shouted with might and main, so that the noise thereof was altogether astonishing; for they had hardly hoped that their champion should have proved so extraordinarily strong and skilful.

Meanwhile, those of King Ryence's Court ran immediately to the Duke of Umber where he lay upon the earth, and they straightway unlaced his helm for to give him air. And first they thought that he was dead, and then they thought that he was like to die; for, behold! he lay without any life or motion. Nor did he recover from that swoon wherein he lay for the space of full two hours and more.

Now whilst the attendants were thus busied about Duke Mordaunt of North Umber, King Arthur sat his horse, very quietly, observing all that they did. Then, perceiving that his enemy was not dead, he turned him about and rode away from that place.

Nor did he return unto Cameliard at that time, for he deemed that he had not yet entirely done with these enemies to the peace of his realm, wherefore he was minded not yet to return the horse and the armor to the merchant, but to keep them for a while for another occasion.

So he bethought him of how, coming to Cameliard, he had passed through an arm of the forest where certain wood-choppers were at work felling the trees. Wherefore, remembering that place, he thought that he would betake him thither and leave his horse and armor in the care of those rude folk until he would need those things once more. So now he rode away into the country-side, leaving behind him the town and the castle and all the noise of shouting and rejoicing; nor did he once so much as turn his head to look back toward that place where he had so violently overthrown his enemy.

And now you shall presently hear of certain pleasant adventures of a very joyous sort that befell him ere he had accomplished all his purposes. For when a man is a king among men, as was King Arthur, then is he of such a calm and equal temper that neither victory nor defeat may cause him to become either unduly exalted in his own opinion or so troubled in spirit as to be altogether cast down into despair. So if you would become like to King Arthur, then you shall take all your triumphs as he took this victory, for you will not be turned aside from your final purposes by the great applause that many men may give you, but you will first finish your work that you have set yourself to perform, ere you give yourself ease to sit you down and to enjoy the fruits of your victory.

Yea, he who is a true king of men, will not say to himself, "Lo! I am worthy to be crowned with laurels;" but rather will he say to himself, "What more is there that I may do to make the world the better because of my endeavors?"

The White Champion meets two Knights at the Mill.

Chapter Third.

How King Arthur Encountered Four Knights and of What Befell Thereby.

NOW, the day was extraordinarily sweet and pleasant unto one so lusty of frame and so lithe of heart as was good King Arthur. For the bright clouds swam smoothly across the blue sky in prodigious volumes of vapor, and the wind blew across the long grass of the meadow lands, and across the fields of growing wheat, so that a multitude of waves travelled over the hills and valleys like an it were across an entire sea of green. And now all the earth would be darkened with wide shadows from those clouds, and, anon, everything would burst out, of a sudden, into a wonderful radiance of sunlight once more. And the little birds they sang all gayly in the hedge-rows and the leafy thickets as though they would burst their tiny throats with singing, and the cock crowed, strong and lusty, from the farm croft, and all was so blithe and comely that the young King, with the visor of his helmet uplifted to the refreshment of the gentle breeze, would sometimes carol very joyously in his journeying. So travelled King Arthur in all that gay and tender summer season, when the earth was young and the time was of long-gone-by.

Now, you are to remember that when King Arthur had come from Carleon unto the castle of Tintagalon, he had brought with him four young knights for to bear him company. And those knights aforesaid were as follows: There was Sir Gawaine, the son of King Lot and of Queen Margaise, and there was Sir Ewaine, the son of King Uriens and of Queen Morgana la Fay (and these two were nephews, half in blood, unto the King), and there was Sir Pellias, and there was Sir Geraint, the son of Erbin. These were the four noble young knights who had come with King Arthur from Camelot unto Tintagalon.

Now it befell, as King Arthur rode all gayly in the summer time as aforesaid, that he came to a certain part of the road where he beheld before him a tall and comely tower that stood upon a green hillock immediately by the roadside. And lo! there stood upon the balcony of that tower *King Arthur* three fair demoiselles, clad all in green taffeta. And on the *cometh upon a* high road in front of the castle there was a knight clad all in *knight enter-* *taining the* very fine armor. And the knight sat upon a noble war-*ladies in green.* horse, and in his hands he held a lute, and he played upon the lute and sang in a voice of extraordinary sweetness. Whiles he sang those three ladies in green taffeta listened to him with great cheerfulness of mien. And whenever that knight would stint his singing, then those three ladies would clap their hands together with great acclaim, and would bid him to sing to them again; and so he would do with great readiness of spirit.

All this King Arthur beheld, and it appeared to him to be a very pleasant sight, wherefore he rejoiced at it exceedingly.

And as he drew nigh, lo! he beheld that the knight who thus sat upon his horse and played upon the lute and sang unto the accompaniment thereof, was none other than Sir Geraint, the son of Erbin. For that knight wore upon his crest the figure of a gryphon, and the device upon his shield was two gryphons rampant facing one another upon a field azure, and King Arthur knew that this was the crest and the device of Sir Geraint. And when the King perceived who was the knight who sat there and sang, he laughed unto himself and straightway closed his visor and made him ready for such encounter as might, perchance, befall. So he drew nigh to where the knight sang and the ladies listened.

Now when Sir Geraint perceived King Arthur approach, he ceased singing and hung up his lute behind him across his shoulder. Then, casting upward his look to those three fair ladies above him, quoth he: "Mesdames, ye have been pleased to listen to that singing which I have assayed altogether in your honor. Now, likewise, in your honor, I will perform a deed of knightly prowess which I very much hope shall bring great glory to you. For, if ye will be pleased to lend me that encouragement which your very great beauty can so easily afford, ye shall behold me, I doubt not, overthrow yonder knight completely, and that to your great credit and renown."

"Sir Knight," said that lady who spoke for the others, "you are, truly, a lord of noble bearing and exceedingly pleasing of address, wherefore we do wish you great success in this undertaking; and we do believe that you will succeed in that which you assay to do."

Upon these Sir Geraint gave those three demoiselles great thanks for their words, and thereupon he closed the visor of his helmet. So, dressing his spear and shield, and saluting those three ladies with great humility of demeanor, he went forth to meet King Arthur where he now sat at a little distance, very quietly and soberly awaiting his pleasure.

Now Sir Geraint knew not King Arthur because he wore no crest upon his helm and no device upon his shield, wherefore as he saluted him he made speech to him in this wise : " Ha ! Messire, I know not who thou art, seeing that thou bearest neither crest nor device. Ne'theless, I am minded to do thee such honor as I may in running a tilt with thee upon the behalf of those three demoiselles whom thou beholdest yonder upon that balcony. For I do affirm, and am ready to maintain the same with my knightly person, that those ladies are fairer than thy lady, whomsoever she may be."

" Sir Knight," quoth King Arthur, " I will gladly run a course with thee in honor of my lady ; for, I may tell thee, she is a princess, and is held by many to be the most beautiful dame in all of the world. But I will only contend with thee upon one condition, and the condition is this— that he who is overthrown shall yield himself as servant unto the other for seven days, and in that time he shall do all that may be required of him."

" I will accept thy gage, Sir Unknown Knight," quoth Sir Geraint, " and when I have overthrown thee, I will yield thee unto those fair ladies yonder for to be their servant for seven days. And I do tell thee that there are a great many knights who would certainly regard that as being both a pleasant and an honorable task."

" And should I so chance as to overthrow thee," said King Arthur, " I will send thee for to serve my lady for that same period of time, and that will be even a pleasanter and a more honorable task than that which thou hast a mind for me to perform."

So each knight saluted the other, and thereupon each took such a stand as should cast the encounter immediately beneath where those three fair demoiselles looked down from the balcony. Then each knight *King Arthur* dressed his spear and his shield, and, having made ready for *overthrows Sir* the encounter, each sat for a small space entirely prepared. *Geraint.* Then each shouted to his war-horse, and drave spur into its flank, and launched forth with wonderful speed to the assault. So they met in the very midst of the course with a force so vehement that the noise thereof was wonderfully appalling for to hear. And each knight smote the other in the very centre of his defences. And, lo ! the spear of Sir Geraint burst into small pieces, even to the truncheon thereof ; but the spear of King Arthur held, and Sir Geraint was cast so violently backward that both he and his horse were overthrown into the dust with a tumult like to a monstrous roaring of thunder.

And when Sir Geraint had recovered his footing, he was, for awhile, so astonished that he wist not where he stood, for never had he been so overthrown in all of his life before. Then, coming quickly unto himself again, he straightway drew forth his sword and called upon King Arthur with exceeding vehemence for to come down from out of his saddle, and to fight him afoot.

"Nay, not so, Sir Knight," said King Arthur, "I will not have to do with thee in that way. Moreover, thou art not to forget that thou hast promised to give thyself unto me as my servant for seven days, for, assuredly, I have entirely overcome thee in this encounter, and now thou art pledged unto me to be my servant."

Then Sir Geraint knew not what to say, being altogether abashed with shame and vexation at his overthrow. Ne'theless, he perceived that he must uphold his knightly word unto that which he had pledged himself to do; wherefore, he put up his sword again, though with exceeding discontent. "Sir Knight," said he, "I do acknowledge myself to have been overcome in this encounter, wherefore I yield myself now unto thy commands, according to my plighted word."

"Then I do place my commands upon thee in this wise," quoth King Arthur. "My command is, that thou goest straightway unto the Lady Guinevere at Cameliard, and that thou tellest her that thou *King Arthur* hast been overthrown by that knight to whom she gave her *sendeth Sir Ge-* *raint to the Lady* necklace as a token. Moreover, I do desire that thou shalt *Guinevere.* obey her in everything that she may command thee to do, and that for the space of seven days to come."

"Sir Knight," quoth Sir Geraint, "that which thou biddest me to do, I will perform according to thy commands."

Thereupon he mounted his horse and went his way. And King Arthur went his way. And those three ladies who stood upon the balcony of the castle were exceedingly glad that they had beheld so noble an assay-at-arms as that which they had looked down upon.

Now, after King Arthur had travelled forward for the distance of two or three leagues or more, he came to a certain place of moorlands, where were many ditches of water, and where the heron and the marsh-hen sought harborage in the sedge. And here, at sundry points, were several windmills, with their sails all turning slowly in the sunlight before a wind which blew across the level plains of ooze. And at this place there was a long, straight causeway, with two long rows of pollard willows, one upon either hand. Now, when he had come nigh the middle of this causeway, King Arthur perceived two knights, who sat their horses in the shade of a great windmill that stood upon one side of the roadway. And a large shadow of the sails moved ever and anon across the roadway as the wheel of the mill turned slowly afore the wind. And all about the mill, and everywhere about, were great quantities of swallows that darted hither and thither like bees about a hive in midsummer. And King Arthur saw that those two knights, as they sat in the shadow of the mill, were eating of a great loaf of rye bread, fresh baked and of brittle crust ; and they ate fair white cheese, which things the miller, all white with dust, served to them. But when these two knights perceived King Arthur, they immediately ceased eating that bread and cheese, and straightway closed their helmets. As for the miller, when he saw them thus prepare themselves, he went quickly back into the mill and shut the door thereof, and then went and looked out of a window which was over above where the knights were standing.

But King Arthur made very merry unto himself when he perceived that those two knights were Sir Gawaine and Sir Ewaine. For he knew that the one was Sir Gawaine because that the crest of his helmet was a leopard rampant, and because he bore upon his shield *King Arthur cometh upon two* the device of a leopard rampant upon a field gules; and he *knights at the windmill.* knew that the other was Sir Ewaine, because he bore upon his crest an unicorn, and because the device upon his shield was that of a lady holding a naked sword in her hand, which same was upon a field or. Accordingly, whiles he was yet at some distance, King Arthur closed his helmet so that those two young knights might not know who he was.

So, when he had come anear to the two knights, Sir Gawaine rode forward for a little distance for to meet him. "Sir Knight," quoth he, "thou must know that this is soothly parlous ground whereon thou hast ventured ; for there is no byway hence across the morass, and thou mayst not go forward without trying a tilt with me."

"Sir Knight," said King Arthur, "and I am very willing to run a tilt with thee. Ne'theless, I will only encounter thee upon one condition, and that is this : that he who is overthrown shall serve the other entirely for the space of seven full days."

"I do accept thy gage, Sir Knight," quoth Sir Gawaine. For he said unto himself, "Of a surety, so exceedingly strong and skilful a knight as I shall easily encompass the overthrow of this unknown knight."

So each knight immediately took his appointed station, and having dressed his spear and his shield, and having fully prepared *King Arthur* himself in every manner, and having rested for a little space, *overthrows Sir* each suddenly shouted to his horse, and drave spur into the *Gawaine.* flanks thereof, and so rushed to the encounter. And each knight smote the other in the midst of his defence, and lo! the spear of Sir Gawaine burst into fragments. But the spear of King Arthur held, so that Sir Gawaine was lifted entirely out of his saddle and over the crupper of his horse. And indeed he fell with wonderful violence into the dust. Nor could he immediately rise from that fall, but lay all bedazed for a little while. And when he did arise, he perceived that the white knight who had overthrown him sat nigh to him upon his horse.

Then King Arthur spake and said: "Sir Knight, I have altogether overthrown thee, and so thou must now serve me according to thy knightly word."

Then up spake Sir Ewaine, who sat nearby upon his horse. "Not so, Sir Knight," he said; "not so, nor until thou hast had to do with me. For I do make demand of thee that thou shalt straightway joust with me. And if I overthrow thee I will claim of thee that thou shalt release my cousin from that servitude unto which he hath pledged himself. But if thou overthrowst me, then will I serve thee even as he hath pledged himself to serve thee."

"Sir Knight," said King Arthur, "I do accept thy gage with all readiness of spirit!"

So each knight took his assigned place and dressed himself for the encounter. Then they shouted, and drave together, rushing the one upon *King Arthur* the other like unto two rams upon the hillside. And the *overthrows Sir* spear of Sir Ewaine was also shivered into pieces. But King *Ewaine.* Arthur's spear held, so that the girths of Sir Ewaine's saddle were burst apart, and both the saddle and the knight were swept off the horse's back with such violence that a tower falling could not have made a greater noise than did Sir Ewaine when he smote the dust of that causeway.

Then Sir Ewaine arose to his feet and gazed upon him, all filled with entire amazement. To him came King Arthur, and bespake him thus: *King Arthur* "Ha, Sir Knight, meseems that thou hast been fairly over- *sendeth the two* come this day. And so, according to your promises, both *knights to the* *Lady Guine-* thou and yonder other knight must fulfil all my commands *vere.* for the space of full seven days to come. Now this is the command that I set upon ye both: that ye shall straightway go unto the Lady Guinevere at Cameliard and shall take her greeting from her knight. And ye shall say to her that her knight unto whom she gave her necklace, hath sent ye, who are King's sons, for to do obedience unto her. And all that she shall command ye to do in the space of these seven days that are to come, that shall ye perform even unto the smallest grain."

"Sir Knight," said Sir Gawaine, "so we will do according to thy commands, having pledged ourselves thereunto. But when these seven days are passed, I do make my vow that I shall seek thee out and shall carry this combat unto its entire extremity. For it may happen to any knight to be unhorsed as I have been, yet I do believe that I may have a better success with thee an I battle with thee to the extremity of my endeavor."

"Sir Knight," said King Arthur, "it shall be even as thou desirest. Yet I do verily believe that when these seven days are passed thou wilt not have such a great desire for to fight with me as thou now hast."

Having so spoken, King Arthur saluted those two knights and they saluted him. And then he turned his horse and went his way. And whenever he bethought him of how those two good knights had fallen before his assault, and when he thought of how astonished and abashed they had been at their overthrow, he laughed aloud for pure mirth, and vowed unto himself that he had never in all of his life engaged in so joyous an adventure as this.

So when Sir Ewaine had mended the girths of his saddle then he and Sir Gawaine mounted their horses and betook their way toward Cameliard much cast down in spirits.

Then the miller came forth from the mill once more, greatly rejoiced at having beheld such a wonderfully knightly encounter from so safe a place as that from which he had beheld it.

And so King Arthur rode onward with great content of mind until the slanting of the afternoon had come, and by that time he had come nigh to that arm of the forest-land which he had in mind as the proper place where he might leave his horse and his armor.

Now as he drew nigh to this part of the forest skirts, he perceived before him at the roadside a gnarled and stunted oak-tree. And he perceived that upon the oak-tree there hung a shield, and that underneath the shield were written these words in fair large letters:

> "𝔚𝔥𝔬𝔰𝔬 𝔰𝔪𝔦𝔱𝔢𝔱𝔥 𝔲𝔭𝔬𝔫 𝔱𝔥𝔦𝔰 𝔰𝔥𝔦𝔢𝔩𝔡
> 𝔇𝔬𝔢𝔱𝔥 𝔰𝔬 𝔞𝔱 𝔱𝔥𝔢 𝔭𝔢𝔯𝔦𝔩 𝔬𝔣 𝔥𝔦𝔰 𝔟𝔬𝔡𝔶."

Then King Arthur was filled with a great spirit, and, uplifting his spear, he smote upon that shield so that it rang like thunder.

Then immediately King Arthur heard a voice issue out of the forest crying, "Who hath dared to assail my shield!" And straightway there came out thence a knight of large frame, riding upon a horse white, like that which King Arthur himself rode. And the trappings of the horse and of the knight were all white like

King Arthur smites the shield of the White Knight.

unto the trappings of King Arthur and his horse. And the knight bore
upon his helmet as his crest a swan with outspread wings, and upon his
shield he bore the emblazonment of three swans upon a field argent. And
because of the crest and the emblazonment of the shield, King Arthur
knew that this knight was Sir Pellias, who had come with him from Camelot to Tintagalon.

So when Sir Pellias had come nigh to where King Arthur waited for
him, he drew rein and bespake him with great sternness of voice: "Ho!
Ho! Sir Knight," quoted he. "Why didst thou dare to smite upon my
shield! Verily, that blow shall bring thee great peril and dole. Now,
prepare to defend thyself straightway because of what thou hast
done."

"Stay! Stay! Sir Knight," said King Arthur, "it shall be as thou wouldst
have it; and I will do combat with thee. Yet will I not assay this adventure until thou hast agreed that the knight who is overcome in the
encounter shall serve the other in whatsoever manner that other may
desire, for the space of one se' night from this time."

"Sir Knight," said Sir Pellias, "I do accept that risk, wherefore I bid
thee now presently to prepare thyself for the encounter."

Thereupon each knight took his station and dressed his spear and shield.
And when they had prepared themselves, they immediately launched together with a violence like to two stones cast from a catapult. So they
met in the midst of the course, and again King Arthur was entirely successful in that assault which he made. For the spear of Sir Pellias burst
King Arthur to pieces, and the spear of King Arthur held; and Sir Pellias
overthrows Sir was cast with passing violence out of his saddle for the dis-
Pellias. tance of more than half a spear's length behind the crupper
of his horse. Nor did he altogether recover from that fall for a long time,
so that King Arthur had to wait beside him for a considerable while ere
he was able to lift himself up from the ground whereon he lay.

"Ha! Sir Knight," said King Arthur, "assuredly it hath not gone well
with thee this day, for thou hast been entirely overthrown and now thou
must straightway redeem thy pledge to serve me for seven days hereafter.
Wherefore, I now set it upon thee as my command, that thou shalt go
straightway unto Cameliard, and that thou shalt greet the Lady Guinevere
King Arthur from me, telling her that her knight unto whom she gave her
sendeth Sir necklace hath been successful in battle with thee. Likewise I
Pellias to the set it upon thee that thou shalt obey her for the space of seven
Lady Guinevere. days in whatsoever she may command thee to do."

"Sir Knight," said Sir Pellias, "it shall even be as thou dost ordain.

Yet I would that I knew who thou art, for I do declare that I have never yet in all my life been overthrown as thou hast overthrown me. And, indeed, I think that there are very few men in the world who could serve me as thou hast served me."

"Sir Knight," said King Arthur, "some time thou shalt know who I am. But, as yet, I am bound to entire secrecy."

Thereupon he saluted Sir Pellias and turned and entered the forest and was gone.

And Sir Pellias mounted his horse and betook him to Cameliard, much cast down and disturbed in spirit, yet much marvelling who that knight could be who had served him as he had been served.

So that day there came to Cameliard, first Sir Geraint and then Sir Gawaine and Sir Ewaine, and last of all there came Sir Pellias. And when these four beheld one another they were all abashed so that one scarce dared to look the other in the face. And when they came before the Lady Guinevere and made their condition known to her, and told her how that knight who wore her necklace had overthrown them all and had sent them thither to serve her for a se'night, and when she reckoned how great and famous were those four knights in deeds of chivalry, she was exceedingly exalted *The Lady Guinevere is pleased with her champion.* that her knight should have approved himself so great in those deeds of arms which he had undertaken to perform. But she greatly marvelled who that champion could be, and debated those things in her own mind. For it was a thing altogether unheard of that one knight, in one day, and with a single spear, should have overthrown five such well proved and famous knights as Duke Mordaunt of North Umber, Sir Geraint, Sir Gawaine, Sir Ewaine, and Sir Pellias. So she gave herself great joy that she had bestowed the gift of her necklace upon so worthy a knight, and she was exceedingly uplifted with extraordinary pleasure at the thought of the credit he had endowed her withal.

Now after King Arthur had entered the forest, he came by and by to where those wood-choppers, afore spoken of, plied their craft. And he abided with them for that night; and when the next morning had come, he intrusted them with his horse and armor, charging them to guard those things with all care, and that they should be wonder- *King Arthur resumes his disguise.* fully rewarded therefor. Then he took his departure from that place with intent to return unto Cameliard. And he was clad in that jerkin of frieze which he had worn ever since he had left Tintagalon.

And when he had reached the outskirts of the forest, he set his cap of disguise upon his head and so resumed his mean appearance once more. So, his knightliness being entirely hidden, he returned to Cameliard for to be gardener's boy as he had been before.

Four Knights serve the Gardener Lad.

Chapter Fourth.

How the Four Knights Served the Lady Guinevere.

NOW, when King Arthur returned to Cameliard once more (which fell upon the afternoon of a second day), he found the gardener waiting for him, exceedingly filled with wrath. And the gardener had a long birchen rod which he had fetched thither for to punish his boy withal, when that he should have returned to the garden again. So when he saw King Arthur he said: "Thou knave! where- *The gardener* fore didst thou quit thy work to go a-gadding?" And King *chideth his boy.* Arthur laughed and said: "Touch me not." At this, the gardener waxed so exceeding wroth, that he catched the King by the collar of his jerkin with intent to beat him, saying: "Dost thou laugh at me, knave, and make a mock at me? Now I will beat thee well for the offence thou hast committed."

Then, when King Arthur felt that man's hand laid upon him, and when he heard the words that the gardener spake in his wrath, his royal spirit waxed very big within him and he cried out: "Ha, wretch! wouldst thou dare to lay thy hands upon my sacred person?" So saying, he seized the gardener by the wrists, and took the rod straight away from him, and struck him with it across the shoulders. And when that poor knave felt himself thus in the powerful grasp of the angry King, and when he felt the rod upon his shoulders, he straightway lifted up a great outcry, albeit the blow hurt him not a whit. "Now get thee gone!" quoth King Arthur, "and trouble me no more; else will I serve thee in a way that will not at all belike thee." Herewith he loosed that poor man and let him go; and the gardener was so bemazed with terror, that both the earth and the sky swam before him. For King Arthur's eyes had flashed upon him like lightning, and those two hands had held his wrists with wonderful power. Wherefore, when the King let him go he gat him away as quickly as might be, all trembling and sweating with a great fear.

So he went straight to the Lady Guinevere and complained to her of the manner in which he had been treated. "Lady," quoth he, weeping

The gardener complaineth to the Lady Guinevere. with the memory of his terror, "my boy goeth away for a day or more, I know not whither; and when I would whip him for quitting his work he taketh the rod straight away from me and beateth me with it. Wherefore, now, I prithee, deal with him as is fitting, and let several strong men drive him away from this place with rods."

Then the Lady Guinevere laughed. "Let be!" she said, "and meddle with him no more; for, indeed, he appeareth to be a very saucy fellow. As for thee! take thou no heed of his coming or his going, and haply I will deal with him in such a way as shall be fitting."

Whereupon the gardener went his way, greatly marvelling that the Lady Guinevere should be so mild in dealing with that toward knave. And the Lady Guinevere went her way, very merry. For she began to bethink her that there was soothly some excellent reason why it should happen that when the White Champion, who did such wonderful deeds, should come thither, then that gardener's boy should go; and that when that same Champion should go, then the gardener's boy should come thitherward again. Wherefore she suspected many things, and was wonderfully merry and cheerful of spirit.

Now, that day, in the afternoon, the Lady Guinevere chanced to walk in the garden with her damsels, and with her walked those four noble

The Lady Guinevere mocketh the gardener's boy. knights who had been sent thither by her White Champion, to wit, Sir Gawaine, Sir Ewaine, Sir Geraint, and Sir Pellias. And the gardener's lad was digging in the gardens; and as they passed by where he was the Lady Guinevere laughed aloud and cried out: "Look! Look! Messires and Ladies! Yonder is a very saucy fellow for to be a gardener's lad, for he continually weareth his cap, even when he standeth in the presence of lords and ladies."

Then Sir Gawaine up and spake, saying: "Is it even so? Now will I straightway go to yonder knave, and will take his hat off for him, and that in a way so greatly to his misliking, that I do not believe that he will ever offend by wearing it in our presence again."

At this the Lady Guinevere laughed a very great deal. "Let be!" she said, "let be! Sir Gawaine! it would ill beseem one so gentle as thou art to have to do with yonder saucy fellow. Moreover, he doth assure us all that he hath an ugly place upon his head, wherefore let him wear his cap in God's mercy."

Thus the Lady Guinevere, though she suspected a very great deal, was yet pleased to make a mock of him whom she suspected.

Now that day Duke Mordaunt of North Umber had entirely recovered from those sore hurts that he had suffered from his overthrow at the hands of the White Champion. Wherefore, the next morning having come, he appeared again before the castle as he had appeared aforetime—clad all in complete armor. So this time there rode before him two heralds, and when the duke and the two heralds had come to that part of the meadows that lay immediately before the castle of Cameliard, the heralds blew their trumpets exceedingly loud. So at the sound of the trumpets many people came and gathered upon the walls; and King Leodegrance came, and took stand upon a lesser tower that looked down upon the plain where were the Duke of North Umber and the two heralds. Then the Duke of North Umber lifted up his eyes and beheld King Leodegrance where he stood over above him upon the top of that tower, and he *The Duke of* cried out in a loud voice: "What ho! King Leodegrance! *North Umber* Thou shalt not think because I suffered a fall from my horse *issueth a second* through the mischance of an assault at arms, that thou art *challenge.* therefore quit of me. Yet, ne'theless, I do now make this fair proffer unto thee. To-morrow day I shall appear before this castle with six knights-companion. Now if thou hast any seven knights who are able to stand against me and my companions in an assault at arms—whether with spears or swords, or ahorse or afoot—then shall I engage myself for to give over all pretence whatsoever unto the hand of the Lady Guinevere. But if thou canst not provide such champions to contend successfully against me and my knights-companion, then shall I not only lay claim to Lady Guinevere, but I shall likewise seize upon and shall hold for mine own, three certain castles of thine that stand upon the borders of North Umber. And, likewise, I shall seize upon and shall hold for mine own all the lands and glebes appertaining unto those same castles. Moreover, this challenge of mine shall hold only until to-morrow at set of sun; after the which time it shall be null and void. Wherefore, King Leodegrance, thou hadst best look to it straightway to provide thee with such champions as may defend thee from these demands aforesaid."

Hereupon those two heralds blew their trumpets once more, and Duke Mordaunt of North Umber turned his horse about and went away from that place. Then King Leodegrance also went his way, very *King Leode-* sorrowful and downcast in his spirits. For he said to himself: *grance is* "Is it at all likely that another champion shall come unto me *downcast.* like that wonderful White Champion who came two days since, I know not whence, for to defend me against mine enemies? And, touching that same White Champion; if I know not whence he came, so also I know not whither he hath departed; how then shall I know where to seek him to beseech his further aid in this time of mine extremity?" Wherefore he went his way, very sorrowful, and wist not what he was to do for to defend himself. So being thus exceedingly troubled in his spirit, he went straight unto his own room, and there shut himself therein; nor would he see any man nor speak unto anyone, but gave himself over entirely unto sorrow and despair.

Now in this extremity the Lady Guinevere bethought her of those four knights who had been pledged for to serve her for seven days. So she went unto them where they were and she bespoke them in this *The Lady Guin-* wise: "Messires, ye have been sent hither pledged for to *evere beseech-* *eth aid of the* serve me for seven days. Now I do ordain it of thee that you *four knights.* will take this challenge of Duke Mordaunt upon you at my behest, and I do much desire that you go forth to-morrow-day for to meet this Duke of North Umber and his knights-companion in battle. For ye are terribly powerful knights, and I do believe you may easily defend us against our enemies."

But Sir Gawaine said, "Not so, Lady; not so! For though we are pledged unto thy service, yet are we not pledged unto the service of King Leodegrance, thy father. Nor have we quarrel of any sort with this Duke of North Umber, nor with his six knights-companion. For we are knights of King Arthur, his Court, nor may we, except at his command, take any foreign quarrel upon us in the service of another king."

Then was the Lady Guinevere exceedingly angry, wherefore she said with great heat: "Either thou art a wonderfully faithful lord unto thy King, Sir Gawaine, or else thou fearest to meet this Duke of North Umber and his knights-companion."

And at this speech of the Lady Guinevere's, Sir Gawaine was also exceedingly wroth, wherefore he made reply: "An thou wert a knight and not a lady, Dame Guinevere, thou wouldst think three or four times ere thou wouldst find courage to speak those words unto me." Whereupon he arose and went out from that place with a countenance all inflamed with wrath. And the Lady Guinevere went away also from that place and to her bower, where she wept a very great deal, both from sorrow and from anger.

Now all this while King Arthur had been very well aware of everything that passed; wherefore he by and by arose and went out and found the gardener. And he took the gardener strongly by the collar of his coat and held him where he was. And he said to him: "Sirrah! I have a command to set upon thee, and thou shalt perform that command to the letter, else, an thou perform it not, a very great deal of pain may befall thee." Herewith speaking, he thrust his hand into the bosom of his jerkin and brought forth thence that necklace of pearls which the Lady Guinevere had given him from about her neck. And he *King Arthur* said further unto the gardener: "Thou shalt take this necklace *sendeth the* to the Lady Guinevere and thou shalt say to her thus: that she *a mission.* is to send me forthwith bread and meat and wine and comfits from her own table. And thou shalt say unto her that I desire her to summon those four knights—to wit, Sir Gawaine, Sir Ewaine, Sir Geraint, and Sir Pellias—and that she is to bid those four for to come and serve me with those things for my refreshment. And thou art to say unto her that she is to lay her commands upon those knights that they are further to serve me according as I may command, and that they are henceforth to be my servants and not her servants. And these are the commands that I lay upon thee; that thou art to say these things unto the Lady Guinevere."

Now when the gardener heard those words he was so astonished that he wist not what to think, for he deemed that the gardener's lad had gone altogether mad. Wherefore he lifted up his voice and cried aloud, "How now! What is this thou sayest! Verily, should I do such a thing as this thou bidst me to do, either it will cost me my life or else it will cost thee thy life. For who would dare for to say such words unto the Lady Guinevere?"

But King Arthur said: "Ne'theless, thou shalt surely do as I command thee, sirrah. For if thou disobey in one single point, then I do assure thee it will go exceedingly ill with thee. For I have it in my power for to make thee suffer as thou hast never suffered before."

And upon this the gardener said, "I will go." For he said unto himself, "If I do as this fellow biddeth me, then will the Lady Guinevere have him punished in great measure, and so I shall be revenged upon him for what he did unto me yesterday. Moreover, it irks me exceedingly that I should have a lad for to work in the garden who behaves as this fellow does. Wherefore," he said, "I will go." So he took that necklace of pearls that King Arthur gave him, and he went forth and, after awhile, he found the Lady Guinevere where she was. And when he had found her, he bespoke her in this wise:

"Lady, my garden boy hath assuredly gone entirely mad. For, under the threat of certain great harm he would do unto me an I performed not his errand, he hath sent me to offer a very grievous affront unto thee. For he hath sent me with this string of large beads for to give to thee; and he bids me to tell thee that thou art to send to him bread and meat and sweetmeats and wine, such as thou usest at thine own table; and he bids me to tell thee that these things are to be served to him by the four noble knights who came hither the day before yesterday. And he saith that thou art to command those same knights that they are to obey him in whatsoever he may command, for that they are henceforth to be his servants and not thine. And, indeed, Lady, he would listen to naught that I might say to him contrariwise, but he hath threatened me with dire injury an I came not hither and delivered this message unto thee."

Now when the Lady Guinevere heard what the gardener said, and when she beheld the necklace which she had given unto that White Champion, and when she wist that the White Champion and the gardener's boy were indeed one, she was uplifted with an exceeding joy; wherefore she knew not whether to laugh or whether to weep for that pure joy. So she arose and took the necklace of pearls, and she bade the gardener for to come with her. Then she went forth until she found those four knights, and when she had found them she spake unto them thus:

"My Lords, awhile sin when I commanded you for to take my quarrel with Duke Mordaunt of North Umber upon you for my sake, ye would *The Lady Guin-* not do so. And thou, my lord Gawaine, didst speak such *evere commands* angry words as are not fitting that one who serveth should *the four knights* speak unto his mistress, far less that a knight should speak *to serve the* *gardener's boy.* unto the daughter of a king. Accordingly I have it in my mind that ye shall perform a certain thing by way of a penance, which, an ye refuse to do, I will know very well that ye do not intend to fulfil that word which ye plighted to my knight when he overthrew you all four in fair combat. Now my command is this: that ye take certain food prepared for my table—meats and white bread and sweetmeats and wine —and that ye take that food unto my gardener's boy, whose cap, Sir Gawaine, thou didst threaten so valorously for to take away from him this very morning. And ye four are to serve the food unto him as though he were a royal knight. And when ye have so served him, ye are to obey him in whatsoever he may ordain. And this I put upon ye as a penalty because ye took not my quarrel upon ye as true knights should, for hereafter ye are to be servants unto that gardener's boy and not unto me. Wherefore ye are now to go unto the buttery of the castle, and ye are to bid the sewer for to give you meats such as are served upon mine own table. And the food ye are to serve upon silver plates, and the wine ye are to serve in silver cups and goblets. And ye are to minister unto that gardener's boy as though he were a great lord of exceeding fame and renown."

Thus spake the Lady Guinevere, and when she had spoken, she turned and left those four knights, and she took with her the gardener, who was so astonished at that which he had heard, that he wist not whether he had gone mad or whether the Lady Guinevere had gone mad. And the Lady Guinevere bade the gardener to go to the gardener's boy and to tell him that all things should be fulfilled according to his commands. And so the gardener did as he was told.

Now turn we to those four knights whom the Lady Guinevere had left. For they were bemazed and abashed at the singular commands she had set upon them. And when they recovered from their amazement, they were inflamed with exceeding indignation that, for the time, they wist not whether that which they saw with their eyes was the light of day, or whether it was altogether darkness. Nor could one of them look at another in the face, so overcome were they with shame at the affront that had been put upon them. Then up and spake Sir Gawaine, and his voice so trembled with his exceeding anger that he could scarce *The four* contain it for to speak his words. " Messires," quoth he, " do *knights* ye not see how that this lady hath wantonly put a great *are angry.* affront upon us because we would not do that which she this morning bade us to do, and because we would not take up her quarrel against the Duke of North Umber? Now we will indeed serve this gardener's boy even as she hath ordained. For we will serve him with meat and drink as she hath commanded ; and we will render our service unto him as she hath bidden us to do. But observe ye ; we are no longer her servants, but we are his servants ; wherefore we may serve him as we choose for to do. So, when we have fulfilled her commands and have served him with meat and drink, and when we have obeyed all the behests he layeth upon us ; then do I make my vow that I, with mine own hand, shall slay that gardener's boy. And when I have slain him, I will put his head into a bag, and I will send that bag unto the Lady Guinevere by the meanest carrier whom I can find for that purpose. And so this proud lady shall receive an affront as great as that affront which she hath put upon us." And they all said that that which Sir Gawaine had planned should be exactly as he had said.

So those four lords went unto the sewer of the castle, and they asked for the best of that food which was to be served unto the Lady Guinevere —meats and bread and sweetmeats and wine. Then they took *The four* them silver plates and platters and they placed the food upon *knights serve* them ; and they took silver cups and silver goblets and they *the garden-* poured the wine into them ; and they went forth with these *er's boy.* things. And when they had come back of the castle nigh to the stables, they found the gardener's boy, and they bade him sit down and eat and to drink. And they waited upon him as though he had been some great lord. And not one of those four knights wist who he was, nor that he was the great King whose servant they, soothly, were. For he wore his cap of disguise upon his head, wherefore they deemed him to be only a poor peasant fellow.

Now when Sir Ewaine beheld that he still wore his cap before them, he spake unto him with great indignation, saying: "Ha, villian! Wouldst thou wear thy cap even in the presence of great princes and lords such as we be?"

Unto this Sir Gawaine said, "Let be, it matters not." And then he said very bitterly unto the gardener's boy: "Eat thou well, sirrah! For thou shalt hardly eat another meal of food upon this earth."

To this the gardener's boy made reply: "Sir Knight, that, haply, shall lie unto another will than thine for to determine. For maybe, I shall eat many other meals than this. And, maybe, ye shall serve at them as ye are serving me now." And those four lords were astonished beyond measure that he should bespeak them thus so calmly and without any appearance of fear.

Then, after he had eaten, the gardener's boy said unto those knights, "Behold, Messires, I have had enough and am done; and now I have other commands for you to fulfil. And my next command is that ye shall make ready straightway to go abroad with me, and to that end ye shall clothe yourselves with complete armor. And thou, Sir Gawaine, shalt go to the head stable-keeper of this castle, and thou shalt demand of him that he shall make ready the Lady Guinevere's palfrey so that I may straightway ride forth upon it. And when ye are all encased in your armor, and when everything is duly appointed according to my command, ye shall bring that palfrey unto the postern gate of the castle, and there I shall meet ye for to ride forth with you."

And Sir Gawaine said: "It shall be done in every way according as thou dost command. But when we ride forth from this castle it shall be a sorry journey for thee."

And the gardener's boy said: "I think not so, Sir Gawaine."

Then those four went away and did according as the gardener's boy commanded. And when they had made themselves ready in full array of armor, and when they had obtained the Lady Guinevere's palfrey, they went unto the postern gate and there the gardener's boy met them. And when he saw that they sat their horses and that they moved not at his coming, he said: "Ha, Messires! would ye so entreat him whom ye have been ordained to serve? Now I do bid ye, Sir Gawaine and Sir Ewaine, for to come down and to hold my stirrup for me; and I bid ye, Sir Geraint and Sir Pellias, for to come down and to hold my palfrey for me whiles I mount."

Then those four noble knights did as they were commanded. And Sir Gawaine said: "Thou mayst command as thou dost list, and I do bid thee to make the most of it whiles thou mayst do so; for thou shalt have but a little while longer for to enjoy the great honor that hath fallen upon thee. For that honor which hath fallen upon thee—lo! it shall presently crush thee unto death."

And the gardener's boy said: "Not so; I believe I shall not die yet whiles." And again those four lords were greatly astonished at the calmness of his demeanor.

And so they rode forth from that place; and the gardener's boy would not permit that they should ride either before him or beside him, but he commanded them that they should ride behind him whiles they were still servants unto him.

So they rode as he assigned them for a considerable way. Then after they had gone forward a great distance, they drew nigh to a gloomy and dismal woodland that lay entirely beyond the country coadjacent to Cameliard. Then, when they had come nigh unto this woodland, Sir Gawaine rode a little forward, and he said: "Sir Gardener's Boy, seest thou yonder woodland? Now when we come into it thou shalt immediately die, and that by a sword that hath never yet been touched by any but noble or knightly blood."

And King Arthur turned him about in his saddle, and he said: "Ha! Sir Gawaine! Wouldst thou ride forward thus when I bid thee to ride behind me?"

And as he spake he took the cap from off his head, and, lo! they all beheld that it was King Arthur who rode with them. *King Arthur proclaimeth himself to the four knights.*

Then a great silence of pure astonishment fell upon them all, and each man sat as though he were turned into an image of stone. And it was King Arthur who first spake. And he said: "Ha! how now, Sir Knights? Have ye no words of greeting for to pay to me? Certes, ye have served me with a very ill grace this day. Moreover, ye have threatened to slay me; and now, when I speak to you, ye say naught in reply."

Then those four knights immediately cried out aloud; and they leaped down from off their horses, and they kneeled down into the dust of the road. And when King Arthur beheld them kneeling there, he laughed with great joyfulness of spirit, and he bade them for to mount their horses again, for the time was passing by when there was much to do.

So they mounted their horses and rode away, and as they journeyed forward the King told them all that had befallen him, so that they were greatly amazed, and gave much acclaim unto the knightliness with which he had borne himself in those excellent adventures through which he had passed. And they rejoiced greatly that they had a king for to rule over them who was possessed of such a high and knightly spirit.

So they rode to that arm of the forest where King Arthur had left his horse and his armor.

The Gardener Lad takes off his Cap.

Chapter Fifth.

*How King Arthur Overcame the Enemies of King Leodegrance,
and How His Royalty Was Proclaimed.*

NOW, when the next day had come, the Duke of North Umber and six knights-companion appeared upon the field in front of the castle of Cameliard as he had duly declared that he and they would do. And those seven champions appeared in very great estate ; for in front of them there rode seven heralds with trumpets and tabards, and behind them there rode seven esquires, each esquire bearing *The Duke of* the spear, the shield, the crest, and the banneret of the knight *North Umber* who was his lord and master. And the seven heralds blew *and his six com-* *panions appear* their trumpets so exceedingly loud that the sound thereof *before the castle.* penetrated unto the utmost parts of Cameliard, so that the people came running from everywhere. And while the heralds blew their trumpets the seven esquires shouted, and waved the spears and the bannerets. So those seven knights rode in such proud estate that those who looked upon them had hardly ever beheld such a splendid presentment of chivalry.

So they paraded up and down that field three times for its entire length, and, meantime, a great crowd of people, called thither by the blowing of the herald's trumpets, stood upon the walls and gazed therefrom at that noble spectacle. And all the Court of King Ryence came, and stood upon the plain in front of the King's pavilion, and they shouted and cheered the Duke of North Umber and his six knights-companion.

Meanwhile, King Leodegrance of Cameliard was so cast down with trouble and shame that he did not choose to show his face, but hid himself away from all his Court. Nor would he permit anyone for to come into his presence at that time.

Nevertheless, the Lady Guinevere, with sundry of her damsels, went

unto the King's closet where he was, and knocked upon the door thereof,
The Lady Guine- and when the King denied her to come in to him, she
vere cheereth her spake to him through the door, giving him words of good
father. cheer, saying: "My lord King and father, I prithee for to
look up and to take good cheer unto thyself. For I do assure thee that
there is one who hath our cause in his hands, and that one is, certes, a
very glorious champion. And he shall assuredly come by and by ere this
day is done, and when he cometh, he shall certainly overthrow our
enemies."

But King Leodegrance opened not the door, but he said: "My daughter, that which thou sayest thou sayest for to comfort me. For there
is no other help for me in this time of trouble only God, His good strong
help and grace." And she said: "Nay, I say that which is the truth;
and the help that God shall send unto thee he shall certainly send through
a worthy champion who at this moment hath our cause in his hand."

So spake the Lady Guinevere, so that whilst King Leodegrance came
not forth, yet he was greatly comforted at that which she said to him.

Thus passed all that morning and a part of the afternoon, and yet no
one appeared for to take up that challenge which the seven knights had
declared. But, whilst the sun was yet three or four hours high, there
suddenly appeared at a great distance a cloud of dust. And in that cloud
Five knights- of dust there presently appeared five knights, riding at great
defender appear speed, thitherward. And when these had come nigh unto
at the field. the walls, lo! the people beheld that he who rode foremost of
aⅼl was that same White Champion who had aforetime overthrown
the Duke of North Umber. Moreover, they perceived that the four
knights who rode with that White Champion were very famous knights
and of great prowess and glory of arms. For the one was Sir Gawaine,
and the other was Sir Ewaine, and the other was Sir Geraint, and the
other was Sir Pellias. For the people of the castle and the town knew
those four knights, because they had dwelt for two days at Cameliard,
and they were of such exceeding renown that folk crowded from far
and near for to look upon them whensoever they appeared for to walk
abroad.

So when the people upon the walls beheld who those knights were, and
when they perceived that White Champion who had aforetime brought
them such exceeding honor, they shouted aloud for the second time with
a voice mightier than that with which they had the first time shouted.

Now King Leodegrance heard the people shouting, whereupon hope
awoke of a sudden within him. So he straightway came forth with all

speed for to see what was ado, and there he beheld those five noble champions about to enter into the field below the castle walls.

And the Lady Guinevere also heard the shouting and she came forth likewise and, behold! there was that White Champion and those four other knights. So when she beheld that White Knight and his four companions-at-arms, her heart was like to break within her for pure joy and gladness, wherefore she wept for the passion thereof, and laughed the whiles she wept. And she waved her kerchief unto those five noble lords and kissed her hand unto them, and the five knights saluted her as they rode past her and into the field.

Now, when the Duke of North Umber was made aware that those five knights had come against him and his knights-companion for to take up his challenge, he straightway came forth from his pavilion and mounted his horse. And his knights-companion came forth and mounted their horses, and he and they went forth for to meet those who had come against them.

And when the Duke of North Umber had come nigh enough, he perceived that the chiefest of those five knights was the White Champion who had aforetime overthrown him. Wherefore he said unto that White Champion: " Sir Knight, I have once before condescended unto thee who art altogether unknown to me or to anybody else that is here. For without inquiring concerning thy quality, I ran a course with thee and, lo! by the chance of arms thou didst overthrow me. Now this quarrel is more serious than that, wherefore I and my companions-at-arms will not run a course with thee and thy companions; nor will we fight with *The Duke of* thee until I first know what is the quality of him against whom *North Umber* I contend. Wherefore, I bid thee presently declare thyself, *refuseth the combat.* who thou art and what is thy condition."

Then Sir Gawaine opened the umbril of his helmet, and he said: "Sir Knight, behold my face, and know that I am Gawaine, the son of King Lot. Wherefore thou mayst perceive that my condition and estate are even better than thine own. Now I do declare unto thee that yonder White Knight is of such a quality that he condescends unto thee when he doeth combat with thee, and that thou dost not condescend unto him."

"Ho, Sir Gawaine!" quoth the Duke of Umber. "What thou sayest is a very strange thing, for, indeed, there are few in this world who are so exalted that they may condescend unto me. Ne'theless, since thou dost avouch for him, I may not gainsay that which thou sayest. Yet, there is still another reason why we may not fight with ye. For, behold! we are seven well-approved and famous knights, and ye are but five; so, con-

sider how unequal are our forces, and that you stand in great peril in undertaking so dangerous an encounter."

Then Sir Gawaine smiled right grimly upon that Duke of North Umber.
"Gramercy for thy compassion, and for the tenderness which thou
showeth concerning our safety, Sir Duke," quoth he. "But ne'theless,
thou mayst leave that matter unto us with entire content of spirit upon
thy part. For I consider that the peril in which ye seven stand is fully
equal to our peril. Moreover, wert thou other than a belted knight, a
simple man might suppose that thou wert more careful of thine own safety
in this matter, than thou art of ours."

Now at these words the countenance of the Duke of North Umber became altogether covered with red, for he wist that he had, indeed, no
great desire for this battle, wherefore he was ashamed because of the
words which Sir Gawaine spake to him. So, each knight closed his helmet,
and all turned their horses, and the one party rode unto one end of the field,
and the other party rode to the other end of the field, and there each took
stand in the place assigned unto them.

And they arranged themselves thus : In the middle was King Arthur,
and upon either hand were two knights; and in the middle was the Duke
of North Umber, and upon either hand were three knights. So, when
they had thus arrayed themselves they dressed their spears and their shields,
and made them altogether ready for the onset. Then King Arthur and
Duke Mordaunt each shouted aloud, and the one party hurled upon the
other party with such violence that the ground shook and thundered
beneath the hoofs of the horses, and the clouds of dust rose up against the
heavens.

And so they met in the middle of the field with an uproar of such dreadful violence that one might have heard the crashing thereof for the distance of more than a mile away.

And when the one party had passed the other, and the dust of the encounter had arisen, lo ! three of the seven had been overthrown, and not
one of the five had lost his seat.

And one of those who had been overthrown was Duke Mordaunt of
North Umber. And, behold! he never more arose again from the ground
whereon he lay. For King Arthur had directed his spear
King Arthur overturneth the Duke of North Umber. into the very midst of his defences, and the spear had held,
wherefore the point thereof had pierced the shield of the
Duke of North Umber, and had pierced his body armor,
and so violent was the stroke, that the Duke of North Umber had been
lifted entirely out of his saddle, and had been cast a full spear's length be-

hind the crupper of his horse. Thus died that wicked man, for as King Arthur drave past him, the evil soul of him quitted his body with a weak noise like to the squeaking of a bat, and the world was well rid of him.

Now when King Arthur turned him about at the end of the course and beheld that there were but four knights left upon their horses of all those seven against whom he and his companions had driven, he uplifted his spear, and drew rein upon his horse, and bespake his knights in this wise : " Messires, I am aweary of all this coil and quarrelling, and do not care to fight any more to-day, so go ye straightway and engage those knights in battle. As for me, I will abide here, and witness your adventure."

" Lord," said they, " we will do our endeavor as thou dost command."

So those four good knights did as he commanded, and they went forth straightway against those other four, much encouraged that their King looked upon their endeavor. And King Arthur sat with the butt of his spear resting upon his instep, and looked upon the field with great con-tent of spirit, and a steadfast countenance.

As for those four knights-companion that remained of the Duke of North Umber's party, they came not forth to this second encounter with so much readiness of spirit as they had done aforetime. For they were now well aware of how great was the excellent prowess of those other knights, and they beheld that their enemies came forth to this second en-counter very fiercely, and with great valor and readiness of spirit. Where-fore their hearts melted away within them with doubt and anxiety as to the outcome of this second encounter.

Nevertheless, they prepared themselves with such resolve as might be, and came forth as they were called upon to do.

Then Sir Gawaine drave straight up to the foremost knight, who was a very well-known champion, hight Sir Dinador of Montcalm. And when he had come sufficiently nigh to him, he lifted himself up in his stirrups and he smote Sir Dinador so fierce a blow that he cleft the shield of that knight asunder, and he cleft his helmet, and a part of the blade of his sword brake away and remained therein.

And when Sir Dinador felt that blow, his brains swam like water, and he was fain to catch the horn of his saddle for to save himself from falling therefrom. Then a great terror straightway fell upon him, so *The knights-* that he drew rein violently to one side. So he fled away *challenger flee* from that place with the terror of death hanging above him *before the* like to a black cloud of smoke. And when his companions *fender.* beheld that stroke that Sir Gawaine delivered, and when they beheld Sir Dinador flee away from before him, they also drew rein to one side and fled away with all speed, pursued with an entire terror of their enemies. And Sir Gawaine and Sir Ewaine and Sir Geraint and Sir Pellias pursued them as they fled. And they chased them straight through the Court of King Ryence, so that the knights and nobles of that Court scattered hither and thither like chaff at their coming. And they chased those fleeing knights in among the pavilions of King Ryence's Court, and no man stayed them; and when they had chased those knights entirely away, they returned to that place where King Arthur still held his station, steadfastly awaiting them.

Now when the people of Cameliard beheld the overthrow of their enemies, and when they beheld how those enemies fled away from before the faces of their champions, they shouted with might and main, and made great acclaim. Nor did they stint their loud shouting when those four knights returned from pursuing their enemies and came back unto the White Champion again. And still more did they give acclaim when those five knights rode across the drawbridge and into the gateway of the town and into the town.

Thus ended the great bout-at-arms, which was one of the most famous in all the history of chivalry of King Arthur's Court.

Now when King Arthur had thus accomplished his purposes, and when *King Arthur returneth his armor to the merchant.* he had come into the town again, he went unto that merchant of whom he had obtained the armor that he wore, and he delivered that armor back to him again. And he said, "To-morrow-day, Sir Merchant, I shall send thee two bags of gold for the rent of that armor which thou didst let me have."

To this the merchant said: "Lord, it is not needed that thou shouldst recompense me for that armor, for thou hast done great honor unto Cameliard by thy prowess."

But King Arthur said: "Have done, Sir Merchant, nor must thou forbid what I say. Wherefore take thou that which I shall send unto thee."

Thereupon he went his way, and, having set his cap of disguise upon his head, he came back into the Lady Guinevere's gardens again.

Now when the next morning had come the people of Cameliard looked forth and, lo! King Ryence had departed entirely away from before the castle. For that night he had struck his pavilions, and had withdrawn his Court, and had gone away from that place where he and his people had sat down for five days past. And with him he had taken the body of the Duke of North Umber, conveying it away in a litter surrounded by many lighted candles and uplifted by a peculiar pomp of ceremony. But when the people of Cameliard beheld that he was gone, they were exceedingly rejoiced, and made merry, and shouted and sang and laughed. For they wist not how deeply enraged King Ryence was against them; for his enmity aforetime toward King Leodegrance was but as a small flame when compared unto the anger that now possessed him.

Now that morning Lady Guinevere walked into her garden, and with her walked Sir Gawaine and Sir Ewaine, and lo! there she beheld the gardener's boy again.

Then she laughed aloud, and she said unto those two knights, "Messires behold! Yonder is the gardener's boy, who weareth his cap continually because he hath an ugly place upon his head."

Then those two knights, knowing who that gardener's boy was, were exceedingly abashed at her speech, and wist not what to say or whither to look. And Sir Gawaine spake, aside unto Sir Ewaine, and quoth he: "'Fore Heaven, that lady knoweth not what manner of man is yonder gardener's boy; for, an she did, she would be more sparing of her speech."

And the Lady Guinevere heard Sir Gawaine that he spoke, but she did not hear his words. So she turned unto Sir Gawaine, and she said: "Sir Gawaine, haply it doth affront thee that that gardener's boy should wear his cap before us, and maybe thou wilt go and take it off from his head as thou didst offer to do two or three days since."

And Sir Gawaine said: "Peace, Lady! Thou knowest not what thou sayest. Yonder gardener's boy could more easily take my head from off my shoulders than I could take his cap from off his head."

At this the Lady Guinevere made open laughter; but in her heart she secretly pondered that saying and greatly marvelled what Sir Gawaine meant thereby.

Now about noon of that day there came an herald from King Ryence of North Wales, and he appeared boldly before King Leodegrance where the King sat in his hall with a number of his people about him. *King Ryence* And the herald said: "My lord King: my master, King *threatened King* Ryence of North Wales, is greatly displeased with thee. For *Leodegrance.* thou didst set certain knights upon Duke Mordaunt of North Umber, and those knights have slain that excellent nobleman, who was close kin unto King Ryence. Moreover, thou hast made no reply to those demands that my master, King Ryence, hath made touching the delivery unto him of certain lands and castles bordering upon North Wales. Wherefore my master is affronted with thee beyond measure. So my master, King

Ryence, bids me to set forth to thee two conditions, and the conditions
are these: Firstly, that thou dost immediately deliver into his hands that
White Knight who slew the Duke of North Umber; secondly, that thou
makest immediate promise that those lands in question shall be presently
delivered unto King Ryence."

Then King Leodegrance arose from where he sat and spake to that
herald with great dignity of demeanor. "Sir Herald," quoth he, "the
demands that King Ryence maketh upon me pass all bounds for insolence.
That death which the Duke of North Umber suffered, he suffered because
of his own pride and folly. Nor would I deliver that White Knight into
thy master's hands, even an I were able to do so. As for those lands that
thy master demandeth of me, thou mayst tell King Ryence that I will not
deliver unto him of those lands so much as a single blade of grass, or a
single grain of corn that groweth thereon."

And the herald said: "If, so be, that is thine answer, King Leodegrance, then am I bidden for to tell thee that my master, King Ryence of
North Wales, will presently come hither with an array of a great force of
arms, and will take from thee by force those things which thou wilt not
deliver unto him peacefully." Whereupon, so saying, he departed thence
and went his way.

Now after the herald had departed, King Leodegrance went into his
closet, and when he had come there he sent, privily, for the Lady Guinevere. So the Lady Guinevere came to him where he was.
*King Leode-
grance converses* And King Leodegrance said to her: "My daughter, it hath
with the Lady happened that a knight clad all in white, and bearing no crest
Guinevere. or device of any sort, hath twice come to our rescue and hath
overthrown our enemies. Now it is said by everybody that that knight
is thine own particular champion, and I hear say that he wore thy necklace as a favor when he first went out against the Duke of North Umber.
Now I prithee, daughter, tell me who that White Champion is, and where
he may be found."

Then the Lady Guinevere was overwhelmed with a confusion, wherefore she looked away from her father's countenance; and she said: "Verily, my Lord, I know not who that knight may be."

Then King Leodegrance spake very seriously to the Lady Guinevere,
and he took her by the hand and said: "My daughter, thou art now of
an age when thou must consider being mated unto a man who may duly
cherish thee and protect thee from thine enemies. For, lo! I grow apace
in years, and may not hope to defend thee always from those perils that
encompass one of our estate. Moreover, since King Arthur (who is a

very great King indeed) hath brought peace unto this realm, all that noble court of chivalry which one time gathered about me has been scattered elsewhither where greater adventures may be found than in my peaceful realm. Wherefore (as all the world hath seen this week past) I have now not one single knight whom I may depend upon to defend us in such times of peril as these which now overshadow us. Now, my daughter, it doth appear to me that thou couldst not hope to find anyone who could so well safeguard thee as this White Knight; for he doth indeed appear to be a champion of extraordinary prowess and strength. Wherefore it would be well if thou didst feel thyself to incline unto him as he appeareth to incline unto thee."

Then the Lady Guinevere became all rosy red as with a fire even unto her throat. And she laughed, albeit the tears overflowed her eyes and ran down upon her cheeks. So she wept, yet laughed in weeping. And she said unto King Leodegrance: "My Lord and father, an I give my liking unto any one in the manner thou speaketh of, I will give it only unto the poor gardener's boy who digs in my garden."

Then, at these words, the countenance of King Leodegrance became contracted with violent anger, and he cried out: "Ha, Lady! Wouldst thou make a mock and a jest of my words?"

Then the Lady Guinevere said: "Indeed, my Lord! I jest not and I mock not. Moreover, I tell thee for verity that that same gardener's boy knoweth more concerning the White Champion than anybody else in all of the world." Then King Leodegrance said: "What is this that thou tellest me?" And the Lady Guinevere said: "Send for that gardener's boy and thou shalt know." And King Leodegrance said: "Verily, there is more in this than I may at present understand."

So he called to him the chief of his pages, hight Dorisand, and he said to him: "Go, Dorisand, and bring hither the gardener's boy from the Lady Guinevere's garden."

So Dorisand, the page, went as King Leodegrance commanded, and in a little while he returned, bringing with him that gardener's boy. And with them came Sir Gawaine, and Sir Ewaine, and Sir Pellias and Sir Geraint. And those four lords stood over against the door, where they entered; but the gardener's boy came and stood beside the table where King Leodegrance sat. And the King lifted up his eyes and looked upon the gardener's boy, and he said: "Ha! Wouldst thou wear thy cap in our presence?"

Then the gardener's boy said: "I cannot take off my cap."

But the Lady Guinevere, who stood beside the chair of King Leodegrance, spake and said: "I do beseech thee, Messire, for to take off thy cap unto my father."

Whereupon the gardener's boy said: "At thy bidding I will take it off."

So he took the cap from off his head, and King Leodegrance beheld his face and knew him. And when he saw who it was who stood before

King Arthur discovereth himself to King Leodegrance. him, he made a great outcry from pure amazement. And he said: "My Lord and my King! What is this!" Thereupon he arose from where he sat, and he went and kneeled down upon the ground before King Arthur. And he set the palms of his hands together and he put his hands within the hands of King Arthur, and King Arthur took the hands of King Leodegrance within his own. And King Leodegrance said: "My Lord! My Lord! Is it then thou who hast done all these wonderful things?"

Then King Arthur said: "Yea; such as those things were, I have done them." And he stooped and kissed King Leodegrance upon the cheek and lifted him up unto his feet and gave him words of good cheer.

Now the Lady Guinevere, when she beheld those things that passed, was astonished beyond measure. And lo! she understood of a sudden all these things with amazing clearness. Wherefore a great fear fell upon her so that she trembled exceedingly, and said unto herself: "What things have I said unto this great King, and how have I made a mock of him and a jest of him before all those who were about me!" And at the thought thereof, she set her hand upon her side for to still the extreme disturbance of her heart. So, whilst King Arthur and King Leodegrance gave to one another words of royal greeting and of compliment, she withdrew herself and went and stood over against the window nigh to the corner of the wall.

Then, by and by, King Arthur lifted up his eyes and beheld her where she stood afar off. So he went straightway unto her and he took her by the hand, and he said: "Lady, what cheer?"

And she said: "Lord, I am afeard of thy greatness." And he said: "Nay, Lady. Rather it is I who am afeard of thee. For thy kind regard is dearer unto me than anything else in all the world, else had I not served for these twelve days as gardener's boy in thy garden all for the sake of thy good will." And she said: "Thou hast my good will, Lord." And he said: "Have I thy good will in great measure?" And she said: "Yea, thou hast it in great measure."

King Arthur is betrothed to the Lady Guinevere. Then he stooped his head and kissed her before all those who were there, and thus their troth was plighted.

Then King Leodegrance was filled with such an exceeding joy that he wist not how to contain himself therefore.

Now, after these things, there followed a war with King Ryence of North Wales. For Sir Kay and Sir Ulfius had gathered together a great army as King Arthur had bidden them to do, so that when King Ryence came against Cameliard he was altogether routed, and his army dispersed, and he himself chased, an outcast, into his mountains.

Then there was great rejoicing in Cameliard. For, after his victory, King Arthur remained there for awhile with an exceedingly splendid Court of noble lords and of beautiful ladies. And there was feasting and jousting and many famous bouts at arms, the like of which those parts had never before beheld. And King Arthur and the Lady Guinevere were altogether happy together.

Now, one day, whiles King Arthur sat at feast with King Leodegrance —they two being exceedingly expanded with cheerfulness—King Leodegrance said unto King Arthur: " My Lord, what shall I offer thee for a dowery with my daughter when thou takest her away from me for to be thy Queen?"

Then King Arthur turned to Merlin, who stood nigh to him, and he said: " Ha, Merlin! What shall I demand of my friend by way of that dowery?"

Unto him Merlin said: " My lord King, thy friend King Leodegrance hath one thing, the which, should he bestow it upon thee, will singularly increase the glory and renown of thy reign, so that the fame thereof shall never be forgotten."

And King Arthur said: " I bid thee, Merlin, tell me what is that thing."

So Merlin said: " My lord King, I will tell thee a story:

" In the days of thy father, Uther-Pendragon, I caused to be made for him a certain table in the shape of a ring, wherefore men called it the ROUND TABLE. Now, at this table were seats for fifty men, *Merlin telleth* and these seats were designed for the fifty knights who were *of the Round* the most worthy knights in all the world. These seats were *Table.* of such a sort, that whenever a worthy knight appeared, then his name appeared in letters of gold upon that seat that appertained unto him ; and when that knight died, then would his name suddenly vanish from that seat which he had aforetime occupied.

" Now, forty-and-nine of these seats, except one seat, were altogether alike (saving only one that was set aside for the King himself, which same was elevated above the other seats, and was cunningly carved and inlaid with ivory and with gold), and the one seat was different from all the others, and it was called the SEAT PERILOUS. For this seat was unlike the others both in its structure and its significance ; for it was all cunningly inset with gold and silver of curious device, and it was covered with a canopy of satin embroidered with gold and silver; and it was altogether of a wonderful magnificence of appearance. And no name ever appeared upon this seat, for only one knight in all of the world could hope to sit therein with safety unto himself. For, if any other dared to sit therein, either he would die a sudden and violent death within three days' time, or else a great misfortune would befall him. Hence that seat was called the SEAT PERILOUS.

"Now, in the days of King Uther-Pendragon, there sat seven-and-thirty knights at the ROUND TABLE. And when King Uther-Pendragon died, he gave the ROUND TABLE unto his friend, King Leodegrance of Cameliard.

"And in the beginning of King Leodegrance's reign, there sat four-and-twenty knights at the ROUND TABLE.

"But times have changed since then, and the glory of King Leodegrance's reign hath paled before the glory of thy reign, so that his noble Court of knights have altogether quitted him. Wherefore there remaineth now not one name, saving only the name of King Leodegrance, upon all those fifty seats that surround the ROUND TABLE. So now that ROUND TABLE lieth beneath its pavilion altogether unused.

"Yet if King Leodegrance will give unto thee, my lord King, that ROUND TABLE for a dower with the Lady Guinevere, then will it lend unto thy reign its greatest glory. For in thy day every seat of that TABLE shall be filled, even unto the SEAT PERILOUS, and the fame of the knights who sit at it shall never be forgotten."

"Ha!" quoth King Arthur. "That would indeed be a dower worthy for any king to have with his queen."

King Leodegrance bestows the Round Table upon King Arthur. "Then," King Leodegrance said, "that dower shalt thou have with my daughter; and if it bring thee great glory, then shall thy glory be my glory, and thy renown shall be my renown. For if my glory shall wane, and thy glory shall increase, behold! is not my child thy wife?"

And King Arthur said: "Thou sayest well and wisely."

Thus King Arthur became the master of that famous ROUND TABLE. And the ROUND TABLE was set up at Camelot (which some men now call Winchester). And by and by there gathered about it such an array of knights as the world had never beheld before that time, and which it shall never behold again.

Such was the history of the beginning of the ROUND TABLE in King Arthur's reign.

King Arthur meets the Lady Guinevere.

Chapter Sixth.

How King Arthur Was Wedded in Royal State and How the Round Table Was Established.

A ND now was come the early fall of the year; that pleasant season when the meadow-land and the wold were still green with summer that had only just passed; when the sky likewise was as of summer-time—extraordinarily blue and full of large floating clouds; when a bird might sing here and another there, a short song in memory of spring-time, when all the air was tempered with warmth and yet the leaves were everywhere turning brown and red and gold, so that when the sun shone through them it was as though a cloth of gold, broidered with brown and crimson and green, hung above the head. At this season of the year it is exceedingly pleasant to be a-field among the nut-trees with hawk and hound, or to travel abroad in the yellow world, whether it be a-horse or a-foot.

Now this was the time of year in which had been set the marriage of King Arthur and the Lady Guinevere at Camelot, and at that place was extraordinary pomp and glory of circumstance. All the world was astir and in a great ferment of joy, for everybody was exceedingly glad that King Arthur was to have him a Queen.

In preparation for that great occasion the town of Camelot was bedight very magnificently, for the stony street along which the Lady Guinevere must come to the royal castle of the King was strewn thick with fresh-cut rushes smoothly laid. Moreover it was in many places spread with carpets of excellent pattern such as might be fit to lay upon the floor of some goodly hall. Likewise all the houses along the way *How Camelot* were hung with fine hangings of woven texture interwoven *town was* with threads of azure and crimson, and everywhere were *adorned.* flags and banners afloat in the warm and gentle breeze against the blue sky, wherefore that all the world appeared to be alive with bright colors, so that when one looked adown that street, it was as though one beheld a crooked path of exceeding beauty and gayety stretched before him.

Thus came the wedding-day of the King—bright and clear and exceedingly radiant.

King Arthur sat in his hall surrounded by his Court awaiting news that the Lady Guinevere was coming thitherward. And it was about the middle of the morning when there came a messenger in haste riding upon a milk-white steed. And the raiment of that messenger and the trappings of his horse were all of cloth of gold embroidered with scarlet and white, and the tabard of the messenger was set with many jewels of various sorts so that he glistened from afar as he rode, with a singular splendor of appearance.

So this herald-messenger came straight into the castle where the King abided waiting, and he said: "Arise, my lord King, for the Lady Guinevere and her Court draweth nigh unto this place."

Upon this the King immediately arose with great joy, and straightway he went forth with his Court of Knights, riding in great state. And as he went down that marvellously adorned street, all the people shouted aloud as he passed by, wherefore he smiled and bent his head from side to side; for that day he was passing happy and loved his people with wonderful friendliness.

Thus he rode forward unto the town gate, and out therefrom, and so came thence into the country beyond where the broad and well-beaten highway ran winding down beside the shining river betwixt the willows and the osiers.

And, behold! King Arthur and those with him perceived the Court of the Princess where it appeared at a distance, wherefore they made great rejoicing and hastened forward with all speed. And as they came nigh, *Of the Court of the Lady Guinevere.* the sun falling upon the apparels of silk and cloth of gold, and upon golden chains and the jewels that hung therefrom, all of that noble company that surrounded the Lady Guinevere her litter flashed and sparkled with surpassing radiance.

For seventeen of the noblest knights of the King's Court, clad in complete armor, and sent by him as an escort unto the lady, rode in great splendor, surrounding the litter wherein the Princess lay. And the framework of that litter was of richly gilded wood, and its curtains and its cushions were of crimson silk embroidered with threads of gold. And behind the litter there rode in gay and joyous array, all shining with many colors, the Court of the Princess—her damsels in waiting, gentlemen, ladies, pages, and attendants.

So those parties of the King and the Lady Guinevere drew nigh together until they met and mingled the one with the other.

Then straightway King Arthur dismounted from his noble horse and, all clothed with royalty, he went afoot unto the Lady Guinevere's litter, whiles Sir Gawaine and Sir Ewaine held the bridle of his horse. Thereupon one of her pages drew aside the silken curtains of the Lady Guinevere's litter, and King Leode- *King Arthur greets the Lady Guinevere.* grance gave her his hand and she straightway descended therefrom, all embalmed, as it were, in exceeding beauty. So King Leodegrance led her to King Arthur, and King Arthur came to her and placed one hand beneath her chin and the other upon her head and inclined his counte- nance and kissed her upon her smooth cheek—all warm and fragrant like velvet for softness, and without any blemish whatsoever. And when he had thus kissed her upon the cheek, all those who were there lifted up their voices in great acclaim, giving loud voice of joy that those two noble souls had thus met together.

Thus did King Arthur give welcome unto the Lady Guinevere and unto King Leodegrance her father upon the highway beneath the walls of the town of Camelot, at the distance of half a league from that place. And no one who was there ever forgot that meeting, for it was full of extraordinary grace and noble courtliness.

Then King Arthur and his Court of Knights and nobles brought King Leodegrance and the Lady Guinevere with great ceremony unto Camelot and unto the royal castle, where apartments were assigned to all, so that the entire place was alive with joyousness and beauty.

And when high noon had come, the entire Court went with great state and ceremony unto the cathedral, and there, surrounded with wonderful magnificence, those two noble souls were married by the Archbishop. *King Arthur and the Lady Guinevere are wedded.*

And all the bells rang right joyfully, and all the people who stood without the cathedral shouted with loud acclaim, and lo! the King and the Queen came forth all shining, like unto the sun for splendor and like unto the moon for beauty.

In the castle a great noontide feast was spread, and there sat thereat four hundred, eighty and six lordly and noble folk—kings, knights, and nobles—with queens and ladies in magnificent array. And near to the King and the Queen there sat King Leodegrance and Merlin, and Sir Ulfius, and Sir Ector the trustworthy, *Of the feast at the King's castle.* and Sir Gawaine, and Sir Ewaine, and Sir Kay, and King Ban, and King Pellinore and many other famous and exalted folk, so that no man had ever beheld such magnificent courtliness as he beheld at that famous wedding-feast of King Arthur and Queen Guinevere.

And that day was likewise very famous in the history of chivalry, for in the afternoon the famous Round Table was established, and that Round Table was at once the very flower and the chiefest glory of King Arthur's reign.

For about mid of the afternoon the King and Queen, preceded by Merlin and followed by all that splendid Court of kings, lords, nobles and knights in full array, made progression to that place where Merlin, partly by magic and partly by skill, had caused to be builded a very wonderful pavilion above the Round Table where it stood.

And when the King and the Queen and the Court had entered in thereat they were amazed at the beauty of that pavilion, for they perceived, an it *Of the pa-* were, a great space that appeared to be a marvellous land of *vilion of the* Fay. For the walls were all richly gilded and were painted *Round Table.* with very wonderful figures of saints and of angels, clad in ultramarine and crimson, and all those saints and angels were depicted playing upon various musical instruments that appeared to be made of gold. And overhead the roof of the pavilion was made to represent the sky, being all of cerulean blue sprinkled over with stars. And in the midst of that painted sky was an image, an it were, of the sun in his glory. And under foot was a pavement all of marble stone, set in squares of black and white, and blue and red, and sundry other colors.

In the midst of the pavilion was a Round Table with seats thereat exactly sufficient for fifty persons, and at each of the fifty places was a chalice of gold filled with fragrant wine, and at each place was a paten of gold bearing a manchet of fair white bread. And when the King and his Court entered into the pavilion, lo! music began of a sudden for to play with a wonderful sweetness.

Then Merlin came and took King Arthur by the hand and led him away from Queen Guinevere. And he said unto the King, "Lo! this is the Round Table."

Then King Arthur said, " Merlin, that which I see is wonderful beyond the telling."

After that Merlin discovered unto the King the various marvels of the *King Arthur is* Round Table, for first he pointed to a high seat, very wonder- *seated at the* fully wrought in precious woods and gilded so that it was *Round Table.* exceedingly beautiful, and he said, "Behold, lord King, yonder seat is hight the 'Seat Royal,' and that seat is thine for to sit in."

And as Merlin spake, lo! there suddenly appeared sundry letters of gold upon the back of that seat, and the letters of gold read the name,

ARTHUR, KING.

And Merlin said, "Lord, yonder seat may well be called the centre seat of the Round Table, for, in sooth, thou art indeed the very centre of all that is most worthy of true knightliness. Wherefore that seat shall be called the centre seat of all the other seats."

Then Merlin pointed to the seat that stood opposite to the Seat Royal, and that seat also was of a very wonderful appearance as afore told in this history. And Merlin said unto the King: "My lord King, that seat is called the Seat Perilous, for no man but one in all this world shall sit therein, and that man is not yet born upon the earth. And if any other man shall dare to sit therein that man shall either suffer death or a sudden and terrible misfortune for his temerity. Wherefore that seat is called the Seat Perilous."

"Merlin," quoth the King, "all that thou tellest me passeth the bound of understanding for marvellousness. Now I do beseech thee in all haste for to find forthwith a sufficient number of knights to fill this Round Table so that my glory shall be entirely complete."

Then Merlin smiled upon the King, though not with cheerfulness, and said, "Lord, why art thou in such haste? Know that when this Round Table shall be entirely filled in all its seats, then shall thy glory be entirely achieved and then forthwith shall thy day begin for to decline. For when any man hath reached the crowning of his glory, then his work is done and God breaketh him as a man might break a chalice from which such perfect ichor hath been drunk that no baser wine may be allowed to defile it. So when thy work is done and ended shall God shatter the chalice of thy life."

Then did the King look very steadfastly into Merlin's face, and said, "Old man, that which thou sayest is ever of great wonder, for thou speakest words of wisdom. Ne'theless, seeing that I am in God His hands, I do wish for my glory and for His good will to be accomplished even though He shall then entirely break me when I have served His purposes."

"Lord," said Merlin, "thou speakest like a worthy king and with a very large and noble heart. Ne'theless, I may not fill the Round Table for thee at this time. For, though thou hast gathered about thee the very noblest Court of Chivalry in all of Christendom, yet are there but two and thirty knights here present who may be considered worthy to sit at the Round Table."

"Then, Merlin," quoth King Arthur, "I do desire of thee that thou shalt straightway choose me those two and thirty."

"So will I do, lord King," said Merlin.

Then Merlin cast his eyes around and lo! he saw where King Pellinore stood at a little distance. Unto him went Merlin and took him by the hand. "Behold, my lord King," quoth he. "Here is the *Merlin chooseth* knight in all the world next to thyself who at this time is most *the knights* worthy for to sit at this Round Table. For he is both exceed- *of the Round Table.* ingly gentle of demeanor unto the poor and needy and at the same time is so terribly strong and skilful that I know not whether thou or he is the more to be feared in an encounter of knight against knight."

Then Merlin led King Pellinore forward and behold! upon the high seat that stood upon the left hand of the Royal Seat there appeared of a sudden the name,

PELLINORE.

And the name was emblazoned in letters of gold that shone with extraordinary lustre. And when King Pellinore took his seat, great and loud acclaim long continued was given him by all those who stood round about.

Then after that Merlin had thus chosen King Arthur and King Pellinore he chose out of the Court of King Arthur the following knights, two and thirty in all, and these were the knights of great renown in chivalry who did first establish the Round Table. Wherefore they were surnamed "The Ancient and Honorable Companions of the Round Table."

To begin, there was Sir Gawaine and Sir Ewaine, who were nephews unto the King, and they sat nigh to him upon the right hand; there was Sir Ulfius (who held his seat but four years and eight months unto the time of his death, after which Sir Geheris—who was esquire unto his brother, Sir Gawaine—held that seat); and there was Sir Kay the Seneschal, who was foster brother unto the King; and there was Sir Baudwain of Britain (who held his seat but three years and two months until his death, after the which Sir Agravaine held that seat); and there was Sir Pellias and Sir Geraint and Sir Constantine, son of Sir Caderes the Seneschal of Cornwall (which same was king after King Arthur); and there was Sir Caradoc and Sir Sagramore, surnamed the Desirous, and Sir Dinadan and Sir Dodinas, surnamed the Savage, and Sir Bruin, surnamed the Black, and Sir Meliot of Logres, and Sir Aglaval and Sir Durnure, and Sir Lamorac (which three young knights were sons of King Pellinore), and there was Sir Griflet and Sir Ladinas and Sir Brandiles and Sir Persavant of Iron-side, and Sir Dinas of Cornwall, and Sir Brian of Listinoise, and Sir Palomides and Sir Degraine and Sir Epinogres, the son of the King of North Umberland and brother unto the enchantress Vivien, and Sir Lamiel of Cardiff, and Sir Lucan the Bottler and Sir Bedevere his brother (which same bare King Arthur unto the ship of Fairies when he lay so sorely wounded nigh unto death after the last battle which he fought). These two and thirty knights were the Ancient Companions of the Round Table, and unto them were added others until there were nine and forty in all, and then was added Sir Galahad, and with him the Round Table was made entirely complete.

Now as each of these knights was chosen by Merlin, lo! as he took that knight by the hand, the name of that knight suddenly appeared in golden letters, very bright and shining, upon the seat that appertained to him.

But when all had been chosen, behold! King Arthur saw that the seat upon the right hand of the Seat Royal had not been filled, and that it bare no name upon it. And he said unto Merlin: "Merlin, how is this, that the seat upon my right hand hath not been filled, and beareth no name?"

And Merlin said: "Lord, there shall be a name thereon in a very little while, and he who shall sit therein shall be the greatest knight in all the world until that the knight cometh who shall occupy the Seat Perilous. For he who cometh shall exceed all other men in beauty and in strength and in knightly grace."

And King Arthur said: "I would that he were with us now." And Merlin said: "He cometh anon."

Thus was the Round Table established with great pomp and great ceremony of estate. For first the Archbishop of Canterbury blessed each and every seat, progressing from place to place surrounded by his Holy Court, the choir whereof singing most musically in accord, whiles others swung censers from which there ascended an exceedingly fragrant vapor of frankincense, filling that entire pavilion with an odor of Heavenly blessedness.

And when the Archbishop had thus blessed every one of those seats, the chosen knight took each his stall at the Round Table, and his esquire came and stood behind him, holding the banneret with his coat-of-arms upon the spear-point above the knight's head. And all those who stood about that place, both knights and ladies, lifted up their voices in loud acclaim.

Then all the knights arose, and each knight held up before him the cross of the hilt of his sword, and each knight spake word *Of the ceremony* for word as King Arthur spake. And this was the cove- *of installation of* nant of their Knighthood of the Round Table: That they *the Round Table.* would be gentle unto the weak; that they would be courageous unto the strong; that they would be terrible unto the wicked and the evil-doer; that they would defend the helpless who should call upon them for aid; that all women should be held unto them sacred; that they would stand unto the defence of one another whensoever such defence should be re. quired; that they would be merciful unto all men; that they would be gentle of deed, true in friendship, and faithful in love. This was their covenant, and unto it each knight sware upon the cross of his sword, and in witness thereof did kiss the hilt thereof. Thereupon all who stood thereabouts once more gave loud acclaim.

Then all the knights of the Round Table seated themselves, and each knight brake bread from the golden patten, and quaffed wine from the golden chalice that stood before him, giving thanks unto God for that which he ate and drank.

Thus was King Arthur wedded unto Queen Guinevere, and thus was the Round Table established.

CONCLUSION

So endeth this Book of King Arthur which hath been told by me with such joyousness of spirit that I find it to be a very great pleasure, in closing this first volume of my work, to look forward to writing a second volume, which now presently followeth.

In that volume there shall be told the history of several very noble worthies who were of the Court of the King, and it seems to me to be a good thing to have to do with the history of such noble and honorable knights and gentlemen. For, indeed, it might well please anyone to read such an history, and to hear those worthies speak, and to behold in what manner they behaved in times of trial and tribulation. For their example will doubtless help us all to behave in a like manner in a like case.

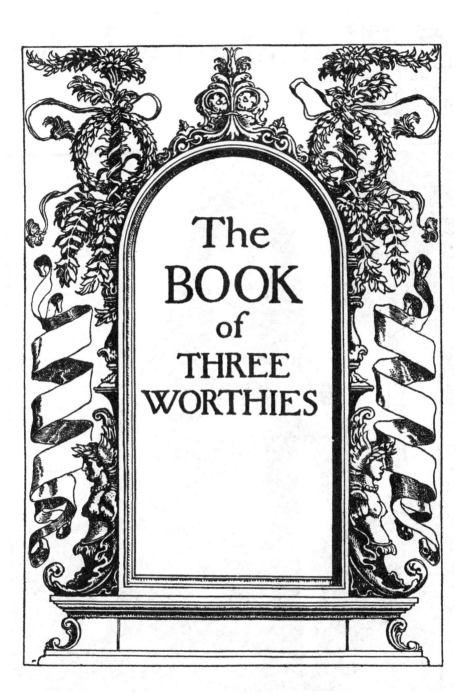

The
BOOK
of
THREE
WORTHIES

he Lady of ye Lake:·

Foreword.

✠   ✠

HERE beginneth the Second Book of the History of King Arthur, called The Book of Three Worthies, because it has to do with three very excellent, honorable Lords of the Court of King Arthur.

Of these three, the first is Merlin the Wise, the second is Sir Pellias, surnamed the Gentle Knight, and the third is Sir Gawaine, the son of King Lot of Orkney and the Isles.

So now presently follows the story of the passing of Merlin the Wise; in the which you shall see how the very wisdom that Merlin possessed in such great measure was the cause of his own undoing. Wherefore I do hope that you yourselves may take that story unto heart so that you shall see that those gifts of mind or *person which God assigns unto you may not be so misused by you or others that they shall become the means of compassing your own downfall.*

For it shall not excuse you in any wise that, as you journey forward in your life, you shall find many men who, like Merlin, have been endowed by the grace of God with very great gifts of talent which they might very easily use to the great benefit of mankind, but which they so misuse as to bring the greater ruin upon themselves and the greater harm unto other men. For, if you shall prove so weak or so wicked as to misuse your talents in that manner unto the harm of others and of yourself, it shall not make your fault the less that others shall have done greater evil than yourself.

Wherefore, let this story of Merlin be a warning unto you, I pray you all. For, though I do not believe that Merlin intended that his talents of magic should do harm unto others, yet, because of his folly, they did as great harm as though he himself had designed to do evil by means of them. Yea; it is hard to tell whether the wickedness or the follies of men do the greater harm in the world; therefore seek to guard yourself well, not only against sin, but against folly and weakness likewise.

The Enchanter Merlin.

Prologue.

UPON a certain day King Arthur sat in the Royal Hall of Camelot with the Queen and all of his Court and all of her Court. And there was great joy and mirth at that place.

Whiles they sat there, there suddenly came an armed knight into the Hall, and his armor was all covered with blood and dust, and he had a great many wounds upon his body. Then all they who were at that place were astonished and affrighted at the aspect of that knight, for his appearance boded no good news to King Arthur. The knight-messenger came to where the King was, *A messenger cometh to the King at Camelot.* and he was nearly fainting with weakness and with the many wounds he had received, and he brought news unto those who were there present that five kings, enemies to King Arthur, had suddenly come into that land and that they were burning and harrying the country upon every side.

And the knight-messenger said that these five kings were the King of Denmark, the King of Ireland, the King of Soleyse, the King of the Vale, and the King of Longtinaise. These had brought with them a great host and were laying waste the land all around about, so that all the realm was in sore travail and sorrow because of their devastations.

Upon this news, King Arthur smote his palms together with great vehemence and cried out, "Alas! who would be a king! Will the time never come when these wars and disturbances shall cease and we shall have entire peace in this land!" Therewith he arose in great agitation and went out from that place, and all who were there were in sore trouble.

So King Arthur immediately sent messengers to two friendly kings who were nearest to him—to wit, to King Pellinore and to King Uriens of Gore—and he bade them to come to his aid without any loss of time. Meantime he himself gathered together a large army with intent to go forth to meet his enemies forthwith.

So he went forth and upon the third day he came with his army unto the forest of Tintagalon and there he stayed with intent to rest for a little

King Arthur asketh aid of King Uriens and of King Pellinore. until King Pellinore and King Uriens should have joined him. But the five kings, his enemies, had news that King Arthur was at that place, and thereupon they made a forced march through North Wales with intent to strike him ere those other two kings could come to his aid. So they came by night to where King Arthur was, and they fell upon him so unexpectedly that there was great danger of his army being put to rout before that assault.

But King Arthur drew his army together by his own courage and large-heartedness, and so they defended themselves with a great spirit until King Pellinore appeared with his army and joined in that battle.

So in the end King Arthur won a great victory over his enemies; for they were put to rout and scattered in every direction. Likewise by

King Arthur is victorious. means of that war, and because of the submissions of these five kings, King Arthur recovered all that realm that had once been his father's, and more besides.

Now in that war eight of the knights of the Round Table lost their lives,

Eight knights of the Round Table are slain in battle. and King Arthur mourned their loss with great dolor; for these were the first knights of the Round Table who had lost their lives in doing battle in his defence. Whilst King Arthur was grieving very sorely for these eight knights, Merlin came unto him, and said, " Be not downcast, lord, for lo! thou hast many excellent knights still left about thee and thou canst certainly not have a very great deal of trouble in filling those eight places that have been thus made empty by death. Now if thou followest my counsel, thou must choose some very worthy adviser from the knights-companion of thy Round Table, and thou wilt consult with him in this matter (for the counsel of two is better than the counsel of one), and between ye ye may fill those places made vacant by war."

This counsel appeared very good to King Arthur, so he did as Merlin advised. For that morning he summoned King Pellinore to his privy closet and laid the matter before him and they two communed together thereupon. In that consultation King Pellinore advised King Arthur in this wise: That there should be four old and worthy knights chosen to fill four of those empty seats, and that there should be four young and ardent knights chosen to fill the other four seats, and in that manner all those eight seats should be filled.

Now that advice appeared to King Arthur to be good, wherefore he said, " Let it be that way." So first they two chose the four *King Arthur* old knights as follows: There was King Uriens of Gore, and *and King Pel-* *linore choose* King Lac, and Sir Hervise de Reuel, and Sir Galliar of Rouge. *eight old and* And from the younger knights of the Court they chose Sir *worthy knights* *for the Round* Marvaise of Leisle, and Sir Lionel, the son of King Ban of *Table.* Benwick, and Sir Cadar of Cornwall. So that there was one place yet to be filled.

Now it was a very hard thing to determine who should fill that place, for there were at that time two very honorable young knights at the Court. One of these was Sir Baudemagus, a young knight, brother of Sir Ewaine and son of King Uriens of Gore and Queen Morgana *They choose* le Fay (which lady was half-sister unto King Arthur as hath *three young* *knights for* been aforetold). And the other young knight was Sir Tor *the Round* who, though late come to the Court, had performed several *Table.* very famous adventures. And Sir Tor was a son of King Pellinore (though not of his Queen), and King Pellinore loved him a very great deal.

Then King Pellinore said to King Arthur, " Lord, there are certainly but two knights in all thy Court to choose from for to fill this eighth seat at the Round Table: one of these is thy sister's son, Sir Baudemagus, and the other is my son, Sir Tor. Now I may not advise thee in this matter, wherefore do thou, Lord, choose the one or the other of these young knights to fill that place. But this I may say, that it will please me very greatly if thy favor should fall upon Sir Baudemagus, for then will all the world believe that I have been above reproach in my dealings in this affair, whereas should Sir Tor be chosen all men would say that I favored mine own son."

Then King Arthur meditated upon this matter for a long while and by and by he spoke and said, " Sir, I have weighed this whole *King Arthur* affair, and it is my belief that Sir Tor is the better knight of *chooseth Sir Tor* those twain. For he hath performed several very excellent *for the Round* *Table.* adventures, whilst Sir Baudemagus, though a worthy knight, hath not yet made manifest any very great achievement in the fields of chivalry. So, in God's name, let Sir Tor be seated as companion of the Round Table."

Then King Pellinore said, "So be it," and thereupon they both arose and went forth from that place.

And, lo! that very moment the names of those eight worthies so chosen appeared each upon the back of the seat at the Round Table that appertained unto him, and so the decision of those two knights was confirmed in the sight of all the world in that manner.

Now when the word of all this reached the ears of Queen Morgana le Fay she was greatly affronted that Sir Baudemagus, her son, should have been passed by and that another should have been chosen in his stead.

Queen Morgana le Fay is affronted with King Arthur. Wherefore she cried out against King Arthur in the hearing of several people, saying: "Ha! how is this! is blood and kinship of no account in the eyes of this King that he passes by so worthy a knight as his own nephew to choose one who is not of lawful birth in his stead? Now, my husband's house has suffered many grievous ills at the hands of King Arthur, for, lo! he hath taken away our royal power and hath made us all little better than captives in his own Court. This in itself is as great an affront as though we were his bitter enemies instead of his nigh of kin. But this that he hath now done to my son in thus passing him by is a greater affront than that other."

And Queen Morgana le Fay spake in this wise not only to King Uriens, who was her husband, but to Sir Ewaine and to Sir Baudemagus, who were her sons. But King Uriens of Gore rebuked her for her speech, for he had grown to love King Arthur very much because of the high nobility of his nature, and likewise Sir Ewaine rebuked her saying that he would listen to no ill thing said of King Arthur, for that not only did he love King Arthur better than anyone else in all the world, but that the King was at once the looking-glass of all knighthood and likewise the very fountain-head of honor.

So spake these two; but Sir Baudemagus hearkened to what his mother, Queen Morgana said, for he was very angry with King Arthur because the King had passed him by. Wherefore he took his departure from the Court without asking leave of King Arthur and went errant in quest of adventure, and at this King Arthur was very sorry.

Now, as aforesaid, Queen Morgana le Fay spake her indignation to several other people of the Court, so that word thereof came at last to the ears of King Arthur and grieved him a very great deal. So when Queen Morgana came to him one day and besought his leave for to quit the Court, he spake to her with great sadness of spirit, saying, "My sister, I am very sorry that you are not pleased with what I have done in this matter, for God knows that I have endeavored to do to the best of my power. And though I would rather a great deal that Sir Baudemagus were fellow of the Round Table, yet it was my very honest belief that, for several reasons, Sir Tor had the best right to a seat at that Table. Now if I chose otherwise than according to my right judgment, what virtue would the Round Table have, seeing that I should have shown favor unto a man because of his kinship to me?"

Then Queen Morgana le Fay said with great heat, "Sir, all that you say only adds to the affront that our house hath sustained at your hands. For now you not only deny my son that seat, but you belittle him by comparing him to his disadvantage with this low-born knight whom you have chosen. Now, the only pleasure that I can have in talking to you is to beseech you to let me go away from this place."

Then King Arthur, speaking with great dignity, said, "Lady, it shall be as you would have it, and you shall go whithersoever it pleases you. For God forbid that I should stay you in your wishes. Moreover, I shall see to it that you shall not depart from this place without such a Court for company as may very well befit one who is the wife of one king and the sister of another."

And so he did as he said he would do, for he sent Queen Morgana le Fay away from his Court with great honor and in high estate of circumstance. But the more patient King Arthur was with her and the more he showed her favor, the more angry Queen Morgana le Fay was with him and the more she hated him.

Queen Morgana le Fay leaveth the Court of King Arthur.

So she betook her way to an estuary of the sea and there she dismissed those whom the King had sent with her and embarked with her own Court in several ships, betaking her way to that enchanted isle, hight Avalon, which was her home.

This island of Avalon was a very strange, wonderful land, such as was not to be seen anywhere else in all the world. For it was like a Paradise for beauty, being covered all over with divers gardens of flowers, intermingled with plantations of fair trees, some bearing fruit and others all a-bloom with blossoms. And besides these were many terraces of lawns, and smooth slopes of grass lying all about the borders of the island, and overlooking the sea from tall white walls of pure marble. And in the midst of these gardens and orchards and plantations and lawns and terraces, were a multitude of castles and towers built up the one above the other—some as white as snow and others very gay with many colors.

And the greatest marvel of that wonderful island was this: that in the midst of all those castles and towers was a single tower built entirely of loadstone. And in that lay the great mystery of that place.

For the island floated upon the surface of the water, and that tower of loadstone possessed such a potency that Avalon would float from place to place according to the will of Queen Morgana le Fay, so that sometimes it would be here, and sometimes it would be there, as that royal lady willed it to be.

Nor was there a very many people who had seen that island, for some-whiles it would be all covered over with a mist of enchantment like to silver, so that no eyes could behold it unless they were fay. But some-times it had been seen, as it were a vision of Paradise. What time he who beheld it would hear gay voices sounding from its lawns and plantations—very thin and clear because of the great distance (for no one ever came nigh to Avalon unless by authority of Queen Morgana le Fay), and he would hear music of so sweet a sort that it was likely that his soul would grow all faint because of the music. Then Avalon would suddenly disappear very marvellously, and he who had seen it would be aware that it was not likely that he would ever see it again.

Such was the island of Avalon, and if you would read of it more particularly you shall find much about it in a certain book written in French and called "Ogier le Danois."

Queen Morgana le Fay loved this island a very great deal, and it is said by many that King Arthur is yet alive in that place, lying there very peacefully and tranquilly whiles he awaits that certain time when he shall return unto the world to make right all that is wrong therein. So it is I have told you of it with these particulars at this place.

PART I

The Story of Merlin

*H*ERE *followeth a particular account of the enchantment of Merlin by a certain damsel, hight Vivien, and of all the circumstances thereunto appertaining.*

Likewise it is to be narrated how King Arthur was betrayed by his own sister, and of how he would certainly have been slain only for the help of that same enchantress Vivien who was the cause of Merlin's undoing.

Also it shall be told how the sheath of Excalibur was lost at that time.

The Enchantress Vivien.

Chapter First.

How Queen Morgana le Fay Meditated Evil Against King Arthur and How She Sent a Damsel to Beguile the Enchanter, Merlin.

NOW Morgana le Fay was a very cunning enchantress, and was so much mistress of magic that she could, by means of potent spells, work her will upon all things, whether quick or dead. For Merlin himself had been her master in times past, and had taught her his arts whilst she was still a young damsel at the Court of Uther-Pendragon. So it was that, next to Merlin, she was, at that time, the most potent enchanter in all the world. Nevertheless she lacked Merlin's foreknowledge of things to happen and his gift of prophecy thereupon, for these things he could not impart unto anyone, wherefore she had not learned them of him.

Now, after Queen Morgana le Fay had come to the Island of Avalon as aforetold, she brooded a great deal over that affront which she deemed King Arthur had placed upon her house; and the more she brooded upon it the more big did it become in her mind. Wherefore, at *Queen Morgana contemplates* last, it seemed to her that she could have no pleasure in life *evil against King Arthur.* unless she could punish King Arthur for that which he had done. Yea; she would have been glad to see him dead at her feet because of the anger that she felt against him.

But Queen Morgana was very well aware that she could never do the King, her brother, an injury so long as Merlin was there to safeguard him, for Merlin would certainly foresee any danger that might threaten the King, and would counteract it, wherefore she was aware that if she would destroy the King, she must first destroy Merlin.

Now, there was at the Court of Queen Morgana le Fay, a certain damsel of such marvellous and bewitching beauty that her like was hardly to be seen in all of the world. This damsel was fifteen years old and of royal blood, being the daughter of the King of Northumberland; and her name was Vivien. This damsel, Vivien, was both wise and cunning beyond all measure for one so young. Moreover, she was without any heart, being cold and cruel to all who were contrary-minded to her wishes. So, because she was so cunning and wise, Queen Morgana liked her and taught her many things of magic and sorcery which she knew. But, notwithstanding all that Queen Morgana did for her, this maiden did not feel any love for her mistress, being altogether devoid of heart.

One day this damsel and Queen Morgana le Fay sat together in a garden of that magic island of Avalon, and the garden was upon a very high terrace and overlooked the sea. And the day was very fair

Queen Morgana talketh with the Damsel Vivien.

and the sea so wonderfully blue that it appeared to be as though the blue sky had melted into water and the water into the sky. As Vivien and the Queen sat in this beautiful place, the Queen said to the damsel, "Vivien, what wouldst thou rather have than anything else in all the world?" To which Vivien replied, "Lady, I would rather have such wisdom as thou hast, than anything else."

Then Queen Morgana laughed and said, "It is possible for thee to be as wise as I am, and wiser too, if so be thou wilt do according to my ordination. For I know a way in which thou mayst obtain wisdom."

"How may I obtain that wisdom, Lady?" said Vivien.

Then Queen Morgana le Fay said, "Hearken and I will tell thee. Thou must know that Merlin, whom thou hast several times seen at the Court of King Arthur, is the master of all the wisdom that it is possible for anyone to possess in this world. All that I know of magic Merlin hath taught me, and he knoweth many things that he did not teach me, but which he withheld from me. For Merlin taught me, when I was a young damsel at the Court of my mother's husband, because I was beautiful in his eyes. For Merlin loveth beauty above all things else in the world, and so he taught me many things of magic and was very patient with me.

"But Merlin hath a gift which belongeth to him and which he cannot communicate to anyone else, for it is instinct with him. That gift is the gift of foreseeing into the future and the power of prophesying thereupon.

"Yet though he may foresee the fate of others, still he is blind to his own fate. For so he confessed to me several times: that he could not tell what was to happen in his own life when that happening concerned himself alone.

"Now thou, Vivien, art far more beautiful than I was at thine age. Wherefore I believe that thou wilt easily attract the regard of Merlin unto thee. And if I give thee, besides, a certain charm which I possess, I may cause it to be that Merlin may love thee so much that he will impart to thee a great deal more of his wisdom than ever he taught me when I was his disciple.

"But thou art to know, Vivien, that in winning this gift of knowledge from Merlin thou wilt put thyself in great peril. For, by and by, when the charm of thy beauty shall have waned with him, then he may easily regret what he hath done in imparting his wisdom to thee; in the which case there will be great danger that he may lay some spell upon thee to deprive thee of thy powers; for it would be impossible that both thou and he could live in the same world and each of ye know so much cunning of magic."

Now unto all this Vivien listened with a great deal of attention, and when Queen Morgana had ended the damsel said, "Dear Lady, all that thou tellest me is very wonderful, and I find myself possessed with a vehement desire to attain such knowledge in magic as that. Wherefore, if thou wilt help me in this matter so that I may beguile his wisdom from Merlin, thou wilt make of me a debtor unto thee for as long as I may live. And touching the matter of any danger that may fall to me in this affair, I am altogether willing to assume that; for I have a great hope that I may be able so to protect myself from Merlin that no harm shall befall me. For when I have drawn all the knowledge that I am able to obtain from him, then I will use that same knowledge to cast such a spell upon him that he shall never be able to harm me or anyone else again. In this I shall play my wit against his wisdom and my beauty against his cunning, and I believe that I shall win at that game."

Then Queen Morgana fell a-laughing beyond all measure, and when she had stinted her laughter, she cried, "Hey, Vivien! certes thou art cunning beyond anything that I ever heard tell of, and I believe that thou art as wicked as thou art cunning. For whoever heard of a child of fifteen years old who would speak such words as thou hast just now spoken;

or whoever could suppose that so young a girl could conceive the thought of compassing the downfall of the wisest magician who hath ever lived."

Then Queen Morgana le Fay set to her lips a small whistle of ivory and gold and blew very shrilly upon it, and in reply there came running a young page of her Court. Queen Morgana commanded him to bring to her a certain casket of alabaster, cunningly carved and adorned with gold and set with several precious stones. And Queen Morgana opened the box and took from within it two rings of pure yellow gold, beautifully wrought and set, the one ring with a clear white stone of extraordinary brilliancy, and the other with a stone as red as blood. Then Queen Morgana said, "Vivien, behold these two rings! They possess each a spell of wonderful potency. For if thou wearest that ring with the white stone, whoever weareth the ring with the red stone shall love thee with such a passion of love that thou mayst do with him whatever thou hast a will to do. So take these rings and go to King Arthur's Court and use them as thy cunning may devise."

Queen Morgana giveth Vivien two enchanted rings.

So Vivien took the two rings and gave Queen Morgana le Fay thanks beyond all measure for them.

Now King Arthur took much pleasure in holding a great feast each Pentecost, at which time his Court was gathered about him with much mirth and rejoicing. At such times it delighted him to have some excellent entertainment for to amuse himself and his Court, wherefore it befell that nearly always something happened that gave much entertainment to the King. So came the Feast of Pentecost, and King Arthur sat at the table with a great many noble and lordly folk and several kings and queens. Now as they all sat at that feast, their spirits greatly expanded with mirth and good cheer, there suddenly came into the hall a very beautiful young damsel, and with her a dwarf, wonderfully misshapen and of a very hideous countenance.

Vivien appears before King Arthur at the Feast of Pentecost.

And the maiden was dressed all in flame-colored satin, very rich, and with beautiful embroidery of gold and embroidery of silver. And her hair, which was red like gold, was coiled into a net of gold. And her eyes were black as coals and extraordinarily bright and glistening. And she had about her throat a necklace of gold of three strands, so that with all that gold and those bright garments she shone with wonderful splendor as she entered the hall. Likewise, the dwarf who accompanied her was clad all in flame-colored raiment, and he bore in his hands a cushion of flame-colored silk with tassels of gold, and upon the cushion he bare a ring of exceeding beauty set with a red stone.

So when King Arthur beheld this beautiful maiden he supposed nothing else, than that there was some excellent entertainment, and at that he rejoiced a very great deal.

But when he looked well at the damsel it appeared to him that he knew her face, wherefore he said to her, "Damsel, who art thou?" "Sir," she said, "I am the daughter of the King of Northumberland, and my name is Vivien," and thereat King Arthur was satisfied.

Then King Arthur said to her, "Lady, what is that thou hast upon yonder cushion, and why hast thou honored us by coming hitherward?" To the which Vivien made reply, "Lord, I have here a very good entertainment for to give you pleasure at this Feast of Pentecost. For here is a ring of such a sort that only he who is the most wise and the most worthy of all men here present may wear it." And King Arthur said, "Let us see the ring."

So Vivien took the ring from the cushion which the dwarf held and she came and brought it unto King Arthur, and the King took the ring into his own hand. And he perceived that the ring was extraordinarily beautiful, wherefore he said, "Maiden, have I thy leave to try this ring upon my finger?" And Vivien said, "Yea, lord."

So King Arthur made attempt to place the ring upon his finger; but, lo! the ring shrank in size so that it would not *King Arthur trieth on the* pass beyond the first joint thereof. Wherefore King Arthur *ring.* said, "It would appear that I am not worthy to wear this ring."

Then the damsel, Vivien, said, "Have I my lord's leave to offer this ring to others of his Court?" And King Arthur said, "Let the others try the ring." So Vivien took the ring to the various folk of the Court, both lords and ladies, but not one of these could wear the ring. Then last of all Vivien came to the place where Merlin sat, and she kneeled upon the ground before him and offered the ring to him; and Merlin, because this concerned himself, could not forecast into the future to know that harm was intended to him. Nevertheless he looked sourly upon the damsel and he said, "Child, what is this silly trick thou offerest me?" "Sir," quoth Vivien, "I beseech you for to try this ring upon your finger." Then Merlin regarded the damsel more closely, and he perceived that she was very beautiful, wherefore his heart softened toward her a great deal. So he spake more gently unto her and he said, "Wherefore should I take the ring?" To the which she made reply, "Because *Merlin secureth the ring.* I believe that thou art the most wise and the most worthy of any man in all this place, wherefore the ring should belong to thee."

Then Merlin smiled, and took the ring and placed it upon his finger, and, lo! it fitted the finger exactly. Thereupon Vivien cried out, "See! the ring hath fitted his finger and he is the most wise and the most worthy." And Merlin was greatly pleased that the ring which the beautiful damsel had given him had fitted his finger in that way.

Then, after a while, he would have withdrawn the ring again but, behold! he could not, for the ring had grown to his finger as though it were a part of the flesh and the bone thereof. At this Merlin became much troubled in spirit and very anxious, for he did not understand what might be meant by the magic of the ring. So he said, "Lady, whence came this ring?" And Vivien said, "Sir, thou knowest all things; dost thou then not know that this ring was sent hitherward from Morgana le Fay?" Then again Merlin was greatly a-doubt, and he said, "I hope there may be no evil in this ring." And Vivien smiled upon him and said, "What evil could there be in it?"

Now by this time the great magic that was in the ring began to work upon Merlin's spirit, wherefore he regarded Vivien very steadily, and suddenly he took great pleasure in her beauty. Then the magic of the ring gat entire hold upon him and, lo! a wonderful passion immediately seized upon his heart and wrung it so that it was pierced as with a violent agony.

And Vivien beheld what passed in Merlin's mind, and she laughed and turned away. And several others who were there also observed the very strange manner in which Merlin regarded her, wherefore they said among themselves, "Of a surety Merlin is bewitched by the beauty of that young damoiselle."

So, after that time the enchantment of the ring of Morgana le Fay so wrought upon Merlin's spirit that he could in no wise disentangle himself from Vivien's witchery; for from that day forth, whithersoever she went, there he might be found not far away; and if she was in the garden, he

The ring work- would be there; and if she was in the Hall, he also would be
eth its charm there; and if she went a-hawking he would also be a-horse-
upon Merlin back. And all the Court observed these things and many
the Wise.
made themselves merry and jested upon it. But, Vivien hated Merlin with all her might, for she saw that they all made merry at that folly of Merlin's, and he wearied her with his regard. But she dissembled this disregard before his face and behaved to him in all ways as though she had a great friendship for him.

Now it happened upon a day that Vivien sat in the garden, and it was wonderfully pleasant summer weather, and Merlin came into the garden and beheld Vivien where she sat. But when Vivien perceived Merlin coming she suddenly felt so great a disregard for him that she could not bear for to be nigh him at that time, wherefore she arose in haste with intent to escape from him. But Merlin hurried and overtook her and he said to her, "Child, do you then hate me?" And Vivien said, "Sir, I do not hate you." But Merlin said, "In very truth I believe that you do hate me." And Vivien was silent.

Then in a little Merlin said, "I would that I knew what I might do for you so that you would cease to hate me, for I find that I have a wonderful love for you." Upon this Vivien looked at Merlin very strangely, and by and by she said, "Sir, if you would only impart your wisdom and your cunning unto me, then I believe that I could love you a very great deal. For, behold! I am but as a young child in knowledge and thou art so old and so wise that I am afraid of thee. If thou wouldst teach me thy wisdom so that I might be thine equal, then haply I might grow to have such a regard for thee as thou wouldst have me feel."

Upon this Merlin looked very steadily at Vivien and he said, "Damsel, thou art, certes, no such foolish child as thou dost proclaim thyself to be; for I see that thine eyes are very bright with a cunning beyond thy years. Now I misdoubt that if I should teach thee the wisdom which thou dost desire to possess, either it would be to thy undoing or else it would be to my undoing."

Then Vivien cried out with a very loud and piercing voice, "Merlin, if thou dost love me, teach me thy wisdom and the cunning of thy magic and then I will love thee beyond anyone else in all the world!"

But Merlin sighed very deeply, for his heart misgave him. Then by and by he said, "Vivien, thou shalt have thy will and I will teach thee all those things of wisdom and magic that thou desirest to know."

Upon this Vivien was filled with such vehement agony of joy that she did not dare to let Merlin look into her countenance lest he should read what was therein written. Wherefore she cast down her eyes and turned her face away from him. Then in a little while she said, "Master, when wilt thou teach me that wisdom?"

To this Merlin made reply, "I shall not teach thee to-day nor to-morrow nor at this place; for I can only teach thee those knowledges in such solitude that there shall be nothing to disturb thy studies. But to-morrow thou shalt tell King Arthur that thou must return unto thy father's kingdom. Then we will depart together accompanied by thy Court; and when we have come to some secluded place, there I will build a habitation by the means of my magic and we shall abide therein until I have instructed thee in wisdom."

Then Vivien made great joy, and she caught Merlin's hand in hers and she kissed his hand with great passion.

So the next day Vivien besought King Arthur that he would give her leave to return unto her father's Court, and upon the third day she and Merlin and a number of attendants who were in service upon the damsel, quitted the Court of King Arthur and departed as though to go upon their way to the Kingdom of Northumberland.

Merlin and Vivien depart from the Court of the King.

But after they had gone some little distance from the Court of the King, they turned to the eastward and took their way toward a certain valley of which Merlin was acquainted, and which was so fair and pleasant a place that it was sometimes called the Valley of Delight, and sometimes the Valley of Joyousness.

ivien bewitches Merlin.

Chapter Second.

How Merlin Journeyed With Vivien Unto the Valley of Joyousness and How He Builded for Her a Castle at That Place. Also, How He Taught Her the Wisdom of Magic and of How She Compassed His Downfall Thereby.

SO, Merlin and Vivien and those who were with them travelled for three days to the eastward, until, toward the end of the third day, they reached the confines of a very dark and dismal forest. And there they beheld before them trees so thickly interwoven together that the eyes could not see anything at all of the sky because of the thickness of the foliage. And they beheld the branches and the roots of the trees that they appeared like serpents all twisted together. Wherefore Vivien said, "Sir, this is a very dismal woodland." "Yea," said Merlin, "so it appeareth to be. Ne'theless there lieth within *Merlin and* this forest that place which is called by some the Valley of *Vivien come to* Joyousness, and by others the Valley of Delight, because of *an enchanted* the great beauty of that place. And there are several path- *forest.* ways extending through this forest by the means of which that valley may be reached by a man, whether a-horse or afoot."

And after a while they found it was as Merlin said, for they came by and by upon one of those pathways and entered it and penetrated into the forest. And, lo! within that doleful woodland it was so dark that it appeared as though night-time had fallen, although it was bright daylight beyond the borders thereof, wherefore many of that party were very much afraid. But Merlin ever gave them good cheer and so they went forward upon their way. So, by and by, they came out at last from that place and into the open again, whereat they were greatly rejoiced and took much comfort.

Now, by this time, the evening had come, very peaceful and tranquil, and they beheld beneath them a valley spread out in that light and it was wonderfully beautiful. And in the centre of the valley was a small lake

Merlin and Vivien comes to the Valley of Joyousness.

so smooth and clear, like to crystal, that it appeared like an oval shield of pure silver laid down upon the ground. And all about the margin of the lake were level meadows covered over with an incredible multitude of flowers of divers colors and kinds, very beautiful to behold.

When Vivien saw this place she cried unto Merlin, " Master, this is, indeed, a very joyous valley, for I do not believe that the blessed meadows of Paradise are more beautiful than this." And Merlin said, " Very well; let us go down into it." So they went down and, as they descended, the night fell apace and the round moon arose into the sky and it was hard to tell whether that valley was the more beautiful in the daytime or whether it was the more beautiful when the moon shone down upon it in that wise.

So they all came at last unto the borders of the lake and they perceived that there was neither house nor castle at that place.

Now upon this the followers of Merlin murmured amongst themselves, saying, " This enchanter hath brought us hitherward, but how will he now provide for us that we may find a resting-place that may shelter us from the inclement changes of the weather. For the beauty of this spot cannot alone shelter us from rain and storm." And Merlin overheard their murmurings and he said, " Peace ! take ye no trouble upon that matter, for I will very soon provide ye a good resting-place." Then he said to them, " Stand ye a little distance aside till I show ye what I shall do." So they withdrew a little, as he commanded them, and he and Vivien remained where they were. And Vivien said, " Master, what wilt thou do ? " And Merlin said, " Wait a little and thou shalt see."

Therewith he began a certain very powerful conjuration so that the earth began for to tremble and to shake and an appearance as of a great red dust arose into the air. And in this dust there began to appear sundry shapes and forms, and these shapes and forms arose very high into the air and by and by those who gazed thereon perceived that there was a great structure apparent in the midst of the cloud of red dust.

Then, after a while, all became quiet and the dust slowly disappeared

Merlin buildeth a castle by the means of his magic.

from the air, and, behold ! there was the appearance of a marvellous castle such as no one there had ever beheld before, even in a dream. For the walls thereof were of ultramarine and vermilion and they were embellished and adorned with figures of gold, wherefore that castle showed in the moonlight like as it were a pure vision of great glory.

Now Vivien beheld all that Merlin had accomplished and she went unto him and kneeled down upon the ground before him and took his hand and set it to her lips. And while she kneeled thus, she said, " Master, this is assuredly the most wonderful thing in the world. Wilt thou then teach me such magic that I may be able to build a castle like this castle out of the elements?" And Merlin said, " Yea; all this will I teach thee and more besides; for I will teach thee not only how thou mayst create such a structure as this out of invisible things, but will also teach thee how thou mayst, with a single touch of thy wand, dissipate that castle instantly into the air; even as a child, with a stroke of a straw, may dissipate a beautiful shining bubble, which, upon an instant is, and upon another instant is not. And I will teach thee more than that, for I will teach thee how to change and transform a thing into the semblance of a different thing; and I will teach thee spells and charms such as thou didst never hear tell of before."

Then Vivien cried out, " Master, thou art the most wonderful man in all of the world!" And Merlin looked upon Vivien and her face was very beautiful in the moonlight and he loved her a very great deal. Wherefore he smiled upon her and said, " Vivien, dost thou still hate me?" And she said, " Nay, master."

But she spake not the truth, for in her heart she was evil and the heart of Merlin was good, and that which is evil will always hate that which is good. Wherefore, though Vivien lusted for the knowledge of necromancy, and though she spake so lovingly with her lips, yet in her spirit she both feared and hated Merlin because of his wisdom. For she wist right well that, except for the enchantment of that ring which he wore, Merlin would not love her any longer in that wise. Wherefore she said in her heart, " If Merlin teaches me all of his wisdom, then the world cannot contain both him and me."

Now Merlin abided with Vivien in that place for a year and a little more, and in that time he taught her all of magic that he was able to impart. So at the end of that time he said unto her, " Vivien, I have now taught thee so much that I believe there is no one in all of the world who knoweth more than thou dost of these things of magic which thou hast studied in this time. For not only hast thou such power of *Merlin teach-* sorcery that thou canst make the invisible elements take form *eth magic to* at thy will, and not only canst thou transform at thy will one *Vivien.* thing into the appearance of an altogether different thing, but thou hast such potent magic in thy possession that thou mayst entangle any living soul into the meshes thereof, unless that one hath some very good talisman to defend himself from thy wiles. Nor have I myself very much more power than this that I have given to thee."

So said Merlin, and Vivien was filled with great joy. And she said in her heart, "Now, Merlin, if I have the good fortune to entangle thee in my spells, then shalt thou never behold the world again."

Now, when the next day had come, Vivien caused a very noble feast to be prepared for herself and Merlin. And by means of the knowledge *Vivien setteth* which Merlin had imparted to her she produced a certain *a feast for* very potent sleeping-potion which was altogether without *Merlin.* taste. This potion she herself infused into a certain noble wine, and the wine she poured into a golden chalice of extraordinary beauty.

So when that feast was ended, and whiles she and Merlin sat together, Vivien said, "Master, I have a mind to do thee a great honor." And Merlin said, "What is it?" "Thou shalt see," said Vivien. Therewith she smote her hands together and there immediately came a young page unto where they were, and he bare that chalice of wine in his hand and gave it unto Vivien. Then Vivien took the chalice and she went to where Merlin sat and kneeled down before him and said, "Sir, I beseech thee to take this chalice and to drink the wine that is within it. For as that wine is both very noble and very precious, so is thy wisdom both very noble and very precious; and as the wine is contained within a chalice of price-less cost, so is thy wisdom contained within a life that hath been beyond all value to the world." Therewith she set her lips to the chalice and kissed the wine that was in it.

Then Merlin suspected no evil, but he took the chalice and quaffed of the wine with great cheerfulness.

After that, in a little, the fumes of that potent draught began to arise into the brains of Merlin and it was as though a cloud descended upon his sight, *Merlin is over-* and when this came upon him he was presently aware that he *come by the wine* was betrayed, wherefore he cried out thrice in a voice, very *that Vivien* bitter and full of agony, "Woe! Woe! Woe!" And then he *giveth him.* cried out, "I am betrayed!" And therewith he strove to arise from where he sat but he could not.

That while Vivien sat with her chin upon her hands and regarded him very steadily, smiling strangely upon him. So presently Merlin ceased his struggles and sank into a sleep so deep that it was almost as though he had gone dead. And when that had happened Vivien arose and leaned over him and set a very powerful spell upon him. And she stretched out her forefinger and wove an enchantment all about him so that it was as though he was entirely encompassed with a silver web of enchantment. And when she had ended, Merlin could move neither hand nor foot nor even so much as a finger-tip, but was altogether like some great insect that a cunning and beautiful spider had enmeshed in a net-work of fine, strong web.

Now, when the next morning had come, Merlin awoke from his sleep and he beheld that Vivien sat over against him regarding him very narrowly. And they were in the same room in which he had *Vivien bewitch-* fallen asleep. And when Vivien perceived that Merlin was *es Merlin.* awake, she laughed and said, " Merlin, how is it with thee?" And Merlin groaned with great passion, saying, " Vivien, thou hast betrayed me."

At this Vivien laughed again very shrilly and piercingly, and she said, " Behold! Merlin, thou art altogether in my power; for thou art utterly inwoven in those enchantments which thou, thyself, hast taught me. For lo! thou canst not move a single hair without my will. And when I leave thee, the world shall see thee no more and all thy wisdom shall be my wisdom and all thy power shall be my power, and there shall be no other in the whole world who shall possess the wisdom which I possess."

Then Merlin groaned with such fervor that it was as though his heart would burst asunder. And he said, " Vivien, thou hast brought me to such shame that even were I released from this spell I could not endure that any man should ever see my face again. For I grieve not for my undoings so much as I grieve at the folly that hath turned mine own wisdom against me to my destruction. So I forgive thee all things that thou hast done to me to betray me; yet there is one thing alone which I crave of thee."

And Vivien said, " Does it concern thee?" And Merlin said, " No, it concerns another." Thereupon Vivien said, " What is it?"

Then Merlin said, " It is this: Now I have received my gift of foresight again, and I perceive that King Arthur is presently in great peril of his life. So I beseech thee Vivien that thou wilt straightway go *Merlin maketh* to where he is in danger, and that thou wilt use thy powers of *one request of* sorcery for to save him. Thus, by fulfilling this one good deed, *Vivien.* thou shalt haply lessen the sin of this that thou hast done to betray me."

Now at that time Vivien was not altogether bad as she afterward became, for she still felt some small pity for Merlin and some small reverence for King Arthur. Wherefore now she laughed and said, " Very well, I will do thy desire in this matter. Whither shall I go to save that King?"

Then Merlin replied, " Go into the West country and unto the castle of a certain knight hight Sir Domas de Noir, and when thou comest there then thou shalt immediately see how thou mayst be of aid to the good King." Upon this Vivien said, " I will do this thing for thee, for it is the last favor that anyone may ever render unto thee in this world."

Therewith Vivien smote her hands together and summoned many of her attendants. And when these had come in she presented Merlin before them, and she said, " Behold how I have bewitched him. Go! See for yourselves! Feel of his hands and his face and see if there be any life in him." And they went to Merlin and felt of him ; his hands and arms and his face, and even they plucked at his beard, and Merlin could not move in any wise but only groan with great dolor. So they all laughed and made them merry at his woful state.

Then Vivien caused it by means of her magic that there should be in that place a great coffer of stone. And she commanded those who were *Vivien places* there that they should lift Merlin up and lay him therein and *Merlin beneath* they did as she commanded. Then she caused it that, by *the stone.* means of her magic, there should be placed a huge slab of stone upon that coffer such as ten men could hardly lift, and Merlin lay beneath that stone like one who was dead.

Then Vivien caused it to be that the magic castle should instantly disappear and so it befell as she willed. Then she caused it that a mist should arise at that place, and the mist was of such a sort that no one could penetrate into it, or sever it asunder, nor could any human eye see what was within. Then, when she had done all this, she went her way with all of her Court from that valley, making great joy in that she had triumphed over Merlin.

Nevertheless she did not forget her promise, but went to the castle of Sir Domas de Noir, and after a while it shall all be told how it befell at that place.

Such was the passing of Merlin, and God grant it that you may not so misuse the wisdom He giveth you to have, that it may be turned against you to your undoing. For there can be no greater bitterness in the world than this : That a man shall be betrayed by one to whom he himself hath given the power of betraying him.

And now turn we unto King Arthur to learn how it fell with him after Merlin had thus been betrayed to his undoing.

Chapter Third.

How Queen Morgana le Fay Returned to Camelot and to the Court With Intent to Do Ill to King Arthur. Also How King Arthur and Others Went a-Hunting and of What Befell Thereby.

NOW, after Merlin had quitted the Court with Vivien in that manner aforetold, Queen Morgana le Fay returned again to Camelot. There she came unto King Arthur and kneeled before him, bowing her face, with an appearance of great humility. And she said, "Brother, I have meditated much upon these matters that have passed and I perceive that I have done very ill to talk against thee as I have done, and to be so rebellious against thy royalty. Wherefore I crave of thee to forgive me my evil words and thoughts against thee."

Then King Arthur was very much moved and he came to Queen Morgana and took her by the hand and lifted her up upon her feet and kissed her brow, and her eyes, saying, "My sister, I have no ill-will against thee, but nothing but love for thee in my heart." And so, Queen Morgana le Fay abode at the Court in the same manner as she had aforetime done, for King Arthur believed that they were reconciled.

Queen Morgana le Fay and King Arthur are reconciled.

Now one day, Queen Morgana and the King fell into a friendly talk concerning Excalibur, and Queen Morgana le Fay expressed a very great desire to see that noble weapon more closely than she had yet done, and King Arthur said he would sometime show it to her. So the next day he said, "Sister, come with me and I will show thee Excalibur." Therewith he took Queen Morgana by the hand and led her into another apartment where was a strong wooden coffer bound with bands of iron. Then the King opened the coffer and therein Queen Morgana le Fay beheld Excalibur where he lay in his sheath. Then King Arthur said to her,

"Lady, take this sword and examine it as you please." Therewith Queen Morgana took Excalibur into her hands and lifted him out of the coffer. And she drew the sword out of the sheath *King Arthur* and, lo! the blade flashed like lightning. Then she said, *showeth Excal-* "Sir, this is a very beautiful sword and I would that I *ibur to Queen* might take it hence and keep it for a little so that I might *Morgana.* enjoy it in full measure."

Now King Arthur was of a mind to show the Queen great courtesy at this time of their reconciliation, wherefore he said to her, "Take it, and be thou its keeper for as long as thou wilt." So Queen Morgana took Excalibur and his sheath and bare them away with her to her inn, and she hid the sword in the bed in which she slept.

Then Queen Morgana sent for sundry goldsmiths, eight in number, and for certain armorsmiths, eight in number, and for certain cunning jewellers, eight in number, and she said unto them, "Make me a sword in every particular like this sword that I have here." And thereupon she showed then Excalibur in his sheath. So these goldsmiths and armorsmiths and lapidaries labored with great diligence, and in a fortnight they had made a sword so exactly like Excalibur that no eye could have told the difference betwixt the one and the other. And Queen Morgana le Fay kept both swords by her until her purposes should have been fulfilled.

It befell upon a certain day that King Arthur proclaimed a hunt, and he and all of his Court were party thereunto.

Now the day before this hunt took place Queen Morgana le Fay came to King Arthur and said, "Brother, I have here for thee a very beautiful and noble horse which I intend to give thee as a gift of love." Therewith she called aloud and there came two grooms bringing a horse as black as jet and all beset with trappings and harness of silver. And the horse was *Queen Morgana* of such extraordinary beauty that neither King Arthur nor *le Fay giveth a* anybody who was with him had ever before seen its like *horse to King* for beauty. So a wonderful delight possessed the King at *Arthur.* sight of the horse and he said, "Sister, this is the noblest gift I have had given to me for this long time." "Ha! brother," quoth Queen Morgana, "doth that horse then belike thee?" "Yea," said King Arthur, "it belikes me more than any horse that I ever beheld before." "Then," quoth Queen Morgana, "consider it as a gift of reconciliation betwixt thee and me. And in sign of that reconciliation I beg of thee that thou wilt ride that horse forth upon the hunt to-morrow day." And King Arthur said, "I will do so."

So the next day he rode forth to the hunt upon that horse as he said that he would do.

Now it happened some time after noon that the hounds started a hart of extraordinary size, and the King and all of his Court followed the chase with great eagerness. But the horse of King Arthur soon out- *King Arthur* stripped all the other horses saving only that of a certain *rideth a-hunt-* very honorable and worthy knight of the Court hight Sir *ing.* Accalon of Gaul. So Sir Accalon and the King rode at a great pace through the forest, and they were so eager with the chase that they wist not whither they were riding. And at last they overtook the hart and found that it was embushed in a certain very thick and tangled part of the forest, and there King Arthur slew the stag, and so the chase was ended.

Now after this had come to pass, the King and Sir Accalon would have retraced their way whither they had come, but in a little they perceived that they were lost in the mazes of the woodland and wist not where they were. For they had followed the chase so far that they were in an alto- gether strange country. So they wandered hither and thither *King Arthur* at great length until eventide, at which time they were op- *and Sir Accalon* pressed with hunger and weariness. Then King Arthur said *of Gaul are lost* to Sir Accalon, " Messire, meseems we shall have nowhere *in the forest.* to rest ourselves to-night unless it be beneath a tree in this forest."

To this Sir Accalon made reply, " Lord, if thou wilt follow my counsel thou wilt let our horses seek their own way through this wilderness, so, haply, because of the instinct of such creatures, they shall bring us unto some place of habitation."

Now this advice appeared to be very good to King Arthur, wherefore he did as Sir Accalon advised and let loose his bridle-rein and allowed his horse to travel as it listed. So King Arthur's horse went along a certain path, and Sir Accalon followed after the King. And they went a great pass in this wise, and the night was descending upon them in the forest.

But, before it was entirely dark, they emerged out of that forest and into an open place where they beheld before them a very wide estuary, as it were an inlet of the sea. And before them was a beach of sand, very smooth, and white, and they two went down to that beach and stood upon the shore, and they wist not what to do, for there was no habitation in sight in any direction.

Now, whiles they stood there a-doubt, they suddenly perceived a ship at a very great distance away. And this ship approached where they were, sailing very rapidly. As the ship drew nigh to that place they perceived that it was of a very strange and wonderful appearance, for it *King Arthur* was painted in many divers colors, very gaudy and brilliant, *and Sir Accalon* and the sails were all of cloth of silk, woven in divers colors *see a wonderful* and embroidered with figures like to the figures of a tapestry ; *ship.* and King Arthur was very greatly amazed at the appearance of that ship.

Now, as they stood so watching the ship, they perceived that it drew nigher and nigher to that place where they were, and in a little it beached itself upon the shore of sand not very far away from them.

Then King Arthur said to Sir Accalon, "Sir, let us go forward to the shore where we may look into this ship, for never did I see its like before in all of my life, wherefore I have a thought that maybe it is fay."

So they two went to where the ship was and they stood upon the shore and looked down into it, and at first they thought that there was no one upon board of the ship, for it appeared to be altogether deserted. But as they stood there marvelling at the wonderfulness of that ship and at the manner in which it had come thither, they beheld, of a sudden, that certain curtains that hung before an apartment at the farther extremity of the ship were parted asunder and there came forth from that place twelve very beautiful damsels. Each of these was clad in a rich garment of scarlet satin very bright and shining, and each wore around her head a circlet of gold, and each had many bracelets of gold upon her arms. These damsels came forward unto where the two knights were and they said, "Welcome, King Arthur!" And they said, "Welcome, Sir Accalon!"

At this King Arthur was very much astonished that they should know him, and he said, "Fair ladies, how is this? Ye appear to know me very well, but I know ye not. Who are ye that know me and my companion and call us by name?"

Unto this the chiefest of those damsels made reply, "Sir, we are part fay and we know all about you ; and we know how that ye have been following a very long chase ; and we know that ye are aweary, anhungered, and athirst. Wherefore we beseech ye that ye come aboard of this ship and rest and refresh yourselves with food and drink."

Now, this appeared to King Arthur to be a very bel-adventure, wherefore he said to Sir Accalon, "Messire, I have a great mind for to go aboard this ship and to follow out this adventure." And Sir Accalon said, "Lord, if thou goest, I will go also."

So those ladies let fall a gangplank from the ship and King Arthur and Sir Accalon drave their horses up the gangplank and aboard the ship, and immediately they did so, the ship withdrew itself from the sands and sailed away as it had come—very swiftly—and it was now the early night-time with the moon very round and full in the sky like to a disk of pure shining silver.

King Arthur and Sir Accalon enter the ship of damoiselles.

Then those twelve damoiselles aided King Arthur and Sir Accalon to dismount; and some took their horses away and others led them into a fair chamber at the end of the ship. And in this chamber King Arthur beheld that a table had been placed as though for their entertainment, spread with a linen cloth and set with divers savory meats, and with manchets of white bread and with several different sorts of excellent wines. And at the sight King Arthur and Sir Accalon were very much rejoiced, for they were very greatly anhungered.

So they immediately sat themselves down at that table and they ate and drank with great heartiness, and whiles they did so some of those damsels served them with food, and others held them in pleasant discourse, and others made music upon lutes and citterns for their entertainment. So they feasted and made very merry.

But, after a while, a very great drowsiness of sleep began to descend upon King Arthur; albeit, he deemed that that drowsiness had come upon him because of the weariness of the chase. So presently he said, "Fair damsels, ye have refreshed us a very great deal and this hath been a very pleasant adventure. But I would now that ye had a place for us to sleep."

Unto this the chiefest of the damsels replied, "Lord, this boat hath been prepared for your refreshment, wherefore all things have been made ready for you with entire fulness."

Therewith some of those twelve damsels conducted King Arthur into a sleeping-chamber that had been prepared for him, and others led Sir Accalon into another chamber prepared for him. And King Arthur marvelled at the beauty of his chamber, for he thought that he had never beheld a more excellently bedight bed-chamber than that one into which he had now entered. So King Arthur laid himself down with much comfort to his body, and straightway he fell into a deep and gentle sleep, without dream or disturbance of any sort.

Now when King Arthur awoke from that sleep, he was astonished beyond all measure so that he wist not whether he was still asleep and dreaming, or whether he was awake. For, lo! he lay upon a pallet in a very dark and dismal chamber all of stone. And he perceived that this chamber was a dungeon, and all about him he heard the sound of many voices in woful complaint.

King Arthur findeth himself in a dreadful prison.

Then King Arthur said to himself, "Where is that ship in which I was last night, and what hath become of those ladies with whom I spake?"

Upon this he looked about him and, behold! he saw that he was indeed in a dungeon and that there were many knights in very sad estate all about him. Wherefore he perceived that they also were captives and that it was they who had made that sound of woful lamentation which he had heard when awaking.

Then King Arthur aroused himself from where he lay and he saw that all those knights who were prisoners there were strangers unto him, and he knew not them and they knew not him. And of these knights there were two and twenty who were prisoners in that place.

Then King Arthur said, "Messires, who are you and where am I at these present?" To the which the chiefest of those knights who were prisoners made reply, "Sir, we are, like yourself, prisoners in a dungeon of this castle, and the castle belongs to a certain knight, hight Sir Domas, surnamed le Noir."

Then King Arthur made great marvel at what had befallen him, wherefore he said, "Messires, here is a very singular thing hath happened to me, for last night I was asleep in a very wonderful ship that I believe was fay, and with me was a knight-companion, and, lo! this morning I awake alone in this dungeon, and know not how I came hither."

"Sir," said the knight who spake for the others, "thou wert last night brought hither by two men clad in black, and thou wert laid down upon yonder pallet without awaking, wherefore it is very plain to me that thou art in the same case that we are in, and that thou art a prisoner unto this Sir Domas le Noir."

Then King Arthur said, "Tell me, who is this Sir Domas, for I declare that I never before heard of him." "I will tell you," said the captive knight, and therewith he did so as follows:

"I believe," said he, "that this Sir Domas is the falsest knight that liveth, for he is full of treason and leasing, and is altogether a coward in his heart. Yet he is a man of very great estate and very powerful in these parts.

"Now there are two brothers, and Sir Domas is one and the other is hight Sir Ontzlake, and Sir Domas is the elder and Sir Ontzlake is the *The knight-* younger. When the father of these two knights died, he left *prisoner telleth* the one an equal patrimony with the other. But now it hath *King Arthur* *concerning* come about that Sir Domas hath nearly all of those estates *Sir Domas.* and that Sir Ontzlake hath only one castle, which same he now holdeth by the force of arms and because of his own courage. For, though Sir Domas is altogether a coward in his heart, yet he hath cunning and guile beyond any man of whom I ever heard tell; wherefore it hath so come about that of his father's patrimony Sir Domas hath everything and Sir Ontzlake hath nothing saving only that one castle and the estate thereunto appertaining.

"Now it would appear to be very strange that Sir Domas is not satisfied with all this, yet he is not satisfied, but he covets that one castle and that small estate that is his brother's, so that he can hardly have any pleasure in life because of his covetousness. Yet he knoweth not how to obtain that estate from his brother, for Sir Ontzlake is a very excellent knight, and the only way that Sir Domas can lay hands upon that estate is by having to do with his brother as man to man in a contest at arms, and this he is afraid to attempt.

"So, for a long time, Sir Domas hath been in search of a knight who may take up his case for him, and do battle against Sir Ontzlake in his behalf. Wherefore all the knights whom he can arrest he bringeth to this castle and giveth them their choice, either to take up his case against his brother, or else to remain in this place as his prisoner without ransom. So he hath arrested all of us, and hath made demand of each that he should do battle in his behalf. But not one of us will take up the case of such an evil-conditioned knight as Sir Domas, so we all remain his prisoners."

"Well," quoth King Arthur, "this is a very wonderful case. But methinks that if Sir Domas maketh his appeal to me, I will take up his case. For I would rather do that than remain a prisoner here for all my life. But if I should take upon me this battle and be successful therein, then I will afterward have to do with Sir Domas himself in such a manner as I do not believe would be very much to his liking."

Now a little while after this the door of that prison-house was opened by the porter, and there entered a very fair young damsel. And this damsel came to King Arthur and she said to him, "What *A damsel* cheer?" "I cannot tell," quoth King Arthur, "but meseems *cometh to* I am in a very sorry pass in this place." "Sir," said the *King Arthur.* damsel, "I am grieved to see so noble-appearing a knight in so dolorous a case. But if you will undertake to defend the cause of the lord of this castle with your person against his enemy, then you shall have *King Arthur* leave to go whithersoever you please." To this King Arthur *consents to* made reply, "Lady, this is a very hard case, that either I must *do battle for* fight a battle I care not for, or else remain a prisoner here *Sir Domas.* without ransom for all of my days. But I would liever fight than live

here all my life, and so I will undertake that adventure as thou wouldst
have me do. But if I do battle for the lord of this castle, and if I should
have Grace of Heaven to win that battle, then it must be that all these,
my companions in imprisonment, shall also go forth with me into free-
dom."

To this the damsel said, "Very well, be it so, for that shall content the
master of this castle."

Then King Arthur looked more closely at the maiden, and he said,
"Damsel, meseems I should know thy face, for I think I have seen thee
somewhere before this." "Nay, sir," said she, "that can hardly be, for I
am the daughter of the lord of this castle."

But in this she was false, for she was one of the damsels of Morgana
le Fay; and she was one of those who had beguiled King Arthur
into the ship the night before; and it was she who had brought him
to that castle and had delivered him into the hands of Sir Domas. And
all these things she had done upon command of Queen Morgana le
Fay.

Then King Arthur said, "But if I do this battle, thou must carry a message for me unto the Court of King Arthur, and that message must be
delivered unto Queen Morgana le Fay into her own hands. Then, when
that is done, I will do this battle for the cause of Sir Domas." And the
damsel said, "It shall be done so."

So King Arthur wrote a sealed letter to Queen Morgana le Fay that she
Queen Morgana should send to him his sword Excalibur; and he sent that
sendeth a message to her. And when Queen Morgana received that
false sword to letter she laughed and said, "Very well, he shall have a sword
King Arthur. that shall please his eye as well as Excalibur." And therewith she sent him that other sword that she had had made exactly like
Excalibur.

So Sir Domas sent word unto his brother Sir Ontzlake, that he had now
a champion for to do battle in his behalf to recover all that portion of their
patrimony which Sir Ontzlake still withheld from him.

Now when Sir Ontzlake received this message he was thrown into great
trouble of spirit, for a little while before he had been very sorely wounded
in a tournament in the which a spear had been thrust through both his
thighs, so that he was then abed with that wound and without power to
arise therefrom. Wherefore he wist not what to do in this case, for he
could not do battle upon his own behalf, and he had no one to do battle
for him.

 ueen Morgana loses
Excalibur his sheath:

Chapter Fourth.

What Befell Sir Accalon, and How King Arthur Fought an Affair-at-Arms With Swords, and How He Came Nigh to Losing His Life Thereby.

HERE followeth the account of what happened unto Sir Accalon the morning after he went aboard that magic ship with King Arthur as aforetold.

Now when Sir Accalon awoke from that same sleep it was with him as it had been with King Arthur; for, at first, he wist not whether he was still asleep and dreaming or whether he was awake. For, lo! he found himself to be lying beside a marble basin of clear water that gushed up very high from a silver tube. And he perceived that not far from this fountain was a large pavilion *Sir Accalon findeth himself beside a fountain.* of parti-colored silk which stood upon the borders of a fair meadow of grass.

So Sir Accalon was altogether astonished to find himself in this place when he had fallen asleep on board that ship, wherefore he was afraid that all this was the fruit of some very evil spell. So he crossed himself and said, "God save King Arthur from any harm, for it seems to me that those damsels upon that ship have wrought some magic upon us for to separate us the one from the other." So saying, he arose from where he lay with intent to inquire further into that matter.

Now, as he made some noise in bestirring himself, there came forth from that pavilion aforementioned a very hideous dwarf, who saluted him with all civility and with high respect. Then Sir Accalon said to the dwarf, "Sirrah, who are you?" Unto which the dwarf made answer, "Messire, I belong unto the lady of yonder pavilion, and she hath sent me to bid you welcome to this place, and to invite you in for to partake of a repast with her." "Ha!" quoth Sir Accalon, "and how was it I came hither?"

"Sir," said the dwarf, "I do not know, but when we looked forth this morning we saw you lying here by the fountain side."

Then Sir Accalon made great marvel at that which had happened to him, and by and by he said, "Who is thy lady?" To which the dwarf replied, "She is hight the Lady Gomyne of the Fair Hair, and she will be passingly glad of your company in her pavilion."

Upon this Sir Accalon arose, and, having laved himself at the fountain
Sir Accalon and so refreshed himself, he went with the dwarf unto the
enters the pavil- pavilion of that lady. And when he had come there he saw
ion of the Lady that in the centre of the pavilion was a table of silver spread
Gomyne. with a fair white cloth and covered with very excellent food
for a man to break his fast withal.

Now immediately Sir Accalon came into the pavilion, the curtains upon the further side thereof were parted and there entered from a further chamber a very beautiful lady and gave Sir Accalon welcome to that place. And Sir Accalon said to her, "Lady, methinks thou art very civil to invite me thus into thy pavilion." "Nay, sir," said the lady, " it took no great effort to be civil unto a knight so worthy as thou." Then she said to Sir Accalon, "Sir, wilt thou sit here at the table with me and break thy fast?"

At this Sir Accalon was very glad, for he was anhungered, and the beauty of the lady pleased him a very great deal, wherefore it afforded him great joy for to be in her company.

So they two sat at the table with a very cheerful and pleasant spirit and the dwarf waited upon them.

Now after Sir Accalon and the Lady of the Pavilion had broken their fasts she spake to him in this wise, " Sir knight, thou appearest to be a very strong and worthy lord and one very well used to feats of arms and to prowess in battle."

To this Sir Accalon made reply, "Lady, it does not beseem me to bespeak of my own worth, but this much I may freely say; I have engaged in several affrays at arms in such measure as a knight with belt and spurs may do, and I believe that both my friends and mine enemies have had reason to say that I have at all times done my devoirs to the best of my powers."

Then the damoiselle said, "I believe you are a very brave and worthy knight, and being such you might be of service to a good worthy knight who is in sad need of such service as one knight may render unto another."

To this Sir Accalon said, "What is that service?" And the damoiselle replied, "I will tell thee: There is, dwelling not far from this place, a

certain knight hight Sir Ontzlake, who hath an elder brother hight Sir
Domas. This Sir Domas hath served Sir Ontzlake very ill in many ways,
and hath deprived him of well nigh all of his patrimony, so that only a little
is left to Sir Ontzlake of all the great possessions that were one time his
father's. But even such a small holding as that Sir Domas begrudges Sir
Ontzlake, so that Sir Ontzlake must needs hold what he hath by such
force of arms as he may himself maintain. Now Sir Domas hath found
himself a champion who is a man of a great deal of strength and prowess,
and through this champion Sir Domas challenges Sir Ontzlake's right to
hold even that small part of those lands which were one time his father's;
wherefore if Sir Ontzlake would retain what is his he must presently do
battle therefore.

"Now this is a very sad case for Sir Ontzlake, for a short time since he
was wounded by a spear at a tournament and was pierced through both of
his thighs, wherefore he is not now able to sit upon his horse and to defend
his rights against assault. Wherefore meseems that a knight could have
no better cause to show his prowess than in the defence of so sad a case as
this."

So spake that lady, and to all she said Sir Accalon listened with great
attention, and when she had ended he said, "Lady, I would be indeed right
willing to defend Sir Ontzlake's right, but, lo! I have no armor nor have
I any arms to do battle withal."

Then that damoiselle smiled very kindly upon Sir Accalon and she said
to him, "Sir, Sir Ontzlake may easily fit thee with armor that shall be
altogether to thy liking. And as for arms, I have in this pavilion a sword
that hath but one other fellow in all the world."

Upon this she arose and went back into that curtained recess from which
she had come, and thence she presently returned, bringing a certain thing
wrapped in a scarlet cloth. And she opened the cloth before Sir Accalon's
eyes, and lo! that which she had there was King Arthur's sword Excalibur in his sheath. Then the damoiselle said, "This sword shall be thine
if thou wilt assume this quarrel upon behalf of Sir Ontzlake."

Now when Sir Accalon beheld that sword he wist not what to think, and
he said to himself, "Certes, either this is Excalibur or else it is his twin
brother." Therewith he drew the blade from out of its shield *The Lady*
and it shined with extraordinary splendor. Then Sir Acca- *Gomyne showeth*
lon said, "I know not what to think for pure wonder, for this *Excalibur to*
sword is indeed the very image of another sword I wot of." *Sir Accalon.*
When he so spake that damoiselle smiled upon him again, and she said,
"I have heard tell that there is in the world another sword like to this."

Then Sir Accalon said, "Lady, to win this sword for myself I would be
willing to fight in any battle whatsoever." And the damoiselle

*Sir Accalon
consents to do
battle for Sir
Ontzlake.*

replied, "Then if thou wilt fight this battle for Sir Ontzlake
thou art free to keep that sword for thine own," at the which
Sir Accalon was rejoiced beyond all measure of gladness.

So it came about that, by the wiles of Queen Morgana le Fay, King
Arthur was brought to fight a battle unknowingly with a knight very
much beloved by him, and that that knight had Excalibur to use against his
master. For all these things had come to pass through the cunning of
Morgana le Fay.

Now a fair field was prepared for that battle in such a place as was convenient both to Sir Domas and to Sir Ontzlake, and thither they came
upon the day assigned, each with his knight-champion and his attendants,
Sir Ontzlake being brought thither in a litter because of the sore wound
in his thighs. Also a great many other folk came to behold the combat,
for the news thereof had gone forth to a great distance around about that
place. So, all being in readiness, the two knights that were to do battle
in that field were brought within the barriers of combat, each fully armed
and each mounted upon a very good horse.

Now King Arthur was clad all in armor of Sir Domas, and Sir Accalon
was clad in armor that belonged to Sir Ontzlake, and the head of each was
covered by his helmet so that neither of those two knew the other.

Then the herald came forth and announced that the battle was toward,
and each knight immediately put himself in readiness for the assault.
Thereupon, the word for assault being given, the two rushed forth, each
from his station, with such speed and fury that it was wonderful to behold.
And so they met in the midst of the course with a roar as of thunder, and
the spear of each knight was burst all into small pieces unto the truncheon
which he held in his hand. Upon this each knight voided his horse with
great skill and address, and allowed it to run at will in that field. And
each threw aside the truncheon of his spear and drew his sword, and
thereupon came, the one against the other, with the utmost fury of battle.

It was at this time that Vivien came to that place upon the behest of
Merlin, and she brought with her such a Court and state of beauty that a

*Vivien cometh
to the field of
battle.*

great many people took notice of her with great pleasure.
So Vivien and her Court took stand at the barriers whence
they might behold all that was toward. And Vivien regarded
those two knights and she could not tell which was King Arthur and
which was his enemy, wherefore she said, "Well, I will do as Merlin

desired me to do, but I must wait and see this battle for a while ere I shall be able to tell which is King Arthur, for it would be a pity to cast my spells upon the wrong knight."

So these two knights came together in battle afoot, and first they foined and then they both struck at the same time and, lo! the sword of King Arthur did not bite into the armor of Sir Accalon, but the sword of Sir Accalon bit very deeply into the armor of King Arthur and wounded him so sorely that the blood ran down in great quantities into his armor. And after that they struck very often and very powerfully, and as it was at first so it was afterward, for the sword of Sir Accalon ever bit into the armor of King Arthur, and the sword of King Arthur bit not at all into his enemy's armor. So in a little while it came that King Arthur's armor was stained all over red with the blood that flowed out from *King Arthur is* a great many wounds, and Sir Accalon bled not at all because *sorely wounded* of the sheath of Excalibur which he wore at his side. And *by Excalibur.* the blood of King Arthur flowed down upon the ground so that all the grass around about was ensanguined with it. So when King Arthur beheld how all the ground was wet with his own blood, and how his enemy bled not at all, he began to fear that he would die in that battle; wherefore he said to himself, "How is this? Hath the virtue departed out of Excalibur and his sheath? Were it not otherwise I would think that that sword which cutteth me so sorely is Excalibur and that this sword is not Excalibur."

Upon this a great despair of death came upon him, and he ran at Sir Accalon and smote him so sore a blow upon the helm that Sir Accalon nigh fell down upon the ground.

But at that blow the sword of King Arthur broke short off at the cross of the handle and fell into the grass among the blood, and the pommel thereof and the cross thereof was all that King Arthur held in his hand.

Now at that blow Sir Accalon waxed very mad, so he ran at King Arthur with intent to strike him some dolorous blow. But when he saw that King Arthur was without weapon, he paused in his assault and he said, "Sir Knight, I see that thou art without weapon and that thou hast lost a great deal of blood. Wherefore I demand thee to yield thyself unto me as recreant."

Then King Arthur was again very much a-dread that his death was near to him; yet, because of his royalty, it was not possible for him to yield to any knight. So he said, "Nay, Sir Knight, I may not yield myself unto thee for I would liever die with honor than yield myself without honor. For though I lack a weapon, there are peculiar reasons why I may not lack worship. Wherefore thou mayst slay me as I am without weapon and that will be thy shame and not my shame."

"Well," said Sir Accalon, "as for the shame I will not spare thee unless thou dost yield to me." And King Arthur said, "I will not yield me." Thereupon Sir Accalon said, "Then stand thou away from me so that I may strike thee." And, when King Arthur had done as Sir Accalon bade him, Sir Accalon smote him such a woful blow that the King fell down upon his knees. Then Sir Accalon raised Excalibur with intent to strike King Arthur again, and with that all the people who were there cried out upon him to spare so worshipful a knight. But Sir Accalon would not spare him.

Then Vivien said unto herself, "Certes, that must be King Arthur who is so near to his death, and I do make my vow that it would be a great pity for him to die after he hath fought so fiercely." So when Sir Accalon raised his sword that second time with intent to strike his enemy, Vivien smote her hands with great force, and emitted at the same time a spell of *Vivien gets a* such potency that it appeared to Sir Accalon upon the instant *spell upon Sir* as though he had received some very powerful blow upon his *Accalon.* arm. For with that spell his arm was benumbed all from the finger-tips unto the hollow of his armpit, and thereupon Excalibur fell out of Sir Accalon's hands and into the grass.

Then King Arthur beheld the sword and he perceived that it was Excalibur and therewith he knew that he had been betrayed. Wherefore he cried out thrice, in a very loud voice, "Treason! Treason! Treason!" and with that he set his knee upon the blade and before Sir Accalon could stay him he had seized it into his hands.

Then it appeared to King Arthur that a great virtue had come into him because of that sword. Wherefore he arose from his knees and ran at Sir Accalon and smote him so sorely that the blade penetrated his armor to the depth of half a palm's breadth. And he smote him again and again and Sir Accalon cried out in a loud voice, and fell down upon his hands *King Arthur* and knees. Then King Arthur ran to him and catched the *overcometh Sir* sheath of Excalibur and plucked it away from Sir Accalon *Accalon.* and flung it away, and thereupon the wounds of Sir Accalon burst out bleeding in great measure. Then King Arthur catched the helmet of Sir Accalon and rushed it off his head with intent to slay him.

Now because King Arthur was blinded with his own blood he did not know Sir Accalon, wherefore he said, "Sir Knight, who art thou who hast betrayed me?" And Sir Accalon said, "I have not betrayed thee. I am

Sir Accalon of Gaul and I am knight in good worship of King Arthur's Court."

But when King Arthur heard this he made great outcry and he said, " How is this? Know you who I am?" And Sir Accalon said, "Nay, I know you not." Then King Arthur said, " I am King Arthur who am thy master." And upon this he took off his helmet and Sir Accalon knew him.

And when Sir Accalon beheld King Arthur he swooned away and lay like one dead upon the ground, and King Arthur said, " Take him hence."

Then when those who were there were aware who King Arthur was, they burst over the barriers and ran toward him with great outcry of pity. And King Arthur would have left this place but upon that he also swooned away because of the great issue of blood that had come from him, wherefore all those who were round about took great sorrow, thinking that he was dying, wherefore they bewailed themselves without stint.

Then came Vivien out into that field and she said, " Let me have him, for I believe that I shall be able to cure his hurts." So she commanded that two litters should be brought and she placed King Arthur in one of the litters and she placed Sir Accalon in the other, and she bore them both away to a priory of nuns that was at no great distance from that place.

So when Vivien had come there she searched the wounds of King Arthur and bathed them with a very precious balsam, so that they immediately began to heal. As for Sir Accalon, she would not have *Vivien healeth* to do with his wounds, but let one of her attendants bathe him *King Arthur.* and dress his hurts.

Now when the next morning had come, King Arthur was so much recovered that he was able to arise, though very weak and sick nigh unto death. So he got up from his couch and he would not permit anyone to stay him, and he wrapped a cloak about him and went to the place where Sir Accalon lay. When he had come there he questioned Sir Accalon very narrowly and Sir Accalon told him all that had happened to him after he had left that ship, and how the strange damsel had given him a sword for to fight with. So when King Arthur heard all that Sir Accalon had to tell him, he said, " Messire, I think that thou art not to be blamed in this matter, but I much do fear me that there is treachery here to compass my ruin."

Then he went out from that place and he found Vivien and he said to her, " Damsel, I beseech thee to dress the wounds of that knight with the same balsam that thou didst use to dress my wounds." " Lord," said Vivien, " I cannot do so, for I have no more of that balsam." But what she said was false, for she did have more of that balsam, but she did not choose to use it upon Sir Accalon.

Sir Accalon dieth of his wounds.   So that afternoon Sir Accalon died of his wounds which he had received in his battle with King Arthur.

And that day King Arthur summoned Sir Domas and Sir Ontzlake into his presence and they came and stood before him, so filled with the terror of his majesty, that they had not the power to stand, but fell down upon their knees unto him.

Then King Arthur said, " I will pardon you, for ye knew not what ye did. But thou, Sir Domas, I believe, art a very false and treasonable knight, wherefore I shall deprive thee of all thy possessions but that one single castle which thy brother had and that I shall give unto thee, but all thy possessions I shall give unto Sir Ontzlake.   And I shall further ordain

King Arthur dealeth with Sir Domas and Sir Ontzlake.   that thou shalt never hereafter have the right to ride upon any horse but a palfrey, for thou art not worthy to ride upon a courser as a true knight hath a right to do.   And I command it of thee that thou shalt presently liberate all those knights who were my companions in captivity, and thou shalt recompense them for all the injury that thou hast done to them according as it shall be decided by a Court of Chivalry."

Therewith he dismissed those two knights, and they were very glad that he had dealt so mercifully with them.

CONCLUSION

Now shortly after that combat betwixt King Arthur and Sir Accalon the news thereof was brought to Queen Morgana le Fay, and the next day thereafter she heard that Sir Accalon was dead, and she wist not how it could be that her designs could have so miscarried. Then she was a-doubt as to how much King Arthur might know of her treachery, so she said to herself, "I will go and see my brother, the King, and if he is *Queen Morgana* aware of my treason I will beseech him to pardon my trans- *cometh to King* gression." So, having made diligent inquiry as to where it *Arthur.* was that King Arthur lay, she gathered together her Court of knights and esquires and went thitherward.

So she came to that place upon the fifth day after the battle, and when she had come there she asked of those who were in attendance what cheer the King had. They answered her, "He is asleep and he must not be disturbed." To the which Queen Morgana le Fay replied, "No matter, I am not to be forbidden, for I must presently see him and speak with him." So they did not dare to stay her because she was the King's sister.

So Queen Morgana went into the chamber where the King lay and he did not waken at her coming. Then Queen Morgana was filled full of hatred and a great desire for revenge, wherefore she said to herself, "I will take Excalibur and his shield and will carry them away with me to Avalon, and my brother shall never see them again." So she went very softly to where King Arthur lay, and she looked upon him as he slept and perceived that he had Excalibur beside him and that he held the handle *Queen Morgana* of the sword in his hand while he slept. Then Queen Morgana *steals the sheath* said, "Alas, for this, for if I try to take Excalibur away from *of Excalibur.* him, haply he will awake and he will slay me for my treason." Then she looked and perceived where the sheath of Excalibur lay at the foot of the couch. So she took the sheath of Excalibur very softly and she wrapped it up in her mantle and she went out thence, and King Arthur did not awaken at her going.

So Queen Morgana came out from the King's chamber and she said to those in attendance, " Do not waken the King, for he sleepeth very soundly." Therewith she mounted her horse and went her way from that place.

Now, after a considerable while, King Arthur awoke and he looked for the sheath of Excalibur, but he perceived that it was gone, wherefore he said immediately, " Who hath been here? " They in attendance made answer, " Queen Morgana le Fay had been here and she came in and saw you and went her way without waking you." Then King Arthur's heart misgave him, and he said, I fear me that she hath dealt treacherously with me from the beginning to the end of these adventures."

Whereupon he arose and summoned all his knights and esquires and mounted his horse for pursuit of Queen Morgana, although he was still passing sick and faint from his sore wounds and loss of blood.

Now, as the King was about ready to depart, Vivien came to him where he was, and she said, " Lord, take me with thee, for if thou dost not do so thou wilt never recover Excalibur his sheath, nor wilt thou ever overtake Queen Morgana le Fay." And King Arthur said, " Come with me, damsel, in God's name." So Vivien went with him in pursuit of Queen Morgana.

Now, by and by, as she fled, Queen Morgana le Fay looked behind her and therewith she perceived that Vivien was with the party of King Arthur, wherefore her heart failed her and she said, " I fear me that I am now altogether ruined, for I have aided that damsel to acquire such knowledge of magic that I shall have no spells to save myself from her counter-spell. But at any rate it shall be that King Arthur shall never have the sheath of Excalibur again for to help him in his hour of need."

Now at that time they were passing beside the margin of a lake of con-

Queen Morgana throweth the sheath of Excalibur into the lake. siderable size. So Queen Morgana le Fay took the sheath of Excalibur in both her hands and swung it by its belt above her head and she threw it a great distance out into the water.

Then, lo! a very singular miracle occurred, for there suddenly appeared a woman's arm out of the water and it was clad in white. And it was adorned with many bracelets. And the hand of the arm catched the sheath of Excalibur and drew it underneath the water and no one ever beheld that sheath again.

So the sheath of Excalibur was lost, and that was a grievous thing for King Arthur in after time, as you may some time read.

Now after Queen Morgana le Fay had thus thrown the sheath of Excalibur into the lake, she went on a little farther to where was a very lonely place with a great many rocks and stones lying about *Queen Morgana* upon the ground. And when she had come to that place she *exercises her* exercised very potent spells of magic that Merlin had taught *magic.* her. So, by means of those spells, she transformed herself and all of her Court and all of their horses into large round stones of divers sizes.

Then in a little while came King Arthur to that place with his knights and esquires, and he was exceedingly heavy of heart, for he had beheld from a great distance how Queen Morgana le Fay had thrown the sheath of Excalibur into that lake.

Now when the King and his Court had come to that spot the damsel Vivien called out upon him to stop and she said to him, " Lord, dost thou behold all those great round stones?" "Yea," said the King, "I do see them." Then Vivien said, "Lo! those stones are Queen Morgana le Fay and the Court who were with her. For this magic that she hath done to change herself and them into stones was a certain thing that Merlin had taught her. Now I myself know that magic, and I also know how to remove that magic at my will. Wherefore, if thou wilt promise to immediately punish that wicked woman for all her treason by depriving her of her life, then will I bring her back unto her true shape again so that thou mayst have her in thy power."

Then King Arthur looked upon Vivien with great displeasure, and he said, "Damsel, thou hast a cruel heart! Thou thyself hast suffered no injury at the hands of Queen Morgana; wherefore, then, wouldst thou have me slay her? Now, but for all thou hast done for me I *King Arthur* would be very much affronted with thee. As for her, I forgive *chideth Vivien.* her all of this, and I shall forgive her again and again and yet again if she sin against me. For her mother was my mother, and the blood which flows in her veins and in my veins cometh from the same fountain-head, wherefore I will do no evil thing against her. Let us return again whence we came."

Then Vivien looked upon King Arthur very bitterly, and she laughed with great scorn, and said, "Thou art both a fool and a dotard," and therewith she vanished from the sight of all.

And after that, because King Arthur had rebuked her for her wickedness in the presence of others, she hated him even more than Morgana le Fay had hated him.

Some time after that, King Arthur heard how Merlin had been beguiled by Vivien, and he sorrowed with great bitterness that Merlin was lost unto the world in that wise.

So endeth the story of the passing of Merlin.

PART II
The Story of Sir Pellias

HERE followeth the story of Sir Pellias, surnamed by many the Gentle Knight.

For Sir Pellias was of such a sort that it was said of him that all women loved him without disadvantage to themselves, and that all men loved him to their great good advantage.

Wherefore, when in the end he won for his beloved that beautiful Lady of the Lake, who was one of the chiefest damoiselles of Faëry, and when he went to dwell as lord paramount in that wonderful habitation which no other mortal than he and Sir Launcelot of the Lake had ever beheld, then were all men rejoiced at his great good fortune—albeit all the Court of King Arthur grieved that he had departed so far away from them never to return again.

So I believe that you will have pleasure in reading the history of the things concerning Sir Pellias hereinafter written for your edification.

ir Pellias, the Gentle
Knight.

Chapter First.

How Queen Guinevere Went a-Maying and of How Sir Pellias Took Upon Him a Quest in Her Behalf.

NOW it befell upon a pleasant day in the spring-time, that Queen Guinevere went a-Maying with a goodly company of Knights and Ladies of her Court. And among those Knights *Queen Guine-* were Sir Pellias, and Sir Geraint, and Sir Dinadan, and Sir *vere goeth* Aglaval, and Sir Agravaine, and Sir Constantine of Cornwall, *a-Maying.* and sundry others, so that the like of that Court was hardly to be found in all of the world, either then or before or since.

The day was exceedingly pleasant with the sunlight all yellow, like to gold, and the breeze both soft and gentle. The small birds they sang with very great joy, and all about there bloomed so many flowers of divers sorts that the entire meadows were carpeted with their tender green. So it seemed to Queen Guinevere that it was very good to be abroad in the field and beneath the sky at such a season.

Now as the Queen and her Court walked in great joy among the blossoms, one of the damsels attendant upon the Lady Guinevere cried out of

There cometh
a damsel to the
May party.

a sudden, "Look! Look! Who is that cometh yonder?"
Thereupon Queen Guinevere lifted up her eyes, and she beheld that there came across the meadows a damsel riding upon
a milk-white palfrey, accompanied by three pages clad in sky-blue raiment.
That damsel was also clad entirely in azure, and she wore a finely wrought
chain of gold about her neck and a fillet of gold about her brows, and her
hair, which was as yellow as gold, was wrapped all about with bands of
blue ribbon embroidered with gold. And one of the pages that followed
the damsel bare a square frame of no very great size, and that the frame
was enveloped and covered with a curtain of crimson satin.

Now when the Queen beheld that goodly company approaching, she bade
one of the knights attendant upon her for to go forth to meet the damsel. And
the knight who went forth in obedience to her command was Sir Pellias.

So when Sir Pellias met the damsel and her three pages, he spake to her

Sir Pellias
talketh with
the damsel.

in this wise: "Fair damsel, I am commanded by yonder
lady for to greet you and to crave of you the favor of your
name and purpose."

"Sir Knight," said the damsel, "I do perceive from your countenance
and address that you are some lord of very high estate and of great
nobility, wherefore I will gladly tell to you that my name is Parcenet,
and that I am a damsel belonging to the Court of a certain very high
dame who dwelleth at a considerable distance from here, and who is
called the Lady Ettard of Grantmesnle. Now I come hitherward desiring
to be admitted into the presence of Queen Guinevere. Accordingly, if
you can tell me whereabout I may find that noble lady, I shall assuredly
be very greatly beholden unto you."

"Ha, Lady!" quoth Sir Pellias, "thou shalt not have very far to go to
find Queen Guinevere; for, behold! yonder she walketh, surrounded by
her Court of Lords and Ladies." Then the damsel said, "I prithee bring
me unto her."

So Sir Pellias led Parcenet unto the Queen, and Queen Guinevere received her with great graciousness of demeanor, saying, "Damsel, what is
it that ye seek of us?"

The damsel
telleth Queen
Guinevere of the
Lady Ettard.

"Lady," quoth the damsel, "I will tell you that very readily.
The Lady Ettard, my mistress, is considered by all in those
parts where she dwelleth to be the most beautiful lady in the
world. Now, of late, there hath come such a report of your
exceeding beauty that the Lady Ettard hath seen fit for to send me hither-

ward to see with mine own eyes if that which is recorded of you is soothly true. And indeed, Lady, now that I stand before you, I may not say but that you are the fairest dame that ever mine eyes beheld unless it be the Lady Ettard aforesaid."

Then Queen Guinevere laughed with very great mirth. And she said, "It appears to me to be a very droll affair that thou shouldst have travelled so great a distance for so small a matter." Then she said, "Tell me, damsel, what is that thy page beareth so carefully wrapped up in that curtain of crimson satin?"

"Lady," quoth the damsel, "it is a true and perfect likeness of the Lady Ettard, who is my mistress."

Then Queen Guinevere said, "Show it to me."

Upon this the page who bore the picture dismounted from his palfrey and, coming to Queen Guinevere, he kneeled down upon one knee and uncovered the picture so that the Queen and her Court might *The damsel* look upon it. Thereupon they all beheld that that picture *showeth the Lady* was painted very cunningly upon a panel of ivory framed with *to the Queen and* gold and inset with many jewels of divers colors. And they *her Court.* saw that it was the picture of a lady of such extraordinary beauty that all they who beheld it marvelled thereat. "Hey, damsel!" quoth Queen Guinevere, "thy lady is, indeed, graced with wonderful beauty. Now if she doth in sooth resemble that picture, then I believe that her like to loveliness is not to be found anywhere in the world."

Upon this Sir Pellias spake out and said, "Not so, Lady; for I do protest, and am willing to maintain my words with the peril of my body, that thou thyself art much more beautiful than that picture."

"Hey day, Sir Knight!" quoth the damsel Parcenet, "it is well that thou dost maintain that saying so far away from Grantmesnle; for at that place is a certain knight, hight Sir Engamore of Malverat, who is a very strong knight indeed, and who maintaineth the contrary to thy saying in favor of the Lady Ettard against all comers who dare to encounter him."

Then Sir Pellias kneeled down before Queen Guinevere, and set his palms together. "Lady," he said, "I do pray thee of thy grace that thou wilt so far honor me as to accept me for thy true knight in this mat- *Sir Pellias as-* ter. For I would fain assay an adventure in thy behalf if I *sumes the ad-* have thy permission for to do so. Wherefore, if thou grantest *venture in* me leave, I will straightway go forth to meet this knight of *honor of the* whom the damsel speaketh, and I greatly hope that when I *Queen.* find him I shall cause his overthrow to the increasing of thy glory and honor."

Then Queen Guinevere laughed again with pure merriment. "Sir," quoth she, "it pleases me beyond measure that thou shouldst take so small a quarrel as this upon thee in my behalf. For if, so be, thou dost assume so small a quarrel, then how much more wouldst thou take a serious quarrel of mine upon thee? Wherefore I do accept thee very joyfully for my champion in this affair. So go thou presently and arm thyself in such a way as may be fitting for this adventure."

"Lady," said Sir Pellias, "if I have thy leave, I will enter into this affair clad as I am. For I entertain hopes that I shall succeed in winning armor and accoutrements upon the way, in the which case this adventure will be still more to thy credit than it would otherwise be."

At this the Queen was very much pleased, that her knight should undertake so serious an adventure clad only in holiday attire; wherefore she said, "Let it be as thou wouldst have it." Thereupon she bade her page, Florian, for to go fetch the best horse that he might obtain for Sir Pellias; and Florian, running with all speed, presently returned with a noble steed, so black of hue that I believe there was not a single white hair upon him.

Then Sir Pellias gave adieu to Queen Guinevere, and her merry Maycourt, and they gave him adieu and great acclaim, and thereupon he mounted his horse and rode away with the damsel Parcenet and the three pages clad in blue.

Now when these had gone some distance the damsel Parcenet said, "Sir, I know not thy name or thy condition, or who thou art?"

Unto this Sir Pellias said, "Damsel, my name is Pellias and I am a knight of King Arthur's Round Table."

At that Parcenet was very much astonished, for Sir Pellias was held by many to be the best knight-at-arms alive, saving only King Arthur and *Sir Pellias and* King Pellinore. Wherefore she cried out, "Messire, it will as-
Parcenet dis- suredly be a very great honor for Sir Engamore to have to do
course together. with so famous a knight as thou." Unto this Sir Pellias said, "Damsel, I think there are several knights of King Arthur's Round Table who are better knights than I." But Parcenet said, "I cannot believe that to be the case."

Then after awhile Parcenet said to Sir Pellias, "Messire, how wilt thou get 'thyself armor for to fight Sir Engamore?" "Maiden," said Sir Pellias, "I do not know at these present where I shall provide me armor; but before the time cometh for me to have to do with Sir Engamore, I have faith that I shall find armor fit for my purpose. For thou must know that it is not always the defence that a man weareth upon his body that bringeth him success, but more often it is the spirit that uplifteth him unto his undertakings."

Then Parcenet said, "Sir Pellias, I do not believe that it is often the case that a lady hath so good a knight as thou for to do battle in her behalf." To which Sir Pellias said very cheerfully, "Damsel, when thy time cometh I wish that thou mayst have a very much better knight to serve thee than I." "Sir," quoth Parcenet, "such a thing as that is not likely to befall me." At the which Sir Pellias laughed with great lightness of heart. Then Parcenet said, "Heigh ho! I would that I had a good knight for to serve me."

To this Sir Pellias made very sober reply, "Maiden, the first one that I catch I will give unto thee for thy very own. Now wouldst thou have him fair or dark, or short or tall? For if thou wouldst rather have him short and fair I will let the tall, dark one go; but if thou wouldst have him tall and dark, I will let go the other sort."

Then Parcenet looked very steadily at Sir Pellias, and she said, "I would have him about as tall as thou art, and with the same color of hair and eyes, and with a straight nose like unto thine, and with a good wit such as thou hast."

"Alas!" said Sir Pellias, "I would that thou hadst told me this before we had come so far from Camelot; for I could easily have got thee such a knight at that place. For they have them there in such plenty that they keep them in wicker cages, and sell them two for a farthing." Whereat Parcenet laughed very cheerfully, and said, "Then Camelot must be a very wonderful place, Sir Pellias."

So, with very merry discourse they journeyed upon their way with great joy and good content, taking much pleasure in the spring-time and the pleasant meadows whereon they travelled, being without care of any sort, and heart-full of cheerfulness and good-will.

That night they abided at a very quaint, pleasant hostelry that stood at the outskirts of the Forest of Usk, and the next morning they departed betimes in the freshness of the early day, quitting that place and entering into the forest shadows.

Now, after they had travelled a considerable distance in that forest, the damsel Parcenet said to Sir Pellias, "Sir, do you know what part of the woods this is?" "Nay," said Sir Pellias. "Well," said Par- *Sir Pellias and* cenet, "this part of the woodland is sometimes called Ar- *Parcenet come* roy, and is sometimes called the Forest of Adventure. For *to the Forest of* *Adventure.* I must tell you it is a very wonderful place, full of magic of sundry sorts. For it is said that no knight may enter into this forest but some adventure shall befall him."

"Damsel," said Sir Pellias, "that which thou tellest me is very good news. For, maybe, if we should fall in with some adventure at this place I may then be able to obtain armor suitable for my purpose."

So they entered the Forest of Adventure forthwith, and then travelled therein for a long way, marvelling greatly at the aspect of that place into which they were come. For the Forest was very dark and silent and wonderfully strange and altogether different from any other place that they had ever seen. Wherefore it appeared to them that it would not be at all singular if some extraordinary adventure should befall them.

So after they had travelled in this wise for a considerable pass they came of a sudden out of those thicker parts of the woodland to where was an opening of considerable extent. And there they beheld before them a *They find an* violent stream of water that flowed very turbulently and with *old woman be-* great uproar of many noises. And they saw that by the side *side the foun-* of the stream of water there was a thorn-tree, and that under-*tain.* neath the thorn-tree was a bank of green moss, and that upon the bank of moss there sat an aged woman of a very woful appearance. For that old woman was extraordinarily withered with age, and her eyes were all red as though with a continual weeping of rheum, and many bristles grew upon her cheeks and her chin, and her face was covered with such a multitude of wrinkles that there was not any place that was free from wrinkles.

Now when that old woman beheld Sir Pellias and Parcenet and the three pages approaching where she sat, she cried out in a loud voice, "Sir, wilt thou not bear me over this water upon thy horse? For, lo! I am very old and feeble and may not cross this river by myself."

Then Parcenet rebuked the old woman, saying, "Peace, be still! Who art thou to ask this noble knight for to do thee such a service as that?"

Then Sir Pellias was not pleased with Parcenet, wherefore he said, "Damsel, thou dost not speak properly in this matter, for that which be-seemeth a true knight is to give succor unto anyone soever who needeth his aid. For King Arthur is the perfect looking-glass of knighthood, and he hath taught his knights to give succor unto all who ask succor of them, without regarding their condition. So saying Sir *Sir Pellias car-* Pellias dismounted from his horse and lifted the old woman *ries the old* up upon the saddle thereof. Then he himself mounted once *woman across* more and straightway rode into the ford of the river and so *the water.* came across the torrent with the old woman in safety to the other side.

And Parcenet followed him, marvelling very greatly at his knightliness, and the three pages followed her.

Now when they had reached the other side of the water, Sir Pellias dismounted with intent to aid the old woman to alight from the horse. But she waited not for his aid, but immediately leaped down very lightly from where she was. And, lo! Sir Pellias beheld that she whom he had thought to be only an aged and withered beldame was, in truth, a very strange, wonderful lady of extraordinary beauty. And, greatly marvelling, he beheld that she was clad in apparel of such a sort as neither *Of the wonder-* he nor any who were there had ever beheld before. And *ful Lady of the* because of her appearance he was aware that she was not like *Lake.* any ordinary mortal, but that she was doubtless of enchantment. For he perceived that her face was of a wonderful clearness, like to ivory for whiteness, and that her eyes were very black and extraordinarily bright, like unto two jewels set into ivory; and he perceived that she was clad all in green from head to foot and that her hair was long and perfectly black and like to fine silk for softness and for glossiness; and he perceived that she had about her neck a collar of opal stones and emeralds inset into gold, and that about her wrists were bracelets of finely wrought gold inset with opal stones and emeralds. Wherefore from all these circumstances he knew that she must be fay.

(For thus was the Lady Nymue of the Lake; and so had she appeared unto King Arthur, and so did she appear unto Sir Pellias and those who were with him.)

So, beholding the wonderful magical quality of that lady, Sir Pellias kneeled down before her and set his hands together, palm to palm. But the Lady of the Lake said, " Sir, why dost thou kneel to me?" " Lady," quoth Sir Pellias, " because thou art so wonderfully strange and beautiful." " Messire," said the Lady of the Lake, " thou hast done a very good service to me and art, assuredly, a very excellent knight. Wherefore, arise and kneel no longer!" So Sir Pellias arose from his knees and stood before her, and he said, " Lady, who art thou?" To the which she made reply, " I am one who holdeth an exceedingly kind regard toward King Arthur and all his knights. My name is Nymue and I am the chiefest of those Ladies of the Lake of whom thou mayst have heard tell. I took upon me that form of a sorry old woman for to test thy knightliness, and, lo! I have not found thee amiss in worthy service." Then Sir Pellias said, " Lady, thou hast assuredly done me great favor in these." Upon that the Lady of the Lake smiled upon Sir Pellias very kindly, and she said, " Sir, I have a mind to do thee a greater favor than that."

The Lady of the   Therewith, so saying, she immediately took from about her
Lake giveth Sir neck that collar of opal stones, of emeralds and gold, and hung
Pellias the col-
lar of gold and it about the shoulders of Sir Pellias, so that it hung down upon
jewels.   his breast with a very wonderful glory of variegated colors.

" Keep this," she said, " for it is of very potent magic."

Upon that she vanished instantly from the sight of those who were there,
leaving them astonished and amazed beyond measure at what had befallen.

And Sir Pellias was like one who was in a dream, for he wist not
whether that which he had beheld was a vision, or whether he had seen it
with his waking eyes. Wherefore he mounted upon his horse in entire
silence, as though he knew not what he did. And likewise in entire silence
he led the way from that place. Nor did any of those others speak at that
time ; only after they had gone a considerable distance Parcenet said,
speaking in a manner of fear, " Messire, that was a very wonderful thing
that befell us." To which Sir Pellias said, " Yea, maiden."

Now that necklace which the Lady of the Lake had hung about the
neck of Sir Pellias possessed such a virtue that whosoever wore it was beloved of all those who looked upon him. For the collar was enchanted
with that peculiar virtue ; but Sir Pellias was altogether unaware of that
circumstance, wherefore he only took joy to himself because of the singular beauty of the jewel which the Lady of the Lake had given him.

ir Pellias encounters the
Sorrowful Lady in Arroy

Chapter Second.

*How Sir Pellias Overcame a Red Knight, Hight Sir Adresack,
and of How He Liberated XXII Captives From That Knight's
Castle.*

NOW, after that wonderful happening, they journeyed continuously for a great while. Nor did they pause at any place until they came, about an hour after the prime of the day, to a certain part of the forest where charcoal-burners were plying their trade. Here Sir Pellias commanded that they should draw rein and rest for a while, and so they dismounted for to rest and to refresh themselves, as he had ordained that they should do.

Now as they sat there refreshing themselves with meat and drink, there came of a sudden from out of the forest a sound of great lamentation and of loud outcry, and almost immediately there appeared from the thickets, coming into that open place, a lady in woful array, riding upon a pied palfrey. And behind her rode a young esquire, clad in colors of green and white and seated *There cometh a sorrowful lady and an esquire into the forest.* upon a sorrel horse. And he also appeared to be possessed of great sorrow, being in much disarray and very downcast of countenance. And the lady's face was all beswollen and inflamed with weeping, and her hair hung down upon her shoulders with neither net nor band for to stay it in place, and her raiment was greatly torn by the brambles and much stained with forest travel. And the young esquire who rode behind her came with a drooping head and a like woful disarray of apparel, his cloak dragging behind him and made fast to his shoulder by only a single point.

Now when Sir Pellias beheld the lady and the esquire in such sad estate, he immediately arose from where he sat and went straightway to the lady and took her horse by the bridle and stayed it where it was. And the lady looked at him, yet saw him not, being altogether blinded by her grief and distraction. Then Sir Pellias said to her, "Lady, what ails thee that thou sorrowest so greatly?" Whereunto she made reply, "Sir, it matters not, for thou canst not help me." "How know ye that?" said Sir Pellias. "I have a very good intention for to aid thee if it be possible for me to do so."

Then the lady looked more narrowly at Sir Pellias, and she perceived him as though through a mist of sorrow. And she beheld that he was not clad in armor, but only in a holiday attire of fine crimson cloth. Wherefore she began sorrowing afresh, and that in great measure, for she deemed that here was one who could give her no aid in her trouble. Wherefore she said, "Sir, thy intentions are kind, but how canst thou look to give me aid when thou hast neither arms nor defences for to help thee in taking upon thee such a quarrel?" But Sir Pellias said, "Lady, I know not how I may aid thee until that thou tellest me of thy sorrow. Yet I have good hope that I may serve thee when I shall know what it is that causes thee such disorder of mind." Thereupon, still holding the horse by the bridle, he brought the lady forward to that place where Parcenet still sat beside the napkin spread with food with which they had been refreshing themselves. And when he had come to that place, he, with all gentleness, constrained the lady for to dismount from her horse. Then, with equal gentleness, he compelled her to sit down upon the grass and to partake of the food. And when she had done so, and had drunk some of the wine, she found herself to be greatly refreshed and began to take to herself more heart of grace. Thereupon, beholding her so far recovered, Sir Pellias again demanded of her what was her trouble and besought her that she would open her heart unto him.

So, being encouraged by his cheerful words, she told to Sir Pellias the trouble that had brought her to that pass.

"Sir Knight," she said, "the place where I dwell is a considerable distance from this. Thence I came this morning with a very good knight, *The sorrowful* hight Sir Brandemere, who is my husband. We have been *lady telleth her* married but for a little over four weeks, so that our happiness *story.* until this morning was as yet altogether fresh with us. Now this morning Sir Brandemere would take me out a-hunting at the break of day, and so we went forth with a brachet of which my knight was wonderfully fond. So, coming to a certain place in the forest, there started up of a sudden from before us a doe, which same the brachet immediately pursued with great vehemence of outcry. Thereupon, I and my lord and this esquire followed thereafter with very great spirit and enjoyment of the chase. Now, when we had followed the doe and the hound for a great distance—the hound pursuing the doe with a great passion of eagerness—we came to a certain place where we beheld before us a violent stream of water which was crossed by a long and narrow bridge. And we beheld that upon the other side of the stream there stood a strong castle with seven towers, and that the castle was built up upon the rocks in such a way that the rocks and the castle appeared to be altogether like one rock.

"Now, as we approached the bridge aforesaid, lo! the portcullis of the castle was lifted up and the drawbridge was let fall very suddenly and with a great noise, and there immediately issued forth from out of the castle a knight clad altogether in red. And all the trappings and the furniture of his horse were likewise of red; and the spear which he bore in his hand was of ash-wood painted red. And he came forth very terribly, and rode forward so that he presently stood at the other end of that narrow bridge. Thereupon he called out aloud to Sir Brandemere, my husband, saying: 'Whither wouldst thou go, Sir Knight?' And unto him Sir Brandemere made reply: 'Sir, I would cross this bridge, for my hound, which I love exceedingly, hath crossed here in pursuit of a doe.' Then that Red Knight cried out in a loud voice, 'Sir Knight, thou comest not upon this bridge but at thy peril; for this bridge belongeth unto me, and whosoever would cross it must first overthrow me or else he may not cross.'

"Now, my husband, Sir Brandemere, was clad at that time only in a light raiment such as one might wear for hunting or for hawking; only that he wore upon his head a light bascinet enwrapped with a scarf which I had given him. Ne'theless, he was so great of heart that he would not abide any challenge such as that Red Knight had given unto him; wherefore, bidding me and this esquire (whose name is Ponteferet) to remain upon the farther side of the bridge, he drew his sword and rode forward to the middle of the bridge with intent to force a way across if he was able so to do. Whereupon, seeing that to be his intent, that Red Knight, clad all in complete armor, cast aside his spear and drew his sword and rode forward to meet my knight. So they met in the middle of the bridge, and when they had thus met that Red Knight lifted himself in his stirrup and smote my husband, Sir Brandemere, upon the crown of his bascinet with his sword. And I beheld the blade of the Red Knight's sword that it cut through the bascinet of Sir Brandemere and deep into his brain-pan, so that the blood ran down upon the knight's face in great abundance. Then Sir Brandemere straightway fell down from his horse and lay as though he were gone dead.

"Having thus overthrown him, that Red Knight dismounted from his horse and lifted up Sir Brandemere upon the horse whence he had fallen so that he lay across the saddle. Then taking both horses by the bridles the Red Knight led them straight back across the bridge and so into his castle. And as soon as he had entered into the castle the portcullis thereof was immediately closed behind him and the drawbridge was raised. Nor did he pay any heed whatever either to me or to the esquire Ponteferet, but he departed leaving us without any word of cheer; nor do I now know whether my husband, Sir Brandemere, is living or dead, or what hath befallen him."

And as the lady spake these words, lo! the tears again fell down her face in great abundance.

Then Sir Pellias was very much moved with compassion, wherefore he said, " Lady, thy case is, indeed, one of exceeding sorrowfulness, and I am greatly grieved for thee. And, indeed, I would fain aid thee to all the *Sir Pellias as-* extent that is in my power. So, if thou wilt lead me to where *sumes an advent-* is this bridge and that grimly castle of which thou speakest, *ure upon relief* I make thee my vow that I will assay to the best of my en-*of the sorrow-* *ful lady.* deavor to learn of the whereabouts of thy good knight, and as to what hath befallen him."

" Sir," said the lady, " I am much beholden unto thee for thy good will. Yet thou mayst not hope for success shouldst thou venture to undertake so grave an adventure as that without either arms or armor for to defend thyself. For consider how grievously that Red Knight hath served my husband, Sir Brandemere, taking no consideration as to his lack of arms or defence. Wherefore, it is not likely that he will serve thee any more courteously." And to the lady's words Parcenet also lifted up a great voice, bidding Sir Pellias not to be so unwise as to do this thing that he was minded to do. And so did Ponteferet, the esquire, also call out upon Sir Pellias, that he should not do this thing, but that he should at least take arms to himself ere he entered upon this adventure.

But to all that they said Sir Pellias replied, " Stay me not in that which I would do, for I do tell you all that I have several times undertaken adventures even more perilous than this and yet I have 'scaped with no great harm to myself." Nor would he listen to anything that the lady and the damsel might say, but, arising from that place, he aided the lady and the damsel to mount their palfreys. Then mounting his own steed, and the esquire and the pages having mounted their steeds, the whole party immediately departed from that place.

So they journeyed for a great distance through the forest, the esquire, Ponteferet, directing them how to proceed in such a way as should bring them by and by to the castle of the Red Knight. So, at last they came to a more open place in that wilderness where was a steep and naked hill before them. And when they had reached to the top of that hill they perceived beneath them a river, very turbulent and violent. *They come to* Likewise they saw that the river was spanned by a bridge, *the castle of the* exceedingly straight and narrow, and that upon the farther *Red Knight.* side of the bridge and of the river there stood a very strong castle with seven tall towers. Moreover the castle and the towers were built up upon the rocks, very lofty and high, so that it was hard to tell where the rocks ceased and the walls began, wherefore the towers and the walls appeared to be altogether one rock of stone.

Then the esquire, Ponteferet, pointed with his finger, and said, "Sir Knight, yonder is the castle of the Red Knight, and into it he bare Sir Brandemere after he had been so grievously wounded." Then Sir Pellias said unto the lady, "Lady, I will presently inquire as to thy husband's welfare."

Therewith he set spurs to his horse and rode down the hill toward the bridge with great boldness. And when he had come nigher to the bridge, lo! the portcullis of the castle was lifted and the drawbridge was let fall with a great noise and tumult, and straightway there issued forth from out of the castle a knight clad all in armor and accoutrements of red, and this knight came forward with great speed toward the bridge's head. Then, when Sir Pellias saw him approaching so threateningly, he said unto those who had followed him down the hill: "Stand fast where ye are and I will go forth to bespeak this knight, and inquire into the matter of that injury which he hath done unto Sir Brandemere." Upon this the esquire, Ponteferet, said unto him, "Stay, Sir Knight, thou wilt be hurt." But Sir Pellias said, "Not so, I shall not be hurt."

So he went forth very boldly upon the bridge, and when the Red Knight saw him approach, he said, "Ha! who art thou who darest to come thus upon my bridge?"

Unto him Sir Pellias made reply, "It matters not who I am, but thou art to know, thou discourteous knight, that I am come to inquire of thee where thou hast disposed of that good knight Sir Brandemere, and to ask of thee why thou didst entreat him so grievously a short time since."

At this the Red Knight fell very full of wrath. "Ha! ha!" he cried vehemently, "that thou shalt presently learn to thy great sorrow, for as I have served him, so shall I quickly serve thee, so that in a little while I shall bring thee unto him; then thou mayst ask him whatsoever thou dost list. But seeing that thou art unarmed and without defence, I would not do thee any bodily ill, wherefore I demand of thee that thou shalt presently surrender thyself unto me, otherwise it will be very greatly to thy pain and sorrow if thou compellest me to use force for to constrain thy surrender."

Then Sir Pellias said, "What! what! Wouldst thou thus assail a knight who is altogether without arms or defence as I am?" And the Red Knight said, "Assuredly shall I do so if thou dost not immediately yield thyself unto me."

"Then," quoth Pellias, "thou art not fit for to be dealt with as be seemeth a tried knight. Wherefore, should I encounter thee, thy overthrow must be of such a sort as may shame any belted knight who weareth golden spurs."

Thereupon he cast about his eyes for a weapon to fit his purpose, and he beheld how that a certain huge stone was loose upon the coping of the bridge. Now this stone was of such a size that five men of usual strength could hardly lift it. But Sir Pellias lifted it forth from its place with great ease, and, raising it with both hands, he ran quickly toward that Red Knight and flung the rock at him with much force. And the stone

Sir Pellias over-throweth the Red Knight with a great stone. smote the Red Knight upon the middle of the shield and drave it back upon his breast, with great violence. And the force of the blow drave the knight backward from his saddle, so that he fell down to the earth from his horse with a terrible tumult and lay upon the bridgeway like one who was altogether dead.

And when they within the castle who looked forth therefrom, saw that blow, and when they beheld the overthrow of the Red Knight, they lifted up their voices in great lamentation so that the outcry thereof was terrible to hear.

But Sir Pellias ran with all speed to the fallen knight and set his knee upon his breast. And he unlaced his helmet and lifted it. And he beheld that the face of the knight was strong and comely and that he was not altogether dead.

So when Sir Pellias saw that the Red Knight was not dead, and when he perceived that he was about to recover his breath from the blow that he had suffered, he drew that knight's misericordia from its sheath and set the point to his throat, so that when the Red Knight awoke from his swoon he beheld death, in the countenance of Sir Pellias and in the point of the dagger.

So when the Red Knight perceived how near death was to him he besought Sir Pellias for mercy, saying, "Spare my life unto me!" Whereunto Sir Pellias said, "Who art thou?" And the knight said, "I am hight Sir Adresack, surnamed of the Seven Towers." Then Sir Pellias said to him, " What hast thou done unto Sir Brandemere and how doth it fare with that good knight?" And the Red Knight replied, " He is not so seriously wounded as you suppose."

Now when Sir Brandemere's lady heard this speech she was greatly exalted with joy, so that she smote her hands together, making great cry of thanksgiving.

But Sir Pellias said, " Now tell me, Sir Adresack, hast thou other captives beside that knight, Sir Brandemere, at thy castle?" To which Sir Adresack replied, " Sir Knight, I will tell thee truly; there are in my castle one and twenty other captives besides him: to wit, eighteen knights and esquires of degree and three ladies. For I have defended this bridge for a long time and all who have undertaken to cross it, those have I taken captive and held for ransom. Wherefore I have taken great wealth and gained great estate thereby."

Then Sir Pellias said, " Thou art soothly a wicked and discourteous knight so to serve travellers that come thy way, and I would do well for to slay thee where thou liest. But since thou hast be- *Sir Pellias layeth* sought mercy of me I will grant it unto thee, though I will do *his injunctions* so only with great shame unto thy knighthood. Moreover, if *upon the Red* *Knight.* I spare to thee thy life there are several things which thou must perform. First thou must go unto Queen Guinevere at Camelot, and there must thou say unto her that the knight who left her unarmed hath taken thine armor from thee and hath armed himself therewith for to defend her honor. Secondly, thou must confess thy faults unto King Arthur as thou hast confessed them unto me and thou must beg his pardon for the same, craving that he, in his mercy, shall spare thy life unto thee. These are the things that thou must perform."

To this Sir Adresack said, " Very well, these things do I promise to perform if thou wilt spare my life."

Then Sir Pellias permitted him to arise and he came and stood before Sir Pellias. And Sir Pellias summoned the esquire, Ponteferet, unto him, and he said, " Take thou this knight's armor from off of his body and put it upon my body as thou knowest how to do." *Sir Pellias* And Ponteferet did as Sir Pellias bade him. For he unarmed *assumes the* Sir Adresack and he clothed Sir Pellias in Sir Adresack's *armor of Sir* *Adresack.* armor, and Sir Adresack stood ashamed before them all. Then Sir Pellias said unto him, " Now take me into thy castle that I may there liberate those captives that thou so wickedly holdest as prisoners." And Sir Adresack said, " It shall be done as thou dost command."

Thereupon they all went together unto the castle and into the castle, which was an exceedingly stately place. And there they beheld a great many servants and attendants, and these came at the command of Sir Adresack and bowed themselves down before Sir Pellias. Then Sir Pellias bade Sir Adresack for to summon the keeper of the dungeon, and Sir Adresack did so. And Sir Pellias commanded the keeper that he should conduct them unto the dungeon, and the keeper bowed down before him in obedience.

Now when they had come to that dungeon they beheld it to be a very lofty place and exceedingly strong. And there they found Sir Brande-mere and those others of whom Sir Adresack had spoken.

Sir Pellias liberates the captives.

But when that sorrowful lady perceived Sir Brandemere, she ran unto him with great voice of rejoicing and embraced him and wept over him. And he embraced her and wept and altogether forgot his hurt in the joy of beholding her again.

And in the several apartments of that part of the castle, there were in all eighteen knights and esquires, and three ladies besides Sir Brande-mere. Moreover, amongst those knights were two from King Arthur's Court: to wit, Sir Brandiles and Sir Mador de la Porte. Whereupon these beholding that it was Sir Pellias who had liberated them, came to him and embraced him with great joy and kissed him upon either cheek.

And all those who were liberated made great rejoicing and gave Sir Pellias such praise and acclaim that he was greatly contented therewith.

Then when Sir Pellias beheld all those captives who were in the dungeon he was very wroth with Sir Adresack, wherefore he turned unto him and said, " Begone, Sir Knight, for to do that penance which I imposed upon thee to perform, for I am very greatly displeased with thee, and fear me lest I should repent me of my mercy to thee."

Thereupon Sir Adresack turned him away and he immediately departed from that place. And he called to him his esquire and he took him and rode away to Camelot for to do that penance which he had promised Sir Pellias to do.

Then, after he was gone, Sir Pellias and those captives whom he had liberated, went through the divers parts of the castle. And there they found thirteen chests of gold and silver money and four caskets of jewels —very fine and of great brilliancy—all of which treasure had been paid in ransom by those captives who had aforetime been violently held prisoners at that place.

And Sir Pellias ordained that all those chests and caskets should be opened, and when those who were there looked therein, the hearts of all were wonderfully exalted with joy at the sight of that great treasure.

Then Sir Pellias commanded that all that treasure of gold and silver should be divided into nineteen equal parts, and when it had been so divided, he said, "Now let each of you who have been held *Sir Pellias* captive in this place, take for his own one part of that treasure *divideth the* as a recompense for those sorrows which he hath endured." *treasures of Sir* Moreover, to each of the ladies who had been held as captives *Adresack among* in that place, he gave a casket of jewels, saying unto her, "Take thou this casket of jewels as a recompense for that sorrow which thou hast suffered. And unto Sir Brandemere's lady he gave a casket of the jewels for that which she had endured.

But then those who were there beheld that Sir Pellias reserved no part of that great treasure for himself, they all cried out upon him: "Sir Knight! Sir Knight! How is this? Behold, thou hast set aside no part of this treasure for thyself."

Then Sir Pellias made answer: "You are right, I have not so. For it needs not that I take any of this gold and silver, or any of these jewels, for myself. For, behold! ye have suffered much at the hands of Sir Adresack, wherefore ye should receive recompense therefore, but I have suffered naught at his hands, wherefore I need no such recompense."

Then were they all astonished at his generosity and gave him great praise for his largeness of heart. And all those knights vowed unto him fidelity unto death.

Then, when all these things were accomplished, Sir Brandemere implored all who were there that they would come with him unto his castle, so that they might refresh themselves with a season of mirth *They abide at* and good faring. And they all said that they would go with *the castle of* him, and they did go. And at the castle of Sir Brandemere *Sir Brandemere.* there was great rejoicing with feasting and jousting for three days.

And all who were there loved Sir Pellias with an astonishing love because of that collar of emeralds and opals and of gold. Yet no one knew of the virtue of that collar, nor did Sir Pellias know of it.

So Sir Pellias abided at that place for three days. And when the fourth day was come he arose betimes in the morning and bade saddle his horse, and the palfrey of the damsel Parcenet, and the horses of their pages.

Then when all those who were there saw that he was minded to depart, they besought him not to go, but Sir Pellias said, "Stay me not, for I must go."

Then came to him those two knights of Arthur's Court, Sir Brandiles and Sir Mador de la Porte, and they besought him that he would let them go with him upon that adventure. And at first Sir Pellias forbade them, but they besought him the more, so that at last he was fain to say, "Ye shall go with me."

So he departed from that place with his company, and all those who remained gave great sorrow that he had gone away.

Parcenet covers **Sir Pellias** with a cloak.

Chapter Third.

How Sir Pellias Did Battle With Sir Engamore, Otherwise the Knight of the Green Sleeves, and of What Befell the Lady Ettard.

NOW, Sir Pellias and his party and the damsel Parcenet and her party travelled onward until after awhile in the afternoon they came unto the utmost boundaries of the forest, where the woodlands ceased altogether and many fields and meadows, with farms and crofts and plantations of trees all a-bloom with tender leaves and fragrant blossoms, lay spread out beneath the sky.

And Sir Pellias said, " This is indeed a very beautiful land into which we have come." Whereat the damsel Parcenet was right well pleased, for she said, " Sir, I am very glad that that which thou seest belikes thee ; for all this region belongeth unto the Lady Ettard, and it is my home. Moreover, from the top of yonder hill one mayst behold the castle of Grantmesnle which lieth in the valley beneath." Then Sir Pellias said, " Let us make haste ! For I am wonderfully desirous of beholding that place."

So they set spurs to their horses and rode up that hill at a hand gallop. And when they had reached the top thereof, lo ! be- *They reach* neath them lay the Castle of Grantmesnle in such a wise that *Grantmesnle.* it was as though upon the palm of a hand. And Sir Pellias beheld that it was an exceedingly fair castle, built altogether without of a red stone, and containing many buildings of red brick within the wall. And behind the walls there lay a little town, and from where they stood they could behold the streets thereof, and the people coming and going upon their businesses. So Sir Pellias, beholding the excellence of that castle, said, " Certes, maiden, yonder is a very fair estate."

" Yea," said Parcenet ; " we who dwell there do hold it to be a very excellent estate."

Then Sir Pellias said to Parcenet : " Maiden, yonder glade of young trees nigh unto the castle appeareth to be a very cheerful spot. Wherefore at that place I and my companions in arms will take up our inn. There, likewise, we will cause to be set up three pavilions for to shelter us by day and by night. Meantime, I beseech of thee, that thou wilt go unto the lady, thy mistress, and say unto her that a knight hath come unto this place, who, albeit he knoweth her not, holdeth that the Lady Guinevere of Camelot is the fairest lady in all of the world. And I beseech thee to tell the lady that I am here to maintain that saying against all comers at the peril of my body. Wherefore, if the lady have any champion for to undertake battle in her behalf, him will I meet in yonder field to-morrow at midday a little before I eat my mid-day meal. For at that time I do propose for to enter into yonder field, and to make parade therein until my friends bid me for to come in to my dinner; and I shall take my stand in that place in honor of the Lady Guinevere of Camelot."

"Sir Pellias," said the damsel, "I will even do as thou desirest of me. And, though I may not wish that thou mayst be the victor in that encounter, yet am I soothly sorry for to depart from thee. For thou art both a very valiant and a very gentle knight, and I find that I have a great friendship for thee."

Then Sir Pellias laughed, and he said, "Parcenet, thou art minded to give me praise that is far beyond my deserving." And Parcenet said, "Sir, not so, for thou dost deserve all that I may say to thy credit."

Thereupon they twain took leave of one another with very good will and much kindness of intention, and the maiden and the three pages went the one way, and Sir Pellias and his two companions and the several attendants they had brought with them went into the glade of young trees as Sir Pellias had ordained.

And there they set up three pavilions in the shade of the trees; the one pavilion of fair white cloth, the second of green cloth, and the third of
Sir Pellias and his knights-companion take up their inn in a glade of trees. scarlet cloth. And over each pavilion they had set a banner emblazoned with the device of that knight unto whom the pavilion appertained: above the white pavilion was the device of Sir Pellias: to wit, three swans displayed upon a field argent; above the red pavilion, which was the pavilion of Sir Brandiles, was a red banner emblazoned with his device: to-wit, a mailed hand holding in its grasp a hammer; above the green pavilion, which was that of Sir Mador de la Porte, was a green banner bearing his device, which was that of a carrion crow holding in one hand a white lily flower and in the other a sword.

So when the next day had come, and when mid-day was nigh at hand, Sir Pellias went forth into that field before the castle as he had promised to do, and he was clad all from head to foot in the red armor which he had taken from the body of Sir Adresack, so that in that armor he presented a very terrible appearance. So he rode up and down before the castle walls for a considerable while crying in a loud voice, " What ho! What ho! Here stands a knight of King Arthur's Court and of his Round Table who doth affirm, and is ready to maintain the same with his body, that the Lady Guinevere, King Arthur's Queen of Camelot, is the most beautiful lady in all of the world, barring none whomsoever. Wherefore, if any knight maintaineth otherwise, let him straightway come forth for to defend his opinion with his body." *Sir Pellias issues challenge to Sir Engamore.*

Now after Sir Pellias had thus appeared in that meadow there fell a great commotion within the castle, and many people came upon the walls thereof and gazed down upon Sir Pellias where he paraded that field. And after a time had passed, the drawbridge of the castle was let fall, and there issued forth a knight, very huge of frame and exceedingly haughty of demeanor. This knight was clad altogether from head to foot in green armor, and upon either arm he wore a green sleeve, whence he was sometimes entitled the Knight of the Green Sleeves.

So that Green Knight rode forward toward Sir Pellias, and Sir Pellias rode forward unto the Green Knight, and when they had come together they gave salute with a great deal of civility and knightly courtesy. Then the Green Knight said unto Sir Pellias, " Sir Knight, wilt thou allow unto me the great favor for to know thy name?"

Whereunto Sir Pellias made reply, " That will I so. I am Sir Pellias, a knight of King Arthur's Court and of his Round Table."

Then the Green Knight made reply, " Ha, Sir Pellias, it is a great honor for me to have to do with so famous a knight, for who is there in Courts of Chivalry who hath not heard of thee? Now, if I have the good fortune for to overthrow thee, then will all thy honor become my honor. Now, in return for thy courtesy for making proclamation of thy name, I give unto thee my name and title, which is Sir Engamore of Malverat, further known as the Knight of the Green Sleeves. And I may furthermore tell thee that I am the champion unto the Lady Ettard of Grantmesnle, and that I have defended her credit unto peerless beauty for eleven months, and that against all comers, wherefore if I do successfully defend it for one month longer, then do I become lord of her hand and of all this fair estate. So I am prepared to do the uttermost in my power in her honor."

Then Sir Pellias said, " Sir Knight, I give thee gramercy for thy words of greeting, and I too will do my uttermost in this encounter." Thereupon each knight saluted each other with his lance, and each rode to his appointed station.

Now a great concourse of people had come down to the lower walls of the castle and of the town for to behold the contest of arms that was toward, wherefore it would be hard to imagine a more worthy occasion where knights might meet in a glorious contest of friendly jousting, wherefore each knight prepared himself in all ways, and dressed him his spear and his lance with great care and circumspection. So when all had been prepared for that encounter, an herald, who had come forth from the castle into the field, give the signal for assault. Thereupon in an instant, each knight drave spurs into his horse and rushed the one against the other, with such terrible speed that the ground shook and trembled beneath the beating of their horses' feet. So they met exactly in the centre of the field of battle, the one knight smiting the other in the midst
Sir Pellias over- of his defences with a violence that was very terrible to
throws Sir En- behold. And the spear of Sir Engamore burst into as many
gamore. as thirty pieces, but the spear of Sir Pellias held so that the Green Knight was hurtled so violently from out of his saddle that he smote the earth above a spear's length behind the crupper of his horse.

Now when those who had stood upon the walls beheld how entirely the Green Knight was overthrown in the encounter, they lifted up their voices in great outcry; for there was no other such knight as Sir Engamore in all those parts. And more especially did the Lady Ettard make great outcry; for Sir Engamore was very much beloved by her; wherefore, seeing him so violently flung down upon the ground, she deemed that perhaps he had been slain.

Then three esquires ran to Sir Engamore and lifted him up and unlaced his helm for to give him air. And they beheld that he was not slain, but only in a deep swoon. So by and by he opened his eyes, and at that Sir Pellias was right glad, for it would have grieved him had he slain that knight. Now when Sir Engamore came back unto his senses once more, he demanded with great vehemence that he might continue that contest with Sir Pellias afoot and with swords. But Sir Pellias would not have it so. "Nay, Sir Engamore," quoth he, "I will not fight thee so serious a quarrel as that, for I have no such despite against thee." And at that denial Sir Engamore fell a weeping from pure vexation and shame of his entire overthrow.

Then came Sir Brandiles and Sir Mador de la Porte and gave Sir Pellias great acclaim for the excellent manner in which he had borne himself in the encounter, and at the same time they offered consolation unto Sir Engamore and comforted him for the misfortune that had befallen him. But Sir Engamore would take but little comfort in their words.

Now whiles they thus stood all together, there issued out from the castle the Lady Ettard and an exceedingly gay and comely Court of esquires and ladies, and these came across the meadow toward where Sir Pellias and the others stood.

Then when Sir Pellias beheld that lady approach, he drew his misericordia and cut the thongs of his helmet, and took the helmet off of his head, and thus he went forward, bareheaded, for to meet her.

But when he had come nigh to her he beheld that she was many times more beautiful than that image of her painted upon the ivory panel which he had aforetime beheld, wherefore his heart went forth unto her with a very great strength of liking. So therewith he kneeled down *Sir Pellias greets* upon the grass and set his hands together palm to palm, *the Lady Ettard* before her, and he said: "Lady, I do very greatly crave thy *in courteous wise.* forgiveness that I should thus have done battle against thy credit. For, excepting that I did that endeavor for my Queen, I would rather, in another case, have been thy champion than that of any lady whom I have ever beheld."

Now at that time Sir Pellias wore about his neck the collar of emeralds and opal stones and gold which the Lady of the Lake had given to him. Wherefore, when the Lady Ettard looked upon him, that necklace drew her heart unto him with very great enchantment. Wherefore she smiled upon Sir Pellias very cheerfully and gave him her hand and caused him to arise from that place where he kneeled. And she said to him, "Sir Knight, thou art a very famous warrior; for I suppose there is not anybody who knoweth aught of chivalry but hath heard of the fame of Sir Pellias, the Gentle Knight. Wherefore, though my champion Sir Engamore of Malverat hath heretofore overthrown all comers, yet he need not feel very much ashamed to have been overthrown by so terribly strong a knight."

Then Sir Pellias was very glad of the kind words which the Lady Ettard spake unto him, and therewith he made her known unto Sir Brandiles and Sir Mador de la Porte. Unto these knights also, the Lady Ettard spake very graciously, being moved thereto by the *Sir Pellias* extraordinary regard she felt toward Sir Pellias. So she be- *and his* sought those knights that they would come into the castle *knights-com-* and refresh themselves, with good cheer, and with that, the *castle of Grant-* knights said that they would presently do so. Wherefore *mesnle.* they returned each knight unto his pavilion, and there each bedight himself with fine raiment and with ornaments of gold and silver in such a fashion that he was noble company for any Court. Then those three knights betook themselves unto the castle of Grantmesnle, and when they had come thither everybody was astonished at the nobility of their aspect.

But Sir Engamore, who had by now recovered from his fall, was greatly cast down, for he said unto himself, "Who am I in the presence of these noble lords?" So he stood aside and was very downcast of heart and oppressed in his spirits.

Then the Lady Ettard set a very fine feast and Sir Pellias and Sir Brandiles and Sir Mador de la Porte were exceedingly glad thereof. And upon her right hand she placed Sir Pellias, and upon her left hand she placed Sir Engamore. And Sir Engamore was still more cast down, for, until now, he had always sat upon the right hand of the Lady Ettard.

Now because Sir Pellias wore that wonderful collar which the Lady of the Lake had given unto him, the Lady Ettard could not keep her regard from him. So after they had refreshed themselves and had gone forth into the castle pleasaunce for to walk in the warm sunshine, the lady would have Sir Pellias continually beside her. And when it came time for those foreign knights to quit the castle, she besought Sir Pellias that he would stay a while longer. Now Sir Pellias was very glad to do that, for he was pleased beyond measure with the graciousness and the beauty of the Lady Ettard.

So by and by Sir Brandiles and Sir Mador de la Porte went back unto their pavilions, and Sir Pellias remained in the castle of Grantmesnle for a while longer.

Now that night the Lady Ettard let to be made a supper for herself and Sir Pellias, and at that supper she and Sir Pellias alone sat at the table, *Sir Pellias and* and the damsel Parcenet waited in attendance upon the lady. *the Lady Ettard* Whiles they ate, certain young pages and esquires played *feast together.* very sweetly upon harps, and certain maidens who were attendant upon the Court of the lady sang so sweetly that it expanded the heart of the listener to hear them. And Sir Pellias was so enchanted with the sweetness of the music, and with the beauty of the Lady Ettard, that he wist not whether he were indeed upon the earth or in Paradise, wherefore, because of his great pleasure, he said unto the Lady Ettard, "Lady, I would that I might do somewhat for thee to show unto thee how high is the regard and the honor in which I hold thee."

Now as Sir Pellias sat beside her, the Lady Ettard had continually held in observation that wonderful collar of gold and of emerald and of opal stones which hung about his neck; and she coveted that collar exceedingly. Wherefore, she now said unto Sir Pellias, " Sir Knight, thou mayst indeed do me great favor if thou hast a mind for to do so." "What favor may I do thee, Lady?" said Sir Pellias. " Sir," said the Lady Ettard, " thou mayst give unto me that collar which hangeth about thy neck."

At this the countenance of Sir Pellias fell, and he said, "Lady, I may not do that; for that collar came unto me in such an extraordinary fashion that I may not part it from me."

Then the Lady Ettard said, "Why mayst thou not part it from thee, Sir Pellias?"

Thereupon Sir Pellias told her all of that extraordinary adventure with the Lady of the Lake, and of how that fairy lady had given the collar unto him.

At this the Lady Ettard was greatly astonished, and she said, " Sir Pellias, that is a very wonderful story. Ne'theless, though thou mayst not give that collar unto me, yet thou mayst let me wear it for a little while. For indeed I am charmed by the beauty of that collar beyond all manner of liking, wherefore I do beseech thee for to let me wear it for a little."

Then Sir Pellias could refuse her no longer, so he said, " Lady, thou shalt have it to wear for a while." Thereupon he took the *Sir Pellias lets* collar from off of his neck, and he hung it about the neck of *the Lady Ettard* the Lady Ettard. *wear the collar.*

Then, after a little time the virtue of that jewel departed from Sir Pellias and entered into the Lady Ettard, and the Lady Ettard looked upon Sir Pellias with altogether different eyes than those with which she had before regarded him. Wherefore she said unto herself: " Hah! what ailed me that I should have been so enchanted with that knight to the discredit of my champion who hath served me so faithfully? Hath not this knight done me grievous discredit? Hath he not come hitherward for no other reason than for that purpose? Hath he not overthrown mine own true knight in scorn of me? What then hath ailed me that I should have given him such regard as I have bestowed upon him?" But though she thought all this, yet she made no sign thereof unto Sir Pellias, but appeared to laugh and talk very cheerfully. Nevertheless, she immediately began to cast about in her mind for some means whereby she might be revenged upon Sir Pellias; for she said unto herself, " Lo! is he not mine enemy and is not mine enemy now in my power? Wherefore should I not take full measure of revenge upon him for all that which he hath done unto us of Grantmesnle?"

So by and by she made an excuse and arose and left Sir Pellias. And

she took Parcenet aside, and she said unto the damsel Parcenet, "Go
and fetch me hither presently a powerful sleeping-draught."

*The Lady
Ettard layeth
plans against
Sir Pellias.*
Then Parcenet said, "Lady, what would you do?" And the
Lady Ettard said, "No matter." And Parcenet said, "Would
you give unto that noble knight a sleeping-draught?" And
the lady said, "I would." Then Parcenet said, "Lady, that would surely
be an ill thing to do unto one who sitteth in peace at your table and eateth
of your salt." Whereunto the Lady Ettard said, "Take thou no care as
to that, girl, but go thou straightway and do as I bid thee."

Then Parcenet saw that it was not wise for her to disobey the lady.
Wherefore she went straightway and did as she was bidden. So she
brought the sleeping-draught to the lady in a chalice of pure wine, and
the Lady Ettard took the chalice and said to Sir Pellias, "Take thou this
chalice of wine, Sir Knight, and drink it unto me according to the measure of that good will thou hast unto me." Now Parcenet stood behind
her lady's chair, and when Sir Pellias took the chalice she frowned and
shook her head at him. But Sir Pellias saw it not, for he was intoxicated
with the beauty of the Lady Ettard, and with the enchantment of the
collar of emeralds and opal stones and gold which she now wore. Wherefore he said unto her, "Lady, if there were poison in that chalice, yet
would I drink of the wine that is in it at thy command."

At that the Lady Ettard fell a-laughing beyond measure, and she said,
"Sir Knight, there is no poison in that cup."

So Sir Pellias took the chalice and drank the wine, and he said, "Lady,
how is this? The wine is bitter." To which the Lady Ettard made
reply, "Sir, that cannot be."

Then in a little while Sir Pellias his head waxed exceedingly heavy as if
it were of lead, wherefore he bowed his head upon the table where he sat.

*Sir Pellias
sleepeth.*
That while the Lady Ettard remained watching him very
strangely, and by and by she said, "Sir Knight, dost thou
sleep?" To the which Sir Pellias replied not, for the fumes of the sleeping-draught had ascended into his brains and he slept.

Then the Lady Ettard arose laughing, and she smote her hands together
and summoned her attendants. And she said to them, "Take this knight
away, and convey him into an inner apartment, and when ye have
brought him thither, strip him of his gay clothes and of his ornaments so
that only his undergarments shall remain upon him. And when ye have
done that, lay him upon a pallet and convey him out of the castle and into
that meadow beneath the walls where he overthrew Sir Engamore, so that
when the morning shall arise he shall become a mock and a jest unto all

who shall behold him. Thus shall we humiliate him in that same field wherein he overthrew Sir Engamore, and his humiliation shall be greater than the humiliation of Sir Engamore hath been."

Now when the damsel Parcenet heard this she was greatly afflicted, so that she withdrew herself apart and wept for Sir Pellias. But the others took Sir Pellias and did unto him as the Lady Ettard had commanded.

Now when the next morning had come, Sir Pellias awoke with the sun shining into his face. And he wist not at all where he was, for his brains were befogged by the sleeping-draught which he had taken. So he said unto himself, " Am I dreaming, or am I awake ? for certes, the last that I remember was that I sat at supper with the Lady Ettard, yet here I am now in an open field with the sun shining upon me."

So he raised himself upon his elbow, and behold ! he lay beneath the castle walls nigh to the postern gate. And above him, upon the top of the wall, was a great concourse of people, who, when they beheld that he was awake, laughed at him and mocked at him. And the Lady Ettard also gazed down at him from a window and he saw that she laughed at him and made herself merry. And lo ! he beheld that he lay there clad only in his linen undervestment, and that he was in his bare feet as though he were prepared to sleep at night. So he sat upon the cot, saying unto himself, " Certainly this must be some shameful dream that oppresses me." Nor was he at all able to recover from his bewilderment.

Now, as he sat thus, the postern gate was opened of a sudden, and the damsel Parcenet came out thence. And her face was all *The damsel* be-wet with tears, and she bare in her hand a flame-colored *Parcenet bring-* mantle. Straightway she ran to Sir Pellias, and said, " Thou *eth succor to Sir* good and gentle knight, take thou this and wrap thyself in it." *Pellias.*

Upon this Sir Pellias wist that this was no dream, but a truth of great shame ; wherefore he was possessed with an extreme agony of shame, so that he fell to trembling, whilst his teeth chattered as though with an ague. Then he said to Parcenet, " Maiden, I thank thee." And he could find no more words to say. So he took the mantle and wrapped himself in it.

Now when the people upon the walls beheld what Parcenet had done, they hooted her and reviled her with many words of ill-regard. So the maiden ran back again into the castle, but Sir Pellias arose and went his way toward his pavilion wrapped in that mantle. And as he went he staggered and tottered like a drunken man, for a great burden of shame lay upon him almost more than he could carry.

So when Sir Pellias had reached his pavilion, he entered it and threw himself on his face upon his couch and lay there without saying anything.

And by and by Sir Brandiles and Mador de la Porte heard of that plight into which Sir Pellias had fallen, and thereupon they hastened to where he lay and made much sorrow over him. Likewise, they were exceedingly wroth at the shame that had been put upon him ; wherefore they said, "We will get us aid from Camelot, and we will burst open yonder castle and we will fetch the Lady Ettard hither to crave thy pardon for this affront. This we will do even if we have to drag her hither by the hair of her head."

Sir Pellias taketh great grief because of his shame.

But Sir Pellias lifted not his head, only he groaned and he said, "Let be, Messires ; for under no circumstance shall ye do that thing, she being a woman. As it is, I would defend her honor even though I died in that defence. For I know not whether I am bewitched or what it is that ails me, but I love her with a very great passion and I cannot tear my heart away from her."

At this Sir Brandiles and Sir Mador de la Porte were greatly astonished, wherefore they said the one to the other, "Certes, that lady hath laid some powerful spell upon him."

Then after a while Sir Pellias bade them go away and leave him, and they did so, though not with any very good will.

So Sir Pellias lay there for all that day until the afternoon had come. Then he aroused himself and bade his esquire for to bring him his armor. Now when Sir Brandiles and Sir Mador de la Porte heard news of this they went to where he was and said, "Sir, what have ye a mind to do?" To this Sir Pellias said, "I am going to try to win me unto the Lady Ettard's presence." Then they said, "What madness is this?" "I know not," said Sir Pellias, "but, meseems, that if I do not behold the Lady Ettard and talk with her I shall surely die of longing to see her." And they say, "Certes, this is madness." Whereunto he replied, "I know not whether it is madness or whether I am caught in some enchantment."

So the esquire fetched unto Sir Pellias his armor as he had commanded, and he clad Sir Pellias in it so that he was altogether armed from head to foot. Thereupon straightway Sir Pellias mounted his horse and rode out toward the castle of Grantmesnle.

Now when the Lady Ettard beheld Sir Pellias again parading the meadow below the castle, she called unto her six of her best knights, and she said unto them, "Behold, Messires, yonder is that knight who brought so much shame upon us yesterday. Now I bid ye for to go forth against him and to punish him as he deserveth."

So those six knights went and armed themselves, and when they had done so they straightway rode forth against Sir Pellias.

Now, when Sir Pellias beheld these approach, his heart overflowed with fury and he shouted in a great voice and drave forward against them. And for a while they withstood him, but he was not to be withstood, but fought with surpassing fury, wherefore they presently brake from before him and fled. So he pursued *Sir Pellias overcometh six knights.* them with great fury about that field and smote four of them down from their horses. Then, when there were but two of those knights remaining, Sir Pellias of a sudden ceased to fight, and he cried out unto those two knights, " Messires, I surrender myself unto ye."

Now at that those two knights were greatly astonished, for they were entirely filled with the fear of his strength, and wist not why he should yield to them. Nevertheless they came and laid hands upon him and took him toward the castle. Upon this Sir Pellias said unto himself, " Now they will bring me unto the Lady Ettard, and I shall have speech with her." For it was for this that he had suffered himself to be taken by those two knights. *Sir Pellias yields himself prisoner.*

But it was not to be as Sir Pellias willed it. For when they had brought him close under the castle, the Lady Ettard called unto them from a window in the wall. And she said, " What do you with that knight?" They say, " We bring him to you, Lady." Upon this she cried out very vehemently, " Bring him not to me, but take him and tie his hands behind his back and tie his feet beneath his horse's belly, and send him back unto his companions."

Then Sir Pellias lifted up his eyes unto that window and he cried out in a great passion of despair, " Lady, it was unto thee I surrendered, and not unto these unworthy knights."

But the Lady Ettard cried out all the more vehemently, " Drive him hence, for I do hate the sight of him."

So those two knights did as the Lady Ettard said; they took Sir Pellias and bound him hand and foot upon his horse. And when they had done so they allowed his horse for to bear him back again unto his companions in that wise. *The Lady Ettard puts shame upon Sir Pellias.*

Now when Sir Brandiles and Sir Mador de la Porte beheld how Sir Pellias came unto them with his hands bound behind his back and his feet tied beneath his horse's belly, they were altogether filled with grief and despair. So they loosed those cords from about his hands and feet, and they cried out upon Sir Pellias, " Sir Knight, Sir Knight, art thou not ashamed to permit such infamy as this?" And Sir Pellias shook and trembled as though with an ague, and he cried out in great despair, " I care not what happens unto me!" They said, " Not unto thyself, Sir

Knight; but what shame dost thou bring upon King Arthur and his Round Table!" Upon this Sir Pellias cried aloud, with a great and terrible voice, "I care not for them, either."

All of this befell because of the powerful enchantment of the collar of emeralds and opal stones and of gold which Sir Pellias had given unto the Lady Ettard, and which she continually wore. For it was beyond the power of any man to withstand the enchantment of that collar. So it was that Sir Pellias was bewitched and brought to that great pass of shame.

he Lady of the Lake sits
by the Fountain in Arroy.

Chapter Fourth.

How Queen Guinevere Quarrelled With Sir Gawaine, and How Sir Gawaine Left the Court of King Arthur For a While.

NOW, in the same measure that Queen Guinevere felt high regard for Sir Pellias, in that same degree she felt misliking for Sir Gawaine. For, though Sir Gawaine was said of many to have a silver tongue, and whiles he could upon occasion talk in such a manner as to beguile others unto his will, yet he was of a proud temper and very stern and haughty. Wherefore he would not always brook that the Lady Guinevere should command him unto her will as she did other knights of that Court. Moreover, she could not ever forget how Sir Gawaine did deny her that time at Cameliard when she besought him and his companions for aid, in her time of trouble, nor how discourteous his speech had been to her upon that occasion. So there was no great liking between these two proud souls, for Queen Guinevere held to her way and Sir Gawaine held to his way under all circumstances.

Now it happened upon an occasion that Sir Gawaine and Sir Griflet and Sir Constantine of Cornwall sat talking with five ladies of the Queen's Court in a pleached garden that lay beneath the tower of the Lady Guinevere, and they made very pleasant discourse *Sir Gawaine* together. For some whiles they would talk and make them *beneath the* merry with jests and contes, and other whiles one or another *Queen's window.* would take a lute that they had with them and would play upon it and would sing.

Now while these lords and ladies sat thus enjoying pleasant discourse and singing in that manner, Queen Guinevere sat at a window that overlooked the garden, and which was not very high from the ground, wherefore she could overhear all that they said. But these lords and ladies were altogether unaware that the Queen could overhear them, so that they talked and laughed very freely, and the Queen greatly enjoyed their discourse and the music that they made.

That day was extraordinarily balmy, and it being well toward the sloping of the afternoon, those lords and ladies were clad in very gay attire. And of all who were there Sir Gawaine was the most gayly clad, for he was dressed in sky-blue silk embroidered with threads of silver. And Sir Gawaine was playing upon the lute and singing a ballad in an exceedingly pleasing voice so that Queen Guinevere, as she sat at the window beside the open casement, was very well content for to listen to him.

Now there was a certain greyhound of which Queen Guinevere was wonderfully fond; so much so that she had adorned its neck with a collar *Sir Gawaine* of gold inset with carbuncles. At that moment the hound *striketh the* came running into that garden and his feet were wet and *Queen's hound.* soiled with earth. So, hearing Sir Gawaine singing and playing upon the lute, that hound ran unto him and leaped upon him. At this Sir Gawaine was very wroth, wherefore he clinched his hand and smote the hound upon the head with the knuckles thereof, so that the hound lifted up his voice with great outcry.

But when Queen Guinevere beheld that blow she was greatly offended, wherefore she called out from her window, "Why dost thou smite my dog, Messire?" And those lords and ladies who were below in the garden were very much surprised and were greatly abashed to find that the Queen was so nigh unto them as to overhear all that they had said and to behold all that they did.

But Sir Gawaine spake up very boldly, saying, "Thy dog affronted me, Lady, and whosoever affronteth me, him I strike."

Then Queen Guinevere grew very angry with Sir Gawaine, wherefore she said, "Thy speech is over-bold, Messire," and Sir Gawaine said, "Not over-bold, Lady; but only bold enough for to maintain my rights."

At this speech the Lady Guinevere's face flamed like fire and her eyes shone very bright and she said, "I am sure that thou dost forget unto *Of the quar-* whom thou speakest, Sir Knight," at the which Sir Gawaine *rel of the* smiled very bitterly and said, "And thou, Lady, dost not re- *Queen and* member that I am the son of a king so powerful that he needs *Sir Gawaine.* no help from any other king for to maintain his rights."

At these words all those who were there fell as silent as though they were turned into stones, for that speech was exceedingly bold and haughty. Wherefore all looked upon the ground, for they durst not look either upon Queen Guinevere nor upon Sir Gawaine. And the Lady Guinevere, also, was silent for a long time, endeavoring to recover herself from that speech, and when she spake, it was as though she was half smothered by her anger. And she said, "Sir Knight, thou art proud and arrogant beyond measure, for I did never hear of anyone who dared to give reply unto his Queen as thou hast spoken unto me. But this is my Court, and I may command in it as I choose; wherefore I do now bid thee for to be-gone and to show thy face no more, either here nor in Hall nor any of the places where I hold my Court. For thou art an offence unto me, wherefore in none of these places shalt thou have leave to show thy face until thou dost ask my pardon for the affront which thou hast put upon me." Then Sir Gawaine arose and bowed very low to the Queen Guinevere and he said, "Lady, I go. Nor will I return thitherward until thou art willing for to tell me that thou art sorry for the discourteous way in which thou hast entreated me now and at other times before my peers."

So saying, Sir Gawaine took his leave from that place, nor did he turn his head to look behind him. And Queen Guinevere went into her cham-ber and wept in secret for anger and for shame. For indeed she was great-ly grieved at what had befallen; yet was she so proud that she would in no wise have recalled the words that she had spoken, even had she been able for to have done so.

Now when the news of that quarrel had gone about the castle it came unto the ears of Sir Ewaine, wherefore Sir Ewaine went straightway unto Sir Gawaine, and asked him what was ado, and Sir Gawaine, who was like one distraught and in great despair, told him everything. Then Sir Ewaine said: "Thou wert certainly wrong for to speak unto the Queen as thou didst. Nevertheless, if thou art banished from this Court, I will go with thee, for thou art my cousin-german and my companion, and my heart cleaveth unto thee." So Sir Ewaine went unto King Arthur, and he said, "Lord, my cousin, Sir Gawaine, hath been banished from this Court by the Queen. And though I may not say that he hath not deserved that punishment, yet I would fain crave thy leave for to go along with him."

At this King Arthur was very grieved, but he maintained a steadfast countenance, and said, "Messire, I will not stay thee from going where it pleases thee. As for thy kinsman, I daresay he gave the Queen such great offence that she could not do otherwise than as she did."

So both Sir Ewaine and Sir Gawaine went unto their inns and com-manded their esquires for to arm them. Then they, with their esquires, went forth from Camelot, betaking their way toward the forest lands. *Sir Gawaine and Sir Ewaine quit the Court.*

There those two knights and their esquires travelled for all that day un-til the gray of the eventide, what time the birds were singing their last songs ere closing their eyes for the night. So, finding the evening draw-ing on apace, those knights were afraid that they would not be able to find kindly lodging ere the night should descend upon them, and they talked together a great deal concerning that thing. But as they came to the top of a certain hill, they beheld below them a valley, very fair and well tilled, with many cottages and farm-crofts. And in the midst of that valley was a goodly abbey very fair to look upon; wherefore Sir Gawaine said unto Sir Ewaine: "If yonder abbey is an abbey of monks, I believe we shall find excellent lodging there for to-night."

They come to an abbey of monks. So they rode down into that valley and to the abbey, and they found a porter at the wicket of whom they learned that it was indeed an abbey of monks. Wherefore they were very glad and made great rejoicing.

But when the abbot of that abbey learned who they were and of what quality and high estate, he was exceedingly pleased for to welcome them, wherefore he brought them into that part of the abbey where he himself dwelt. There he bade them welcome and had set before them a good supper, whereat they were very much rejoiced. Now the abbot was merry of soul, and took great pleasure in discourse with strangers, so he diligently inquired of those two knights concerning the reason why they were errant. But they told him naught concerning that quarrel at Court, but only that they were in search of adventure. Upon this the abbot said, "Ha, Messires, if ye are in search of adventures, ye may find one not very far from this place."

The abbot telleth the knights of a good adventure. So Sir Gawaine said, "What adventure is that?" And the abbot replied, "I will tell ye; if ye will travel to the eastward from this place, ye will come, after a while, to a spot where ye shall find a very fair castle of gray stone. In front of that castle ye will find a good level meadow, and in the midst of the meadow a sycamore-tree, and upon the sycamore-tree a shield to which certain ladies offer affront in a very singular manner. If ye forbid those ladies to affront that shield you will discover a very good adventure."

Then Sir Gawaine said, "That is a very strange matter. Now, to-morrow morning we will go to that place and will endeavor to discover of what sort that adventure may be." And the abbot said, "Do so," and laughed in great measure.

So when the next morning had come, Sir Gawaine and Sir Ewaine gave adieu unto the abbot, and took their leave of that place, riding away unto the eastward, as the abbot had advised. And after they had ridden in that direction for two or three hours or more they beheld before them the borders of a forest all green and shady with foliage, and very cheerful in the warmth of the early summer day. And, lo! immediately at the edge of the woodland there stood a fair, strong castle of gray stone, with windows of glass shining very bright against the sky.

Then Sir Gawaine and Sir Ewaine beheld that everything was as the abbot had said; for in front of the castle was a smooth, level meadow with a sycamore-tree in the midst thereof. And as they drew near they perceived that a sable shield hung in the branches of the tree, and in a little they could see that it bore the device of three white goshawks displayed. But that which was very extraordinary was that in front of *Sir Gawaine* that shield there stood seven young damsels, exceedingly fair *and Sir Ewaine* of face, and that these seven damsels continually offered a *behold the dam-* *sels assailing* great deal of insult to that shield. For some of those damsels *the shield.* smote it ever and anon with peeled rods of osier, and others flung lumps of clay upon it, so that the shield was greatly defaced therewith. Now nigh to the shield was a very noble-appearing knight clad all in black armor, and seated upon a black war-horse, and it was very plain to be seen that the shield belonged unto that knight, for otherwise he had no shield. Yet, though that was very likely his shield, yet the knight offered no protest either by word or by act to stay those damoiselles from offering affront thereunto.

Then Sir Ewaine said unto Sir Gawaine, "Yonder is a very strange thing that I behold; belike one of us is to encounter yonder knight." And Sir Gawaine said, "Maybe so." Then Sir Ewaine said, "If it be so then I will undertake the adventure." "Not so," said Sir Gawaine, "for I will undertake it myself, I being the elder of us twain, and the better seasoned in knighthood." So Sir Ewaine said, "Very well. Let it be that way, for thou art a very much more powerful knight than I, and it would be a pity for one of us to fail in this undertaking." Thereupon Sir Gawaine said, "Let be, then, and I will undertake it."

So he set spurs to his horse and he rode rapidly to where those damsels offered affront in that way to the sable shield. And he set his spear in rest and shouted in a loud voice, "Get ye away! Get ye away!" So when those damsels beheld the armed knight riding at them in that wise they fled away shrieking from before him.

Then the Sable Knight, who sat not a great distance away, rode forward in a very stately manner unto Sir Gawaine, and he said, "Sir Knight, why dost thou interfere with those ladies?" Whereunto Sir Gawaine replied, "Because they offered insult unto what appeared to me to be a noble and knightly shield." At this the Sable Knight spake very haughtily, saying, "Sir Knight, that shield belongeth unto me and I do assure thee that I am very well able for to take care of it without the interference of any other defender." To which Sir Gawaine said, " It would appear not, Sir Knight."

Then the Sable Knight said, " Messire, an thou thinkest that thou art better able to take care of that shield than I, I think that thou wouldst do very well to make thy words good with thy body." To this Sir Gawaine said, " I will do my endeavor to show thee that I am better able to guard that shield than thou art who ownest it."

Upon this the Sable Knight, without further ado, rode unto the sycamore-tree, and took down from thence the shield that hung there.

Sir Gawaine and the Black Knight engage in battle. And he dressed the shield upon his arm and took his spear in hand and made him ready for defence. And Sir Gawaine likewise made him ready for defence, and then each knight took such station upon the field as appeared unto him to be fitting.

Now, when the people of that castle perceived that a combat of arms was toward, they crowded in great numbers to the walls, so that there were as many as twoscore ladies and esquires and folk of different degrees looking down upon that field of battle from the walls.

So when those knights were altogether prepared, Sir Ewaine gave the signal for encounter and each knight shouted aloud and drave spurs into his charger and rushed forward to the assault with a noise like thunder for loudness.

Now, Sir Gawaine thought that he should easily overcome his adversary in this assault and that he would be able to cast him down from out of his saddle without much pains, for there was hardly any knight in that realm equal to Sir Gawaine for prowess. And, indeed, he had never yet been unhorsed in combat excepting by King Arthur. So when those two rode to the assault, the one against the other, Sir Gawaine thought of a surety that his adversary would fall before him. But it was not so, for in that

The Black Knight over-throweth Sir Gawaine. attack Sir Gawaine's spear was broken into many pieces, but the spear of the Sable Knight held, so that Sir Gawaine was cast with great violence out of the saddle, smiting the dust with a terrible noise of falling. And so astonished was he at that fall that it appeared unto him not as though he fell from his saddle, but as though the earth rose up and smote him. Wherefore he lay for a while all stunned with the blow and with the astonishment thereof.

But when he heard the shouts of the people upon the castle wall, he immediately aroused himself from where he lay in the dust, and he was so filled with rage and shame that he was like one altogether intoxicated. Wherefore he drew his sword and rushed with great fury upon his enemy with intent to hew him down by main strength. Then that other knight, seeing him come thus at him, immediately voided his own saddle and drew his sword and put himself in posture either for assault or for defence. So they lashed together, tracing this way and that, and smiting with such fury that the blows they gave were most terrible for to behold. But when Sir Ewaine beheld how fierce was that assault, he set spurs unto his horse and pushed him between the knights-contestant, crying out aloud, "Sir Knights! Sir Knights! what is this? Here is no cause for such desperate battle." But Sir Gawaine cried out very furiously, "Let be! let be! and stand aside! for this quarrel concerns thee not." And the Sable Knight said, "A-horse or afoot, I am ready to meet that knight at any time."

But Sir Ewaine said, "Not so; ye shall fight no more in this quarrel. For shame, Gawaine! For shame to seek such desperate quarrel with a knight that did but meet thee in a friendly fashion in a fair contest!"

Then Sir Gawaine was aware that Sir Ewaine was both just and right; wherefore he put up his sword in silence, albeit he was like to weep for vexation at the shame of his overthrow. And the Sable Knight put up his sword also, and so peace was made betwixt those two.

Then the Sable Knight said, "I am glad that this quarrel is ended, for I perceive, Messires, that ye are assuredly knights of great nobility and gentleness of breeding; wherefore I would that we might henceforth be friends and companions instead of enemies. Wherefore I do beseech ye for to come with me a little ways from here where I have taken up my inn, so that we may rest and refresh ourselves in my pavilion."

Unto this Sir Ewaine said, "I give thee gramercy for thy courtesy, Sir Knight; and we will go with thee with all the pleasure that it is possible to feel." And Sir Gawaine said, "I am content." So these three knights straightway left the field of battle.

And when they had come to the edge of the forest Sir Gawaine and Sir Ewaine perceived a very fine pavilion of green silk set up beneath the tree. And about that pavilion were many attendants of divers sorts *Sir Gawaine* all clad in colors of green and white. So Sir Gawaine per- *and Sir Ewaine* ceived that the knight who had overthrown him was certainly *vilion of the* someone of very high estate, wherefore he was very greatly *Black Knight.* comforted. Then the esquires of those three knights came and removed the helmet, each esquire from his knight, so that the knight might be made comfortable thereby. And when this was done Sir Gawaine and Sir Ewaine perceived that the Sable Knight was very comely of countenance, being ruddy of face and with hair like to copper for redness. Then Sir Ewaine said unto the knight, "Sir Unknown Knight, this knight, my companion, is Sir Gawaine, son of King Urien of Gore, and I am Ewaine, the son of King Lot of Orkney. Now, I crave of thee that wilt make thyself known unto us in like manner."

"Ha," said the other; "I am glad that ye are such very famous and royal knights, for I am also of royal blood, being Sir Marhaus, the son of the King of Ireland."

Then Sir Gawaine was very glad to discover how exalted was the quality of that knight who overthrew him and he said unto Sir Marhaus, "Messire, I make my vow, that thou art one of the most terrible knights in the world. For thou hast done unto me this day what only one knight in all the world hath ever done, and that is King Arthur, who is my uncle and my lord. Now thou must certainly come unto the Court of King Arthur, for he will be wonderfully glad for to see thee, and maybe he will make thee a Knight of his Round Table—and there is no honor in all of the world that can be so great as that." Thus he spoke unthinkingly; and then he remembered. Wherefore he smote his fist against his forehead, crying out, "Aha! aha! who am I for to bid thee to come unto the Court of King Arthur, who only yesterday was disgraced and banished therefrom?"

Then Sir Marhaus was very sorry for Sir Gawaine, and he inquired concerning the trouble that lay upon him, and Sir Ewaine told Sir Marhaus all about that quarrel; at that Sir Marhaus was still more sorry for Sir Gawaine, wherefore he said, "Messires, I like ye both wonderfully well, and I would fain become your companion in the adventures ye are to undertake. For now I need remain here no longer. Ye must know that I was obliged to defend those ladies who assailed my shield until I had overthrown seven knights in their behalf. And I must tell ye that Sir Gawaine was the seventh knight I have overthrown. Wherefore, since I have now overthrown him, I am now released from my obligation and may go with ye."

Then Sir Gawaine and Sir Ewaine were very much astonished that any knight should lie beneath so strange an obligation as that—to defend those who assailed his shield—and they besought Sir Marhaus to tell them why he should have been obliged to fulfil such a pledge. So Sir Marhaus *Sir Marhaus* said, "I will tell ye. The case was this: Some whiles ago I *telleth his story.* was travelling in these parts with a hawk upon my wrist. At that time I was clad very lightly in holiday attire, to wit: I wore a tunic of green silk, and hosen one of green and one of white. And I had nothing upon me by way of defence but a light buckler and a short sword. Now, coming unto a certain stream of water, very deep and rapid, I perceived before me a bridge of stone crossing that stream, but so narrow that only one horseman might cross the bridge at a time. So I entered upon that bridge and was part way across it, when I perceived a knight in armor coming the other way. And behind the knight there sat upon a pillion a very fair lady with golden hair and very proud of demeanor. Now, when that knight perceived me upon the bridge, he cried aloud, ' Get back! get back! and suffer me to pass!' But this I would not do, but said, ' Not so, Sir Knight, for, having advanced so far upon this bridge, I have certes the right of way to complete my passage, and it is for you to wait and to permit me to cross.' But the knight would not do so, but immediately put himself in posture of offence and straightway came against me upon the bridge with intent either to slay me or to drive me back unto the other extremity of the bridge. But this he was not able to do, for I defended myself very well with my light weapons. And I so pushed my horse against his horse that I drave him backward from off the bridge and into the water, whereinto the horse and the knight and the lady all of them fell with a terrible uproar.

"At this the lady shrieked in great measure and both she and the knight were like to drown in the water, the knight being altogether clad in armor, so that he could not uplift himself above the flood. Wherefore, beholding their extremity, I leaped from off my horse and into the water, and with great ado and with much danger unto myself, I was able to bring them both unto the land.

"But that lady was very greatly offended with me, for her fair raiment was altogether wet and spoiled by the water, wherefore she upbraided me with great vehemence. So I kneeled down before her and besought her pardon with all humility, but she still continued to upbraid me. Then I offered unto her for to perform any penance that she might set upon me. At this the lady appeared to be greatly mollified, for she said, ' Very well, I will set thee a penance,' and when her knight had recovered she said, ' Come with us,' and so I mounted my horse and followed them. So after we had gone a considerable distance we came to this place and here she commanded me as follows: 'Sir Knight,' quoth she, ' this castle belongeth unto me and unto this knight who is my lord. Now, this shall be the penance for the affront thou hast given me: thou shalt take thy shield and hang it up in yonder sycamore-tree and every day I will send certain damsels of mine own out from the castle. And they shall offend against that shield and thou shalt not only suffer whatever offence they may offer, but thou shalt defend them against all comers until thou hast overcome seven knights.'

"So I have done until this morning, when thou, Sir Gawaine, camest hither. Thou art the seventh knight against whom I have contended, and as I have overcome thee, my penance is now ended and I am free."

Then Sir Gawaine and Sir Ewaine gave Sir Marhaus great joy that his penance was completed, and they were very well satisfied each party with the others. So Sir Gawaine and Sir Ewaine abided that night in the pavilion of Sir Marhaus and the next morning they arose and, having laved themselves in a forest stream, they departed from that place where they were.

So they entered the forest land once more and made their way by certain paths, they knew not whitherward ; and they travelled all that morning and until the afternoon was come.

Now, as they travelled thus Sir Marhaus said of a sudden, " Messires, know ye where we are come to ? " " Nay," they said, " we know not."

The three knights enter the Forest of Adventure. Then Sir Marhaus said, " This part of the forest is called Arroy and it is further called ' The Forest of Adventure.' For it is very well known that when a knight, or a party of knights enter this forest, they will assuredly meet with an adventure of some sort, from which some come forth with credit while others fail therein." And Sir Ewaine said, " I am glad that we have come hither. Now let us go forward into this forest."

So those three knights and their esquires continued onward in that woodland where was silence so deep that even the tread of their horses upon the earth was scarcely to be heard. And there was no note of bird and no sound of voice and hardly did any light penetrate into the gloom of that woodland. Wherefore those knights said unto one another, " This is soothly a very strange place and one, maybe, of enchantment."

Now when they had come into the very midst of these dark woodlands, they perceived of a sudden, in the pathway before them, a fawn as white *They behold a white fawn in the forest.* as milk. And round the neck of the fawn was a collar of pure gold. And the fawn stood and looked at them, but when they had come nigh to it, it turned and ran along a very narrow path. Then Sir Gawaine said, " Let us follow that fawn and see where it goeth." And the others said, " We are content." So they followed that narrow path until of a sudden they came to where was a little open lawn very bright with sunlight. In the midst of the lawn was a fountain of water, and there was no fawn to be seen, but, lo ! beside the fountain there *They behold a beautiful lady in the forest.* sat a wonderfully beautiful lady, clad all in garments of green. And the lady combed her hair with a golden comb, and her hair was like to the wing of a raven for blackness. And upon her arms she wore very wonderful bracelets of emeralds and of opal stones inset into cunningly wrought gold. Moreover, the face of the lady was like ivory for whiteness and her eyes were bright like jewels set in ivory. Now, when this lady perceived the knights she arose and laid aside her golden comb and bound up the locks of her hair with ribbons of scarlet silk, and thereupon, she came to those knights and gave them greeting.

Then those three knights gat them down straightway from off their horses, and Sir Gawaine said, " Lady, I believe that thou art not of mortal sort, but that thou art of faërie." Unto this the lady said, " Sir Gawaine, thou art right," and Sir Gawaine marvelled that she should know his name so well. Then he said to her, " Lady, who art thou ? " and she made answer, " My name is Nymue and I am the chiefest of those Ladies of the Lake of whom thou mayst have heard. For it was I who gave unto King Arthur his sword Excalibur; for I am very friendly unto King Arthur and to all the noble Knights of his Court. So it is that I know ye all. And I know that thou, Sir Marhaus, shall become one of the most famous Knights of the Round Table." And all they three marvelled at the lady's words. Then she said, " I prithee tell me what it is that ye seek in these parts ? " And they say, " We seek adventure." " Well," said she, " I will bring you unto adventure, but it is Sir Gawaine who must undertake it." And Sir Gawaine said, " That is very glad news." Then the lady said, " Take me behind you upon your saddle, Sir Gawaine, and I will show unto you that adventure." So Sir Gawaine took the lady up behind him upon the saddle, and lo! she brought with her a fragrance such as he had never known before ; for that fragrance was so subtle that it seemed to Sir Gawaine that the forest gave forth that perfume which the Lady of the Lake brought with her.

So the Lady of the Lake brought them by many devious ways out from that part of the forest; and she brought them by sundry roads and paths until they came out into an open country, very fruitful and pleasant to behold; and she brought them up a very high hill, and from the top of the hill they looked down upon a fruitful and level plain as upon a table spread out before them. And they beheld that in the midst of the plain was a noble castle built all of red stone and of red bricks; and they beheld that there was a small town built also of red bricks.

Now as they sat their horses there on top of the hill they perceived of a sudden a knight clad all in red armor who came forth from a glade of trees. And they saw that the knight paraded the meadow that lay in front of the castle, and they saw that he gave challenge to those within the castle. Then they perceived that the drawbridge of the castle was let fall of a sudden and that there issued from thence ten knights clad in complete armor. And they beheld those ten knights assail the one knight in red armor, and they beheld the one knight assail the ten. And they beheld that for a while those ten withstood the one, but that he assailed them so terribly that he smote down four of them very quickly. Then they beheld that the rest brake and fled from before that one, and that the Red Knight pursued the others about the meadow with great fury. And they saw that he smote down one from out his saddle and another and another until but two of those knights were left.

The three knights behold a very singular assault-at-arms.

Then Sir Gawaine said, " That is certainly a very wonderful sight for to see." But the Lady of the Lake only smiled and said, "Wait a little."

So they waited and they saw that when the Red Knight had smitten down all of his enemies but those two, and that when he had put those two in great peril of their lives, he of a sudden sheathed his sword and surrendered himself unto them. And they saw that those two knights brought the Red Knight to the castle, and that when they had brought him there a lady upon the wall thereof bespake that Red Knight as with great violence of language. And they beheld that those two knights took the Red Knight and bound his hands behind his back, and that they bound his feet beneath his horse's belly, and that they drave him away from that place.

All this they beheld from the top of that hill, and the Lady of the Lake said unto Sir Gawaine, " There thou shalt find thy adventure, Sir Gawaine." And Sir Gawaine said, " I will go," and the Lady of the Lake said, " Do so."

Thereupon, lo! she vanished from their sight and they were greatly amazed.

Sir Gawaine sups with ÿ Lady Ettard

Chapter Fifth.

How Sir Gawaine Met Sir Pellias and How He Promised to Aid Him With the Lady Ettard.

NOW, after that wonderful lady had disappeared from their sight in that manner, those three knights stood for a little while altogether astonished, for they wist not how to believe what their eyes had beheld. Then, by and by, Sir Gawaine spake, saying, "Certes, that was a very wonderful thing that happened to us, for in all my life I never knew so strange a miracle to befall. Now, it is very plain that some excellent adventure lieth in what we have seen, wherefore let us descend into yonder valley, for there we shall doubtless discover what that signifies which we have just now beheld. For I make my vow that I have hardly ever seen so terribly powerful a knight as he who has just now fought yonder battle, wherefore I can in no wise understand why, when he should so nearly have obtained a victory over his enemies, he should have surrendered himself to them as he did."

And Sir Ewaine and Sir Marhaus agreed that it would be well to go down and inquire what was the meaning of that which they had beheld.

So they three and their attendants rode down into the valley.

And they rode forward until they had come to a certain glade of trees and there they beheld three goodly pavilions that stood there: the one pavilion of white cloth, the second pavilion of green cloth, and the third pavilion of scarlet cloth.

Now, as the three knights-companion drew nigh to the pavilions, there came forth two knights to meet them. And when Sir Gawaine and Sir Ewaine saw the shields of the two, they immediately knew that they were Sir Brandiles and Sir Mador de la Porte. And in the same manner Sir Brandiles and Sir Mador de la Porte knew Sir Gawaine and Sir Ewaine, and each party was very much

The three knights meet the two.

astonished at thus meeting the other in so strange a place. So when they came together they gave one another very joyful greeting and clasped hands with strong love and good fellowship.

Then Sir Gawaine made Sir Marhaus acquainted with Sir Brandiles and Sir Mador de la Porte and thereupon the five knights all went together into those three pavilions, discoursing the while with great amity and pleasure. And when they had come into the pavilion of Sir Brandiles they found there spread a good refreshment of white bread and wine of excellent savor.

Then after a while Sir Gawaine said to Sir Brandiles and Sir Mador de la Porte, "Messires, we observed a little while ago a very singular thing; for, as we stood together at the top of yonder hill and looked down into this plain we beheld a single knight clad all in red armor who did battle with ten knights. And that one knight in red armor combated the ten with such fury that he drave them all from before him, though they were so many and he but one. And truly I make my vow that I have hardly ever seen a knight show such great prowess in arms as he. Yet, when he had overcome all but two of those knights, and was in fair way to win a clear victory, he suddenly yielded himself unto the two and suffered them to take him and bind him and drive him with great indignity from the field. Now, I pray ye, tell me what was the meaning of that which we beheld, and who was that knight who fought so great a battle and yet yielded himself so shamefully."

At this Sir Brandiles and Sir Mador de la Porte made no answer, but directed their looks another way, for they knew not what to say. But when Sir Gawaine beheld that they were abashed he began more than ever to wonder what that thing meant; wherefore he said, "What is this? Why do ye not answer me? I bid ye tell me what is the meaning of your looks, and who is that red knight!"

Then after a while Sir Mador de la Porte said, "I shall not tell you, but you may come and see."

Then Sir Gawaine began to think maybe there was something in this that it would be better not to publish, and that, haply, he had best examine further into the matter alone. So he said unto the other knights, "Bide ye here a little, Messires, and I will go with Sir Mador de la Porte."

So Sir Gawaine went with Sir Mador de la Porte, and Sir Mador led him unto the white pavilion. And when they had come there Sir Mador drew aside the curtains of the pavilion, and he said, "Enter!" and Sir Gawaine entered.

Now, when he had come into the pavilion he perceived that a man sat upon a couch of rushes covered with an azure cloth, and in a little he perceived that man was Sir Pellias. But Sir Pellias saw not him immediately, but sat with his head bowed, like one altogether overwhelmed by a great despair. *Sir Mador de la Porte bringeth Sir Gawaine to Sir Pellias.*

But when Sir Gawaine beheld who it was that sat upon the couch, he was greatly amazed and cried out, " Ha! is it thou, Sir Pellias? is it thou?"

But when Sir Pellias heard Sir Gawaine's voice, and when he perceived who it was that spake to him, he emitted an exceedingly bitter cry. And sprang to his feet and ran as far away as the walls of the pavilion would let him, and turned his face unto the walls thereof.

Then, after a while, Sir Gawaine spoke very sternly to Sir Pellias, saying, " Messire, I am astonished and very greatly ashamed that a Knight of King Arthur's Royal Court and of his Round Table should behave in so dishonorable a manner as I saw thee behave this day. For it is hardly to be believed that a knight of *Sir Gawaine rebukes Sir Pellias.* such repute and nobility as thou would suffer himself to be taken and bound by two obscure knights as thou didst suffer thyself this day. How couldst thou bring thyself to submit to such indignity and insult? Now, I do demand of thee that thou wilt explain this matter unto me."

But Sir Pellias was silent and would not make any reply. Then Sir Gawaine cried out very fiercely, " Ha! wilt thou not answer me?" and Sir Pellias shook his head.

Then Sir Gawaine said, still speaking very fiercely, " Messire! thou shalt answer me one way or another! For either thou shalt tell me the meaning of thy shameful conduct, or else thou shalt do extreme battle with me. For I will not suffer it that thou shalt bring such shame upon King Arthur and his Round Table without myself defending the honor and the credit of him and of it. One while thou and I were dear friends, but unless thou dost immediately exculpate thyself I shall hold thee in contempt, and shall regard thee as an enemy."

Upon this Sir Pellias spake like unto one that was nigh distracted, and he said, " I will tell thee all." Then he confessed everything unto Sir Gawaine, telling all that had befallen since that time when he had left the May Court of Queen Guinevere to enter upon this adventure, and Sir Gawaine listened unto him with great amazement. And when Sir Pellias had made an end of telling all that had befallen him, Sir Gawaine said, " Certes, this is very wonderful. Indeed, I cannot understand how thou camest to be so entangled in the charms of this lady unless she hath bewitched thee with some great enchantment."

Unto this Sir Pellias said, " Yea, I believe that I have been bewitched, for I am altogether beside myself in this, and am entirely unable to contain my passion."

Then Sir Gawaine bethought him for a long while, considering that matter very seriously; and by and by he said, " I have a plan, and it is this: I will go unto the Lady Ettard myself, and will inquire diligently into this affair. And if I find that anyone hath entangled thee in enchantments, it will go hard with me but I will punish that one with great dolor. For I shall not have it that another enchanter shall beguile thee as one hath already beguiled Merlin the Wise."

Then Sir Pellias said unto Sir Gawaine, " How wilt thou accomplish this matter so as to gain into the presence of the Lady Ettard ? "

Thereupon Sir Gawaine replied, " That I will tell thee. We twain shall exchange armor, and I will go unto the castle in thy armor. When

Sir Gawaine advises with Sir Pellias
I have come there I shall say that I have overcome thee in an encounter, and have taken thine armor away from thee. Then they will haply admit me into the castle to hear my story, and I shall have speech with her."

Then Sir Pellias said, " Very well; it shall be as thou dost ordain."

So Sir Pellias summoned an esquire, and Sir Gawaine summoned his esquire, and those two removed the armor from Sir Pellias, and clad Sir Gawaine therein. After they had done that Sir Gawaine mounted upon the horse of Sir Pellias, and rode openly into that field wherein Sir Pellias had aforetime paraded.

Now, it happened that the Lady Ettard was at that time walking upon a platform within the castle walls, from which place she looked down into that meadow. So when she beheld a red knight parading in the meadow, she thought it was Sir Pellias come thither again, and at that she was vexed and affronted beyond all measure. Wherefore she said unto those nigh her, " That knight vexes me so wofully that I fear me I shall fall ill of vexation if he cometh here many more times. I would that I knew how to rid myself of him; for already, and only an hour ago, I sent ten good knights against him, and he overcame them all with great despatch and with much dishonor unto them and unto me."

So she beckoned to the Red Knight, and when he had come nigh to the walls of the castle, she said to him, " Sir Knight, why dost thou come hitherward to afflict me and to affront me thus? Canst thou not understand that the more often thou comest to tease me in this manner, the more do I hate thee? "

Then Sir Gawaine opened the umbril of his helmet and showed his face, and the Lady Ettard saw that the Red Knight was not Sir Pellias. And Sir Gawaine said, " Lady, I am not that one whom thou supposest me to be, but another. For, behold! I have thine enemy's armor upon my body, wherefore thou mayst see that I have overcome him. For thou mayst suppose that it is hardly to be thought that I could wear his armor unless I took it from him by force of arms. Wherefore thou needst trouble thyself no more about him."

Then the Lady Ettard could not think otherwise than this knight (whom she knew not) had indeed overthrown Sir Pellias in a bout of arms, and had taken his armor away from him. And indeed she was exceedingly astonished that such a thing could have happened; for it appeared to her that Sir Pellias was one of the greatest knights in the world; wherefore she marvelled who this knight could be who had overthrown him in battle. So she gave command to sundry of those in attendance upon her that they should go forth and bring that red knight into the castle and that they should pay him great honor; for that he must assuredly be one of the very greatest champions in the world.

Thus Sir Gawaine came into the castle and was brought before the Lady Ettard where she stood in a wonderfully large and noble hall. For that hall was illuminated by seven tall windows of colored *Sir Gawaine* glass, and it was hung around with tapestries and hangings, *entereth Grant-* very rich and of a most excellent quality, wherefore Sir Ga- *mesnle.* waine was greatly astonished at the magnificence of all that he beheld in that place.

Now, Sir Gawaine had taken the helmet from off his head, and he bore it under his arm and against his hip, and his head was bare so that all who were there could see his face very plainly. Wherefore they all perceived that he was exceedingly comely, that his eyes were as blue as steel, his nose high and curved, and his hair and beard very dark and rich in color. Moreover, his bearing was exceedingly steadfast and haughty, so that those who beheld him were awed by the great knightliness of his aspect.

Then the Lady Ettard came to Sir Gawaine and gave him her hand, and he kneeled down and set it to his lips. And the lady bespoke him very graciously, saying, " Sir Knight, it would give me a great deal of pleasure if thou wouldst make us acquainted with thy name, and if thou wouldst proclaim thy degree of estate unto us."

Unto this Sir Gawaine made reply, " Lady, I cannot inform you of these things at these present, being just now vowed unto secrecy upon those points, wherefore I do crave your patience for a little."

Then the Lady Ettard said, " Sir Knight, it is a great pity that we may not know thy name and degree; ne'theless, though we are as yet in ignorance as to thy quality, I yet hope that thou wilt give us the pleasure of thy company awhile, and that thou wilt condescend to remain within this poor place for two days or three, whiles we offer thee such refreshment as we are able to do."

Now here a very untoward thing befell. To wit, it was this: The Lady Ettard had come to love that necklace of emeralds and of opal stones and

The magical necklace enchanteth Sir Gawaine. of gold that she had borrowed from Sir Pellias, and that to such a degree that she never let it depart from her whether by day or by night. Wherefore she wore it at that moment hanging about her neck and her throat. So, as she talked to Sir Gawaine, he looked upon that necklace, and the enchantment thereof began to take a very great hold upon him. For he presently began to feel as though his heart was drawn with exceeding ardency out of his bosom and unto the Lady Ettard; so much so that, in a little while, he could not at all keep his regard withdrawn from her. And the more that he looked upon the necklace and the lady the more did the enchantment of the jewel take hold upon his spirits. Accordingly, when the Lady Ettard spake so graciously unto him, he was very glad to accept of her kindness; wherefore he said, gazing very ardently at her the whiles, "Lady, thou art exceedingly gentle to extend so great a courtesy unto me; wherefore I shall be glad beyond measure for to stay with thee for a short while."

At these words the Lady Ettard was very greatly pleased, for she said to herself, "Certes, this knight (albeit I know not who he may be) must be a champion of extraordinary prowess and of exalted achievement. Now, if I can persuade him to remain in this castle as my champion, then shall I doubtless gain very great credit thereby; for I shall have one for to defend my rights who must assuredly be the greatest knight in all the world." Wherefore she set forth every charm and grace of demeanor to please Sir Gawaine, and Sir Gawaine was altogether delighted by the kindness of her manner.

Now, Sir Engamore was there present at that time, wherefore he was very greatly troubled in spirit. For in the same degree that Sir Gawaine received courtesy from the Lady Ettard, in that same degree Sir Engamore was cast down into great sorrow and distress—so much so that it was a pity for to see him. For Sir Engamore said to himself, "Aforetime, ere these foreign knights came hitherward, the Lady Ettard was very kind to me, and was willing to take me for her champion and lord. But first came Sir Pellias and overthrew me, and now cometh this strange knight and overthroweth him, wherefore, in the presence of such a great champion as this, I am come to be as nothing in her sight." So Sir Engamore withdrew himself from that place and went unto his closet, where he sat himself down alone in great sorrow.

Now the Lady Ettard had given command that a very noble and splendid feast should be prepared for Sir Gawaine and for herself, and whilst it was preparing she and Sir Gawaine walked together in the pleasaunce of the castle. For there was a very pleasant shade in the place, and flowers grew there in great abundance, and many birds sang very sweetly in among the blossoms of the trees. And as Sir Gawaine and the lady walked thus together, the attendants stood at a little distance and regarded them. And they said to one another, "Assuredly it would be a very good thing if the Lady Ettard would take this knight for her champion, and if he should stay here in Grantmesnle forever."

So Sir Gawaine and the lady walked together, talking very cheerfully, until sunset, and at that time the supper was prepared and they went in and sat down to it. And as they supped, a number of pages, very fair of face, played upon harps before them; and sundry damsels sang very sweetly in accord to that music, so that the bosom of Sir Gawaine was greatly expanded with joy. Where- *Sir Gawaine and the Lady Ettard feast together.* fore he said to himself, "Why should I ever leave this place? Lo! I have been banished from King Arthur's Court; why then should I not establish here a Court of mine own that might, in time, prove to be like to his for glory?" And the Lady Ettard was so beautiful in his eyes that this seemed to him to be a wonderfully pleasant thought.

Now turn we unto Sir Pellias:

For after Sir Gawaine had left him, the heart of Sir Pellias began to misgive him that he had not been wise; and at last he said to himself, "Suppose that Sir Gawaine should forget his duty to me when he meeteth the Lady Ettard. For it seems that haply *Sir Pellias is a-doubt.* she possesses some potent charm that might well draw the heart of Sir Gawaine unto her. Wherefore if Sir Gawaine should come within the circle of such enchantment as that, he may forget his duty unto me and may transgress against the honor of his knighthood."

And the more that Sir Pellias thought of this the more troubled he grew in his mind. So at last, when evening had fallen, he called an esquire unto him and he said, "Go, and fetch me hither the garb of a black friar, for I would fain go unto the castle of Grantmesnle in disguise." So the esquire went as he commanded and brought him such a garb, and Sir Pellias clad himself therein.

Now, by that time, the darkness had come entirely over the face of the earth so that it would not have been possible for anyone to know Sir Pellias, even if they had seen his face. So he went unto the castle, and they who were there, thinking that he was a black friar, as he appeared to be, admitted him into the castle by the postern gate.

So, as soon as Sir Pellias had come into the castle, he began to make diligent inquiry concerning where he might find that knight who had come thither in the afternoon, and those within the castle, still think-

Sir Pellias cometh to the castle in disguise. ing him to be a friar of black orders, said unto him, "What would ye with that knight?" To the which Sir Pellias said, "I have a message for him." They of the castle said, "Ye cannot come at that knight just now, for he is at supper with the Lady Ettard, and he holds her in pleasant discourse."

At this Sir Pellias began to wax very angry, for he greatly misliked the thought that Sir Gawaine should then make merry with the Lady Ettard. So he said, speaking very sternly, "I must presently have speech with that knight, wherefore I bid ye to bring me unto him without delay." Then they of the castle said, "Wait and we will see if that knight is willing to have you come to him."

So one of the attendants went unto that place where Sir Gawaine sat at supper with the Lady Ettard, and he said, "Sir Knight, there hath come hither a black friar who demandeth to have present speech with thee, and he will not be denied, but continually maketh that demand."

At this Sir Gawaine was greatly troubled in his conscience, for he knew that he was not dealing honorably by Sir Pellias, and he pondered whether or not this black friar might be a messenger from his friend. But yet he could not see how he might deny such a messenger speech with him. So, after a while of thought, he said, "Fetch the black friar hither and let him deliver his message to me."

So Sir Pellias, in the garb of a black friar, was brought by the attendants into the outer room of that place where Sir Gawaine sat at supper with the lady. But for a little time Sir Pellias did not enter the room, but stood behind the curtain of the ante-room and looked upon them, for he desired to make sure as to whether or no Sir Gawaine was true to him.

Now everything in that room where the knight and the lady sat was bedight with extraordinary splendor, and it was illuminated by a light of several score of waxen tapers that sent forth a most delightful perfume as they burned. And as Sir Pellias stood behind the curtains, he beheld Sir Gawaine and the Lady Ettard as they sat at the table together, and he saw that they were filled with pleasure in the company of one another.

And he saw that Sir Gawaine and the lady quaffed wine out of the same chalice and that the cup was of gold. And as he saw those two making merry with one another, he was filled with great anger and indignation, for he now perceived that Sir Gawaine had betrayed him.

So, by and by, he could contain himself no longer, wherefore he took five steps into that room and stood before Sir Gawaine and the Lady Ettard. And, when they looked upon him in great surprise, he cast back the hood from his face and they knew him. Then the Lady Ettard shrieked with great vehemence, crying out, "I have been betrayed!" and Sir Gawaine sat altogether silent, for he had not a single word to say either to the lady or to Sir Pellias.

Then Sir Pellias came close to the Lady Ettard with such a fell countenance that she could not move for fear. And when he had come nigh to her he catched that necklace of emeralds and opal stones and gold with such violence that he brake the clasp thereof and so plucked it from her neck. Then he said, "This is mine and thou hast no right to it!" And therewith he thrust it into his bosom. Then he turned upon Sir Gawaine where he sat, and he said, "Thou art false both unto thy knighthood and unto thy friendship, for thou hast betrayed me utterly." There- *Sir Pellias* upon he raised his arm and smote Sir Gawaine upon the face *places affront* with the back of his hand so violently that the mark of his *upon Sir Ga-* fingers was left in red all across the cheek of Sir Gawaine. *waine.*

Then Sir Gawaine fell as pale as ashes and he cried out, "Sir, I have in sooth betrayed thee, but thou hast offered such affront to me that our injury is equal." To the which Sir Pellias made reply, "Not so; for the injury I gave to thee is only upon thy cheek, but the injury thou gavest to me is upon my heart. Ne'theless, I will answer unto thee for the affront I have done thee. But thou also shalt answer unto me for the offence thou hast done unto me, in that thou hast betrayed me."

Then Sir Gawaine said, "I am willing to answer unto thee in full measure." And Sir Pellias said, "Thou shalt indeed do so." Thereupon he turned and left that place, nor did he so much as look again either at Sir Gawaine or at the Lady Ettard.

But, now that the Lady Ettard no longer had the magic collar about her neck, Sir Gawaine felt nothing of the great enchantment that had afore-time drawn him so vehemently unto her. Accordingly, he now suffered a misliking for her as great as that liking which had aforetime drawn him unto her. Wherefore he said to himself, "How was it possible that for this lady I could have so betrayed my knighthood and have done so much harm unto my friend!" So he pushed back his chair very violently and arose from that table with intent to leave her.

But when the Lady Ettard saw his intent she spake to him with very great anger, for she was very much affronted in that he had deceived her when he said that he had overcome Sir Pellias. Wherefore she said with

Sir Gawaine and the Lady Ettard speak bitterly together.
great heat, "Thou mayst go, and I am very willing for to have thee do so, for thou didst say false when thou didst tell me that thou hadst overcome Sir Pellias. For now I perceive that he is both a stronger and a nobler knight than thou. For he smote thee as though thou wert his servant, and thou yet bearest the marks of his fingers upon thy cheek."

At this Sir Gawaine was exceedingly wroth and entirely filled with the shame of that which had befallen him, wherefore he said, " Lady, I think thou hast bewitched me to bring me to such a pass of dishonor. As for Sir Pellias, look forth into that meadow to-morrow and see if I do not put a deeper mark upon him than ever he hath put upon me." Thereupon he left that place and went down into the court-yard and called upon the attendants who were there for to fetch him his horse. So they did as he commanded and he straightway rode forth into the night.

And he was very glad of the darkness of the night, for it appeared to him that it was easier to bear his shame in the darkness, wherefore when he had come to the glade of trees he would not enter the pavilion where his friends were. And also, when Sir Ewaine and Sir Marhaus came out unto him and bade him to come in, he would not do so, but stayed without in the darkness; for he said unto himself, " If I go in where is a light, haply they will behold the mark of Sir Pellias his hand upon my face."

So he stayed without in the darkness and bade them to go away and leave him alone.

But when they had gone he called his esquire unto him and he said, " Take this red armor off me and carry it into the pavilion of Sir Pellias, for I hate it." So the esquire did as Sir Gawaine commanded, and Sir Gawaine walked up and down for the entire night, greatly troubled in spirit and in heart.

The Lady of the Lake finds Sr. Pellias wounded.

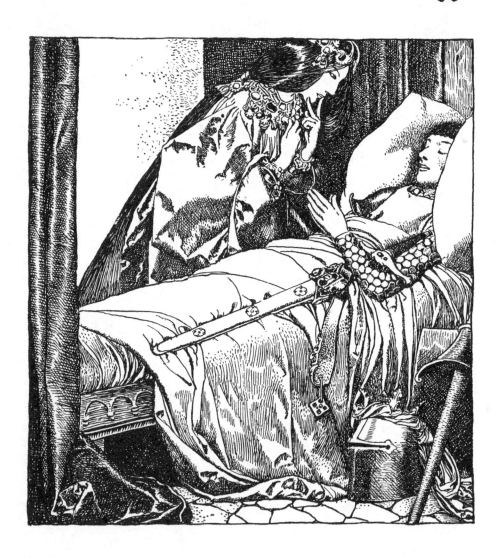

Chapter Sixth.

How the Lady of the Lake Took Back Her Necklace From Sir Pellias.

NOW, when the next morning had come, Sir Gawaine summoned his esquire unto him and said, "Fetch hither my armor and case me in it." And the esquire did so. Then Sir Gawaine said, "Help me unto my horse," and the esquire did so. And the morning was still very early, with the grass all lustrous and sparkling with dew, and the little birds singing with such vehemence that it might have caused anyone great joy to be alive. Wherefore, when Sir Gawaine was seated a-horseback and in armor, he began to take more courage unto himself, and the dark vapors that had whilom overshadowed him lifted themselves a little. So he bespoke his esquire with stronger Sir Gawaine voice, saying, "Take this glove of mine and bear it to Sir *issues challenge* Pellias and tell him that Sir Gawaine parades in the meadow *to Sir Pellias.* in front of the castle and that he there challenges Sir Pellias for to meet him a-horse or afoot, howsoever that knight may choose."

At these that esquire was very much astonished, for Sir Gawaine and Sir Pellias had always been such close friends that there was hardly their like for friendship in all that land, wherefore their love for one another had become a byword with all men. But he held his peace concerning his thoughts and only said, "Wilt thou not eat food ere thou goest to battle?" And Sir Gawaine said, "Nay, I will not eat until I have fought. Wherefore do thou go and do as I have bid thee."

So Sir Gawaine's esquire went to Sir Pellias in his pavilion and he gave unto that knight the glove of Sir Gawaine, and he delivered Sir Gawaine's message to him. And Sir Pellias said, "Tell thy master that I will come forth to meet him as soon as I have broken my fast."

Now, when the news of that challenge had come to the ears of Sir Brandiles and Sir Mador de la Porte and Sir Ewaine and Sir Marhaus, those knights were greatly disturbed thereat, and Sir Ewaine said to the others, " Messires, let us go and make inquiries concerning this business." So the four knights went to the white pavilion where Sir Pellias was breaking his fast.

And when they had come into the presence of Sir Pellias, Sir Ewaine said to him, " What is this quarrel betwixt my kinsman and thee ? " And Sir Pellias made reply, " I will not tell thee, so, let be and meddle not with it."

Then Sir Ewaine said, " Wouldst thou do serious battle with thy friend ? " To which Sir Pellias said, " He is a friend to me no longer."

Then Sir Brandiles cried out, " It is a great pity that a quarrel should lie betwixt such friends as thou and Sir Gawaine. Wilt thou not let us make peace betwixt you ? " But Sir Pellias replied, " Ye cannot make peace, for this quarrel cannot be stayed until it is ended."

Then those knights saw that their words could be of no avail and they went away and left Sir Pellias.

So when Sir Pellias had broken his fast he summoned an esquire named Montenoir, and he bade him case him in that red armor that he had worn for all this time, and Montenoir did so. Then, when Sir Pellias was clad in that armor, he rode forth into the meadow before the castle where Sir Gawaine paraded. And when he had come thither those four other knights came to him again and besought him that he would let peace be made betwixt him and Sir Gawaine, but Sir Pellias would not listen to them, and so they went away again and left him, and he rode forth into the field before the castle of Grantmesnle.

Now a great concourse of people had come down upon the castle walls for to behold that assault-at-arms, for news thereof had gone all about that place. And it had also come to be known that the knight that would do combat with Sir Pellias was that very famous royal knight hight Sir Gawaine, the son of King Lot of Orkney, and a nephew of King Arthur; wherefore all the people were very desirous to behold so famous a knight do battle.

Likewise the Lady Ettard came down to the walls and took her stand in a lesser tower that overlooked the field of battle. And when she had taken her stand at that place she beheld that Sir Pellias wore that necklace of emeralds and opal stones and gold above his body armor, and her heart went out to him because of it, wherefore she hoped that he might be the victor in that encounter.

Then each knight took his station in such place as seemed to him to be fitting, and they dressed each his spear and his shield and made him ready for the assault. Then, when they were in all ways prepared, Sir Marhaus gave the signal for the assault. Thereupon each knight in- *Sir Pellias and* stantly quitted that station which he held, dashing against the *Sir Gawaine* other with the speed of lightning, and with such fury that the *do battle.* earth thundered and shook beneath their horses' hoofs. So they met fairly in the centre of the course, each knight striking the other in the very midst of his defences. And in that encounter the spear of Sir Gawaine burst even to the hand-guard, but the spear of Sir Pellias held, so *Sir Pellias* that Sir Gawaine was cast out of his saddle with terrible vio- *overthroweth* lence, smiting the earth with such force that he rolled thrice *Sir Gawaine.* over in the dust and then lay altogether motionless as though bereft of life.

At this, all those people upon the walls shouted with a great voice, for it was an exceedingly noble assault-at-arms.

Then the four knights who stood watching that encounter made all haste unto Sir Gawaine where he lay ; and Sir Pellias also rode back and sat his horse nigh at hand. Then Sir Ewaine and Sir Gawaine's esquire unlaced the helmet of Sir Gawaine with all speed, and, behold ! his face was the color of ashes and they could not see that he breathed.

Thereupon Sir Marhaus said, "I believe that thou hast slain this knight, Sir Pellias," and Sir Pellias said, "Dost thou think so?" "Yea," quoth Sir Marhaus, "and I deem it a great pity." Unto which Sir Pellias made reply, "He hath not suffered more than he deserved."

At these words Sir Ewaine was filled with great indignation, wherefore he cried out, "Sir Knight, I think that thou forgettest the quality of this knight. For not only is he a fellow-companion of the Round Table, to whom thou hast vowed entire brotherhood, but he is also the son of a king and the nephew of King Arthur himself."

But to this Sir Pellias maintained a very steadfast countenance and replied, "I would not repent me of this were that knight a king in his own right instead of the son of a king."

Then Sir Ewaine lifted up his voice with great indignation, crying out upon Sir Pellias, "Begone ! or a great ill may befall thee." "Well," said Sir Pellias, "I will go."

Upon this he turned his horse and rode away from that place and entered the woodland and so was gone from their sight.

Then those others present lifted up Sir Gawaine and bare him away unto the pavilion late of Sir Pellias, and there they laid him upon the couch of Sir Pellias. But it was above an hour ere he recovered *Sir Pellias* himself again ; and for a great part of that while those nigh *departs into* unto him believed him to have been dead. *the forest.*

But not one of those knights wist what was the case; to wit, that Sir Pellias had been so sorely wounded in the side in that encounter that it *Sir Pellias is* was not to be hoped that he could live for more than that day. *sore wounded.* For, though the spear of Sir Gawaine had burst, and though Sir Pellias had overthrown him entirely, yet the head of Sir Gawaine's spear had pierced the armor of Sir Pellias, and had entered his side and had there broken off, so that of the iron of the spear, the length of the breadth of a palm had remained in the body of Sir Pellias a little above the midriff. Wherefore, while Sir Pellias sat there talking so steadfastly unto those four knights, he was yet whiles in a great passion of pain, and the blood ran down into his armor in abundance. So, what with the loss of the blood, and of the great agony which he suffered, the brain of Sir Pellias swam as light as a feather all the time that he held talk with those others. But he said not a word unto them concerning the grievous wound he had received, but rode away very proudly into the forest.

But when he had come into the forest he could not forbear him any longer, but fell to groaning very sorely, crying out, "Alas! alas! I have certes got my death-wound in this battle!"

Now it chanced that morn that the damsel Parcenet had ridden forth to fly a young gerfalcon, and a dwarf belonging to the Lady Ettard had ridden with her for company. So, as the damsel and the dwarf rode through a certain part of the forest skirt, not a very great distance from Grantmesnle, where the thicker part of the woodland began and the thinner part thereof ceased, the damsel heard a voice in the woodlands, lamenting with very great dolor. So she stopped and harkened, and by and by she heard that voice again making a great moan. Then Parcenet said to the dwarf, "What is that I hear? Certes, it is the voice of someone in lamentation. Now let us go and see who it is that maketh such woful moan." And the dwarf said, "It shall be as thou sayest."

So the damsel and the dwarf went a little way farther and there they beheld a knight sitting upon a black horse beneath an oak-tree. And that *How Parcenet* knight was clad altogether in red armor, wherefore, Parcenet *findeth Sir Pel-* knew that it must be Sir Pellias. And she saw that Sir Pel-*lias wounded* lias leaned with the butt of his spear upon the ground and so *in the forest.* upheld himself upon his horse from which he would otherwise have fallen because of his great weakness, and all the while he made that great moan that Parcenet had heard. So, seeing him in this sorry condition, Parcenet was overcome with great pity, and she made haste to him crying out, "Alas! Sir Pellias, what ails thee?"

Then Sir Pellias looked at her as though she were a great way removed from him, and, because of the faintness of his soul, he beheld her, as it were, through thin water. And he said, very faintly, "Maiden, I am sore hurt." Thereupon she said, "How art thou hurt, Sir Pellias?" And he replied, "I have a grievous wound in my side, for a spear's point standeth therein nigh a palm's breadth deep so that it reaches nearly to my heart, wherefore, meseems that I shall not live for very long."

Upon this the maiden cried out, "Alas! alas! what is this!" and she made great lament and smote her hands together with sorrow that that noble knight should have come to so grievous an extremity.

Then the dwarf that was with Parcenet, seeing how greatly she was distracted by sorrow, said, "Damsel, I know of a certain place in this forest (albeit it is a considerable distance from this) where there dwelleth a certain very holy hermit who is an extraordinarily skilful leech. Now, an we may bring this knight unto the chapel where that hermit dwelleth, I believe that he may be greatly holpen unto health and ease again."

Upon this Parcenet said, "Gansaret"—for Gansaret was the dwarf's name—"Gansaret, let us take this knight unto that place as quickly as we are able. For I tell thee sooth when I say that I have a very great deal of love for him." "Well," said the dwarf, "I will show thee where that chapel is."

So the dwarf took the horse of Sir Pellias by the bridle-rein and led the way through that forest, and Parcenet rode beside Sir Pellias and upheld him upon his saddle. For some whiles Sir Pellias fainted with sickness and with pain so that he would else have fallen had she not upheld him. Thus they went forward very sorrowfully and at so slow a pace that it was noontide ere they came to that certain very dense and lonely part of the forest where the hermit abided.

And when they had come unto that place the dwarf said, "Yonder, damsel, is the chapel whereof I spake."

Then Parcenet lifted up her eyes and she beheld where was a little woodland chapel built in among the leafy trees of the forest. And around this chapel was a little open lawn bedight with flowers, and nigh to the door of the hermitage was a fountain of water as clear as crystal. And this was a very secret and lonely place and withal very silent and peaceful, for in front of the chapel they beheld a wild doe and her fawn browsing upon the tender grass and herbs without any fear of harm. And when the dwarf and the maiden and the wounded knight drew nigh, the doe and the fawn looked up with great wide eyes and spread their large ears with wonder, yet fled not, fearing no harm, but by and by began their browsing again. Likewise all about the chapel in the branches of the trees were great quantities of birds, singing and chirping very cheerfully. And those birds were waiting for their mid-day meal that the hermit was used to cast unto them.

(Now this was that same forest sanctuary whereunto King Arthur had come that time when he had been so sorely wounded by Sir Pellinore as hath been aforetold in this history.)

As the maiden and the dwarf and the wounded knight drew nigh to this chapel, a little bell began ringing very sweetly so that the sound thereof echoed all through those quiet woodlands, for it was now the hour of noon. And Sir Pellias heard that bell as it were a great way off, and first he said, " Whither am I come? " and then he made shift to cross himself. And Parcenet crossed herself and the dwarf kneeled down and crossed himself. Then when the bell had ceased ringing, the dwarf cried out in a loud voice, " What ho! what ho! here is one needing help! "

Then the door of the sanctuary was opened and there came forth from that place a very venerable man with a long white beard as it were of *Parcenet and the* finely carded wool. And, lo! as he came forth, all those *dwarf bring Sir* birds that waited there flew about him in great quantities, for *Pellias to the* *hermit of the* they thought that he had come forth for to feed them; where- *forest.* fore the hermit was compelled to brush those small fowls away with his hands as he came unto where the three were stationed.

And when he had come unto them he demanded of them who they were and why they had come thither with that wounded knight. So Parcenet told him how it was with them, and of how they had found Sir Pellias so sorely wounded in the forest that morning and had brought him hither-ward.

Then, when the hermit had heard all of her story, he said, " It is well and I will take him in." So he took Sir Pellias into his cell, and when they had helped lay him upon the couch, Parcenet and the dwarf went their way homeward again.

After they had gone, the hermit examined the hurt of Sir Pellias, and Sir Pellias lay in a deep swoon. And the swoon was so deep that the hermit beheld that it was the death-swoon, and that the knight was nigh to his end. So he said, " This knight must assuredly die in a very little while, for I can do naught to save him." Wherefore he immediately quitted the side of Sir Pellias and set about in haste to prepare the last sacrament such as might be administered unto a noble knight who was dying.

Now whiles the hermit was about this business the door opened of a

sudden and there came into that place a very strange lady clad all in green
and bedight around the arms with armlets of emeralds and *The Lady of the*
opal stones inset into gold.   And her hair, which was very *Lake cometh to*
soft, was entirely black and was tied about with a cord of *Sir Pellias.*
crimson ribbon.   And the hermit beheld that her face was like to ivory
for whiteness and that her eyes were bright, like unto jewels set into ivory,
wherefore he knew that she was no ordinary mortal.

And this lady went straight to Sir Pellias and leaned over him so that
her breath touched his forehead.   And she said, "Alas! Sir Pellias, that
thou shouldst lie so."   "Lady," said the hermit, "thou mayst well say
'Alas,' for this knight hath only a few minutes to live."   To this the lady
said, "Not so, thou holy man, for I tell thee that this knight shall have a
long while yet to live."   And when she had said this she stooped and took
from about his neck that necklace of emeralds and opal stones and gold
that encircled it and she hung it about her own neck.

Now when the hermit beheld what she did, he said, "Lady, what is this
that thou doest, and why dost thou take that ornament from a dying man?"

But the lady made reply very tranquilly, "I gave it unto him, wherefore I do but take back again what is mine own.   But now I prithee let
me be with this knight for a little while, for I have great hope that I may
bring back life unto him again."

Then the hermit was a-doubt and he said, "Wilt thou endeavor to heal
him by magic?"   And the lady said, "If I do, it will not be by magic that
is black."

So the hermit was satisfied and went away, and left the lady alone with
Sir Pellias.

Now when the lady was thus alone with the wounded knight she immediately set about doing sundry very strange things.   For first she brought
forth a loadstone of great power and potency and this she set to the
wound.   And, lo! the iron of the spear-head came forth from the wound;
and as it came Sir Pellias groaned with great passion.   And when the
spear-point came forth there burst out a great issue of blood like to
a fountain of crimson.   But the lady immediately pressed a fragrant napkin of fine cambric linen to the wound and stanched the blood, and it bled
no more, for she held it within the veins by very potent spells of magic.
So, the blood being stanched in this wise, the lady brought *The Lady of the*
forth from her bosom a small crystal phial filled with an elixir *Lake healeth*
of blue color and of a very singular fragrance.   And she *Sir Pellias.*
poured some of this elixir between the cold and leaden lips of the knight;
and when the elixir touched his lips the life began to enter into his body

once more; for, in a little while, he opened his eyes and gazed about him with a very strange look, and the first thing that he beheld was that lady clad in green who stood beside him, and she was so beautiful that he thought that haply he had died and was in Paradise, wherefore he said, "Am I then dead?"

"Nay, thou art not dead," said the lady, "yet hast thou been parlously nigh to death." "Where then am I?" said Sir Pellias. And she replied, "Thou art in a deep part of the forest, and this is the cell of a saint-like hermit of the forest." At this Sir Pellias said, "Who is it that hath brought me back to life?" Upon this the lady smiled and said, "It was I."

Now for a little while Sir Pellias lay very silent, then by and by he spake and said, "Lady, I feel very strangely." "Yea," said the lady, "that is because thou hast now a different life." Then Sir Pellias said, "How is it with me?" And the lady said, "It is thus: that to bring thee back to life I gave thee to drink of a certain draught of an *elixir vitæ* so that thou art now only half as thou wert before; for if by the one half thou art mortal, by the other half thou art fay."

Then Sir Pellias looked up and beheld that the lady had about her neck the collar of emeralds and opal stones and gold which he had *Sir Pellias loveth the Lady of the Lake.* aforetime worn. And, lo! his heart went out to her with exceeding ardor, and he said, "Lady, thou sayest that I am half fay, and I do perceive that thou art altogether fay. Now, I pray thee to let it be that henceforth I may abide nigh unto where thou art." And the lady said, "It shall be as thou dost ask, for it was to that end I have suffered thee nearly to die, and then have brought thee back unto life again."

Then Sir Pellias said, "When may I go with thee?" And she said, "In a little when thou hast had to drink." "How may that be?" said Sir Pellias, "seeing that I am but yet like unto a little child for weakness." To the which the lady made reply, "When thou hast drunk of water thy strength shall return unto thee, and thou shalt be altogether well and whole again."

So the Lady of the Lake went out, and presently returned, bearing in her hand an earthen crock filled with water from the fountain near at hand. And when Sir Pellias had drunk that water he felt, of a sudden, his strength come altogether back to him.

Yet he was not at all as he had been before, for now his body felt as light as air, and his soul was dilated with a pure joy such as he had never felt in his life before that time. Wherefore he immediately uprose from his couch of pain, and he said, "Thou hast given life unto me again, now do I give that life unto thee forever."

Then the lady looked upon him and smiled with great loving-kindness. And she said, "Sir Pellias, I have held thee in tender regard ever since I beheld thee one day in thy young knighthood drink a draught of milk at a cottager's hut in this forest. For the day was warm and thou hadst set aside thy helmet, and a young milkmaid, brown of face and with bare feet, came and brought thee a bowl of milk, which same thou didst drink of with great appetite. That was the first time that I beheld thee—although thou didst not see me. Since that time I have had great friendship for all thy fellowship of King Arthur's Court and for King Arthur himself, all for thy sake."

Then Sir Pellias said, "Lady, wilt thou accept me for thy knight?" and she said, "Aye." Then Sir Pellias said, "May I salute thee?" And she said, "Yea, if it pleasures thee." So Sir Pellias kissed her upon the lips, and so their troth was plighted.

Now return we unto Parcenet and the dwarf:

After those two had left that hermitage in the woodland, they betook their way again toward Grantmesnle, and when they had come nigh out of the forest at a place not far from the glade of trees wherein *Parcenet bring-* those knights-companion had taken up their inn, they met *eth news of Sir* one of those knights clad in half-armor, and that knight was *Pellias to Sir* Sir Mador de la Porte. Then Parcenet called upon him by *Mador de la Porte.* name, saying, "Alas! Sir Mador, I have but this short time quitted a hermit's cell in the forest where I left Sir Pellias sorely wounded to death, so I fear me he hath only a little while to live."

Then Sir Mador de la Porte cried out, "Ha! maiden, what is this thou tellest me? That is a very hard thing to believe; for when Sir Pellias quitted us this morn he gave no sign of wound or disease of any sort."

But Parcenet replied, "Ne'theless, I myself beheld him lying in great pain and dole, and, ere he swooned his death-swoon, he himself told me that he had the iron of a spear in his side."

Then Sir Mador de la Porte said, "Alas! alas! that is sorry news! Now, damsel, by thy leave and grace, I will leave thee and hasten to my companions to tell them this news." And Parcenet said, "I prithee do so."

So Sir Mador de la Porte made haste to the pavilion where were his companions, and he told them the news that he had heard.

Now at this time Sir Gawaine was altogether recovered from the violent overthrow he had suffered that morning, wherefore when he heard the news that Sir Mador de la Porte brought to him, he smote his hands together and cried out aloud, "Woe is me! what have I done! For first

I betrayed my friend, and now I have slain him. Now I will go forth straightway to find him and to crave his forgiveness ere he die."

But Sir Ewaine said, "What is this that thou wouldst do? Thou art not yet fit to undertake any journey."

Sir Gawaine said, "I care not, for I am determined to go and find my friend." Nor would he suffer any of his companions to accompany him;
Sir Gawaine but when he had summoned his esquire to bring him his horse,
departeth to find he mounted thereon and rode away into the forest alone, be-
Sir Pellias. taking his way to the westward, and lamenting with great sorrow as he journeyed forward.

Now when the afternoon had fallen very late, so that the sun was sloping to its setting, and the light fell as red as fire through the forest leaves, Sir Gawaine came to that hermit's cell where it stood in the silent and solitary part of the forest woodland. And he beheld that the hermit was outside of his cell digging in a little garden of lentils. So when the hermit saw the armed knight come into that lawn all in the red light of the setting sun, he stopped digging and leaned upon his trowel. Then Sir Gawaine drew nigh, and, as he sat upon his horse, he told the holy man of the business whereon he had come.

To this the hermit said, "There came a lady hither several hours ago, and she was clad all in green, and was of a very singular appearance, so that it was easy to see that she was fay. And by means of certain charms of magic that lady cured thy friend, and after she had healed him, the two rode away into the forest together."

Then Sir Gawaine was very much amazed, and he said, "This is a very strange thing that thou tellest me, that a knight who is dying should be brought back to life again in so short a time, and should so suddenly ride forth from a bed of pain. Now, I prithee tell me whither they went." The hermit said, "They went to the westward." Whereupon, when Sir Gawaine heard this, he said, "I will follow them."

So he rode away and left the hermit gazing after him. And as he rode forward upon his way, the twilight began to fall apace, so that the woodlands after a while grew very dark and strange all around him. But as the
Sir Gawaine darkness descended a very singular miracle happened, for, lo!
follows a singu- there appeared before Sir Gawaine, a light of a pale blue
lar light. color, and it went before him and showed him the way, and he followed it, much marvelling.

Now after he had followed the light for a very long time he came at last, of a sudden, to where the woodland ceased, and where there was a wide, open plain of very great extent. And this plain was all illuminated by a singular radiance which was like that of a clear full moonlight, albeit no moon was shining at that time. And in that pale and silver light Sir Gawaine could see everything with wonderful distinctness; wherefore he beheld that he was in a plain covered all over with flowers of divers sorts, the odors whereof so filled the night that it appeared to press upon the bosom with a great pleasure. And he beheld that in front of him lay a great lake, very wide and still. And all those things appeared so strange in that light that Sir Gawaine wotted that he had come into a land of faëry. So he rode among tall flowers toward that lake in a sort of fear, for he wist not what was to befall him.

Now as he drew near the lake he perceived a knight and a lady approaching him; and when they had come nigh he beheld that the knight was Sir Pellias, and that his countenance was exceedingly strange. And he beheld that the lady was she whom he had aforetime seen all clad in green apparel when he had travelled in the Forest of Adventure with Sir Ewaine and Sir Marhaus.

Now when Sir Gawaine first beheld Sir Pellias he was filled with a great fear, for he thought it was a spirit that he saw. But when he perceived that Sir Pellias was alive, there came into his bosom a joy as great as that fear had been; wherefore he made haste toward Sir Pellias. And when he had come near to Sir Pellias, he leaped from off of his horse, crying out, "Forgive! Forgive!" with great vehemence of passion. Then he would have taken Sir Pellias into his arms, *Sir Gawaine findeth Sir Pellias.* but Sir Pellias withdrew himself from the contact of Sir Gawaine, though not with any violence of anger. And Sir Pellias spake in a voice very thin and of a silvery clearness as though it came from a considerable distance, and he said, "Touch me not, for I am not as I was aforetime, being not all human, but part fay. But concerning my forgiveness: I do forgive thee whatsoever injury I may have suffered at thy hands. And more than this I give unto thee my love, and I greatly hope for thy joy and happiness. But now I go away to leave thee, dear friend, and haply I shall not behold thee again, wherefore I do leave this with thee as my last behest; to wit, that thou dost go back to King Arthur's Court and make thy peace with the Queen. So thou mayst bring them news of all that hath happened unto me."

Then Sir Gawaine cried out in great sorrow, "Whither wouldst thou go?"

And Sir Pellias said, "I shall go to yonder wonderful city of gold and azure which lieth in yonder valley of flowers."

Then Sir Gawaine said, "I see no city but only a lake of water."

Whereupon Sir Pellias replied, "Ne'theless, there is a city yonder and thither I go, wherefore I do now bid thee farewell."

Then Sir Gawaine looked into the face of Sir Pellias and beheld again that strange light that it was of a very singular appearance, for, lo! it was white like to ivory and his eyes shone like jewels set in ivory, and a smile lay upon his lips and grew neither more nor less, but always remained the same. (For those who were of that sort had always that singular appearance and smiled in that manner—to wit, the Lady of the Lake, and Sir Pellias, and Sir Launcelot of the Lake.)

Then Sir Pellias and the Lady of the Lake turned and left Sir Gawaine *Sir Pellias dis-* where he stood, and they went toward the lake, and they *appeareth into* entered the lake, and when the feet of the horse of Sir Pellias *the lake.* had touched the water of the lake, lo! Sir Pellias was gone and Sir Gawaine beheld him no more, although he stood there for a long time weeping with great passion.

So endeth the story of Sir Pellias.

But Sir Gawaine returned unto the Court of King Arthur as he had promised Sir Pellias to do, and he made his peace with Queen Guinevere and, thereafter, though the Queen loved him not, yet there was a peace betwixt them. And Sir Gawaine published these things to the Court of King Arthur and all men marvelled at what he told.

And only twice thereafter was Sir Pellias ever seen of any of his aforetime companions.

And Sir Marhaus was made a Companion of the Round Table and became one of the foremost knights thereof.

And the Lady Ettard took Sir Engamore into favor again, and that summer they were wedded and Sir Engamore became lord of Grant-mesnle.

So endeth this story.

PART III

The Story of Sir Gawaine

*H*ERE *followeth the story of Sir Gawaine and of how he discovered such wonderful faithfulness unto King Arthur, who was his lord, that I do not believe that the like of such faithfulness was ever seen before.*

For indeed, though Sir Gawaine was at times very rough and harsh in his manner, and though he was always so plain-spoken that his words hid the gentle nature that lay within him, yet, under this pride of manner, was much courtesy; and at times he was so urbane of manner and so soft of speech that he was called by many the Knight of the Silver Tongue.

So here ye shall read how his faithfulness unto King Arthur brought him such high reward that almost anyone in all the world might envy him his great good fortune.

 ir Gawaine the Son of
Lot, King of Orkney:

Chapter First.

How a White Hart Appeared Before King Arthur, and How Sir
Gawaine and Gaheris, His Brother, Went in Pursuit Thereof,
and of What Befell Them in That Quest.

UPON a certain time King Arthur, together with Queen Guinevere
and all of his Court, were making progression through that part of
his kingdom which was not very near to Camelot. At this time
the King journeyed in very great state, and Queen Guinevere had her
Court about her, so there were many esquires and pages; wherefore, what
with knights, lords, and ladies in attendance, more than six score of people
were with the King and Queen.

Now it chanced that at this time the season of the year was very warm,
so that when the middle of the day had come the King commanded that
a number of pavilions should be spread for their accommodation, wherein
that they might rest there until the heat of the day had passed. So the
attendants spread three pavilions in a pleasant glade upon the outskirts
of the forest.

When this had been done, the King gave command that the tables, whereat they were to eat their mid-day meal, should be spread beneath the shadow of that glade of trees; for there was a gentle wind blowing and there were many birds singing, so that it was very pleasant to sit in the open air.

Accordingly the attendants of the Court did as the King commanded, and the tables were set upon the grass beneath the shade, and the King and Queen and all the lords and ladies of their Courts sat down to that cheerful repast.

Now whiles they sat there feasting with great content of spirit, and with much mirth and goodly talk among themselves, there came of a sudden a *A white hart* great outcry from the woodland that was near by, and there- *and a white* with there burst forth from the cover of that leafy wilderness *hound appear* *before King Ar-* a very beautiful white hart pursued by a white brachet of *thur at feast.* equal beauty. And there was not a hair upon either of these animals that was not as white as milk, and each wore about its neck a collar of gold very beautiful to behold.

The hound pursued the white hart with a very great outcry and bellow-ing, and the hart fled in the utmost terror. In this wise they ran thrice around the table where King Arthur and his Court sat at meat, and twice in that chase the hound caught the hart and pinched it on its haunch, and there-with the hart leaped away, and all they who sat there observed that there was blood at two places upon its haunch where the hound had pinched it. But each time the hart escaped from the hound, and the hound followed after it with much outcry of yelling so that King Arthur and Queen Gui-nevere and all their Court were annoyed at the noise and tumult that those two creatures made. Then the hart fled away into the forest again by another path, and the hound pursued it and both were gone, and the bay-ing of the hound sounded more and more distant as it ran away into the woodland.

Now, ere the King and Queen and their Court had recovered from their astonishment at these things, there suddenly appeared at that part of the forest whence the hart and the hound had emerged, a knight and a lady, and the knight was of very lordly presence and the lady was exceedingly beautiful. The knight was clad in half-armor, and the lady was clad in green as though for the chase; and the knight rode upon a charger of dapple gray, and the lady upon a piebald palfrey. With them were two esquires, also clad for the chase.

These, seeing the considerable company gathered there, paused as though in surprise, and whilst they stood so, there suddenly appeared an-other knight upon a black horse, clad in complete armor, and he seemed to be very angry. For he ran upon the half-armed knight and smote him so sorry a blow with his sword, that the first knight fell down from his horse and lay upon the ground as though dead; whereat the lady who was with him shrieked with great dolor.

Then the full-armed knight upon the black horse ran to the lady and catched her, and he lifted her from her palfrey and laid her across the horn of his saddle, and thereupon he rode back into the forest again. The lady screamed with such vehemence of violent outcry, that it was a great pity to hear her, but the knight paid no attention to her shrieking, but bore her away by main force into the forest.

King Arthur and his Court behold a knight carry off a lady prisoner.

Then, after he and the lady had gone, the two esquires came and lifted up the wounded knight upon his horse, and then they also went away into the forest and were gone.

All this King Arthur and his Court beheld from a distance, and they were so far away that they could not stay that knight upon the black horse from doing what he did to carry away the lady into the forest; nor could they bring succor to that other knight in half-armor whom they had beheld struck down in that wise. So they were very greatly grieved at what they had beheld and knew not what to think of it. Then King Arthur said to his Court, "Messires, is there not some one of you who will follow up this adventure and discover what is the significance of that which we have seen, and compel that knight to tell why he behaved as he did?"

Upon this Sir Gawaine said, "Lord, I shall be very glad indeed to take upon me this adventure if I have thy leave to do so." And King Arthur said, "Thou hast my leave." Then Sir Gawaine said, "Lord, I would that thou would also let me take my younger brother, Gaheris, with me as mine esquire in this undertaking, for he groweth apace unto manhood, and yet he hath never beheld any considerable adventure at arms." So King Arthur said, "Thou hast my leave to take thy brother with thee."

Sir Gawaine and Gaheris undertake the adventure of these things.

At this Gaheris was very glad, for he was of an adventurous spirit, wherefore the thought of going with his brother upon this quest gave him great pleasure.

So they two went to the pavilion of Sir Gawaine, and there Gaheris aided Sir Gawaine as his esquire to don his armor. Then they rode forth upon that quest which Sir Gawaine had undertaken.

Now they journeyed onward for a very considerable distance, following that direction which they had seen the hart take when it had sped away from before the hound, and when, from time to time, they would meet some of the forest folk, they would inquire of them whither had fled that white brachet and the white hart, and whither had fled the knight and the lady, and so they followed that adventure apace.

By and by, after a long pass—it being far advanced in the afternoon—they were suddenly aware of a great uproar of conflict, as of a fierce battle in progress. So they followed this sound, and after a while they came to an open meadow-land with very fair and level sward. Here they beheld two knights fighting with great vehemence of passion, and with a very deadly purpose. Then Sir Gawaine said, "What is this? Let us go see." So he and Gaheris rode forward to where those two knights were *They behold* engaged, and as they approached, the two knights paused in *two knights* their encounter, and rested upon their weapons. Then Sir *fighting.* Gawaine said, "Ha! Messires, what is to do and why do ye fight with such passion, the one against the other, in that wise?" Then one of the knights said to Sir Gawaine, "Sir, this does not concern you;" and the other said, "Meddle not with us, for this battle is of our own choosing."

"Messires," said Sir Gawaine, "I would be very sorry to interfere in your quarrel, but I am in pursuit of a white hart and a white brachet that came this way, and also of a knight who hath carried off a lady upon the same pass. Now I would be greatly beholden to ye if you would tell me if ye have seen aught of one or the other."

Then that knight who had first spoken said, "Sir, this is a very strange matter, for it was upon account of that very white hart and that brachet, *One of the* and of the knight and the lady that we two were just now en- *knights tells* gaged in that battle as thou didst behold. For the case is *their story.* this: We two are two brothers, and we were riding together in great amity when that hart and that hound came hitherward. Then my brother said he very greatly hoped that the white hart would escape from the hound, and I said that I hoped that the hound would overtake the hart and bring it to earth. Then came that knight with that lady, his captive, and I said that I would follow that knight and rescue the lady, and my brother said that he would undertake that adventure.

"Upon these points we fell into dispute; for it appeared to me that I felt great affection for that hound, and my brother felt as extraordinary regard for the white hart, and that as I had first spoken I should have the right to follow that adventure; but my brother felt affection for the hart, and he considered that as he was the elder of us twain, he had the best right to the adventure. So we quarrelled, and by and by we fell to upon that fight in which thou did see us engaged."

At this Sir Gawaine was very greatly astonished, and he said, "Messires, I cannot understand how so great a quarrel should have arisen from so small a dispute ; and, certes, it is a great pity for two brothers to quarrel as ye have done, and to give one another such sore cuts and wounds as I perceive you have both received."

"Messires," said the second knight, "I think thou art right, and I now find myself to be very much ashamed of that quarrel." And the other said, "I too am sorry for what I have done."

Then Sir Gawaine said, "Sirs, I would be very glad indeed if you would tell me your names." And the one knight said, "I am called Sir Sorloise of the Forest." And the other said, "I am called Sir Brian of the Forest."

Then Sir Sorloise said, "Sir Knight, I would deem it a very great courtesy if thou wouldst tell me who thou art."

"I would be very glad to do that," said Sir Gawaine, and therewith he told them his name and condition. Now, when they heard who Sir Gawaine was, those two knights were very greatly astonished and pleased ; for no one in all the courts of chivalry was more famous than Sir Gawaine, the son of King Lot of Orkney. Wherefore those two brothers said, "It is certainly a great joy to us to meet so famous a knight as thou art, Sir Gawaine."

Then Sir Gawaine said, "Sir Knights, that hart and that hound came only a short while ago to where King Arthur and Queen Guinevere and their Courts of lords and ladies were at feast, and there, likewise, all we beheld that knight seize upon the lady and make her captive. Wherefore, I and my brother have come forth upon command of King Arthur for to discover what is the meaning of that which we beheld. Now I shall deem it a very great courtesy upon your part if you will cease from this adventure and will go in amity unto the Court of the King, and will tell him of what ye beheld and of how you quarrelled and of how we met. For otherwise I myself will have to engage ye both, and that would be a great pity ; for ye are weary with battle and I am fresh."

Then these two knights said, "Sir, we will do as you desire, for we have no wish to have to do with so powerful a knight as you."

Thereupon those two knights departed and went to the Court of King Arthur as Sir Gawaine ordained, and Sir Gawaine and his brother rode forward upon their adventure.

Now, by and by they came nigh to a great river, and there they beheld before them a single knight in full armor, who carried a spear in his hand and a shield hanging to his saddle-bow. Thereupon Sir Gawaine

made haste forward and he called aloud to the knight, and the knight
paused and waited until Sir Gawaine had overtaken him.   And
Sir Gawaine when Sir Gawaine came up to that knight he said, " Sir Knight,
and Gaheris hast thou seen a white hart and a white hound pass by this way?
meet a knight
beside the river. And hast thou seen a knight bearing off a captive lady?"
Unto this the knight said, " Yea, I beheld them both, and I am even now
following after them with intent to discover whither they are bound."
Then Sir Gawaine said, " Sir Knight, I bid thee not to follow this adventure
farther, for I myself am set upon it.   Wherefore I desire thee for to give
it over so that I may undertake it in thy stead."   " Sir," said the other
knight, speaking with a very great deal of heat, " I know not who thou
art, nor do I care a very great deal.   But touching the pursuance of this
adventure, I do tell thee that I myself intend to follow it to the end and
so will I do, let who will undertake to stay me."
Thereupon Sir Gawaine said, " Messire, thou shalt not go forward upon
this adventure unless thou hast first to do with me."   And the knight said,
" Sir, I am very willing for that."
So each knight took such stand upon that field as appeared to him to be
best, and each put himself into a posture of defence and dressed his shield
and his spear.   Then, when they were thus prepared in all ways, they immediately launched forth, the one against the other, rushing together with
great speed and with such an uproar that the ground trembled and shook
Sir Gawaine beneath them.   So they met together in the midst of the
overthroweth course and the spear of the strange knight burst all into small
the knight. pieces, but the spear of Sir Gawaine held; wherefore he
hurled that knight out of his saddle with such violence that he smote the
ground with a blow like an earthquake.
Then Sir Gawaine rode back to where his enemy was (for that knight
was unable to arise), and he removed the helmet from the head of the
fallen knight and beheld that he was very young and comely.
Now, when the fresh air smote upon the knight's face, he presently
awoke from his swoon and came back unto his senses again, whereupon
Sir Gawaine said, " Dost thou yield unto me?"   And the knight said, " I
do so."   Then Sir Gawaine said, " Who art thou?"   And the knight said,
" I am called Sir Alardin of the Isles."   " Very well," said Sir Gawaine;
" then I lay my command upon thee in this wise: that thou shalt go to
the Court of King Arthur and deliver thyself to him as a captive of my
prowess.   And thou art to tell him all that thou knowest of the hart and
the hound and the knight and the lady.   And thou shalt tell him all that
hath befallen thee in this assault."

So the knight said that he would do that, and thereupon they parted, the one party going the one way and the other party going the other way.

After that Sir Gawaine and his brother, Gaheris, rode a considerable distance until they came, by and by, through a woodland into an open plain, and it was now about the time of sunset. And they beheld in the midst of the plain a very stately and noble castle with five towers and of very great strength.

And right here they saw a sight that filled them with great sorrow, for they beheld the dead body of that white brachet lying beside the road like any carrion. And they saw that the hound was pierced through with three arrows, wherefore they wist that it had been slain very violently. *Sir Gawaine and Gaheris behold the dead brachet.*

Now when Sir Gawaine beheld that beautiful hound lying dead in that wise, he was filled with great sorrow. " What a pity it is," he cried, "that this noble hound should be slain in this wise; for I think that it was the most beautiful hound that ever I saw in all my life. Here hath assuredly been great treachery against it; for it hath been foully dealt with because of that white hart which it pursued. Now, I make my vow that if I can find that hart I will slay it with mine own hands, because it was in that chase that this hound met its death."

After that they rode forward toward that castle, and as they drew nigh, lo! they beheld that white hart with the golden collar browsing upon the meadows before the castle.

Now, as soon as the white hart beheld those two strangers, it fled with great speed toward the castle, and it ran into the court-yard of the castle. And when Sir Gawaine beheld the stag, he gave chase in pursuit of it with great speed, and Gaheris followed after his brother.

So Sir Gawaine pursued the white hart into the court-yard of the castle and from thence it could not escape. Then Sir Gawaine leaped him down from his horse and drew his sword and slew the hart with a single blow of his weapon. *Sir Gawaine slayeth the white hart.*

This he did in great haste, but when he had done that and it was too late to mend it, he repented him of what he had done very sorely.

Now with all this tumult, there came out the lord and the lady of that castle ; and the lord was one of very haughty and noble aspect, and the lady was extraordinarily graceful and very beautiful of appearance. And Sir Gawaine looked upon the lady and he thought he had hardly ever seen so beautiful a dame, wherefore he was more sorry than ever that, in his haste, he had slain that white hart.

But when the lady of the castle beheld the white hart, that it lay dead upon the stone pavement of the court-yard, she smote her hands together and shrieked with such shrillness and strength, that it pierced the ears to hear her. And she cried out, "Oh, my white hart, art thou then dead?" And therewith she fell to weeping with great passion. Then Sir Gawaine said, "Lady, I am very sorry for what I have done, and I would that I could undo it." Then the lord of that castle said to Sir Gawaine, "Sir, didst thou slay that stag?" "Yea," said Sir Gawaine. "Sir," said the lord of the castle, "thou hast done very ill in this matter, and if thou wilt wait a little I will take full vengeance upon thee." Unto which Sir Gawaine said, "I will wait for thee as long as it shall please thee."

Then the lord of the castle went into his chamber and clad himself in his armor, and in a little while he came out very fiercely. "Sir," said Sir Gawaine, "what is thy quarrel with me?" And the lord of the castle said, "Because thou hast slain the white hart that was so dear to my lady." To the which Sir Gawaine said, "I would not have slain the white hart *The knight of* only that because of it the white brachet was so treacherously *the castle assail-* slain." Upon this the lord of the castle was more wroth than *eth Sir Gawaine.* ever, and he ran at Sir Gawaine and smote him unawares, so that he clave through the epaulier of his armor and cut through the flesh and unto the bone of the shoulder, so that Sir Gawaine was put to a great agony of pain at the stroke. Then Sir Gawaine was filled with rage at the pain of the wound, wherefore he smote the knight so woful a blow that he cut through his helmet and into the bone beneath, and thereupon the knight fell down upon his knees because of the fierceness of the blow, and he could not rise up again. Then Sir Gawaine catched his helmet and rushed it off from his head.

Upon this the knight said in a weak voice, "Sir Knight, I crave mercy of you, and yield myself to you."

Sir Gawaine But Sir Gawaine was very furious with anger because of *maketh to slay* that unexpected blow which he had received and because of *the knight of* the great agony of the wound, wherefore he would not have *the castle.* mercy, but lifted up his sword with intent to slay that knight.

Then the lady of the castle beheld what Sir Gawaine was intent to do, and she brake away from her damsels and ran and flung herself upon the knight so as to shield him with her own body. And in that moment Sir Gawaine was striking and could not stay his blow; nevertheless, he *Sir Gawaine* was able to turn his sword in his hand so that the edge thereof *striketh the lady* did not smite the lady. But the flat of the sword struck her *of the castle* upon the neck a very grievous blow, and the blade cut her a *without intent.* little, so that the blood ran down her smooth white neck and over her kerchief; and with the violence of the blow the lady fell down and lay upon the ground as though she were dead.

Now when Sir Gawaine beheld that, he thought that he had slain that lady in his haste, and he was all a-dread at what he had done, wherefore he cried, "Woe is me! what have I done?"

"Alas!" said Gaheris, "that was a very shameful blow that thou didst strike; and the shame of it is mine also because thou art my brother. Now I wish I had not come with thee to this place."

Then Sir Gawaine said to the lord of that castle, "Sir, I will spare thy life, for I am very sorry for what I have done in my haste."

But the knight of the castle was filled with great bitterness, because he thought that his lady was dead, wherefore he cried out as in despair, "I will not now have thy mercy, for thou art a knight without mercy and without pity. And since thou hast slain my lady, who is dearer to me than my life, thou mayst slay me also. For that is the only service which thou canst now render me."

But by now the damsels of the lady had come to her where she lay, and the chiefest of these cried out to the lord of the castle, "Ha, sir, thy lady is not dead, but only in a swoon from which she will presently recover."

Then when the lord of the castle heard that, he fell to weeping in great measure from pure joy; for now that he knew his lady was alive he could not contain himself for joy. Therewith Sir Gawaine came to him and lifted him up from the ground where he was, and kissed him upon the cheek. Then certain others came and bare the lady away into her chamber, and there in a little while she recovered from that swoon and was but little the worse for the blow she had received.

That night Sir Gawaine, and his brother, Gaheris, abided with the knight and the lady, and when the knight learned who Sir Gawaine was, he felt it great honor to have so famous a knight in that place. So they feasted together that evening in great amity.

Now, after they had refreshed themselves, Sir Gawaine said, "I beseech you, sir, to tell me what was the meaning of the white hart and the white brachet which led me into this adventure."

To this the lord of the castle (whose name was Sir Ablamor of the Marise) said, "I will do so." And therewith he spake as follows:

"You must know, sir, that I have a brother who hath always been very dear to me, and when I took this, my lady, unto wife, he took her sister as his wife.

"Now, my brother dwelt in a castle nigh to this, and we held commerce

together in great amity. But it befell upon a day that my lady and my
The lord of the brother's lady were riding through this forest together dis-
castle telleth the coursing very pleasantly. What time there appeared a lady
story of the
white hart and unto them, exceedingly beautiful, and of very strange appear-
the white hound. ance, for I do not think that either my lady or her sister ever
beheld her like before.

"This strange lady brought unto those two ladies a white hart and a
white brachet, and the hart and the hound she held each by a silver chain
attached to a golden collar that encircled its neck. And the white hart
she gave unto my lady and the white brachet she gave unto my lady's
sister. And then she went away leaving them very glad.

"But their gladness did not last for very long, for ever since that time
there hath been nothing else but discord between my brother and myself,
and between my lady and her sister, for the white hound hath ever sought
the white hart for to destroy it, wherefore I and my lady have entertained
very great offence against my brother and his lady because they did not
keep the white brachet at home. So it has come to pass that a number of
times we have sought to destroy the hound, so that my brother and his
lady have held equal offence against us.

"Now this day it chanced I was toward the outskirts of the forest to the
east of us, when I heard a great outcry in the woodland, and by and by
the white hart that belonged to my lady came fleeing through the woodland, and the white brachet that belonged to my brother's lady was in
pursuit of it ; and my brother and his lady and two esquires followed
rapidly after the hart and the brachet.

"Then I was very greatly angered, for it seemed to me that they were
chasing that white hart out of despite of my lady and myself, wherefore I
followed after them with all speed.

"So I came upon them at the outskirts of the woodland, nigh to
where there were a number of pavilions pitched in the shade of a glade of
trees in the midst of the meadow, and there, in mine anger, I struck my
brother a great blow so that I smote him down from his horse. And I
catched his lady and I threw her across the horn of my saddle and I bore
her here away to this castle, and here I have held her out of revenge
because they pursued the white hart which belonged to my lady. For
my lady loved that hart as she loved nothing else in the world, excepting
myself."

"Sir," said Sir Gawaine, "this is a very strange matter. Now I beseech
thee to tell me of what appearance was that lady who gave the white hart
and the white hound unto those two ladies?" "Messire," said the knight,

"she was clad all in crimson, and about her throat and arms were a great many ornaments of gold beset with stones of divers colors, and her hair was red like gold and was enmeshed in a net of gold, and her eyes were very black and shone with exceeding brightness, and her lips were like coral, so that she possessed a very strange appearance."

"Ha!" said Sir Gawaine, "from this description methinks that lady could have been none other than the sorceress Vivien. For now she spendeth all of her time in doing such mischief as this by means of her enchantment, out of pure despite. And, indeed, I think it would be a very good thing if she were put out of this *Sir Gawaine heareth of Vivien.* world so that she could do no more such mischief. But tell me, Messire, where now is that lady, thy wife's sister?" "Sir," said the knight, "she is in this castle and is a prisoner of honor." "Well," quoth Sir Gawaine, "since now both the hart and the hound are dead, ye can assuredly bear no more enmity toward her and your brother, wherefore I do beseech you that you will let her go free, and will enter again into a condition of amity and good-will the one with the other, in such a manner as hath afore obtained between you." And the lord of the castle said, "Sir, it shall be so."

And so he set the lady free at that time, and thereafter there was amity between them as Sir Gawaine had ordained.

And the next day Sir Gawaine and his brother, Gaheris, returned unto this Court of the King and he told King Arthur and his Court all that had befallen, hiding nothing from them.

Now, Queen Guinevere was very much displeased when she heard how Sir Gawaine would show no mercy to that knight and how he had struck the lady with his sword. Wherefore she said aside to one of those who stood nigh to her, "It seems to me to be a very strange thing for a belted knight to do, to refuse to give mercy unto a fallen enemy and to strike a lady with his sword; for I should *Queen Guinevere is displeased with Sir Gawaine.* think that any sword that had drawn blood from a lady in such wise would be dishonored for aye; and I cannot think that anyone who would strike a lady in that wise would hold himself guiltless unto his vow of knighthood."

This Sir Gawaine overheard and he was exceedingly wroth thereat. But he concealed his anger at that time. Only after he had gone away he said to Gaheris, his brother, "I believe that lady hateth me with all her heart; but some time I will show to her that I have in me more courtesy and am more gentle than she believes me to be. As for my sword, since she deemeth it to be dishonored by *Sir Gawaine breaketh his sword.* that blow, I will not use it any more." So he took the sword out of its sheath and brake it across his knee and flung it away.

Now all this hath been told to set forth that which follows; for there ye shall learn what great things of nobility Sir Gawaine could do when it behooved him to do them.   For, haply, ye who have read this story may feel as Queen Guinevere did, that Sir Gawaine was not rightwise courteous as a belted knight should have been in that adventure aforetold.

King Arthur findeth ye olds woman in ye hut:

Chapter Second.

How King Arthur Became Lost in the Forest, and How He Fell Into a Very Singular Adventure in a Castle Unto Which He Came.

NOW, it befell upon a time some while after this, that King Arthur was at Tintagalon upon certain affairs of state. And Queen Guinevere and her Court and the King's Court made progression from Camelot unto Carleon, and there they abided until the King should be through his business at Tintagalon and should join them at Carleon.

Now that time was the spring of the year, and all things were very jolly and gay, wherefore King Arthur became possessed with a great desire for adventure. So he called unto him a certain favorite esquire, hight Boisenard, and he said to him, "Boisenard, this day is so pleasant that I hardly know how I may contain myself because of the joy I take in it, for it seems to be that my heart is nigh ready to burst with a great pleasure of desiring. So I am of a mind to go a-gadding with only thee for companion."

To this Boisenard said, "Lord, I know of nothing that would give to me a greater pleasure than that."

So King Arthur said, "Very well, let us then go away from this place in such a manner that no one will be aware of our departure. And so we will go to Carleon and surprise the Queen by coming unexpectedly to that place."

So Boisenard brought armor, without device, and he clad the King in that armor; and then they two rode forth together, and no one wist that they had left the castle.

And when they came forth into the fields, King Arthur whistled and sang and jested and laughed and made himself merry; for he *King Arthur* was as a war-horse turned forth upon the grass that taketh *sets forth with* glory in the sunshine and the warm air and becometh like *his esquire.* unto a colt again.

So by and by they came into the forest and rode that way with great content of spirit; and they took this path and they took that path for no reason but because the day was so gay and jolly. So, by and by, they lost their way in the mazes of the woodland and knew not where they were.

Now when they found themselves to be lost in that wise they journeyed with more circumspection, going first by this way and then by that, but in *They are lost in* no manner could they find their way out from their entangle-*the forest.* ment. And so fell night-time and they knew not where they were; but all became very dark and obscure, with the woodland full of strange and unusual sounds around about them.

Then King Arthur said, " Boisenard, this is a very perplexing pass and I do not know how we shall find lodging for this night."

To this Boisenard said, " Lord, if I have thy permission to do so, I will climb one of these trees and see if I can discover any sign of habitation in this wilderness." And King Arthur said, " Do so, I pray thee."

So Boisenard climbed a very tall tree and from the top of the tree he *Boisenard be-* beheld a light a great distance away, and he said, " Lord, I *holdeth a light.* see a light in that direction." And therewith he came down from the tree again.

So King Arthur and Boisenard went in the direction that Boisenard had beheld the light, and by and by they came out of the forest and into an open place where they beheld a very great castle with several tall towers, very grim and forbidding of appearance. And it was from this castle that the light had appeared that Boisenard had seen. So they two rode up to the castle and Boisenard called aloud and smote upon the gate of the castle. Then immediately there came a porter and demanded of them what they would have. Unto him Boisenard said, " Sirrah, we would come in to lodge for to-night, for we are a-weary." So the porter said, " Who are you?"—speaking very roughly and rudely to them, for he could not see of what condition they were because of the darkness. Then Boisenard said, " This is a knight of very good quality and I am his esquire, and we have lost our way in the forest and now we come hither seeking shelter."

" Sir," said the porter, " if ye know what is good for you, ye will sleep in the forest rather than come into this place, for this is no very good retreat for errant knights to shelter themselves."

Upon this King Arthur bespake the porter, for that which the porter said aroused great curiosity within him. So he said, " Nay, we will not go away from here and we demand to lodge here for this night."

Then the porter said, " Very well; ye may come in." And thereupon he opened the gate and they rode into the court-yard of that castle.

Now at the noise of their coming, there appeared a great many lights within the castle, and there came running forth divers attendants. Some of these aided King Arthur and Boisenard to dismount, *King Arthur* and others took the horses, and others again brought basins *and his esquire* of water for them to wash withal. And after they had *enter the castle.* washed their 'aces and hands, other attendants brought them into the castle.

Now as they came into the castle, they were aware of a great noise of very many people talking and laughing together, with the sound of singing and of harping. And so they came into the hall of the castle and beheld that it was lighted with a great number of candles and tapers and torches. Here they found a multitude of people gathered at a table spread for a feast, and at the head of the table there sat a knight, well advanced in years and with hair and beard white as milk. Yet he was exceedingly strong and sturdy of frame, having shoulders of wonderful broadness and a great girth of chest. This knight was of a very stern and forbidding appearance, and was clad altogether in black, and he wore around his neck a chain of gold, with a locket of gold hanging pendant from it.

Now when this knight beheld King Arthur and Boisenard come into the hall, he called aloud to them in a very great voice bidding them to come and sit with him at the head of the table; and they did so, and those at the head of the table made place for them, and thus they sat there beside the knight.

Now King Arthur and Boisenard were exceedingly hungry, wherefore they ate with great appetite and made joy of the entertainment which they received, and meantime the knight held them in very pleasant discourse, talking to them of such things as would give them the most entertainment. So after a while the feast was ended and they ceased from eating.

Then, of a sudden, the knight said to King Arthur, " Messire, thou art young and lusty of spirit and I doubt not but thou hath a great heart within thee. What say you now to a little sport betwixt *The knight of* us two?" Upon this King Arthur regarded that knight *the castle chal-* very steadily and he believed that his face was not so old *lenges King* as it looked; for his eyes were exceedingly bright and *adventure.* shone like sparks of light; wherefore he was a-doubt and he said, " Sir, what sport would you have?" Upon this the knight fell a-laughing in great measure and he said, " This is a very strange sport that I have in mind, for it is this: That thou and I shall prove the one unto the other what courage each of us may have." And King Arthur said, " How shall we prove that?" Whereunto the knight made reply, " This is what we shall do: Thou and I shall stand forth in the middle of this hall, and thou shalt have leave to try to strike off my head; and if I can receive that blow without dying therefrom, then I shall have leave to strike thy head off in a like manner."

Upon this speech King Arthur was greatly a-dread and he said, " That is very strange sport for two men to engage upon."

Now when King Arthur said this, all those who were in the hall burst out laughing beyond all measure and as though they would never stint from their mirth. Then, when they had become in a measure quiet again, the knight of that castle said, " Sir, art thou afraid of that sport?" Upon which King Arthur fell very angry and he said, " Nay, I am not afeared, for no man hath ever yet had reason to say that I showed my-self afeared of anyone." " Very well," said the knight of the castle; " then let us try that sport of which I spake." And King Arthur said, " I am willing."

Then Boisenard came to King Arthur where he was, and he said, " Lord, do not thou enter into this thing, but rather let me undertake this venture in thy stead, for I am assured that some great treachery is meditated against thee." But King Arthur said, " Nay; no man shall take my danger upon himself, but I will assume mine own danger without calling upon any man to take it." So he said to the knight of the castle, " Sir, I am ready for that sport of which thou didst speak, but who is to strike that first blow and how shall we draw lots therefor?" " Messire," said the knight of the castle, " there shall be no lots drawn. For, as thou art the guest of this place, so shall thou have first assay at that sport."

Therewith that knight arose and laid aside his black robe, and he was clad beneath in a shirt of fine linen very cunningly worked. And he wore hosen of crimson. Then he opened that linen undergarment at the throat and he turned down the collar thereof so as to lay his neck bare to the blow. Thereupon he said, " Now, Sir Knight, thou shalt have to strike well if thou wouldst win at this sport."

But King Arthur showed no dread of that undertaking, for he arose and drew Excalibur so that the blade of the sword flashed *King Arthur* *cuts off the head* with exceeding brightness. Then he measured his distance, *of the knight of* and lifted the sword, and he smote the knight of the castle *the castle.* with all his might upon the neck. And, lo! the blade cut through the neck of the knight of the castle with wonderful ease, so that the head flew from the body to a great distance away.

But the trunk of the body of that knight did not fall, but instead of that it stood, and it walked to where the head lay, and the hands of the trunk picked up the head and they set the head back upon the body, and, lo! that knight was as sound and whole as ever he had been in all his life.

Upon this all those of the castle shouted and made great mirth, and they called upon King Arthur that it was now his turn to try that sport. So the King prepared himself, laying aside his surcoat and opening his under-garment at the throat, as the knight of the castle had done. And at that Boisenard made great lamentation. Then the knight of the castle said, "Sir, art thou afeared?" And King Arthur said, "No, I am not afeared, for every man must come to his death some time, and it appears that my time hath now come, and that I am to lay down my life in this foolish fashion for no fault of mine own."

Then the knight of the castle said, "Well, stand thou away a little distance so that I may not strike thee too close, and so lose the virtue of my blow."

So King Arthur stood forth in the midst of the hall, and the knight of the castle swung his sword several times, but did not strike. Likewise, he several times laid the blade of the sword upon King Arthur's *The knight tor-* neck, and it was very cold. Then King Arthur cried out *ments King* in great passion, "Sir, it is thy right to strike, but I be- *Arthur.* seech thee not to torment me in this manner." "Nay," said the knight of the castle, "it is my right to strike when it pleases me, and I will not strike any before that time. For if it please me I will torment thee for a great while ere I slay thee." So he laid his sword several times more upon King Arthur's neck, and King Arthur said no more, but bore that torment with a very steadfast spirit.

Then the knight of the castle said, "Thou appearest to be a very courageous and honorable knight, and I have a mind to make a covenant with thee." And King Arthur said, "What is that covenant?" "It is this," said the knight of the castle, "I will spare thee thy life for a year and a day if thou wilt pledge me thy knightly word to return hither at the end of that time."

Then King Arthur said, "Very well; it shall be so." And therewith he pledged his knightly word to return at the end of that time, swearing to that pledge upon the cross of the hilt of Excalibur.

Then the knight of the castle said, "I will make another covenant with

thee." "What is it?" said King Arthur. "My second covenant is this," quoth the knight of the castle, "I will give to thee a riddle, and if thou
The knight of the castle sets King Arthur a riddle. wilt answer that riddle when thou returnest hither, and if thou makest no mistake in that answer, then will I spare thy life and set thee free." And King Arthur said, "What is that riddle?" To which the knight made reply, "The riddle is this: What is it that a woman desires most of all in the world?"

"Sir," said King Arthur, "I will seek to find the answer to that riddle, and I give thee gramercy for sparing my life for so long a time as thou hast done, and for giving me the chance to escape my death." Upon this the knight of the castle smiled very sourly, and he said, "I do not offer this to thee because of mercy to thee, but because I find pleasure in tormenting thee. For what delight canst thou have in living thy life when thou knowest that thou must, for a surety, die at the end of one short year? And what pleasure canst thou have in living even that year when thou shalt be tormented with anxiety to discover the answer to my riddle?"

Then King Arthur said, "I think thou art very cruel." And the knight said, "I am not denying that."

So that night King Arthur and Boisenard lay at the castle, and the next day they took their way thence. And King Arthur was very heavy and troubled in spirit; ne'theless he charged Boisenard that he should say nothing concerning that which had befallen, but that he should keep it in secret. And Boisenard did as the King commanded, and said nothing concerning that adventure.

Now in that year which followed, King Arthur settled his affairs. Also he sought everywhere to find the answer to that riddle. Many there were who gave him answers in plenty, for one said that a woman most desired wealth, and another said she most desired beauty, and one said she desired power to please, and another said that she most desired fine raiment; and one said this, and another said that; but no answer appeared to King Arthur to be good and fitting for his purpose.

So the year passed by, until only a fortnight remained; and then King Arthur could not abide to stay where he was any longer, for it seemed to him his time was very near to hand, and he was filled with a very bitter anxiety of soul, wherefore he was very restless to be away.

So he called Boisenard to him, and he said, "Boisenard, help me to arm, for I am going away."

Then Boisenard fell a-weeping in very great measure, and he said, "Lord, do not go."

At this King Arthur looked very sternly at his esquire, and said, "Boisenard, how is this? Wouldst thou tempt me to violate mine honor? It is not very hard to die, but it would be very bitter to live my life in dishonor; wherefore tempt me no more, but do my bidding and hold thy peace. And if I do not return in a month from this time, then mayst thou tell all that hath befallen. And thou mayst tell Sir Constantine of Cornwall that he is to search the papers in my cabinet, and that there he will find all that is to be done should death overtake me."

So Boisenard put a plain suit of armor upon King Arthur, though he could hardly see what he was about for the tears that flowed down out of his eyes in great abundance. And he laced upon the armor *King Arthur* of the King a surcoat without device, and he gave the King *set forth to return to the castle* a shield without device. Thereupon King Arthur rode away *of the evil* without considering whither his way took him. And of every- *knight.* one whom he met he inquired what that thing was that a woman most desired, and no one could give him an answer that appeared to him to be what it should be, wherefore he was in great doubt and torment of spirit.

Now the day before King Arthur was to keep his covenant at that castle, he was wandering through the adjacent forest in great travail of soul, for he wist not what he should do to save his life. As he wandered so, he came of a sudden upon a small hut built up under an overhanging oak-tree so that it was very hard to tell where the oak-tree ended and the hut began. And there were a great many large rocks all about covered with moss, so that the King might very easily have passed by the hut only that he beheld a smoke to arise therefrom as from a fire that burned within. So he went to the hut and opened the door and entered. At first he thought there was no one there, but when he looked again he beheld an old woman sitting bent over a small fire that burned upon the *King Arthur* hearth. And King Arthur had never beheld such an ugly *cometh to the* beldame as that one who sat there bending over that fire, for *hut of an old* her ears were very huge and flapped, and her hair hung down *woman.* over her head like to snakes, and her face was covered all over with wrinkles so that there were not any places at all where there was not a wrinkle; and her eyes were bleared and covered over with a film, and the eyelids were red as with the continual weeping of her eyes, and she had but one tooth in her mouth, and her hands, which she spread out to the fire, were like claws of bone.

Then King Arthur gave her greeting and she gave the King greeting, and she said to him, "My lord King, whence come ye? and why do ye come to this place?"

Then King Arthur was greatly astonished that that old woman should know him, who he was, and he said, "Who are you that appeareth to know me?" "No matter," said she, "I am one who meaneth you well; so tell me what is the trouble that brings you here at this time." So the King confessed all his trouble to that old woman, and he asked her if she knew the answer to that riddle, "What is it that a woman most desires?" "Yea," said the old woman, "I know the answer to that riddle very well, but I will not tell it to thee unless thou wilt promise me something in return."

At this King Arthur was filled with very great joy that the old woman should know the answer to that riddle, and he was filled with doubt of what she would demand of him, wherefore he said, "What is it thou must have in return for that answer?"

Then the old woman said, "If I aid thee to guess thy riddle aright, thou must promise that I shall become wife unto one of the knights of thy Court, whom I may choose when thou returnest homeward again."

"Ha!" said King Arthur, "how may I promise that upon the behalf of anyone?" Upon this the old woman said, "Are not the knights of thy Court of such nobility that they will do that to save thee from death?" "I believe they are," said King Arthur. And with that he meditated a long while, saying unto himself, "What will my kingdom do if I die at this time? I have no right to die." So he said to the old woman, "Very well, I will make that promise."

The old woman telleth King Arthur to answer the riddle. Then she said unto the King, "This is the answer to that riddle: That which a woman most desires is to have her will." And the answer seemed to King Arthur to be altogether right.

Then the old woman said, "My lord King, thou hast been played upon by that knight who hath led thee into this trouble, for he is a great conjurer and a magician of a very evil sort. He carrieth his life not within his body, but in a crystal globe which he weareth in a locket hanging about his neck; wherefore it was that when thou didst cut the head from off his body, his life remained in that locket and he did not die. But if thou hadst destroyed that locket, then he would immediately have died."

"I will mind me of that," said King Arthur.

So King Arthur abided with that old woman for that night, and she refreshed him with meat and drink and served him very well. And the next morning he set forth unto that castle where he had made his covenant, and his heart was more cheerful than it had been for a whole year.

Chapter Third.

How King Arthur Overcame the Knight-Enchanter, and How Sir Gawaine Manifested the High Nobility of His Knighthood.

NOW, when King Arthur came to the castle, the gateway thereof was immediately opened to him and he entered. And when he had entered, sundry attendants came and conducted him into the hall where he had aforetime been. There he beheld the knight of that castle and a great many people who had come to witness the conclusion of the adventure. And when the knight beheld King Arthur he said to him, "Sir, hast thou come to redeem thy pledge?" "Yea," said King Arthur, "for so I made my vow to thee." Then the knight of the castle said, "Sir, hast thou guessed that riddle?" And King Arthur said, "I believe that I have." The knight of the castle said, "Then let me hear thy answer thereto. But if thou makest any mistake, or if thou dost not guess aright, then is thy life forfeit." "Very well," said King Arthur, "let it be that way. Now this is the answer to thy riddle: That which a woman most desires is to have her will."

King Arthur returneth to the castle of the evil knight.

Now when the lord of the castle heard King Arthur guess aright he wist not what to say or where to look, and those who were there also perceived that the King had guessed aright.

Then King Arthur came very close to that knight with great sternness of demeanor, and he said, "Now, thou traitor knight! thou didst ask me to enter into thy sport with thee a year ago, so at these present it is my turn to ask thee to have sport with me. And this is the sport I will have, that thou shalt give me that chain and locket that hang about thy neck, and that I shall give thee the collar which hangeth about my neck."

At this, the face of that knight fell all pale, like to ashes, and he emitted a sound similar to the sound made by a hare when the hound lays hold upon it. Then King Arthur catched him very violently by the arm, and he catched the locket and brake it away from about the knight's neck, and

upon that the knight shrieked very loud, and fell down upon his knees and
besought mercy of the King, and there was great uproar in that place.

*King Arthur
slayeth the
knight of
the castle.*
Then King Arthur opened the locket and lo! there was a ball
as of crystal, very clear and shining. And King Arthur said,
"I will have no mercy," and therewith he flung the ball violently down upon the stone of the pavement so that it brake
with a loud noise. Then, upon that instant, the knight-conjurer gave a
piercing bitter cry and fell down upon the ground; and when they ran to
raise him up, behold! he was entirely dead.

Now when the people of that castle beheld their knight thus suddenly
dead, and when they beheld King Arthur how he stood in the fury of his
kingly majesty, they were greatly afeared so that they shrunk away from
the King where he stood. Then the King turned and went out from that
castle and no one stayed him, and he mounted his horse and rode away,
and no one gave him let or hindrance in his going.

Now when the King had left the castle in that wise, he went straight to
the hut where was the old beldame and he said to her, "Thou hast holpen
me a very, great deal in mine hour of need, so now will I fulfil that pledge
which I made unto thee, for I will take thee unto my Court and thou shalt
choose one of my knights for thy husband. For I think there is not one
knight in all my Court but would be very glad to do anything that lieth in
his power to reward one who hath saved me as thou hast done this day."

Therewith he took that old woman and he lifted her up upon the crupper of his horse; then he himself mounted upon his horse, and so they

*King Arthur
taketh the old
woman away
with him.*
rode away from that place. And the King comported himself
to that aged beldame in all ways with the utmost consideration as though she had been a beautiful dame of the highest
degree in the land. Likewise he showed her such respect
that had she been a lady of royal blood, he could not have shown greater
respect to her.

So in due time they reached the Court, which was then at Carleon. And
they came there nigh about mid-day.

Now about that time it chanced that the Queen and a number of the
lords of the Court, and a number of the ladies of the Court, were out in
the fields enjoying the pleasantness of the Maytime; for no one in all the
world, excepting the esquire, Boisenard, knew anything of the danger that
beset King Arthur; hence all were very glad of the pleasantness of the
season. Now as King Arthur drew nigh to that place, these lifted up their
eyes and beheld him come, and they were astonished beyond all measure
to see King Arthur come to them across that field with that old beldame

behind him upon the saddle, wherefore they stood still to wait until King Arthur reached them.

But when King Arthur had come to them, he did not dismount from his horse, but sat thereon and regarded them all very steadfastly; and Queen Guinevere said, "Sir, what is this? Hast thou a mind to play some merry jest this day that thou hast brought hither that old woman?"

"Lady," said King Arthur, "excepting for this old woman it were like to have been a very sorry jest for thee and for me; for had she not aided me I would now have been a dead man and in a few days you would doubtless all have been in great passion of sorrow."

Then all they who were there marvelled very greatly at the King's words. And the Queen said, "Sir, what is it that hath befallen thee?"

Thereupon King Arthur told them all that had happened to him from the very beginning when he and Boisenard had left the castle of Tintagalon. And when he had ended his story, they were greatly amazed.

Now there were seventeen lords of the Court there present. So when King Arthur had ended his story, he said unto these, "Messires, I have given my pledge unto this aged woman that any one of you whom she may choose, shall take her unto him as his wife, and shall treat her with all the regard that it is possible for him to do; for this was the condition that she laid upon me. Now tell me, did I do right in making unto her my pledge that I would fulfil that which she desired?" And all of those who were present said, "Yea, lord, thou didst right, for we would do all in the world for to save thee from such peril as that from which thou hast escaped."

Then King Arthur said to that old woman, "Lady, is there any of these knights here whom you would choose for to be your husband?" Upon this, the old woman pointed with her very long, bony finger *The old woman* unto Sir Gawaine, saying, "Yea, I would marry that lord, for *chooseth* I see by the chain that is around his neck and by the golden *Sir Gawaine.* circlet upon his hair and by the haughty nobility of his aspect, that he must be the son of a king."

Then King Arthur said unto Sir Gawaine, "Sir, art thou willing to fulfil my pledge unto this old woman?" And Sir Gawaine said, "Yea, lord, whatsoever thou requirest of me, that will I do." So Sir Gawaine came to the old woman and took her hand into his and set it to his lips; and not one of all those present so much as smiled. Then they all turned their faces and returned unto the King's castle; and they were very silent and downcast, for this was sore trouble that had come upon that Court.

Now after they had returned unto the Court, they assigned certain apartments therein to that old woman, and they clad her in rich raiment such as a queen might wear, and they assigned unto her a Court such as

Sir Gawaine taketh the old woman to wife.

was fit for a queen; and it seemed to all the Court that, in the rich robes which she wore, she was ten times more ugly than she was before. So when eleven days had passed, Sir Gawaine was wedded to that old woman in the chapel of the King's Court with great ceremony and pomp of circumstance, and all of those who were there were as sad and as sorrowful as though Sir Gawaine had been called upon to suffer his death.

Afterward that they were married, Sir Gawaine and the old woman went to Sir Gawaine's house and there Sir Gawaine shut himself off from all the world and suffered no one to come nigh him; for he was proud beyond all measure, and in this great humiliation he suffered in such a wise that words cannot tell how great was that humiliation. Wherefore he shut himself away from the world that no one might behold his grief and his shame.

And all the rest of that day he walked continually up and down his chamber, for he was altogether in such despair that it came unto his mind

Sir Gawaine is in great sorrow.

that it would be well if he took his own life; for it seemed to him impossible for to suffer such shame as that which had come upon him. So after a while it fell the dark of the early night and therewith a certain strength came to Sir Gawaine and he said, " This is a shame for me for to behave in this way; for since I have married that lady she is my true wedded wife and I do not treat her with that regard unto which she hath the right." So he went out of that place and sought the apartment of that old woman who was his wife, and by that time it was altogether dark. But when Sir Gawaine had come into that place where she was, that old woman upbraided him, crying out upon him, " So, Sir! You have treated me but ill upon this our wedding-day, for you have stayed all the afternoon away from me and now only come to me when it is dark night." And Sir Gawaine said, "Lady, I could not help it, for I was very sore oppressed with many cares. But if I have disregarded thee this day, I do beseech thy forgiveness therefore, and I will hold myself willing to do all that is in my power to recompense thee for any neglect that I have placed upon thee." Then the lady said, " Sir, it is very dark in this place; let us then have a light." " It shall be as thou dost desire," said Sir Gawaine, " and I, myself, will go and fetch a light for thee."

So Sir Gawaine went forth from that place and he brought two waxen tapers, one in either hand, and he bore them in candlesticks of gold; for he was minded to show all respect unto that old woman. And when he came into the room he perceived that she was at the farther end of the apartment and he went toward her, and she arose and stood before him as he approached.

But when the circle of light fell upon that old woman, and when Sir Gawaine beheld her who stood before him, he cried out aloud in a very great voice because of the great marvel and wonder of that which he saw. For, instead of that old woman whom he had left, he beheld a lady of extraordinary beauty and in the very flower of her youth. And he beheld that her hair was long and *Of the beautiful lady who appeareth to Sir Gawaine.* glossy and very black, and that her eyes were likewise black like to black jewels, and that her lips were like coral, and her teeth were like pearls. So, for a while, Sir Gawaine could not speak, and then he cried out, "Lady! lady! who art thou?"

Then that lady smiled upon Sir Gawaine with such loving-kindness that he wist not what to think, other than that this was an angel who had descended to that place out of paradise. Wherefore he stood before her for a long time and could find no more words to say, and she continued to smile upon him very kindly in that wise. Then by and by Sir Gawaine said to her, "Lady, where is that dame who is my wife?" And the lady said, "Sir Gawaine, I am she." "It is not possible," cried out Sir Gawaine, "for she was old and extraordinarily ugly, but I believe that thou art beautiful beyond any lady whom I have beheld." And the lady said, "Nevertheless, I am she and because thou hast taken me for thy wife with thine own free will and with great courtesy, so is a part of that enchantment that lay upon me removed from me. For I will now be able to appear before thee in mine own true shape. For whiles I was a little while ago so ugly and foul as thou didst behold me to be, now am I to be as thou seest me, for one-half the day—and the other half thereof I must be ugly as I was before."

Then Sir Gawaine was filled beyond all words with great joy. And with that joy there came an extreme passion of loving regard for that lady. So he cried out aloud several times, "This is surely the most wonderful thing that ever befell any man in all the world." Therewith he fell down upon his knees and took that lady's hands into his own hands, and kissed her hands with great fervor, and all the while she smiled upon him as she had done at first.

Then again the lady said, "Come, sit thee down beside me and let us consider what part of the day I shall be in the one guise, and what part of the day I shall be in the other guise; for all day I may have the one appearance, and all night I may have the other appearance."

Then Sir Gawaine said, "I would have thee in this guise during the night time, for then we are together at our own inn; and since thou art of this sort that I now see thee, I do not at all reckon how the world may regard thee."

Upon this the lady spake with great animation, saying, "No, sir, I would not have it in that wise, for every woman loveth the regard of the world, and I would fain enjoy such beauty as is mine before the world, and not endure the scorn and contempt of men and women."

To this Sir Gawaine said, "Lady, I would have it the other way."

And she said, "Nay, I would have it my way."

Sir Gawaine giveth the lady her will. Then Sir Gawaine said, "So be it. For since I have taken thee for my wife, so must I show thee respect in all matters; wherefore thou shalt have thy will in this and in all other things."

Then that lady fell a-laughing beyond all measure and she said, "Sir, I did but put this as a last trial upon thee, for as I am now, so shall I always be."

Upon this Sir Gawaine was so filled with joy that he knew not how to contain himself.

So they sat together for a long time, hand in hand. Then after a while Sir Gawaine said, "Lady, who art thou?" Unto which she made reply, "I am one of the Ladies of the Lake; but for thy sake I have become mortal like to other women and have quit that very beautiful home where I one time dwelt. I have kept thee in my heart for a considerable while, for I was not very far distant at that time when thou didst bid adieu to Sir Pellias beside the lake. There I beheld how thou didst weep and bewail thyself when Sir Pellias left thee, wherefore my heart went out to thee with great pity. So, after a while, I quitted that lake and became mortal for thy sake. Now, when I found the trouble into which King Arthur had fallen I took that occasion to have him fetch me unto thee so that I might test the entire nobility of thy knighthood; and, lo! I have found it all that I deemed it possible to be. For though I appeared to thee so aged, so ugly, and so foul, yet hast thou treated me with such kind regard that I do not believe that thou couldst have behaved with more courtesy to me had I been the daughter of a king. Wherefore it doth now afford me such pleasure for to possess thee for my knight and my true lord, that I cannot very well tell thee how great is my joy therein."

Then Sir Gawaine said, "Lady, I do not think it can be so great as my joy in possessing thee." And thereupon he came to her and laid his hand upon her shoulder and kissed her upon the lips.

Then, after that, he went forth and called with a great voice all through that house, and the people of the house came running from everywhere. And he commanded that the people should bring lights and refreshments, and they brought the lights, and when they had brought them and beheld that beautiful lady instead of the aged dame, they were filled with great wonder and joy; wherefore they cried out aloud and clapped *Sir Gawaine* their hands together and made much sound of rejoicing. And *lets make* they set a great feast for Sir Gawaine and his lady, and in *great rejoicing.* place of the sorrow and darkness that had been, there was joy and light, and music and singing; wherefore those of the King's Court, beholding this from a distance, said, "It is very strange that Sir Gawaine should have taken so much joy of having wedded that old beldame."

But when the next morning had come, that lady clad herself in raiment of yellow silk, and she hung about her many strands of precious stones of several colors, and she set a golden crown upon her head. And Sir Gawaine let call his horse, and he let call a snow-white palfrey for the lady, and thereupon they rode out from that place and entered the Court of the King. But when the King and the Queen and their several Courts beheld that lady, they were filled with such great astonishment that they wist not what to say for pure wonder. And when they heard all that had happened, they gave great joy and loud acclaim so that all their mourning was changed into rejoicing. And, indeed, there was not one knight there of all that Court who would not have given half his life to have been so fortunate in that matter as was Sir Gawaine, the son of King Lot of Orkney.

Such is the story of Sir Gawaine, and from it I draw this significance: as that poor ugly beldame appeared unto the eyes of Sir Gawaine, so doth a man's duty sometimes appear to him to be ugly and exceedingly ill-favored unto his desires. But when he shall have wedded himself unto that duty so that he hath made it one with him as a bridegroom maketh himself one with his bride, then doth that duty become of a sudden very beautiful unto him and unto others.

So may it be with ye that you shall take duty unto yourselves no matter how much it may mislike ye to do so. For indeed a man shall hardly have any real pleasure in his life unless his inclination becometh wedded unto his duty and cleaveth unto it as a husband cleaveth unto his wife. For when inclination is thus wedded unto duty, then doth the soul take great joy unto itself as though a wedding had taken place betwixt a bridegroom and a bride within its tabernacle.

Likewise, when you shall have become entirely wedded unto your duty, then shall you become equally worthy with that good knight and gentleman Sir Gawaine; for it needs not that a man shall wear armor for to be a true knight, but only that he shall do his best endeavor with all patience and humility as it hath been ordained for him to do. Wherefore, when your time cometh unto you to display your knightness by assuming your duty, I do pray that you also may approve yourself as worthy as Sir Gawaine approved himself in this story which I have told you of as above written.

CONCLUSION

So endeth this volume wherein hath been told, with every circumstance of narration, the history of those Three Worthies who were of the Court of King Arthur.

And now, if God will give me the grace to do so, I will some time, at no very great time from this, write the further history of sundry other knights and worthies of whom I have not yet spoken.

And among the first of these shall be Sir Launcelot, whom all the world knoweth to have been the greatest knight in prowess of arms of any who has lived, excepting Sir Galahad, who was his son. And I shall tell you the story of Sir Ewaine and Sir Geraint, and of Sir Percival and of sundry others.

But of this another time. For now, with great regret I bid you adieu and bring this history unto a close.

So may God grant us to come together at another time with such happiness and prosperity that you may have a free and untroubled heart to enjoy the narrated history of those excellent men which I shall then set before you. Amen.